I0637831

A DAUGHTER OF THE RICH

BOOKS BY

MARY E. WALLER

The Wood-carver of 'Lympus

A Daughter of the Rich

The Little Citizen

Sanna

Our Benny

A Year out of Life

Flamsted Quarries

Through the Gates of the
Netherlands

A

Daughter of the Rich

BY

M. E. WALLER

AUTHOR OF "THE WOODCARVER OF 'LYMPUS," "SANNA,"
"THE LITTLE CITIZEN," "THROUGH THE GATES
OF THE NETHERLANDS," ETC.

ILLUSTRATED BY
ELLEN BERNARD THOMPSON

BOSTON
LITTLE, BROWN, AND COMPANY
1911

Copyright, 1903, 1905,
BY LITTLE, BROWN, AND COMPANY.

All rights reserved

Thirteenth Printing

Printers

S. J. PARKHILL & CO., BOSTON, U. S. A.

To

"MARTIE"

CONTENTS

LIST OF ILLUSTRATIONS

A DAUGHTER OF THE RICH

I

MOLASSES TEA

"Good-night, Martie," called a sweet voice down the stairway.

"Good-night, Rose dear; I thought you were asleep."

"Good-night, Martie," duetted the twins, in the shrillest of treble and falsetto.

"Good-night, you rogues; go to sleep; you'll wake baby."

"Dood-night, mummy," chirped a little voice from the adjoining room.

There was a shout of laughter from the twins.

"Shut up," growled March from the attic over the kitchen. "Good-night, mother." His growl ended in a squeak, for March was at that interesting period of his life indicated by a change of voice. At the sound, a prolonged snicker from somewhere was answered by a corresponding giggle from another-where.

"Now, children," said Mrs. Blossom, speaking up the stairway, "do be quiet, or baby will be wide awake."

"Tum tiss me, mummy," piped the little voice a second time, with no sound of sleep in it.

" Yes, darling, I 'll come ; " as she turned to go into the bedroom adjoining the kitchen, there was the sound of a jump overhead, a patter of bare feet, a squabble on the stairs, and Budd and Cherry, the irrepressible ten-year-old twins, tumbled into the room.

" I 'll haul those kids back to bed for you, mother," shouted March, and flung himself out of bed to join the fray, while Rose was not behindhand in making her appearance.

Mrs. Blossom came in with little May in her arms, and that was the signal for a wholesale kissing-party in which May was hostess.

" Children, children, you 'll smother me ! " laughed their mother.   " Here, sit down on the rug and warm your toes, — coming over those bare stairs this cold night ! "   And down they sat, Rose and March, Budd and Cherry and little May, in thick white and red flannel night-dresses and gray flannel pajamas.

Budd coughed consumptively, and Cherry followed suit. March shivered and shook like a small earthquake, and Rose looked up laughingly at her mother.

" We know what that means, don't we, Martie," she said.   " Shall I help ? "

" No, no, dear, — in your bare feet ! "

Mrs. Blossom took a lamp from the shelf over the fire-place, and, leaving the five with their fifty toes turned and wriggling before the cheering warmth of the blazing hickory logs, disappeared in the pantry.

" Oh, bully," said Budd, rubbing his flannel pajamas

just over his stomach; " I wish 't was a cold night every day, then we could have molasses tea all the time, don't you, Cherry? "

" Mm," said Cherry, too full of the anticipated treat for articulate speech.

" There's nothing like it to warm up your insides," said March; " mother's a brick to let us get up for it. She would n't, you know, if father were at home."

" My tummy's told," piped May, frantically patting her chest in imitation of Budd, and all the children shouted to see the wee four-year-old maiden trying to manufacture a shiver in the glow of the cheerful fire.

Mrs. Blossom had never told her recipe for her "hot molasses tea;" but it had been famed in the family for more than a generation. She had it from her mother. The treat was always reserved for a bitterly cold night, and the good things in it of which one had a taste — molasses, white sugar, lemon-peel, butter, peppermint, boiled raisins, and mysterious unknowns — were compounded with hot water into a palate-tickling beverage.

When Mrs. Blossom reappeared, with a kettle sending forth a small cloud of fragrant steam in one hand and a tray filled with tin cups in the other, the delighted " Ohs " and " Ahs " repaid her for all her extra work at the close of a busy, weary day.

Budd rolled over on the rug in his ecstasy, and Cherry was about to roll on top of him, when March interfered, and order was restored.

As they sat there on the big, braided square of woollen

rag-carpet, sipping and ohing and ahing with supreme satisfaction, Mrs. Blossom broached the subject of valentines.

"It's the first of February, children, and time to begin to make valentines. You're not going to forget the Doctor *this* year, are you?"

"No, indeed, Martie," said Rose. "He deserves the prettiest we can make. I've been thinking about it, and I'm going to make him a shaving-case, heart-shaped, with birch-bark covers, and if March will decorate it for me, I think it will be lovely; will you, March?"

"Course I will; the Doctor's a brick. I'll tell you what, Martie, I can pen and ink some of those spruces and birches that the Doctor was so fond of last summer; how'll that do?"

"Just the thing," said his mother; "I know it will please him. What are you thinking, Cherry?" for the "other half" of Budd was gazing dreamily into the fire, forgetting her tea in her revery.

"Fudge!" said Cherry, shortly. March and Rose laughed.

"Keep still making fun of Cherry," said Budd, ruffling at the sound; and to emphasize his admonishing words, he dug his sharp elbow so suddenly into March's ribs that some hot molasses tea flew from the cup which his brother had just put to his mouth and spattered on his bare feet.

March deliberately set down his tin cup on the hearth near the fire beside his brother's, and turned upon Budd.

Budd tried to dodge, but had no room. In a trice, March had his arms around him, and was hugging him in a bear-like embrace. " Say you 're sorry ! " he demanded.

" Au-ow ! "

" Say you 're sorry ! " he roared at him, hugging harder.

" Au-ow-ee-ow ! "

" Quick, or I 'll squeeze you some more ! "

Budd was squirming and twisting like an eel.

" O-ee-wau-au-*Au !* "

" There," said March, releasing him and setting him down with a thump on the rug; " I 'll teach you to poke me in the ribs that way and scald my feet. — You 're game, though, old fellow," he added patronizingly, as he heard a suspicious sniff from Cherry. " You and Cherry make a whole team any day."

Cherry's sniff changed to a smile, for March did not condescend to praise either of them very often.

" Well," she said meditatively, " I suppose it did sound funny to say that, but I was thinking that if Budd would make me a little heart-shaped box of birch-bark, I 'd make some maple-sugar fudge, — you know, Martie, the kind with butternuts in it, — and that could be my valentine for the Doctor."

" Why, that 's a bright idea, Cherry," said Mrs. Blossom; and, " Bully for you, Cherry," said Budd; " we 'll begin to-morrow and crack the butternuts."

" What will May do ? " asked Mrs. Blossom, lifting the little girl, who was already showing signs of being over-come with molasses tea and sleep. May nestled in her mother's arms, leaned her head, running over with golden curls, on her mother's breast, and murmured drowsily, —

"'Ittle tooties — tut with mummy's heart-tutter — tutter — tooties — tut —" The blue-veined eyelids closed over the lovely eyes; and Mrs. Blossom, holding up her finger to hush the children's mirth at May's inspired utterance, carried her back into the bedroom.

One after another the children crept noiselessly upstairs, with a whispered, "Good-night, Martie," and in ten minutes Mary Blossom knew they were all in the land of dreams.

II

MRS. BLOSSOM'S VALENTINE

IT was a bitter night. Mrs. Blossom refilled the kitchen stove, and threw on more hickory in the fireplace in anticipation of her husband's late return from the village. She drew her little work-table nearer to the blaze, and sat down to her sewing. Then she sighed, and, as she bent over the large willow basket filled with stockings to be darned and clothes to be mended, a tear rolled down her cheek and plashed on the edge.

There was so much she wanted to do for her children — and so little with which to do it! There was March, an artist to his finger-tips, who longed to be an architect; and Rose, lovely in her young girlhood and giving promise of a lovelier womanhood, who was willing to work her way through one of the lesser colleges, if only she could be prepared for entrance. Mary Blossom saw no prospect of being able to do anything for either of them.

And the father! He must be spared first, if he were to be their future bread-winner. Mary Blossom could never forget that day, a year ago this very month, when her husband was brought home on a stretcher, hurt, as they thought, unto death, by a tree falling the wrong way in the woods where he was directing the choppers.

What a year it had been! All they had saved had gone to pay for the extra help hired to carry on the farm and finish the log-cutting. A surgeon had come from the nearest city to give his verdict in the case and help if he could.

The farm was mortgaged to enable them to pay the heavy bills incident to months of sickness and medical attendance; still the father lay helpless, and Mary Blossom's faith and courage were put to their severest test, when both doctor and surgeon pronounced the case hopeless. He might live for years, they said, but useless, so far as his limbs were concerned.

This was in June; and then it was that Mary Blossom, leaving Rose in charge of her father and the children, left her home, and walked bareheaded rapidly up the slope behind the house, across the upland pastures and over into the woodlands, from which they had hoped to derive a sufficient income to provide not only for their necessities, but for their children's education and the comforts of life.

Deep into the heart of them she made her way; and there, in the green silence, broken only by the note of a thrush and the stirring of June leafage above and about her, she knelt and poured out her sorrow-filled heart before God, and cast upon Him the intolerable burden that had rested so long upon her soul.

The shadows were lengthening when at last she turned homewards. Cherry and Budd met her in the pasture, for Rose had grown anxious and sent them to find her.

" Why, where have you been, Martie? " exclaimed the twins. " We were so frightened about you, because you did n't come home."

" You need n't have been; I 've been talking with a Friend." And more than that she never said. The children's curiosity was roused, but when they told Rose and asked her what mother meant, Rose's eyes filled with tears, and she kept silence; for she alone knew with Whom her mother had talked that June afternoon.

" Run ahead, Budd, and tell Malachi to harness up Bess. I want him to take a letter down to the village so that it may go on the night mail." Budd flew rather than ran; for there was a look in his mother's face that he had never seen before, and it awed him.

That night a letter went to Doctor Heath, a famous nerve specialist of New York City. It was a letter from Mary Blossom, his old-time friend and schoolmate in the academy at Barton's River. In it she asked him if he would give her his advice in this case, saying she could not accept the decision of the physician and surgeon unless it should be confirmed by him.

" I cannot pay you now," she wrote, " but it was borne in upon me this afternoon to write to you, although you may have forgotten me in these many years, and I have no claim of present friendship, even, upon your time and service; but I must heed the inner command to appeal to you, whatever you may think of me, — if I disobeyed *that*, I should be disobeying God's voice in my life," — and signed herself, " Yours in childhood's remembrance."

The next day a telegram was brought up from the village; and the day after the Doctor himself followed it.

It was an anxious week; but the wonderful skill conquered. The pressure on a certain nerve was removed, and for the last six months Benjamin Blossom had been slowly but surely coming back to his old-time health and strength. But again this winter the extra help had been necessary, and it had taxed all Mary Blossom's ingenuity to make both ends meet; for there was the interest on the mortgage to be paid every six months, and the ready money had to go for that.

In the midst of her thoughts, her recollections and plans, she caught the sound of sleigh-bells. The tall clock was just striking ten. Smoothing every line of care and banishing all look of sadness from her face, she met her husband with a cheery smile and a, " I 'm so glad you 've got home, Ben; it 's just twenty below, and the molasses tea is ready for you and Chi."

"Chi!" called Mr. Blossom towards the barn.

"Whoa!" shouted a voice that sounded frosty in spite of itself. "Whoa, Bess!"

"Come into the kitchen before you turn in; there 's some hot molasses tea waiting for us."

"Be there in a minute," he shouted back, and Bess pranced into the barn.

"Oh, Mary, this *is* good," said Mr. Blossom, as he slipped out of his buffalo-robe coat and into his warm house-jacket, dropped his boots outside in the shed, and put on his carpet-slippers that had been waiting for him on the hearth.

"It is home, Ben," said his wife, bringing out clean tin cups from the pantry, and putting them to warm beside the kettle on the hearth.

"Yes, with you in it, Mary," he said with the smile that had won him his true-love eighteen years before.

"Come in, Chi," he called towards the shed, whence came sounds as if some one were dancing a double-shuffle in snow-boots.

"'Fraid I'll thaw 'n' make a puddle on the hearth, Mis' Blossom. I'm as stiff as an icicle: guess I'll take my tea perpendic'lar; I ain't fit to sit down."

"Sit down, sit down, Chi," said Mrs. Blossom. "You'll enjoy the tea more; and give yourself a thorough heating before you go to bed. I've put the soapstone in it," she added.

"Well, you beat all, Mis' Blossom; just as if you did n't find enough to do for yourself, you go to work 'n' make work." He broke off suddenly, "George Washin'ton!" he exclaimed, "most forgot to give you this letter that come on to-night's mail."

He handed Mrs. Blossom the letter, which, with some difficulty, owing to his stiffened fingers, he extracted from the depths of the tail-pocket of his old overcoat. Then he helped himself to a brimming cup of the tea, and apparently swallowed its contents without once taking breath.

"Why, it's from Doctor Heath!" exclaimed Mrs. Blossom, recognizing the handwriting. "Is it a valentine, I wonder?" she said, feigning to laugh, for her heart sank within her, fearing it might be the bill, — and yet, and yet, the Doctor had said — she got no further with these thoughts, so intent was she on the contents of the letter.

Chi, with an eye to prolonging his stay till he should know the why and wherefore of a letter from the great Doctor at this season of the year, took another cup of the tea.

"Ben, oh, Ben!" cried Mrs. Blossom, in a faint, glad voice; and therewith, to her husband's amazement, she handed him the letter, put both arms around his neck, and, dropping her head on his shoulder, sobbed as if her heart would break.

Chi softly put down his half-emptied cup and tiptoed with creaking boots from the room.

"Can't stand that, nohow," he muttered to himself in the shed; and, forgetting to light his lantern, he felt his way up the backstairs to his lodging in the room overhead, blinded by some suspicious drops of water in his eyes, which he cursed for frost melting from his bushy eyebrows.

"Oh, Ben, think of it!" she cried, when her husband had soothed and calmed her. "Twenty-five dollars a week; that makes a little more than twelve hundred a year. Why, we can pay off all the mortgage and be free from that nightmare."

For answer her husband drew her closer to him, and late into the night they sat before the dying fire, talking and planning for the future.

"Children," she said at breakfast next morning, and her voice sounded so bright and cheery that the room seemed full of sunshine, although the sky was a hard, cold gray,

"I've had one valentine already; it came last night from the Doctor."

Chi listened with all his ears.

"Mother!" burst from the children, "where is it?" "Show it to us." "Why didn't you tell us before breakfast?"

"I can't show it to you yet; it's a live one."

"A live one!" chorussed the children.

"You're fooling us, mother," said March.

"Do I look as if I were?" replied his mother.

And March was obliged to confess that she had never looked more in earnest.

Rose left her seat and stole to her father's side. "What does it mean, pater?" she whispered.

"Ask your mother," was all the satisfaction she received, and walked, crestfallen, back to her chair; for when had her father refused her anything?

"When will you tell us, anyway?" said Budd, a little gruffly. He hated a secret.

"I can't tell you that either," said his mother, "and I don't know that I shall tell you until the very last, if you ask in that voice."

Budd screwed his mouth into a smile, and, unbeknown to the rest of the family, reached under the cloth for his mother's hand. He sat next to her, and that had been his way of saying "Forgive me," ever since he was a tiny boy.

He had a squeeze in return and felt happier.

"I say, let's guess," said Cherry. "If I don't do something, I shall burst."

"You express my feelings perfectly, Cherry," said March, gravely, and the guessing began.

"A St. Bernard puppy ? " said Budd, who coveted one.

"A Shetland pony," said Cherry.

"The Doctor's coming up here, himself." That was Rose's guess.

"'T ain't likely," growled Budd.

"A tunning 'ittle baby," chirped May.

March failed to think of any live thing the Doctor was likely to send unless it might be a Wyandotte blood-rooster, such as he and the Doctor had talked about last summer.

"You're all cold, cold as ice," laughed their mother, using the words of the game she had so often played with them when they were younger.

"Oh, mother ! " they protested. They were almost indignant.

Chi rose and left the table. "Beats me," he muttered, as he took down his axe from a beam in the woodshed. "What in thunder can it be? I ain't goin' to ask questions, but I'll ferret it out, — by George Washin'ton ; " and that was Chi's most solemn oath.

III

" WHAT is it, dear ? "

" Bothered — bothered."

" A case ? "

" Yes, and I must get it off my mind this evening."

The Doctor set down his after-dinner coffee untasted on
the library table, and rose with a half sigh from his easy
chair before the blazing wood-fire. His heavy eyebrows
were drawn together into a straight line over the bridge of
his nose, and that, his wife knew full well, was an ominous
sign.

" Must you go to-night? It's such a fearful storm;
just hear it ! "

" Yes, I must; just to get it off my mind. I sha'n't be
gone long, and I 'll tell you all about it when I get home."
The Doctor stooped and kissed the detaining hand that his
wife had laid lovingly on his arm; then, turning to the
telephone, he bespoke a cab.

As the vehicle made its way up Fifth Avenue in the teeth
of a February, northeast gale that drove the sleet rattling
against the windows, Doctor Heath settled back farther
into his corner, growling to himself, " I wish some people
would let me manage their affairs for them; it would

show their common sense to let me show them some of mine."

A few blocks north of the park entrance, the cab turned east into a side street, and stopped at Number 4.

" Mr. Clyde in, Wilkins?" asked the Doctor of the colored butler, who opened the door.

" Yes, sah; jes' up from dinner, sah, to see Miss Hazel."

" Tell him I want to see him in the library."

" Yes, sah." He took the Doctor's cloak and hat, hesitating a moment before leaving, then turning, said: " 'Scuse me, sah, but Miss Hazel ain't more discomposed? "

" No, no, Wilkins; Miss Hazel is doing fairly well."

" Thank you, sah ; " and Wilkins ducked his head and sprang upstairs.

" Why, Dick," said Mr. Clyde, as he entered the library hurriedly, " what 's wrong ? "

" The world in general, Johnny, and your world in particular, old fellow."

" Is Hazel worse ? " The father's anxiety could be heard in the tone with which he put the question.

" I 'm not satisfied, John, and I 'm bothered."

When Doctor Heath called his friend " John," Mr. Clyde knew that the very soul of him was heavily burdened. The two had been chums at Yale : the one a rich man's son ; the other a country doctor's one boy, to whom had been bequeathed only a name honored in every county of his native state, a good constitution, and an ambition to follow his father's profession. The boy had become one of the leading physicians of the great city in which he made his home; his friend one of the most sought-after men in the whirling gayeties of the great metropolis.   As he stood on the hearth with his back to the mantel waiting for the physician's next word, he was typical of the best culture of the city, and the Doctor looked up into the fine face with a deep affection visible in his eyes.

" Going out, as usual, John?"

" Only to the Pearsells' reception.   Don't keep me waiting, old fellow; speak up."

" How the deuce am I to make things plain to you, John?   Here, draw up your chair a little nearer mine, as you used in college when you knew I had a four A. M. lecture awaiting you, after one of your larks."

The two men helped themselves to cigars; and the Doctor, resting his head on the back of the chair, slowly let forth the smoke in curling rings, and watched them dissolve and disperse.

" Come, Dick, go ahead; I can stand it if you can."

" Well, then, I 've done all I can for Hazel, and shall have to give up the case unless you do all *you* can for her."

Now the Doctor had not intended to make his statement in such a blunt fashion, and he could not blame Mr. Clyde for the touch of resentment that was so quick to show in his answer.

" I did n't suppose you went back on your patients in this way, Richard; much less on a friend.   I have done everything I can for Hazel.   If there is anything I 've omitted, just tell me, and I 'll try to make it good."

2

The Doctor nodded penitently. "I know, John, I've said it badly; and I don't know but that I shall make it worse by saying you've done too much."

"Too much! That is not possible. Did n't you order last year's trip to Florida and the summer yachting cruise?"

Doctor Heath groaned. "I'm getting in deeper and deeper, John; you can't understand, because you are you; born and bred as you are — Look here, John, did it ever occur to you that Hazel is a little hot-house plant that needs hardening?"

"No, Richard."

"Well, she is; she needs hardening to make her any kind of a woman physically and, and — " The Doctor stopped short. There were some things of which he rarely spoke.

"My Hazel needs hardening!" exclaimed the amazed father. "Why, Richard, have n't you impressed upon me again and again that she needs the greatest care?"

The Doctor groaned again and smote his friend solidly on the knee.

"Oh, you poor rich — you poor rich! 'Eyes have ye, and ye see not; ears have ye, and hear not.' John, the girl must go away from you, who over-indulge her, from this home-nest of luxury, from this private-school business and dancing-class dissipation, from her young-grown-up lunch-parties and matinée-parties, from her violin lessons and her indoor gymnastics — curse them!"

This was a great deal for the usually self-contained

physician, and Mr. Clyde stared at him, but half comprehending.

"Go away? Do you mean, Richard, that she must leave me?"

"Yes, I mean just that."

"Well,"—it was a long-drawn, thinking "well,"—"I will ask my sister to take her this summer. She returns from Egypt soon and has just written me she intends to open her place, 'The Wyndes,' in June."

Again the Doctor groaned: "And kill her with golf and picnics and coaching among all those fashionable butterflies! Now, hear to me, John," he laid his hand on his friend's shoulder, "send her away into the country, that is country,—something, by the way, which you know precious little about. Let me find her a place up among those life-giving Green Hills, and do you do without her for one year. Let *me* prescribe for her *there;* and I'll guarantee she returns to you hale and hearty. Trust her to me, John; you'll thank me in the end. I can do no more for her here."

"Do you mean, Richard, to put her away into real country conditions?"

"Yes, just that; into a farmer's family, if possible,—and I know I can make it possible,—and let her be as one of them, work, play, go barefoot, eat, sleep, be merry—in fact, be what the Lord intended her to be; and you'll find out that is something very different from what she is, if only you'll hear to me."

The Doctor was pacing the room in his earnestness.

He was not accustomed to beg thus to be allowed to prescribe for his patients. His one word was law, and he
was not required to explain his motives.

Mr. Clyde's eyes followed him; then he broke the prolonged silence.

"Richard, you have asked me the one thing to which
her mother would never have consented. How, then,
can I ? "

"Think it over, John, and let me know."

The two men clasped hands.

"Let me take you along in my cab to the reception; it's inhuman to take out your horses on such a
night."

"Thank you, no; I think I 'll give it up; I 'm not in
the mood for it. Good-night, old fellow."

"Good-night, Johnny."

The next morning, at breakfast, the Doctor took up a
note that lay beside his plate, and after reading it
beamed joyously while he stirred his coffee vigorously
without drinking it. When, finally, he looked up, his
wife elevated her eyebrows over the top of the coffee urn,
and the Doctor laughed.

"To be sure, wifie, read the note." And this is what
she read : —

DEAR RICHARD, — I 've had a hard night, trying to look at
things from your point of view and see my own duty towards
Hazel. Things have grown rather misty, looking both backwards and forwards, and I have concluded I can't do better
than to take you at your word, — trust her to you, and accept

the guarantee of her return to me with her physical condition such as it should be.

This decision will, as you well know, raise a storm of protest among the relations. The whole swarm will be about my ears in less than no time. Stand by me. The whole responsibility rests upon you, — and tell Hazel; I'm too much of a coward. This is a confession, but you will understand. Let me know the details of your plans so soon as possible. I have never been able to give you such a proof of friendship. Have you ever asked another man for such ? I mistrust you, old fellow.   Yours,

JOHN.

IV

"GABRIELLE."

"Oui, mademoiselle Hazel," came in shrill yet muffled tones from the depths of the dressing-room closet.

"Bring me my white silk kimono."

"Oui, mademoiselle."

The order, in French, was given in a weak and slightly fretful voice that issued from the bed at the farther end of a large room from which the dressing-room opened. The apartment was, in truth, what Doctor Heath had called it, "a nest of luxury."

It was a bitter Saint Valentine's Day which succeeded the Doctor's evening visit. The wood-fire, blazing cheerily in the ample fireplace, sent its warmth and light far out into the room, flashing red reflections in the curiously twisted bars of the brass bedstead. At the left of the fireplace stood a small round tea-table, and upon it a little silver tea-kettle on a standard of the same metal. Dainty cups and saucers of egg-shell china were grouped about it; a miniature silver tray held a sugar-dish and a cream-pot and a half-dozen gold-lined souvenir spoons.

On the richly carved mantel stood an exquisite plate-glass clock, the chimes of which were just striking nine, and, keeping it company to right and left, were two dainty figures of a shepherd and shepherdess in Dresden china. The remaining mantel space was filled with tiny figures in bisque, — a dachshund, a cat and kittens, a porcelain box, heart-shaped, the top covered with china forget-me-nots, a silver drinking-cup, a small oval portrait on ivory of a beautiful young woman, framed in richly chased gold, the inner rim set round with pearls. A blue pitcher of Cloisonné and a tray of filigree silver heaped with dainty cotillion favors stood on one end; on the other, a crystal vase filled with white tulips.

Soft blue and white Japanese rugs lay upon the polished floor; delicate blue and white draperies hung at the windows. Dressing-case and writing-desk of white curled maple were each laden with articles for the toilet and for writing, in solid silver, engraved with the monogram H. C. A couch, upholstered in blue and white Japanese silk, stood at the right of the fireplace, and all about the room were dainty wicker chairs enamelled in white, and cushioned to match the hangings.

The bed was canopied in pale blue covered with white net and edged with lace, and the coverlet was of silk of the same delicate color, embroidered with white violets and edged like the canopy, only with a deeper frill of lace. The occupant of this couch, fit for a princess royal, was the little mistress of all she surveyed, as well as the mansion of which the room formed a small part; and a woebegone-looking little girl she was, who called again, and this time impatiently: —

" Gabrielle, hurry, do."

" Oui, oui, mademoiselle Hazel ; " and Gabrielle tripped across the room with the white kimono in one hand and fresh towels in the other. She had just slipped it upon Hazel when there was a knock at the door. Gabrielle opened it, and Wilkins asked in a voice intended to be low, but which proved only husky : —

" Nuss say she mus' jes' speak wif Marse Clyde 'fo' she come up, an' wan's to know if Miss Hazel will haf her breffus now or wait till she come up herse'f."

Before Gabrielle could answer, Hazel called out, " You may bring it up now, Wilkins ; and has the postman come yet ? "

Wilkins' broad smile sounded in his voice, as it came out of its huskiness.

" Yes, Miss Hazel, ben jes' 'fo' I come up. I ain't seen no hearts, but dey 's thicker 'n spatter by de feel, an' a heap o' boxes by 'spress ! "

" Oh, bring them up quick, Wilkins, and tell papa to be sure and come up directly after breakfast."

" Yes, for sho', Miss Hazel," said Wilkins, delighted to have a word with the little daughter of her whom he had carried in his arms thirty-two years ago up and down the jasmine-covered porch of an old New Orleans mansion.

In a few minutes, he reappeared with two large silver trays, on one of which was the tempting breakfast of Hamburg grapes, a dropped egg, a slice of golden-brown toast, half of a squab broiled to the melting-point, and a cup of cocoa. On the other were boxes large and small, and white envelopes of all sizes.

Gabrielle cut the string and opened the boxes, while Hazel looked on, pleased to be remembered, but finding nothing unusual in the display; for Christmas and Easter and birthdays and parties brought just about the same collection, minus "the hearts," which Wilkins had felt through the covers. The only fun, after all, was in the guessing.

Just then Mr. Clyde entered.

"Oh, papa! I'm so glad you have come; it's no fun guessing alone." She put up her peaked, sallow little face for the good-morning kiss; and her father, with the thought of his last night's struggle, took the face in both hands and kissed brow and mouth with unusual tenderness.

"Why, papa!" she exclaimed, "that kiss is my best valentine; you never kissed me that way before."

"Well, it's time I began, Birdie; let's see what you have for nonsense here. What's this — from Cambridge?"

"Oh, that's Jack, I'm sure; he always sends me violets; but what is that in the middle of the bunch?" With a smile she drew out a tiny vignette of her Harvard Sophomore cousin. It was framed in a little gold heart, and on a slip of paper was written, "For thee, I'm all 'art."

"Jack's a gay deceiver," laughed her father; "he's all ' 'art' for a good many girls, big and little. What's this? — and this?"

One after another he took out the contents of envelopes and boxes, — candy hearts by the pound in silver bonbon boxes, silk hearts, paper hearts, a flower heart of real roses ("That's from you, Papa Clyde!" she exclaimed, and her father did not deny the pleasant accusation), hollow gilt hearts stuffed with sentiments, a silver châtelaine heart for change, and last, but not least, an enormous envelope, a foot square, containing a white paper heart all written over with "sentiments" from the girls in her class at school.

"Come now, Birdie," said her father, after the last one had been opened and guessed over, "eat your breakfast, or nurse will scold us both for putting play before business."

"I don't think I want any, papa," said Hazel, languidly, for, after all, the valentines had proved to be almost too much excitement for the little girl, who was just recovering from weeks of slow fever; "and, Gabrielle, take the flowers away, they make my head ache, — and the other things, too," she added, turning her head wearily on the pillow.

"But you *must* eat, Hazel dear," said her father, gently but firmly; and therewith he took a grape and squeezed the pulp between her lips. Hazel laughed, — a faint sound.

"Why, papa, if you feed me that way, I shall be a real Birdie. Yes," she nodded, "that's good; I'll take another;" and her father proceeded to feed her slowly, now coaxing, now urging, then commanding, till a few grapes and a half egg were disposed of.

"There, now, I won't play tyrant any longer," he said, "for your real tyrant of a doctor is coming soon, and I must be out of the way."

"Are you going to be at home for luncheon to-day, papa?"

"No, dear, I've promised to go out to Tuxedo with the Masons, but I shall be at home before dinner, just to look in upon you. I dine with the Pearsells afterwards. Good-bye." A kiss, — two, three of them; and the merry, handsome young father, still but thirty-seven, had gone, and with him much of the brightness of Hazel's day.

But she was used to this. Ever since she could remember anything, she had been petted and kissed and — left with her nurse, her governess, or a French maid.

Her young mother, a Southern belle, lived more out of her home than in it, with the round of gayeties in the winter months interrupted and continued by winter house-parties at Lenox, a yachting cruise in the Mediterranean, an early spring-flitting to the mountains of North Carolina, and the later household moving to Newport.

In all these migrations Hazel accompanied her parents; in fact, was moved about as so much goods and chattels, from New York to the Berkshires, from the Berkshires to Malta, from Malta to the Great Smokies, from the mountains to the sea; her appurtenances, the governess and French maid, went with her; and the routine of her home in New York, the study, the promenade, the all-alone breakfasts and dinners went on with the regularity of clockwork, whether on the yacht, in the mountains, or in the villa on the Cliff.

So now, although she wished her father would stay and entertain her, it never occurred to her to tell him so; and

likewise it never occurred to the father that his child
needed or wished him to stay. Nor had it ever occurred
to the young mother that she was not doing her whole
duty by her child; for she never omitted to go upstairs
and kiss her little daughter good-night, whether the child
was awake or asleep, before going out to dinner, theatre,
or reception.

She died when Hazel was nine, and it was a lovely
memory of "mamma" that Hazel cherished: a vision of
loveliness in trailing white silk, or velvet, or lace, — her
mother always wore white, it was her Southern inheritance,
— with a single dark-red rose among the folds of Vene-
tian point of the bertha; always a gleam of white neck
and arms banded with flashing, many-faceted diamonds,
or roped with pearls; always a sense of delicious white
warmth and fragrance, as the vision bent over her and
pressed a light kiss upon her cheek. And if, in her bliss,
she opened her sleepy eyes, she looked always into laughing brown depths, and putting up her hand caressed
shining masses of brown hair.

But it was always a good-night vision. In the morning
mamma did not breakfast until ten, and Hazel was off to
the little private school at half-past nine. At noon
mamma was either out at lunch or giving a lunch-party;
and in the afternoon there was the promenade in the
Park with the governess, and sometimes, as a treat, a drive
with mamma on her round of calls, when Hazel and the
maid sat among the furs in the carriage. Then Hazel
played at being grown up, and longed for the time when

she could wear a reception dress like mamma's, of white broadcloth and sable, and trip up the steps of the various houses, and trip down again with a bevy of young girls laughing and chatting so merrily.

All that had ceased when Hazel was nine, and the young father had made her mistress in her mother's place. It was such a great house! and there were so many servants! and the housekeeper was so strict! and it was so queer to sit at the round table in the big dining-room and try to look at papa over the silver épergne in the centre!

When she was eleven, she entered one of the large private schools which many of her little mates attended. Soon it came to be the "girls of our set" with Hazel; and then there followed music-lessons, and violin-lessons, and riding-lessons, and dancing-class, and riding-days in the Park, and lunch-parties with the girls, and theatre-matinée-parties, and concerts at Carnegie Hall, and birthday parties, and sales — school and drawing-room affairs — and Lenten sewing-classes; until gradually her little society life had become an epitome of her mother's, and when she began to shoot up like a bean-sprout, lose her round face and the delicate pink from her cheeks, uncles and aunt and cousin and friends whispered of her mother's frail constitution, and that it was time to take heed.

Then it was that the physician, who had helped to bring her into the world, was summoned hastily to prevent her early departure from it. This was the "curious case" that so bothered him; and this pale, languid girl of thirteen in the blue-canopied bed was the one he intended to transplant into another soil.

A short, sharp tap announced his arrival. The nurse opened the door.

" Good-morning, little girl — ah, ah ! Saint Valentine's Day ? I had forgotten it; all those came this morning ? " he said cheerily, pointing to a table on which Gabrielle had placed all the remembrances but the flowers.

" Yes, Doctor Heath ; but my best valentine, you know, is papa, and after him, you."

" Hm, flatterer ! " growled the Doctor, feeling her pulse. " Pretty good, pretty good. Think we can get you up for half a day. What do you say, nurse ? "

" I think it will do her good, Doctor Heath ; she has no appetite yet, and a little exercise might help her to it."

" No appetite ? " The two eyebrows drew together in a straight line over the bridge of his nose, and, from under them, a pair of keen eyes looked at Hazel.

" Well, I 've planned something that will give you a splendid one, Hazel, — the best kind of a tonic — "

" Oh, I don't want to take any more tonics. I am so sick of them," said Hazel, in a despairing tone, for although she adored the Doctor, she despised his medicines.

" You won't get sick of this tonic so soon, I 'll warrant," he said, unbending his brows and letting the full twinkle of his fine eyes shine forth, — " at least not after you are used to it. I won't say but that it may cause a certain kind of sickness at first; in fact, I 'm sure of it."

" Oh, will it nauseate me ? " cried Hazel, dreading to suffer any more.

" No, no, it won't do that, but — "

" But what *do* you mean, Doctor Heath ? Are you joking ? "

" Never was more in earnest in my life," replied the Doctor, rubbing his hands in glee, much to Hazel's amazement. " Hazel," he turned abruptly to her, " papa is a splendid fellow; did you know that ? "

Hazel laughed aloud, a real girl's laugh, — Doctor Heath was so queer at times.

" Have you just found that out ? " she retorted.

" No, you witch, — don't be impertinent to your elders, — I have n't ; but really he is, take it all in all, just about the most common-sense fellow in New York City."

" What has he done now, that you are praising him so ? "

" Just heard to me, my dear, and agreed to do just as I want him to," said the Doctor, demurely.

" Why," laughed Hazel, " that 's just when I think he is a most splendid fellow, when he does just what I want him to. Is n't it funny you and I think just alike ! " And she gave his hand a malicious little pat. The Doctor caught the five slender digits and held them fast.

" Now we 're agreed that you have the most splendid, common-sense father in the world, I want you to prove to me that your father has the most splendid, common-sense daughter in it, as well."

Again Hazel laughed. She was used to her friend's ways.

"That means that you want me to take that old, new tonic of yours."

"Yes, just that," said the Doctor, emphatically; "and now, as you don't appear to care to hear about it, I'm going to make a long call and tell you its entire history."

"Have you brought it with you?" asked Hazel, somewhat mystified.

"No, I can't carry around with me in a cab five children, a hundred acres of pine woods, a whole mountain-top, and a few Jersey cows."

"What *do* you mean? You *are* joking."

Then the physician clasped the thin hand a little more closely and told her of the country plan.

At first, Hazel failed to comprehend it. She gazed at the speaker with large, serious eyes, as if she half-feared he had taken leave of his senses.

"Did papa know it this morning?" was her first question.

"Yes, my dear."

"Then that is why he kissed me the way he did," she said thoughtfully. "But," her lip quivered, "I sha'n't have him to kiss me up there, and — and — oh, dear!" A wail went up from the canopied bed that made the Doctor turn sick at heart, and even the nurse hurried away into the dressing-room.

Somehow Doctor Heath could not exhort Hazel, as he had her father, to use common-sense. He preferred to use diplomacy.

"You see, Hazel, a year won't be so very long, and it will give your hair time to grow; and perhaps you would not mind wearing a cap for a time up there, while if you were here you certainly would not care about going to dancing-school or parties in that rig; now would you?"

Hazel sniffed and looked for her handkerchief. As she failed to find it, the Doctor applied his own huge square of linen to the dripping, reddened eyes, and tenderly stroked the smooth-shaven head.

Hazel had her vanities like all girls, and her long dark braids had been one of them. After the fever, she had been shorn of what scanty locks had been left to her, and many a time she had wondered what the girls would say when they saw her. After all, the new plan might be endured, for the sake of the hair and her looks.

She sniffed again, and this time a good many tears were drawn up into her nose. The Doctor, taking no notice of the subsiding flood, proceeded, —

"My patients always look so comical when the fuzz is coming out. It's like chicken-down all over the head — "

"Fuzz!" exclaimed Hazel, with a dismayed, wide-eyed look; "must I have fuzz for hair?"

"Why, of course, for about five months," was the Doctor's matter-of-fact reply. "Then," he continued, apparently unheeding the look of relief that crept over Hazel's face, "you are apt to have the hair come out curly."

"Oh!"

"Yes, and it really grows very fast — that is," he said, resorting to wile, "if any one is strong and well; but if the general health is not good, why — hem! — the hair isn't apt to grow!"

"Goodness! I don't want to be bald all my life!"

"No, I thought not, and for that very reason it did seem the best thing for you to get into the country where you can get well and strong as fast as ever you can."

"Shall I have to eat my breakfast and dinner alone up there?" was her next question.

Doctor Heath laughed. "What! With all those five children! You will never want for company, I can assure you of that. And now I'll be off; as it's Saint Valentine's Day, which I had forgotten, I'll wager I have five valentines from those very children waiting for me at home."

"Will you show them to me, if you have?"

"To be sure I will. Now sit up for half a day, and get yourself strong enough to let me take you up there by the middle of March."

"Oh, are you going to take me? What fun! Are they friends of yours?" she added timidly.

"Every one," said the Doctor, emphatically. He turned at the door. "You haven't said yet whether you will honor me with your company up there."

"I suppose I must," she said, with something between a sigh and a laugh. "But I don't know what Gabrielle will do; she'll be so homesick."

"Gabrielle!" cried the Doctor, in a voice loud with amazement; "you don't think you are going to take Gabrielle with you, do you?"

Before Hazel had time to recover from her astonishment, Gabrielle, hearing her name called so loudly, came tripping into the room.

"Oui, oui, monsieur le docteur;" and Doctor Heath beat a hasty retreat to avoid further misunderstandings.

In the afternoon, Hazel received a box by messenger, with, "Please return by bearer," on the wrapper. On opening it, she found the Doctor's valentines with the following sentiments appropriately attached.

I

By Rose-pose made, by March adorned,
'T is not a Heart that one should scorn:
For use each day, the whole year through,
Where find a Valentine so true?

II

Cherry Blossom made this fudge
(Buddie made the box).
Eat it soon, or you will judge,
She made it all of rocks.

III

Baby May has made this cookie;
Mother baked it — but, by hookey!
I can't find another rhyme
To match with this your valentine.
    Your loving Valentines,

ROSE, MARCH, " BUDD AND CHERRY," MAY BLOSSOM.
(We're one.)

MOUNT HUNGER, February 14, 1896.

V

It was the middle of April, yet the drifts still blocked the ravines, and great patches of snow lay scattered thickly on the northern and eastern slopes of the mountains.

Not a bud had thought of swelling; not a fern dared to raise its downy ball above the sodden leaves. Day after day a keen wind from the north chased dark clouds across a watery blue sky, and now and then a solitary crow flapped disconsolately over the upland pastures and into the woods.

But in the farmhouse on the mountain, every Blossom was a-quiver with excitement, for the " live Valentine " was to arrive that day.

According to what Doctor Heath had written first, Mrs. Blossom had expected Hazel to come the middle of March. She had told the children about it a week before that date, and ever since, wild and varied and continuous had been the speculations concerning the new member of the family.

Both father and mother were much amused at the different ways in which each one accepted the fact, and commented upon it. At the same time they were slightly anxious as to the outcome of such a combination.

"They 'll work it out for themselves, Mary," said Mr. Blossom, when his wife was expressing her fears on account of the attitude of March and Cherry.

"I hope with all my heart they will, without friction or unpleasantness for the poor child," replied his wife, thoughtfully, for March's looks and words returned to her, and they foreboded trouble.

Her husband smiled. "Perhaps the 'poor child' will have her ways of looking at things up here, which may cause a pretty hard rub now and then for our children. But let them take it; it will do them good, and show us what stuff is in them for the future."

Mrs. Blossom tried to think so, but March's words on that afternoon she had told the children came back to her.

They were dumb at first through sheer surprise. Then Rose spoke, flinging aside her Virgil she had been studying by the failing light at the window.

"Oh, mother! we 've been so happy — just by ourselves."

"Will you be less happy, Rose, in trying to make some one else share our happiness?"

Rose said nothing, but leaned her forehead against the pane, and the tears trickled adown it and froze halfway.

Mrs. Blossom proceeded, in the silence that followed, to tell them something of Hazel's life. Then Budd spoke up like a man.

"I 'm awful sorry for her; she 's a little brick to be willing to come away from her father and live with folks she don't know. I 'd be a darned coward about leaving my Popsey."

There was no tablecloth handy to hide the squeeze he wanted to give his mother's hand, and Mrs. Blossom, knowing how he hated any public demonstration of affection, reserved her approving kiss for the dark and bedtime. But she looked at him in a way that sent Budd whistling, "I won't play in your back-yard," over to the kitchen stove, where he stared inanely at his own reflection in the polished pipe.

For the first time in her life, Cherry did not echo her twin's sentiment. She was already insanely jealous of the new-comer who seemed to claim so much of her mother's sympathy and affection. And she was n't even here! What would it be when she was here for good and all?

At this miserable thought, and all that it appeared to involve, Cherry began to cry.

Now to see Cherry Blossom cry generally afforded great fun for the whole family; for there never was a girl of ten who could cry in quite such a unique manner as this same round-faced, pug-nosed, brown-eyed Cherry, whose red hair curled as tightly as corkscrews all over her head, and bobbed and danced and quivered and shook with every motion and emotion.

First, her nose grew very red at the tip; then, her small mouth screwed itself around by her left ear; gradually, her round face wrinkled till it resembled a withered crab-apple; and finally, if one listened intently and watched closely, one could hear small sniffs and see two infinitesimal drops of water issue from the nearly closed and wrinkled eyes.

But to-day no one noticed, and Cherry sat down in her mother's lap, and mumbled out her woe between sniffs.

"I can't help it if Budd does want her; *I* don't, Martie. Budd will play with her, and you'll kiss her just as you do us, and it won't be comfy any more."

"That does not sound like mother's Cherry Blossom," said Mrs. Blossom, smiling in spite of herself. "I think I'll tell you all why it comes to mother and father as a blessing."

Then Mrs. Blossom told them of the mortgage on the farm; how it had been made necessary, and what it meant, and how it was her duty to accept what had been sent to her as a means of paying it off.

Rose came over from the window. "Oh, why didn't you tell us before, Martie," she cried, sobbing outright this time, "and let us help you to earn something towards it during all this dreadful year? To think you have been bearing all this, and just going about the same, smiling and cheer — oh, dear!" Rose sat down on the hearth-rug at her mother's feet, and her sobs mingled with Cherry's sniffs.

March, who had listened thus far in silence, rose from the settle where he had flung himself in disgust, and, going over to his mother, stood straight and tall before her. His gray eyes flashed.

"I've been a fool, mother, not to see it all before this. You ought to have told *me*. I'm your eldest son, and come next after father in 'home things.'" And with this assertion he made a mighty resolve, then and there to put away boyish things and be more of a man. His mother, looking at him, felt the change, and tears of thankfulness filled her eyes.

"What could you do, children? You were too young to have your lives burdened with work."

"I'd have found something to do, mother, if you had only told me. About the girl — " he hesitated — "of course I'll look at it from the money side, but it'll never be the same after she comes — never!" And with that he went off into the barn.

His mother sighed, for March was looking at the matter in the very way which, to her, was abhorrent.

"Don't sigh so, Martie," cried Rose; "I'll take back what I said, and do everything I can to help you by making it pleasant for her. Budd has made me ashamed of myself."

"That's my own daughter Rose," said Mrs. Blossom, leaning over to kiss her parting, for Cherry was awkwardly in the way.

"Did you hear Rose, Cherry?" whispered her mother.

"Ye-es," sniffed Cherry.

"And won't you try to help mother, and make Hazel happy?"

"N-o," said Cherry, still obdurate.

"Very well; then I must depend on Rose and Budd and little May," replied her mother, putting her down from her knee. By which Cherry knew she was out of favor, and, not having Budd to flee to for sympathy, ran blindly out into the woodshed and straight into Chi, who was bringing

in two twelve-quart milk pails filled to overflowing with
their creamy contents.

"Hi there! Cherry Bounce! Steady, steady — without
you want to mop up this woodshed."

"O Chi! I'm just as miser'ble; a new little girl's
coming to live with us always, and we'll have no more
good times."

"That's queer," said Chi, balancing the pails deftly as
Cherry fluttered about, rather uncertain as to where she
should betake herself in the cold. "I should think it
would be the more, the merrier. When's she comin'?"

"This very month," said Cherry, opening her eyes a little
wider, and forgetting to sniff in her delight at telling some
news. "She's a rich little girl, but very poor, too, mother
says, and she's been sick and is coming here to get well. I
suppose she's lost all her flesh while she's been sick, like
Aunt Tryphosa; don't you? That's why she's so poor."

"Hm! — rich 'n' poor too; that's bad for children," said
Chi, soberly.

"Why?" asked Cherry, surprised into drying her small
tears and forgetting to sniff.

"Coz 'tis. You see, all you children are rich 'n' poor
too; so she'll keep you comp'ny, as she's poor where
you're rich as Crœsus, 'n' you're poor as Job's turkey
where she's rich."

"Why, what do you mean, Chi?"

"You wait awhile, 'n' you'll find out." And with that,
Cherry had to be content.

As the woodshed was too cold to be long comfortably

mournful in, — Cherry decided to go inside and set the table for tea, wondering, meanwhile, what Chi meant. Ordinarily she would have gone straight to her mother to find out; but just to-night Cherry felt there was an abyss separating them, and she hated the very thought of the newcomer having caused this break between her adored Martie and herself before having stepped foot in the house.

But Hazel's arrival had been delayed a whole month: first, on account of the unusually cold weather of March, and then on account of the Doctor's pressing engagements. To-night, however, this long waiting was to be at an end.

Mr. Blossom had harnessed Bess and Bob into the two-seated wagon, and driven down three miles for them to the " Mill Settlement ; " and there he was to meet the stage from Barton's River, the nearest railway station.

As the time approached for the light of the lantern on the wagon to glimmer on the lower mountain road, which ran in view of the house, the excitement of Budd and Cherry grew intense. March intended to be indifferent, yet tolerant, but even he went twice to the door to listen. As for Rose, she was thinking almost more of Doctor Heath, with whom she was a great favorite, than of the coming guest. Chi had done up the chores early with March's help, and sat whistling and whittling in the shed door with his eye on the lower road.

" They 're coming; they 're coming ! " screamed the twins, making a wild dash for the woodshed, that they might have the first glimpse as the wagon drove up to the kitchen porch.

"Chi, they're coming!" they shrieked in his ear, as they flew past him.

"Well, I ain't deaf, if they are," said Chi, gathering himself together, and going out to help unload.

"Chi, how are you?" said the Doctor, in a hearty tone, grasping the horny hand held out to him.

"First-rate, 'n' glad to see you back on the Mountain."

"Here, lend a hand, will you? and take out a little somebody who has to be handled rather gently for a week or two."

"I ain't much used to handlin' chiny," he replied, "but I'll be careful."

He reached up his long arms and, gently as a woman, lifted Hazel out of the wagon on to the porch.

By this time, Budd had found his bearings and had the Doctor by the hand.

"Halloo, Budd! here you are handy. Just take Hazel's bag, and run into the house with her; she mustn't stand a minute in this keen air."

Budd's heart was going pretty fast, but he faced the music.

"Come along, Hazel; we've been waiting a month to see you."

"And I've been waiting longer than that to see you, Budd." The gentle voice made Budd her vassal forever after.

"Here, Martie, here's Hazel!" he shouted quite unnecessarily, for his mother had come to the door to welcome her guests. Cherry, hearing the shout, disappeared in the pantry, and was invisible until called to supper.

In the confusion of glad welcome that followed, Hazel was conscious of stepping into a large, warm, lighted room, of some one's arms about her, and of a loving voice, saying:

"Come in, dear; you must be so tired with your long journey and this cold ride;" and then a kiss that made her half forget the lonely, strange feeling she had had during the stage and wagon ride, despite the doctor's cheerfulness and care of her.

Then some one untied her brown velvet hood and loosened her long sealskin coat.

"Let me take off your things," said Rose.

Hazel looked up and into the loveliest face she ever remembered to have seen.

"I 'm Rose, and this is May. May, this is the valentine Martie told us of."

"I tiss 'oo," said May, winningly, and held up her rosy bud of a face to Hazel. Hazel stooped to give her, not one, but a half-dozen kisses. There was no resisting such a little blossom.

May put up her hand and stroked the little silk skull-cap.

"What 'oo wear tap for ? "

"Sh! baby," said Rose, horrified, putting her hand on May's mouth.

"Oh, don't do that," said Hazel, "I 'm so used to it now; I don't mind what people say or think. But I did at first."

May's lip began to quiver and roll over; Hazel sat down on the settle, and, drawing May up beside her, said gently: —

"There, there, little May Blossom, don't you cry, and I'll tell you all about it. It's because I have n't any hair. I lost it all when I was sick so long. Sometime I'll show you how funny my head looks, all covered with fuzz. Doctor Heath says it's like a little chicken's." And May was comforted and won once and for all to the Valentine, who gave her the tiny châtelaine watch to play with.

Budd had been hanging about to get the first glimpse of Hazel by lamplight, and now rushed off to the barn and Chi to give vent to his feelings.

"I say, Chi, where are you?"

"In the harness room," replied Chi. "What do you want?" as he appeared.

"I say, Chi, she's a peach. She is n't a bit stuck up, as March said she would be."

"Good-lookin'?" queried Chi.

"N-o," said Budd, hesitating, "n-o, but I think she will be when she gets some hair."

"Ain't got any hair!" exclaimed Chi. "How does that happen?"

"She said she'd been sick an' lost it all, an' 't was like chicken fuzz."

"Said that, did she?" exclaimed Chi, laughing; then, with the sudden change from gayety to absolute solemnity that was peculiar to him, he said: —

"She's no fool, I can tell you that, Budd; 'n' I'll bet

my last red cent she 'll come out an A Number 1 beauty;
'n' March Blossom had better hold his tongue till he cuts
all his wisdom teeth." And with that Chi went into the
shed room to " wash up."

What a supper that was! And what a room in which
to eat it!

But for the Doctor's cheery voice, Hazel, as she sat in a
corner of the settle, might have thought herself in another
world, so unaccustomed were her city-bred eyes to all that
was going on before her. The room itself was so queer,
and, in a way new to her, delightful.

The farmhouse was an old one, strong of beam and solid
of foundation. It had been divided at first according to
the fashion of the other century in which it was built. But
as his family increased, Mr. Blossom found the need of a
large, general living-room. It was then that he took down
the wall between the front square room and the kitchen,
and threw them into one. It was this arrangement that
made the apartment unique.

At one end was the huge fireplace that was originally
in the front room. At the left of the fireplace was the
jog into which the front door opened, formerly the little
entry.

This was the sitting-room end of the low forty-foot-long
apartment; and it showed to Hazel the fireplace, the old-
fashioned crane, with the hickory back-log glowing warm
welcome, the long red-cushioned settle, a set of shelves
filled with books, a little round work-table, Mrs. Blossom's
special property, a large round table of cherry that had

turned richly red with age, and wooden armchairs and rockers, with patchwork cushions.

The middle portion served for dining-room. In it were the family table of hard pine, the wooden chairs, and Mrs. Blossom's grandmother's tall pine dresser.

At the kitchen end, next the woodshed, were the sink, the stove, the kitchen shelves for pots and pans, and the kitchen table with its bread-trough and pie-board, all of which Rose kept scoured white with soap and sand.

This living-room, sitting-room, dining-room, and kitchen in one had six windows facing south and east. Every window had brackets for plants; for this evening Rose had turned the blossom-side inwards to the room, and the walls glowed and gleamed with the velvety crimson of gloxinias, the red of fuchsias, the pink and white and scarlet of geraniums, the cream of wax-plant and begonia. Upon all this radiance of color, the lamplight shone and the fire flashed its crimson shadows. The kettle sang on the stove, and the delicious odor of baked potatoes came from the open oven.

"Why, March!" said the Doctor, coming down from the spare room at the call for supper, "waiting for an introduction? I did n't know you stood on ceremony in this fashion. Allow me," he said with mock gravity to Hazel, and presented March in due form.

Hazel greeted him exactly as she would have greeted a new boy at dancing-school. "Little Miss Finicky," was March's scornful thought of her, as he bowed rather awkwardly and thrust his hands into his pockets, racking his brains for something to say.

" What a handsome boy ! As handsome as Jack," was Hazel's first impression ; then, missing the cordiality with which the other members of the family had welcomed her, she said in thought, " I 'm sure he does not want me here by the way he acts ; I think he 's horrid."

Doctor Heath sat down by Hazel. " I 'm not going to let you sit down to tea with all these mischiefs, little girl, not to-night, for you can't eat baked potatoes and the other good things after that long journey, so I 'll ask Rose to give you a bite right here on the settle."

" I 'll speak to Rose," said March, glad to get away.

" Thank you," said the Doctor, looking after him with a puzzled expression in his keen eyes. Just then Mr. Blossom and Chi came in, and the whole family sat down at the table.

" Why, where 's Cherry ? " exclaimed the Doctor.

"Budd, where 's Cherry ? " said his father.

" I promised her I would n't tell where she hides till she was twelve, an' now she 's ten, an' she 's been so mean about Haz — "

" Budd," said his father, sternly, " answer me directly."

"She 's under the pantry shelf behind the meal-chest," said Budd, meekly.

There was a shout of laughter that caused Cherry to crawl out pretty quickly and open the pantry door, — for it was hard to hear the fun and not be in it.

" Come, Cherry," said her mother, still laughing, and

Cherry slipped into her seat beside Doctor Heath with a murmured, "How do you do?" and her face bent so low over her plate that nothing was visible to Hazel but a round head running over with tight red curls that bobbed and trembled in a peculiarly funny way.

"Well, Cherry," said the Doctor, trying to speak gravely, with only the red tip of a nose in view, "you seem to be rather low in your mind. I shall have to prescribe for you. Chi, suppose you drive me down to the Settlement to-morrow morning, and on the way to the train I will send up a cure-all for low spirits. I've something for March, too. I think he needs it." He drew his eyebrows together over the bridge of his nose and cast a sharp glance at the boy, who felt the doctor had read him.

"That means you've got something for us," said Budd, bluntly.

"Guess Budd's hit the nail on the head this time," said Chi. "Shouldn't wonder if 'twas some pretty lively stuff."

"You're right there, Chi," replied the Doctor, laughing. "There's plenty of good strong bark in it —"

Thereupon there was a shout of joy from Budd which brought Cherry's head into position at once.

"I know, I know, it's a St. Bernard puppy!"

"Oh — ee," squealed Cherry, in her delight, and forthwith put her arm through the Doctor's and squeezed it hard against her ribs.

"Guess there's a good deal of crow-foot in the other, ain't there?" said Chi, with a wink at March, who deliber-

4

ately left his seat after saying, " Excuse me " most gravely
to his mother, and turned a somersault in the kitchen end
just to relieve his feelings. Then, with his hands in his
pockets, he went up to Doctor Heath, his usually clear,
pale face flushing with excitement.

" Do you mean, Doctor Heath, you're going to give me
a full-blooded Wyandotte cock?" he demanded.

" That is just what I mean, March," replied the Doctor,
with great gravity, "and twelve full-blooded wives are at
this moment looking in vain for a roost beside their lord
and master in the express office down at Barton's River."

" Oh, glory!" cried March, wringing the Doctor's hand
with both his, and then going off to execute another
somersault. "You've done it now!"

" Done what, March?" asked Doctor Heath, really
touched by the boy's grateful enthusiasm.

" Made my fortune," he replied, dropping into his seat
again, breathless with excitement; and to the Doctor's
amazement he saw tears, actual tears, gather in the boy's
eyes, before he looked down in his plate and busied himself
with his baked potato.

Hazel saw them too. " What a strange boy," she thought,
" and how different this is from eating my dinner all alone!"
Then she slipped up to the Doctor's side with her small tray
containing nothing but empty dishes, for the keen air and
the sight of so many others eating and enjoying themselves
had given her a good appetite.

" Are you satisfied with me *now?*" she said, presenting
her tray.

"I should think so," he exclaimed. "Two glasses of milk, two slices of toasted brown bread, one piece of sponge cake, and a baked apple with cream! I've gone out of business with you; my last 'tonic' is going to work well, — don't you think so?"

"I'm sure it is," she said quietly, but there was such a depth of meaning in the sweet voice and the few words that the Doctor threw his arm around her as they rose from the table, and kept her beside him until bedtime.

At nine o'clock, Mrs. Blossom helped her to undress, and then, saying she would come back soon, left her alone in the little bedroom off the kitchen.

Hazel looked about her in amazement. This was her little room! A small single bed, looking like a snow drift, so white and feathery and high was it; one window curtained with a square of starched white cotton cloth that drew over the panes by means of a white cord on which it was run at the top; a tiny wash-stand with an old-fashioned bowl and pitcher of green and white stone-ware, and over it an old-fashioned gilt mirror; a small splint-bottomed chair and large braided rug of red woollen rags. That was all, except in one corner, where some cleats had been nailed to the ceiling and a clothes-press made by hanging from them full curtains of white cloth.

For the first time in her life, Hazel unpacked her own travelling-bag and took out the silver toilet articles with the pretty monogram. But where should she put them? No bureau, no dressing-case, no bath-room! — For a few minutes Hazel felt bewildered, then, laughing, she put them back again into her bag, and, leaving her candle in the tin candlestick on the wash-stand, she gave one leap into the middle of the high feather-bed.

Just then Mrs. Blossom returned from saying good-night to her own children. She tucked Hazel in snugly, and to the young girl's surprise, knelt by the bed saying, " Let us repeat the Lord's Prayer together, dear ; " and together they said it, Hazel fearing almost the sound of her own voice. When they had finished, Mary Blossom, still kneeling, asked that Father to bless the coming of this one of His little ones into their home, and asked it in such a loving, trustful way, that Hazel's arm stole out from the coverlet and around Mrs. Blossom's neck ; her head, soft and silky as a new-born baby's, cuddled to her shoulder; and when Mrs. Blossom kissed her good-night, she said suddenly, but half-timidly, " Do you say *this* with Rose every night ? "

" Yes, dear, every night."

" And how old is Rose ? "

" She will be seventeen next August."

" Do you with Budd and Cherry, too ? "

" Yes, with all my children, even March and May."

" March ! " exclaimed Hazel.

" Why not ? " laughed his mother. " I 'm sure he needs it, as you 'll find out; now good-night, and don't get up to our early breakfast to-morrow, for the Doctor goes on the first morning train, and you 're not quite strong enough yet to do just as we do. Good-night again."

" Good-night," said Hazel, thinking she could never have enough of this kind of putting to bed.

Meanwhile March and Budd, in their bedroom over the " long-room," were discussing in half-whispers Wyandotte cocks, St. Bernard puppies, and the new-comer, for they were too excited to sleep.

Just behind March's bed, near the head, there was a large knot in the boards of the flooring, which for four years had served him many a good turn, when Budd and Cherry were planning, below in the kitchen, how they could play tricks upon him. March had carefully removed the knot, and with his eye, or ear, at the hole, he had been able, entirely to the mystification of the twins, to overthrow their conspiracies and defeat their flank movements. When his espionage was over, he replaced the knot, and no one in the household was the wiser for his private detective service.

To-day, late in the afternoon, he had taken out the knot, intending to have a view of the new arrival, unbeknown to the rest of the household; but so interested had he become in the general welcome and in the anticipation of the Doctor's gifts, that he had forgotten both to look through the hole and to replace the knot.

Hazel, too, could not sleep at first. It was all so strange, and yet she was so happy. Her thoughts were in New York, and she was already planning for a visit from her father, when suddenly she remembered that she had left the little châtelaine watch he had given her on her last birthday, lying on the settle where May had been playing with it. She must wind it regularly, that was her father's stipulation when he gave it to her. She sprang out of bed, tiptoed to the door, listened; all was still, but not wholly dark. The embers beneath the ashes in the fire-place sent a dull glow into the room. Softly she stole out; found her watch, then, half-way to her own door, stopped, startled by a voice issuing apparently from the rafters overhead. It was March, who, forgetting his open knot-hole, turned over towards the wall with a prolonged yawn and said, evidently in answer to Budd: —

"Oh, go to sleep; don't talk about her. I think she's a perfect guy."

VI

MALACHI

It was a month after the eventful day for the Blossoms, and Saturday morning. Rose, with her sleeves rolled up above her elbows, was kneading bread and singing, as she worked: —

> "'Oh, a king would have loved and left thee,
> And away thy sweet love cast:
> But I am thine
> Whilst the stars shall shine, —
> To the — last — ' "

Just here, she gave the round mass of dough a toss up to the ceiling and caught it deftly on her right fist as it came down, finishing her octave with high C, while again the bread spun aloft and dropped in safety on her left fist — " to the last! "

Then she proceeded with her kneading and singing: —

> "' I told thee when love was hopeless;
> But now he is wild and sings —
> That the stars above [up went the bread again] —
> Shine ever on Love — ' "

A peal of merry laughter close behind her made her jump, and the bread came down kerchunk into the kneading trough.

"Gracious, Hazel! how you frightened me! I thought you were off with Budd and Cherry."

"So I was; but they wanted me to come in and tell you there is to be a secret meeting of the N. B. B. O. O. Society in the usual place. They said you would know where it is."

"Of course I do; do you?"

"No, they would n't tell. They said it is against the rules to allow any one in who has n't been initiated. They said they 'd initiate me, if I wanted to join."

"Well, do you want to?"

"Of course I do, if you belong," said Hazel, eagerly.

"Tell them I 'll be out after I 've put the bread to rise and cleared up; but be sure and tell them not to do anything till I come."

"Yes," cried Hazel, joyfully, skipping through the wood-shed and encountering Chi with a bag of seed-beans.

"Where you goin', Lady-bird?" (This was Chi's name for her from the first day.) "Seems to me you 're gettin' over the ground pretty fast."

"The Buds" (for so Hazel had nicknamed the children) "are going to have a meeting somewhere of the N. B. B. O. O. Society, and I 'm to be initiated, Chi. What does that mean?"

"Initiated, hey? Into a secret society? Well, that depends. — Sometimes it means being tossed sky-high in a blanket, and then again you 're dropped lower than the bottomless pit; and you can't most always tell beforehand which way you 're goin'."

Hazel's face fairly lost the rich color she had gained in

the past month. This was more than she had bargained for.

"Oh, Chi! They would n't do such things to me!" she exclaimed in dismay.

"Well, no — I don't know as they 'd carry it *that* far; but those children mean mischief every time."

"But they would n't hurt me, Chi. They would n't be as mean as that; besides, Rose would n't let them."

"Well, I don't know as she would. But children are children, and Rose ain't grown any wings yet."

"Was Rose initiated?" was Hazel's next rather anxious question.

"Yes, she was," said Chi, taking up a handful of beans and letting them run through his fingers into the open bag.

"How do you know, Chi?"

"Coz I initiated her myself."

"You, Chi? Why, do you belong?"

"First member of the N. B. B. O. O. Society."

"Well, that 's funny. Who initiated you?"

Chi set down the bag of beans, and for a moment shook with laughter; then, growing perfectly sober, he said solemnly: —

"I initiated myself. But they was all on hand when I did it."

"What did you do, Chi?"

"Just hear her!" said Chi to himself, but aloud, he said, "I 'll tell you this much, if it is a secret society. They try 'n' see what stuff you 're made of."

" ' Sugar and spice
And all that 's nice,
That 's what little girls are made of,' "

Hazel interrupted, singing merrily.

" There was n't much 'sugar 'n' spice' in that Rose Blossom when she put me to the test. You ain't heard a screech-owl yet; but when you do, you 'll come running home to find out whose bein' killed in the woods."

Hazel looked at him half in fear, but Chi went on stolidly : —

" 'N' those children told me I 'd got to go up into the woods at twelve o'clock at night, when the screech-owls was yellin' bloody murder, to show I was n't scairt of nothin'; 'n' I went."

" Oh, Chi, was n't it awful ? "

" Kinder scarey; but they gave me the dinner horn 'n' told me to blow a blast on that when I was up there, so they 'd hear, 'n' know I was *clear* into the woods ; for they was all on hand watchin' from the back attic window — what they could in a pitch-black night — to see if I 'd back down."

" And you did n't, Chi ? " said Hazel, eagerly.

" You bet I did n't, 'n' I brought home an old screecher just to prove I was game."

" How did you catch him, Chi ? "

Chi clapped his hands on his knees, and shook with laughter; then he grew perfectly sober : —

" I took a dark lantern along with me, just to kind of feel my way in the woods — but the children did n't

know about that — 'n' when an old screecher gave a blood-
curdlin' yell, just as near my right ear as the engine down
on the track when you 're standin' at the depot at Barton's
River, — just then I turned on the light full tilt, and the
feller sat right still on the branch, kind of dazed like, 'n'
I took him just as easy as I 'd take a hen off the roost
after dark, 'n' brought him home. 'N' just as I was goin'
up into the attic in the dark, the shed stairs' way, 'n' the
children was all listenin' at the top in the dark, the
dummed bird gave such a screech that the children all
tumbled over one another tryin' to get back to their beds,
'n' such screamin' 'n' hollerin' you never heard — the bird
was n't in it."

Again Chi laughed at the recollection, and Hazel joined
him.

" Did they make you do anything more, Chi ? "

" By George Washin'ton ! I should think they did,"
said Chi, soberly. " That last was March's idea, but
Rose went him one more."

" What could Rose think of worse than that ? " demanded
Hazel.

" Well, she did. She blindfolded my eyes 'n' took me
by the hand, 'n' turned me round 'n' round till I was most
dizzy ; 'n' then she gave me a rope, 'n' she took one end
of it 'n' made me take the other, 'n' kept leadin' me 'n'
leadin' me, 'n' the children all caperin' round me, screamin'
'n' laughin'. Pretty soon — I calculated I 'd walked about
a quarter of a mile — the rope grew slack ; all of a sudden the laughin' 'n' screamin' stopped, 'n' I — walked

right off the bank into the big pool down under the pines, ker — splash! 'n' the children, after they'd got me in, was so scairt for fear I'd lose my breath — I could n't drown coz there was n't more than five feet of water in it — that they hauled on the rope with all their might, 'n' pulled me out; 'n' I let 'em pull," said Chi, grimly.

"I hope they were satisfied after that," said Hazel, soberly.

"They appeared to be," said Chi, contentedly, "for they said I should be president, coz I was so brave. But there's other things harder to do than that."

"What are they, Chi?"

"You've got to keep the by-laws."

"What are those?"

"Rules of the Society. One of 'em's, you must n't be afraid to tell the truth. 'N' another is, you must be scairt to tell a lie."

Hazel grew scarlet at her own thoughts.

"Another is, to help other folks all you can; 'n' the fourth 'n' last is, that no boy or girl as lives in this great, free country of ours ought to be a coward."

Hazel drew a long breath.

"Those must be hard to keep."

"Well, they ain't always easy, that's a fact; but they re mighty good to live by," he added, picking up the bean-bag. "I lived with Ben Blossom's father when I was a little chap as chore boy, 'n' he gave me my schoolin' 'n' clothes; 'n' I've lived with his son ever since he was married, 'n' he's been the best friend a man could have, 'n'

I 've always got along with him in peace and lovin'-kind-
ness; 'n' those four by-laws his father wrote on my boy-
hood; 'n' by those four by-laws I 've kept my manhood;
'n' so I think it 'll do anybody good to join the Society."

" Well," said Hazel, stoutly, " I 'll show them I 'm not
afraid of some things, if I did run away from the turkey-
gobbler."

" That 's right," said Chi, heartily, " 'n' more than that
— betwixt you 'n' me — you 've no cause to be scairt *whatever* they do; now mark my words, *whatever they do*,"
repeated Chi, emphatically.

" I don't care what they do so long as you 're there, Chi,"
said Hazel, looking up into his weather-roughened, deeply-
lined face with such utter trust in her great eyes that Chi
caught up the bag over his shoulder and hurried out to
the barn, muttering to himself: —

" George Washin'ton! How she manages to creep into
the softest corner of a man's heart, I don't know; I expect it 's those great eyes of hers, 'n' that voice just like a
brook winnerin' 'n' gurglin' over its stones in August. —
Guess there 's luck come to this house with Lady-bird!"
And he went about his work.

VII

"Now, Hazel, we 're ready," said Rose, after the dinner dishes had been washed and the children's time was their own. Hazel submitted meekly to the blindfolding process.

She had tried in vain to find out something of what the children intended to do, but they were too clever for her to gain the smallest hint as to the initiation. March had been busy in the ice-house, and Cherry had been ironing the aprons for the family, — that was her Saturday morning duty. Budd and the St. Bernard puppy were off with Chi in the fields.

Rose led her through the woodshed and out of doors — Hazel knew that by the rush of soft air that met her face — and away, somewhither. At last she was helped to climb a ladder; Chi's hand grasped hers, and she felt the flooring under her feet. Then she was left without support of any kind, not daring to move with Chi's story in her thoughts.

"Guess we 'll have the roll-call first," said Chi, solemnly. There was not a sound to be heard except now and then a rush of wings and the twitter of swallows.

" Molly Stark."

" Here," said Rose.

" Markis de Lafayette."

" Here," from March.

" Marthy Washin'ton."

" Present," said Cherry, forgetting she was not in school. Budd snickered, and the president called him to order.

" Fine of two cents for snickerin' in meetin'." Budd looked sober.

" Ethan Allen."

" Here," said Budd, in a subdued voice.

" Old Put, — Here," said Chi, addressing and answering himself. " Now, Markis, read the by-laws."

" Number One. — We pledge ourselves not to be afraid to tell the truth."

" Number Two. — We pledge ourselves to be afraid to tell a lie.

" Number Three. — We pledge ourselves to try to help others whenever we can, wherever we can, however we can, as long as ever we can.

" Number Four. — We, as American boys and girls, pledge ourselves never to play the coward nor to disgrace our country."

" Molly Stark, unfurl the flag," said Chi.

Hazel heard a rustle as Rose unrolled the banner of soft red, white, and blue cambric.

" Put Old Glory round the candidate's shoulders," commanded the president, and Hazel felt the soft folds being draped about her.

"There now, Lady-bird, you're dressed as pretty as you're ever goin' to be; it don't make a mite of difference whether you're the Empress of Rooshy, or just plain every-day folks; 'n' now you've got that rig on, we're ready to give you the hand of fellowship. Markis, you have the floor."

"What name does the candidate wish to be known by?" asked March, with due gravity; then, forgetting his rôle, he added, "You must take the name of some woman who has been just as brave as she could be."

Hazel, feeling the folds of the flag about her, suddenly recalled her favorite poem of Whittier's.

"Barbara Frietchie," she said promptly and firmly.

The various members shouted and cheered themselves hoarse before order was restored.

"What'd I tell you, Budd?" said Chi, triumphantly; then there was another shout, for Chi had broken the rules in speaking thus.

"Two cents' fine!" shouted Budd, "for speaking out of order in meeting."

"Sho! I forgot," said Chi, humbly; "well, proceed."

"Do you, Barbara Frietchie, pledge yourself to try to keep these by-laws?"

"Yes," said Hazel, but rather tremulously.

"Well, then, we'll put you to the test. Molly Stark will extend the first hand of fellowship to Barbara Frietchie — No, hold out your hand, Hazel; way out — don't you draw it back that way!"

"I did n't," retorted Hazel.

" Yes, you did, I saw you ! "

" You did n't, either."

" I did."

" You did n't."

" I did, too."

" He did n't, did he, Chi ? " said Hazel, furious at this charge of apparent timidity.

" I don't believe you drew it back even if March does think he saw you," said Chi, pouring oil both ways on the troubled waters ; " 'n' I never thought 't was just the thing for a boy to tell a girl she was a coward before she 'd proved to be one — specially if he belongs to this Society."

The Marquis de Lafayette hung his head at this rebuke ; but in the action his cocked hat of black and gilt paper lurched forward and drew off with it his white cotton-wool wig. Budd and Cherry, forgetting all rules, fines, and sense of propriety, rolled over and over at the sight ; Rose sat down shaking with laughter, and even Chi lost his dignity.

" I wish you would let me *see,* or do something," said Hazel, plaintively, when she could make herself heard.

" 'T ain't fair to keep Hazel waiting so," declared Budd, and the president called the meeting to order again.

" Put out your hand, Hazel," said Rose. " Now shake."

Hazel grasped a hand, cold, deathly cold, and clammy. The chill of the rigid fingers sent a corresponding shiver down the length of her backbone, and the goose-flesh rose all over her arms and legs. She thought she must shriek ; but she recalled Chi's words, set her teeth hard, and shook the awful thing with what strength she had, never uttering a sound.

"Bully for you, Hazel! I knew you'd show lots of pluck," cried Budd.

"Got grit every time," said Chi, proudly. "Now let's have the other test and get down to business. Guess all three of you'll have to have a finger in this pie. Hurry up, Marthy Washin'ton!" Cherry scuttled down the ladder, and in a few minutes labored, panting, up again.

"What did you bring two for?" demanded Budd.

"'Cause March said 't would balance me better on the ladder," replied Cherry, innocently. At which explanation Chi laughed immoderately, much to Cherry's discomfiture.

"Now, Hazel, roll up your sleeve and hold out your bare arm," said the Marquis. Hazel obeyed, wondering what would come next.

"Here, Budd, you hold it; all ready, Cherry?"

"Ye-es — wait a minute; now it's all right."

"This we call burning in the Society's brand, — N. B. B. O. O.;" the voice of the Marquis was solemn, befitting the occasion.

Hazel drew her breath sharply, uncertain whether to cry out or not. There was a sharp sting across her arm, as if a hot curling-iron had been drawn quickly across it; then a sound of sizzling flesh, and the odor of broiled beefsteak rose up just under her nostrils.

There was a diabolical thud of falling flat-irons; Rose tore the bandage from Hazel's eyes, and the bewildered candidate for membership, when her eyes grew somewhat

wonted to the dim light, found herself in a corner of the
loft in the barn, with the elegant figure of the Marquis in
cocked hat, white wig, yellow vest, blue coat, and yellow
knee-breeches dancing frantically around her; Ethan Allen
in white woollen shirt, red yarn suspenders, and red, white,
and blue striped trousers, turning back-hand somersaults
on the hay; Chi standing at salute with his great-great-
grandfather's Revolutionary musket, his old straw hat
decorated with a tricolor cockade, and Cherry in a white
cotton-wool wig, a dark calico dress of her mother's and a
white neckerchief, flat on the floor beside two six-pound
flat-irons.

A piece of raw beef on a tin pan, some bits of ice, and a
kid glove stuffed with ice and sawdust, lay scattered about.
They told the tale of the initiation.

"Three cheers for Barbara Frietchie!" shouted Budd,
as he came right side up. The barn rang with them.

"Now we'll give the right hand of true fellowship," said
Chi, rapping with the butt of his musket for order.

Rose gave Hazel's hand a squeeze. "I'm so glad you're
to be one of us," she said heartily; and Hazel squeezed
back.

March came forward, bowed low, and said, "I apologize
for my distrust of your pluck," and held out his hand with
a look in the flashing gray eyes that was not one of mock-
ery; indeed, he looked glad, but never a word of welcome
did he speak.

"I could flog that proud feller," muttered Chi to himself.

Hazel hesitated a moment, then put out her hand a little reluctantly. March caught the gesture and her look.

"Oh, you're not obliged to," he said haughtily, and turned on his heel. But Hazel put her hand on his arm.

"I'm afraid we are both breaking some of the by-laws, March. I do want to shake hands, but I was thinking just then that you did n't mean the apology — not really and truly; and if you did mean it, there was something else you needed to apologize for more than that!"

March flushed to the roots of his hair. Then his boy's honor came to the rescue.

"I *do* want to now, Hazel — and forgive and forget, won't you?" he said, with the winning smile he inherited from his father, but which he kept for rare occasions.

Hazel put her hand in his, and felt that this had been worth waiting for. She knew that at last March had taken her in.

Budd gripped with all his might, Cherry shook with two fingers, and Chi's great hand closed over hers as tenderly as a woman's would have done.

This was Hazel's initiation into the Nobody's Business But Our Own Society. It was the second meeting of the year.

"Now, March, I'll make you chairman and ask you to state the business of this meetin', as you've called it. Must be mighty important?"

"It is," replied March, gravely, all the fun dying out of his face. "You remember, all of you, — don't you ? — what mother told us that night she said Hazel was coming ? ”

“ Yes,” chorussed the children.

“ Well, I 've been thinking and thinking ever since how I could help — ”

“ So 've I, March,” interrupted Rose.

“ And I have, too,” said Budd.

“ What 's all this mean ? ” said Chi, somewhat astonished, for he had not known why the meeting had been called.

“ Why, you see, Chi, we never knew till then that the farm had been mortgaged on account of father's sickness, and that it had been so awful hard for mother all this year — ”

Chi cleared his throat.

“ — And we want to do something to help earn. If we could earn just our own clothes and books and enough to pay for our schooling, it would be something.”

“ Guess 't would,” said Chi, clearing his throat again. “ Kind of workin' out the third by-law, ain't you ? ”

“ Trying to,” answered March, with such sincerity in his voice that Chi's throat troubled him for full a minute. “ And what I want to find out, without mother's knowing it, or father either, is how we can earn enough for those things. If anybody 's got anything to say, just speak up.”

“ What you goin' to do with those Wyandottes ? ”

“ I knew you 'd ask that, Chi. I 'm going to raise a fine breed and sell the eggs at a dollar and a half for thirteen; but I can't get any chicken-money till next fall, and no egg-money till next spring, and I want to begin now."

"Hm —" said Chi, taking off his straw hat and slowly scratching his head. "Well," he said after a pause in which all were thinking and no one talking, "why don't all of you go to work raisin' chickens for next Thanksgivin'?"

"By cracky!" said Budd, "we could raise three or four hundred, an' fat 'em up, an' make a pile, easy as nothing."

"I don't know about it's bein' so easy; but children have the time to tend 'em, and I don't see why it won't work, seein' it's a good time of year."

"But where 'll we get the hens to set, Chi?" said March.

"Oh, there's enough of 'em settin' round now on the bare boards," Chi replied.

"Can I raise some, too?" asked Hazel, rather timidly.

"Don't know what there is to hinder," said Chi, with a slow smile.

"And can I buy some hens for my very own?"

"Why, of course you can; just say the word, 'n' you 'n' I 'll go settin'-hen hunting within a day or so."

"Oh, what fun!" cried Hazel, clapping her hands. "But I want some that will sit and lay too, Chi; then I can sell the eggs."

There was a shout of laughter, at which Hazel felt hurt.

"There now, Lady-bird, we won't laugh at your city ways of lookin' at things any more. The hens ain't quite so accommodatin' as *that*, but we 'll get some good setters first, 'n' then see about the layin' afterwards."

"But, Chi, it will take such a lot of corn to fatten them. We don't want to ask father for anything."

"That's right, Rose. Be independent as long as you can; I thought of that, too. Now, there's a whole acre on the south slope I ploughed this spring, — nice, hot land, just right for corn-raisin'; 'n' if you children 'll drop 'n' cover, I 'll help you with the hoein' 'n' cuttin' 'n' huskin'; 'n' you 'll have your corn for nothin'."

"Good for you, Chi; we 'll do it, won't we?" cried March.

"You bet," said Budd.

"I can pick berries," said Rose, "and we can always sell them at the Inn, or at Barton's River."

"Yes, and we can begin in June," said Cherry; "the pastures are just red with the wild strawberries, you know, Rose."

"It's an awful sight of work to pick 'em," said Budd, rather dubiously.

"Well, you can't get your money without workin', Budd; 'n' work don't mean 'take it easy.'"

"I 'm sure we can get twenty-five cents a quart for them right in the village. I 've heard folks say they make the best preserve you can get, and you can't buy them for love nor money," said Rose. "Mother makes beautiful ones."

"Was n't that what we had last Sunday night when the minister was here to tea?" asked Hazel.

"Yes," said Rose.

"I never tasted any strawberries like them at home, and the housekeeper buys lots of jams and jellies in the fall."

Hazel thought hard for a minute. Suddenly she jumped
to her feet, clapped her hands, and spun round and round
like a top, crying out, " I have it !   I have it ! "

The N. B. B. O. O. Society was amazed to see the new
member perform in this lively manner, for Hazel had been
rather quiet during the first month. Now she caught up
her skirts with a dainty tilt, and danced the Highland
Fling just to let her spirits out through her feet. Up and
down the floor of the loft she charged, hands over her head,
hands swinging her skirts, light as a fairy, bending, sway-
ing, and bowing, till, with a big "cheese," she sat down
almost breathless by Chi. Was this Hazel? The members
of the N. B. O. O. looked at one another in amazement,
and March's eyes flashed again, as they had done once
before during the afternoon.

" Now all listen to me," she said, as if, after a month of
silence, she had found her tongue. " I 've an idea, and
when I have one, papa says it 's worth listening to, — which
is n't often, I 'm sure. We 'll pick the strawberries, and
get Mrs. Blossom to show Rose how to do them up ; and
I 'll write to papa and Doctor Heath's wife and to our
housekeeper and Cousin Jack, and see if they don't want
some of those delicious preserves that they can't get in the
city. I 'll find out from Mrs. Scott — that 's the housekeeper — how much she pays for a jar in New York, and
then we 'll charge a little more for ours because the strawberries are a little rarer. Are n't there any other kinds of
berries that grow around here ? "

" Guess you 'd better stop 'n' take breath, Lady-bird ;

there's a mighty lot of plannin' in all that. What'd I tell you, Budd?" Chi asked again.

Budd looked at Hazel in boyish admiration, but said nothing.

"I think that's splendid, Hazel," said Rose, "if they'll only want them."

"I know they will; but are there any other berries?"

"Berries! I should think so; raspberries and black-berries by the bushel on the Mountain, and they say they're the best anywhere round here," said March.

"Oh, dear!" sighed Cherry, "I wish we could go to work right now."

"Well, so you can," said Chi, "only you can't go berryin' just yet. You can begin to drop that corn this very after-noon; better be inside the ground pretty soon, with all those four hundred chickens waitin' to join the Thanks-givin' procession."

"Oh, Chi, you're making fun of us," laughed Rose.

"Don't you believe it, Rose-pose; never was more in earnest in my life. Come along, 'n' I'll show you."

VIII

It was a trial of patience to have to wait twenty-one days before the first of the "four hundred" could be expected to appear.

"You'll have to be kind of careful 'bout steppin' round in the dark, Mis' Blossom, 'n' you, too, Ben," said Chi, "for you'll find a settin' hen most anywheres nowadays."

Mrs. Blossom laughed. "Oh, Chi, what dear children they are, even if they aren't quite perfect."

"Can't be beat," replied Chi, earnestly. "Look at them now, will you?"

Mrs. Blossom stepped out on the porch, and looked over to the south slope and the corn-patch. "What if her father were to see her now!" She laughed again, both at her thoughts and the sight.

"'T would give him kind of a shock at first," Chi chuckled, "but he'd get over it as soon as he'd seen that face."

"It is wonderful how she has improved. I shouldn't be surprised if he came up here soon to see Hazel."

"Well, he'll find somethin' worth lookin' at. See there, now!"

The girls had been making scarecrows to protect the young corn, stuffing old shirts and trousers with hay and straw, while March and Budd had been getting ready the cross-tree frames. In dropping and covering the corn that Saturday afternoon after the initiation, the girls had found their skirts and petticoats not only in the way as they bent over their work, but greatly soiled by contact with the soft, damp loam. So they had begged to wear overalls of blue denim like Chi's and the boys'. The request had been gladly granted. "It will save no end of washing," said Mrs. Blossom, and forthwith made up three pairs on the machine.

The girls found it great fun. They tucked in their petticoats and buttoned down their shoulder-straps with right good will. Then Mr. Blossom presented them with broad, coarse straw hats, such as he and Chi used, and with these on their heads they rushed off to the corn-patch. There now they were, — five good-looking boys with hands joined, dancing and capering around a scarecrow, that looked like a gentleman tramp gone entirely to seed, and singing at the top of their voices Budd's favorite, "I won't play in your back yard."

At that very hour, when the gentleman scarecrow of the corn-patch was looking amiably, although slightly squint-eyed, out from under his tattered straw hat (for March had drawn rude features on the white cloth bag stuffed with cotton-wool which served for a head, and on it Rose had sewed skeins of brown yarn to imitate hair) at the antics of the five pairs of blue overalls, Mr. Clyde, having finished his nine o'clock breakfast, asked for the mail.

"Yes, Marse John" (so Wilkins always called Mr. Clyde when they were alone), "'spect dere's one from Miss Hazel by de feel an' de smell."

Mr. Clyde smiled. "How can you tell by the 'feel and the smell,' Wilkins?"

"Case it's bunchy lake in de middle, an' de vi'lets can't hide dere bref."

"Well, we'll see," said Mr. Clyde, willing to indulge his faithful servant's childish curiosity. Wilkins busied himself quietly about the breakfast-room.

As Mr. Clyde opened the envelope, the crushed blue and white violets fell out. Suddenly he burst into such a hearty laugh that Wilkins had hard work to suppress a sympathetic chuckle.

"I shall have to carry this letter over to the Doctor, Wilkins," he said, still laughing. "I shall be in time to find him a few minutes alone before office hours." He rose from the table.

Wilkins followed him out to give his coat a last touch with the brush; he was fearful Mr. Clyde might leave without revealing anything of the contents of the letter from his beloved Miss Hazel.

"'Scuse me, Marse John," he said in desperation, as Mr. Clyde went towards the front door, "but Miss Hazel ain't no wusser case yo' goin' to de Doctah's?"

"Oh, Wilkins, I forgot; you want to know how Miss Hazel is. She is doing finely; as happy as a bird, and sends her love to you in a postscript. I think I'll run up and see her soon."

Wilkins ducked and beamed. " 'Pears lake dis yere house ain't de same place wif de little missus gone."

" You 're right, Wilkins," said Mr. Clyde, earnestly. " I shall not open the Newport cottage this year; it would be too lonesome without her."

" Well, Dick," he said gayly, as he entered the Doctor's office, " I shall hold you responsible for some of the lives of the 'Four Hundred.' Here, read this letter."

MOUNT HUNGER, MILL SETTLEMENT, BARTON'S
RIVER, VERMONT, May 19, 1896.

DEAREST PAPA, — Good-morning! I am answering your long letter a little sooner than I expected to, because I want you to do something for me in a business way; that's the way March says it must be.

I don't know how to begin to tell you, but I 've joined the N. B. B. O. O. Society and one of the by-laws is that we must help others all we can and just as much as we can. I wish you 'd been at the initiashun. (I don't know about that spelling, and I 'm in a hurry, or I 'd ask.) I had the hand of fellowship from a supposed corpse's hand first, and then I was branded on the arm. And afterwards they all took me in, and now we 're raising four hundred chickens to help others; I 'll tell you all about it when you come. Chi, that's the hired man, but he is really our friend, took me sitting-hen hunting day before yesterday, for I am to own some myself; and we drove all over the hills to the farmhouses and found and bought twelve, or rather Chi did, for I had to borrow the money of him, as I felt so bad when I kissed you good-bye that I forgot to tell you my quarterly allowance was all gone, and I know you won't like my borrowing of Chi, for you have said so many times never to owe anybody and I've always tried to pay for everything except when I had to borrow of Gabrielle, or Mrs. Scott, when I forgot my purse.

But truly the hens were in such an awful hurry to sit, that it did seem too bad to keep them waiting even three days till I could get some money from you; and then, too, we've all of us, March and Rose and Budd and Cherry and me, bet on which hen would get the first chicken, and that chicken is going to be a prize chicken and especially fatted, and of course, if I waited for the money to come from you, I couldn't stand a chance of coming out ahead in our four hundred chicken race, so I borrowed of Chi. The hens came to just $4 and eighty cents. I'll pay you back when I earn it, and don't you think it would have been a pity to lose the chance for the prize chicken just for that borrow?

Please send the money by return mail. I've other letters to write, so please excuse my not paragraphing and so little punctuation, but I've so much to do and this must go at once.

Your loving and devoted daughter,

HAZEL CLYDE.

P. S. The hens are sitting around everywhere. Give my love to Wilkins. H. C.

The Doctor shouted; then he stepped to the dining-room door and called, " Wifie, come here and bring that letter."

Mrs. Heath came in smiling, with a letter in her hand, which, after cordially greeting Mr. Clyde, she read to him, — an amazed and outwitted father.

MOUNT HUNGER, MILL SETTLEMENT, BARTON'S RIVER, VERMONT, May 19, 1896.

MY DEAR MRS. HEATH, — Please thank my dear Doctor Heath for the note he sent me two weeks ago. I ought to write to him instead of to you, for I don't owe you a letter (your last one was so sweet I answered it right off), but he never allows his patients strawberry preserve and jam, so it would be no use to ask his help just now, as this is pure business, March says.

We are trying to help others, and the strawberries — wild ones — are as thick as spatter — going to be — all over the pastures, and we 're going to pick quarts and quarts, and Rose is going to preserve them, and then we 're going to sell them.

Do you think of anybody who would like some of this preserve? If you do, will you kindly let me know by return mail?

I can't tell just the price, and March says that is a great drawback in real business, and this *is* real — but it will not be more than $1 and twenty-five cents a quart. They will be fine for luncheon. *I* never tasted any half so good at home.

My dear love to the Doctor and a large share for yourself from

Your loving friend,

HAZEL CLYDE.

P. S. Rose says it is n't fair for people to order without knowing the quality, so we 've done up a little of Mrs. Blossom's in some Homeepatic (I don't know where that "h" ought to come in) pellet bottles, and will send you a half-dozen "for samples," March says, to send to any one to taste you think would like to order. H. C.

"The cure is working famously," said Doctor Heath, rubbing his hands in glee.

"Well," said Mr. Clyde, laughing, "I may as well make the best of it; but I can't help wondering whether the wholesale grocers in town have been asked to place orders with Mount Hunger, or the Washington Market dealers for prospective chickens! There 's your office-bell; I won't keep you longer, but if this 'special case' of yours should develop any new symptoms, just let me know."

"I 'll keep you informed," rejoined the Doctor. "Better run up there pretty soon, Johnny," he called after him.

"I think it's high time, Dick. Good-bye."

At that very moment, a symptom of another sort was developing in Z—— Hall, Number 9, at Harvard.

Jack Sherrill and his chum were discussing the last evening's Club theatricals. "I saw that pretty Maude Seaton in the third or fourth row, Jack; did she come on for that, — which, of course, means you?"

"Wish I might think so," said Jack, half in earnest, half in jest, pulling slowly at his corn-cob pipe.

"By Omar Khayyam, Jack! you don't mean to say you're hit, at last!"

"Hit, — yes; but it's only a flesh-wound at present, — nothing dangerous about it."

"She's got the style, though, and the pull. I know a half-dozen of the fellows got dropped on to-night's cotillion."

"Kept it for me," said Jack, quietly.

"No, really, though — " and his chum fell to thinking rather seriously for him.

Just then came the morning's mail, — notes, letters, special delivery stamps, all the social accessories a popular Harvard man knows so well. Jack looked over his carelessly, — invitations to dinner, to theatre parties, "private views," golf parties, etc. He pushed them aside, showing little interest. He, like his Cousin Hazel, was used to it.

The morning's mail was an old story, for Sherrill was worth a fortune in his own right, as several hundred mothers and daughters in New York and Boston and Philadelphia knew full well.

Moreover, if he had not had a penny in prospect, Jack Sherrill would have attracted by his own manly qualities and his exceptionally good looks. His riches, to which he had been born, had not as yet wholly spoiled him, but they cheated him of that ambition that makes the best of young manhood, and Life was out of tune at times — how and why, he did not know, and there was no one to tell him.

He had rather hoped for a note from Maude Seaton, thanking him, in her own charming way, for the flowers he had sent her on her arrival from New York the day before. True, she had worn some in her corsage, but, for all Jack knew, they might have been another man's; for Maude Seaton was never known to have less than four or five strings to her bow. It was just this uncertainty about her that attracted Jack.

" Hello! Here 's a letter for you by mistake in my pile," said his chum.

" Why, this is from my little Cousin Hazel, who is rusticating just now somewhere in the Green Mountains." Jack opened it hastily and read, —

MOUNT HUNGER, MILL SETTLEMENT, BARTON'S
RIVER, VERMONT, May 19, 1896.

DEAREST COUSIN JACK, — It is perfectly lovely up here, and I've been inishiated into a Secret Society like your Dicky Club, and one of the by-laws is to help others all we can and wherever we can and as long as ever we can, and so I've thought of that nice little spread you gave last year after the foot-ball game,

6

and how nice the table looked and what good things you had, but I don't remember any strawberry jam or preserves, do you?

We're hatching four hundred chickens to help others, — I mean we have set 40 sitting hens on 520 eggs, not all the 40 on the five hundred and twenty at once, you know; but, I mean, each one of the 40 hens are sitting on 13 eggs apiece, and March says we must expect to lose 120 eggs — I mean, chickens, — as the hens are very careless and sit sideways — I've seen them myself — and so an extra egg is apt to get chilly, and the chickens can't stand any chilliness, March says. But Chi, that's my new friend, says some eggs have a double yolk, and maybe, there'll be some twins to make up for the loss.

Anyway, we want 400 chickens to sell about Thanksgiving time, and, of course, we can't get any money till that time. So now I've got back to your spread again and the preserves, and while we're waiting for the chickens, we are going to make preserves — *dee*-licious ones! I mean we are going to pick them and Rose is going to preserve them. We've decided to ask $1 and a quarter a quart for them; Rose — that's Rose Blossom — says it is dear, but if you could see my Rose-pose, as Chi calls her, you'd think it cheap just to eat them if she made them. She's perfectly lovely — prettier than any of the New York girls, and when she kneads bread and does up the dishes, she sings like a bird, something about love. I'll write it down for you, sometime. *I'm* in love with her.

Please ask your college friends if they don't want some jam and *wild* strawberry preserves. If they do, March says they had better order soon, as I've written to New York to see about some other orders.

Yours devotedly,

HAZEL.

P. S. I've sent you a sample of the strawberry preserve in a homeepahtic pellet bottle, to taste; Rose says it is n't fair to ask people to buy without their knowing what they buy. I saw that Miss Seaton just before I came away; she came to call on me and brought some flowers. She said I looked like you — which was an awful whopper because I had my head shaved, as you know; I asked her if she had heard from you, and she said she had. She is n't half as lovely as Rose-pose. H. C.

IX

THE PRIZE CHICKEN

THERE was wild excitement, as well as consternation, in the farmhouse on the Mountain.

On the next day but one after Hazel had sent her letters, Chi had brought up from the Mill Settlement a telegram which had come on the stage from Barton's. It was addressed to, " Hazel Clyde, Mill Settlement, Barton's River, Vermont," and ran thus : —

CAMBRIDGE, May 20, 1 P.M.

Hope to get in our order ahead of New York time. Seventeen dozen of each kind. Letter follows.

JACK.

" Seventeen dozen ! " screamed Rose, on hearing the telegram.

" Seventeen dozen of *each kind !* " cried Budd.

" Oh, quick, March, do see what it comes to ! " said Hazel.

Then such an arithmetical hubbub broke loose as had never been heard before on the Mountain.

" Seventeen times twelve," said Rose, — " let me see ; seven times two are fourteen, one to carry — do keep still, March ! " But March went on with : —

"Twelve times four are forty-eight — seventeen times forty-eight, hm — seven times eight are fifty-six, five to carry — Shut up, Budd; I can't hear myself think." But Budd gave no heed, and continued his computation.

"Four times seventeen are — four times seven are twenty-eight, two to carry; four times one are four and two are — I say, you 've put me all out!" shouted Budd, and, putting his fingers in his ears, he retired to a corner. Rose continued to mumble with her eyes shut to concentrate her mind upon her problem, threatening Cherry impatiently when she interrupted with her peculiar solution, which she had just thought out: —

"If one quart cost one dollar and twenty-five cents, twelve quarts will cost twelve times one dollar and twenty-five cents, which is, er — twelve times one are twelve; twelve times twenty-five! Oh, gracious, that's awful! What 's twelve times twenty-five, March?"

"Shut up," growled March; "you 've put me all off the track."

"Me, too," said Rose, in an aggrieved tone.

Mrs. Blossom had been listening from the bedroom, and now came in, suppressing her desire to smile at the reddened and perplexed faces. "Here 's a pencil, March, suppose you figure it out on paper."

A sigh of relief was audible throughout the room, as March sat down to work out the result. "Eight hundred and sixteen quarts at one dollar twenty-five a quart," said March to himself; then, with a bound that shook the long-room, he shouted, "One thousand and twenty dollars!" and therewith broke forth into singing: —

"Glory, glory, halleluia!
Glory, glory, halleluia!
Glory, glory, halleluia,
For the N. B. B. O. O.!"

The rest joined in the singing with such goodwill that the noise brought in Chi from the barn. When he was told the reason for the rejoicing, he looked thoughtful, then sober, then troubled.

"What's the matter, Chi? Cheer up! You have n't got to pick them," said March.

"'T ain't that; but I hate to throw cold water on any such countin'-your-chickens-'fore-they're-hatched business," said Chi.

"'T is n't chickens; it's preserves, Chi," laughed Rose.

"I know that, too," said Chi, gravely. "But suppose you do a little figuring on the hind-side of the blackboard."

"What *do* you mean, Chi?" asked Hazel.

"Well, I'll figure, 'n' see what you think about it. Seventeen dozen times four, how much, March?"

"Eight hundred and sixteen."

"Hm! eight hundred and sixteen glass jars at twelve and a half cents apiece — let me see: eight into eight once; eight into one no times 'n' one over. There now, your jars 'll cost you just one hundred and two dollars."

There was a universal groan.

"'N' that ain't all. Sugar's up to six cents a pound, 'n' to keep preserves as they ought to be kept takes about a pound to a quart. Hm, eight hundred 'n' sixteen pounds of sugar at six cents a pound — move up my point 'n' mul-

tiply by six — forty-eight dollars 'n' ninety-six cents; added
to the other — "

"Oh, don't, Chi!" groaned one and all.

"It spoils everything," said Rose, actually ready to cry
with disappointment.

"Well, Molly Stark, you've got to look forwards and
backwards before you *promise* to do things," said Chi,
serenely; and Rose, hearing the Molly Stark, knew just
what Chi meant.

She went straight up to him, and, laying both hands on
his shoulders, looked up smiling into his face. "I'll be
brave, Chi; we'll make it work somehow," she said gently;
and Chi was not ashamed to take one of the little hands
and rub it softly against his unshaven cheek.

"That's my Rose-pose," he said. "Now, don't let's
cross the bridges till we get to them; let's wait till we
hear from New York."

They had not long to wait. The next day's mail brought
three letters, — from Mrs. Heath, Mr. Clyde, and Jack.
Hazel could not read them fast enough to suit her audience.
There was an order from Mrs. Heath for two dozen of each
kind, and the assurance that she would ask her friends, but
she would like her order filled first.

Mr. Clyde wrote that he was coming up very soon and
would advance Hazel's quarterly allowance; at which
Hazel cried, "Oh-ee!" and hugged first herself, then Mrs.
Blossom, but said not a word. She wanted to surprise
them with the glass jars and the sugar. Her father had

enclosed five dollars with which to pay Chi, and he and Hazel were closeted for full a quarter of an hour in the pantry, discussing ways and means.

Jack wrote enthusiastically of the preserves and chickens, and, like Hazel, added a postscript as follows:

" Don't forget you said you would write down for me the song about Love that Miss Blossom sings when she is kneading bread.   Miss Seaton is just now visiting in Boston.   I 'm to play in a polo match out at the Longmeadow . grounds next week, and she stays for that."   This, likewise, Hazel kept to herself.

Meanwhile, the strawberry blossoms were starring the pastures, but only here and there a tiny green button showed itself.   It was a discouraging outlook for the other Blossoms to wait five long weeks before they could begin to earn money; and the thought of the chickens, especially the prize chicken, proved a source of comfort as well as speculation.

As the twenty-first day after setting the hens drew near, the excitement of the race was felt to be increasing.   Hazel had tied a narrow strip of blue flannel about the right leg of each of her twelve hens, that there might be no mistake; and the others had followed her example, March choosing yellow; Cherry, white; Rose, red; and Budd, green.

The barn was near the house, only a grass-plat with one big elm in the centre separated it from the end of the woodshed.   As Chi said, the hens were sitting all around everywhere; on the nearly empty hay-mow there were some twenty-five, and the rest were in vacant stalls and feed-boxes.

It was a warm night in early June. Hazel was thinking over many things as she lay wakeful in her wee bedroom. To-morrow was the day; somebody would get the prize chicken. Hazel hoped she might be the winner. Then she recalled something Chi had said about hens being curious creatures, set in their ways, and never doing anything just as they were expected to do it, and that there was n't any time-table by which chickens could be hatched to the minute. What if one were to come out to-night! The more she thought, the more she longed to assure herself of the condition of things in the barn. She tossed and turned, but could not settle to sleep. At last she rose softly; the great clock in the long-room had just struck eleven. She looked out of her one window and into the face of a moon that for a moment blinded her.

Then she quietly put on her white bath-robe, and, taking her shoes in her hand, stepped noiselessly out into the kitchen.

There was not a sound in the house except the ticking of the clock. Softly she crept to the woodshed door and slipped out.

Chi, who had the ears of an Indian, heard the soft "crush, crush," of the bark and chips underneath his room. He rose noiselessly, drew on his trousers, and slipped his suspenders over his shoulders, took his rifle from the rack, and crept stealthily as an Apache down the stairs. Chi thought he was on the track of an enormous woodchuck that had baffled all his efforts to trap, shoot, and decoy him, as well as his attempts to smoke and drown him out. But nothing was moving in or about the shed. He stepped outside, puzzled as to the noise he had heard.

"By George Washin'ton!" he exclaimed under his breath, "what's up now?" for he had caught sight of a little figure in white fairly scooting over the grass-plat under the elm towards the barn. In a moment she disappeared in the opening, for on warm nights the great doors were not shut.

"Guess I'd better get out of the way; 't would scare her to death to see a man 'n' a gun at this time of night. It's that prize chicken, I'll bet." And Chi chuckled to himself. Then he tiptoed as far as the barn door, looked in cautiously, and, seeing no one, but hearing a creak overhead, he slipped into a stall and crouched behind a pile of grass he had cut that afternoon for the cattle.

He heard the feet go "pat, pat, pat," overhead. He knew by the sound that Hazel was examining the nests. Then another noise — Cherry's familiar giggle — fell upon his ear. He looked out cautiously from behind the grass. Sure enough; there were the twins, robed in sheets and barefooted. Snickering and giggling, they made for the ladder leading to the loft.

"The Old Harry's to pay to-night," said Chi, grimly, to himself. "When those two get together on a spree, things generally hum! I'd better stay where I'm needed most."

Hazel, too, had caught the sound of the giggle and snicker, and recognized it at once.

" Goodness ! " she thought, " if they should see me, 't would frighten Cherry into fits, she 's so nervous. I 'd better hide while they 're here. They 've come to see about that chicken, just as I have ! " Hazel had all she could do to keep from laughing out loud. She lay down upon a large pile of hay and drew it all over her. " They can't see me now, and I can watch them," she thought, with a good deal of satisfaction.

Surely the proceedings were worth watching. The moonlight flooded the flooring of the loft, and every detail could be plainly seen.

" Nobody can hear us here if we do talk," said Budd. " You 'll have to hoist them up first, to see if there are any chickens, and be sure and look at the rag on the legs; when you come to a green one, it 's mine, you know."

" Oh, Budd ! I can't hoist them," said Cherry, in a distressed voice.

" They do act kinder queer," replied Budd, who was trying to lift a sleeping hen off her nest, to which she seemed glued. " I 'll tell you what 's better than that; just put your ear down and listen, and if you hear a ' peep-peep,' it 's a chicken."

Cherry, the obedient slave of Budd, crawled about over the flooring on her hands and knees, listening first at one nest, then at another, for the expected "peep-peep."

" I don't hear anything," said Cherry, in an aggrieved tone, " but the old hens guggling when I poke under them. Oh ! but here 's a green rag sticking out, Budd."

" And a speckled hen? " said Budd, eagerly.

" Yes."

" Well, that's the one I've been looking for ; it's dark over here in this corner.   Lemme see."

Budd put both hands under the hen and lifted her gently.   " Ak — ok — ork — ach," gasped the hen, as Budd took her firmly around the throat; but she was too sleepy to care much what became of her, and so hung limp and silent.

" I'll hold the hen, Cherry, and you take up those eggs one at a time and hold them to my ear."

" What for? " said Cherry.

" Now don't be a loony, but do as I tell you," said Budd, impatiently.   Cherry did as she was bidden ; Budd listened intently.

" By cracky! there's one! " he exclaimed. , " Here, help me set this hen back again, and keep that one out."

" What for? " queried Cherry, forgetting her former lesson.

" Oh, you ninny! — here, listen, will you? " Budd put the egg to her ear.

" Why, that's a chicken peeping inside.   I can *hear* him," said Cherry, in an awed voice.

" Yes, and I'm going to let him out," said Budd, triumphantly.

" But then you'll have the prize chicken, Budd," said Cherry, rather dubiously, for she had wanted it herself.

"Of course, you goosey, what do you suppose I came out here for?" demanded Budd.

"But, Budd, will it be fair?" said Cherry, timidly.

"Fair!" muttered Budd; "it's fair enough if it's out first. It's their own fault if they don't know enough to get ahead of us."

"Did you think it all out yourself, Budd?" queried Cherry, admiringly, watching Budd's proceeding with wide-open eyes.

"Yup," said Budd, shortly.

They were not far from Hazel's hiding-place, and, by raising her head a few inches, she could see the whole process.

First Budd listened intently at one end of the egg, then at the other. He drew out a large pin from his pajamas and began very carefully to pick the shell.

"Oh, gracious, Budd! what are you doing?" cried Cherry.

"What you see," said Budd, a little crossly, for his conscience was not wholly at ease.

He picked and picked, and finally made an opening. He examined it carefully.

"Oh, thunder!" he exclaimed under his breath, "I've picked the wrong end."

"What do you mean?" persisted Cherry.

"I wanted to open the 'peep-peep' end first, so he could breathe," replied Budd, intent upon his work. Cherry watched breathlessly. At last the other end was opened, and Budd began to detach the shell from something which

might have been a worm, a fish, a pollywog, or a baby white
mouse, for all it looked like a chicken. It lay in Budd's
hand.

"Oh, Budd, you 've killed it!" cried Cherry, beginning
to sniff.

"Shut up, Cherry Blossom, or I'll leave you," threat-
ened Budd. Just then the moon was obscured by a passing
cloud, and the loft became suddenly dark and shadowy.
Cherry screamed under her breath.

"Oh, Budd, don't leave me; I can't see you!"

There was a soft rapid stride over the flooring; and
before Budd well knew what had happened, he was seized
by the binding of his pajamas, lifted, and shaken with such
vigor that his teeth struck together and he felt the jar in
the top of his head.

As the form loomed so unexpectedly before her, Cherry
screamed with fright.

"I'll teach you to play a business trick like this on us,
you mean sneaking little rascal!" roared March. "Do
you think I did n't see you creeping out of the room along
the side of my bed on all fours? You did n't dare to
walk out like a man, and I might have known you were
up to no good!" Another shake followed that for a
moment dazed Budd. Then, as he felt the flooring beneath his feet, he turned in a towering passion of guilt
and rage on March.

"You 're a darned sneak yourself," he howled rather
than cried. "Take that for your trouble!" Raising his
doubled fist, he aimed a quick, hard blow at March's

stomach.   But, somehow, before it struck, one strong
hand — not March's — held his as in a vice, and another,
stronger, hoisted him by the waist-band of his pajamas
and held him, squirming and howling, suspended for a
moment; then he felt himself tossed somewhere.   He fell
upon the hay under which Hazel had taken refuge, and
landed upon her with almost force enough to knock the
breath from her body.   Cherry, meanwhile, had not ceased
screaming under her breath, and, as Budd descended so
unexpectedly upon Hazel, a great groan and a sharp wail
came forth from the hay, to the mortal terror of all but
Chi, who grew white at the thought of what might have
happened to his Lady-bird, and, unintentionally, through
him.

That awful groan proved too much for the children.
Gathering themselves together in less time than it takes
to tell it, they fled as well as they could in the dark, —
down the ladder, out through the barn, over the grass-
plat, into the house, and dove into bed, trembling in every
limb.

" What on earth is the matter, children?" said Mrs.
Blossom, appearing at the foot of the stairs.   " Did one
of you fall out of bed?"

Budd's head was under the bedclothes, his teeth chattering through fear; likewise Cherry.   March assumed as
firm a tone as he could.

" Budd had a sort of nightmare, mother, but he's all
right now."   March felt sick at the deception.

" Well, settle down now and go to sleep; it's just

twelve." And Mrs. Blossom went back into the bedroom where Mr. Blossom was still soundly sleeping.

Meanwhile, Chi was testing Hazel to see that no harm had been done.

"Oh, I'm all right," said Hazel, rather breathlessly. "But it really knocked the breath out of my body." She laughed. "I never thought of your catching up Budd that way and plumping him down on top of me!"

"Guess my wits had gone wool-gatherin', when I never thought of your hidin' there," said Chi, recovering from his fright. "But that boy made me so pesky mad, tryin' to play such a game on all of us, that I kind of lost my temper 'n' did n't see straight. Well—" he heaved a sigh of relief, "he 's got his come-uppance!"

"Where do you suppose that poor little chicken is?"

"We 'll look him up; the moon 's comin' out again."

There, close by the nest, lay the queer something on the floor. "I 'll tuck it in right under the old hen's breast, 'n' then, if there 's any life in it, it 'll come to by mornin'." He examined it closely. "I 'll come out 'n' see. Come, we 'd better be gettin' in 'fore 't is dark again—"

He put the poor mite of a would-be chicken carefully under the old hen, where it was warm and downy, and as he did so, he caught sight of the rag hanging over the edge of the nest. He looked at it closely; then slapping his thigh, he burst into a roar of laughter.

"What is it, Chi?" said Hazel, laughing, too, at Chi's mirth.

"Look here, Lady-bird! you 've got the Prize Chicken,

after all. That boy could n't tell green from blue in the moonlight, 'n' he's hatched out one of yours. By George Washin'ton! that's a good one, — serves him right," he said, wiping the tears of mirth from his eyes.

The chicken lived, but never seemed to belong to any one in particular; and as Chi said solemnly the next morning, "The less said on this Mountain about prize chickens, the better it'll be for us all."

X

AN UNEXPECTED MEETING

It was a busy summer in and about the farmhouse on
Mount Hunger. What with tending the chickens — there
were four hundred and two in all — and strawberry-pick-
ing and preserving, and in due season a repetition of the
process with raspberries and blackberries, the days seemed
hardly long enough to accomplish all the young people
had planned.

Mr. Clyde came up for two days in June, and upon his
return told Doctor Heath that he, too, felt as if he needed
that kind of a cure.

Hazel was the picture of health and fast becoming what
Chi had predicted, "an A Number 1" beauty. Her dark
eyes sparkled with the joy of life; on her rounded cheeks
there was the red of the rose; the skull-cap had been discarded, and a fine crop of soft, silky rings of dark brown
hair had taken its place.

"Never, no, never, have I had such good times," she
wrote to her Cousin Jack at Newport. "We eat on the
porch, and make believe camp out in the woods, and we
ride on Bess and Bob all over the Mountain. We've
about finished the preserves and jams, and Rose has only
burnt herself twice. The chickens, Chi says, are going to

be prime ones ; it 's awfully funny to see them come flying and hopping and running towards us the minute they see us — March says it 's the ' Charge of the Light Brigade.'

" I wish you could be up here and have some of the fun, — but I 'm afraid you 're too old. I enclose the song Rose sings which you asked me for. I don't understand it, but it 's perfectly beautiful when she sings it."

Hazel had asked Rose for the words of the song, telling her that her Cousin Jack at Harvard would like to have them. Rose looked surprised for a moment.

" What can he want of them ? " she asked in a rather dignified manner ; and Hazel, thinking she was giving the explanation the most reasonable as well as agreeable, replied : —

" I don't know for sure, but I think — you won't tell, will you, Rose ? "

" Of course I won't. I don't even know your cousin, to begin with."

" I think he is going to be engaged, or is, to Miss Seaton of New York. All his friends think she is awfully pretty, and papa says she is fascinating. I think Jack wanted them to give to her."

" Oh," said Rose, in a cool voice with a circumflex inflection, then added in a decidedly toploftical tone, " I 've no objection to his making use of them. I 'll copy them for you."

" Thank you, Rose," said Hazel, rather puzzled and a little hurt at Rose's new manner.

This conversation took place the first week in August,

and the verses were duly forwarded to Jack, who read them over twice, and then, thrusting them into his breast-pocket, went over to the Casino, whistling softly to himself on the way. There, meeting his chum and some other friends, he proposed a riding-trip through the Green Mountain region for the latter part of August.

"The Colonel and his wife will go with us, I'm sure, and any of the girls who can ride well will jump at the chance," said his chum. "It's a novelty after so much coaching."

"I'll go over and see Miss Seaton about it," said Jack, and walked off singing to himself, —

> " ' — the stars above
> Shine ever on Love '—"

His friend turned to the others. "That's a go; I've never seen Sherrill so hard hit before." Then he fell to discussing the new plan with the rest.

Jack was wily enough, as he laid the plan before Maude Seaton, to attempt to kill two birds with one stone. He had had a desire, ever since the first letter of Hazel's, to see his little cousin in her new surroundings, and this desire was immeasurably strengthened by his curiosity to see a girl who sang Barry Cornwall's love-lyrics on Mount Hunger. Consequently, in planning the high-roads to be followed through the Green Mountains, he had not omitted to include Barton's River, as it boasted a good inn.

"Here's Woodstock, — just here," he explained to pretty Maude Seaton, as they sat on the broad morning-porch of the palatial Newport cottage, with a map of Vermont on the table between them. "We can stop there a day or two, and make our next stop at Barton's River; I've heard it's a beautiful place, with glorious mountain rides within easy distance. Suppose we arrange to stop three or four days there and take it all in? I've been told it's the finest river-valley in New England."

"Oh, do let's! The whole thing is going to be delightful. I'm so tired of coaching; I believe nobody enjoys it now, unless it's the one who holds the reins, and then all the others are bored. But with fine horses this will be no end of fun. We can send on our trunks ahead, can't we?"

"Oh, yes, that's easily arranged. By the way, what horse will you take? Remember," he said, looking her squarely in the eyes with a flattering concern, "it's a mountain country, and we can't afford to have anything happen to you."

"No danger for me," laughed Maude, meeting his look as squarely. "And I can't worry about you after seeing the polo game you played yesterday," she added with frank admiration.

"It was a good one, was n't it?" said Jack, his eyes kindling at the remembrance. "It was my mascot did the business — see?" He put his hand in his breast-pocket, expecting to draw forth a ribbon bow of Maude's that she had given him for "colors;" but, to his amazement, and to Miss Seaton's private chagrin, he drew forth only the slip of paper with Barry Cornwall's love-song in Rose Blossom's handwriting.

Where the dickens was that bow? Jack felt the absurdity of hunting in all his pockets for something he had
intended should express one phase, at least, of his sentiments. He felt the blood mounting to the roots of his
hair, and, laughing, put a bold face on it.

He held out the slip of paper. " It looks innocent,
does n't it? " he said mischievously, and enjoyed to the
full Maude's look of discomfiture, which, only for a second,
she could not help showing. " She 'll know now how a
fellow feels when he has sent her flowers and sees her
wearing another man's offering," he thought. He turned
to the map again.

" Well, what horse will you ride ? "

" I 'll take Old Jo; he 's safe, and splendid for fences.
Of course you 'll take Little Shaver? "

" Yes, he and I don't part company very often. So it 's
settled, is it ? " he asked, feeling cooler than he did.

" So far as I am concerned, it is; and I know the Colonel
and Mrs. Fenlick will go; it 's just the thing they like."

" Well, I 'll leave you to speak to the other girls, and
I 'll go over and see Mrs. Fenlick. Good-bye." He held
out his hand, but Miss Seaton chose to be looking down
the avenue at that moment.

" Oh, there are the Graysons beckoning to me ! " she
exclaimed eagerly. " Excuse me, and good-bye — I must
run down to see them." As she walked swiftly and grace-
fully over the lawn, she knew Jack Sherrill was watching
her. " Yes, it 's settled," she thought, as she hurried on;
" and something else is settled, too, Mr. Sherrill ! You 've

been hanging fire long enough — and the idea of his
forgetting that bow! "

The Graysons thought they had never seen Maude
Seaton quite so pretty as she was that morning, when she
stood chatting and laughing with all in general, and fascinating each in particular. The result was, the Graysons
joined the riding-party in a body, and Sam Grayson vowed
he would cut Jack Sherrill out if he had to fight for it.

It was a glorious first of September when the riding-
party, ten in number, cantered up to the inn at Barton's
River, and it was a merry group in fresh toilets that gathered after dinner and a rest of an hour or two in their rooms,
on the long, narrow, vine-covered veranda of the inn. It
had been a warm day, and the afternoon shadows were
gratefully cooling.

"Will you look at that load coming down the street?"
said Mrs. Fenlick. "I never saw anything so funny!"

The whole party burst out laughing, as the vehicle, an
old apple-green cart, apparently filled with bobbing calico
sunbonnets and straw hats, shackled and rattled up to the
side door of the inn.

"I shall call them the Antediluvians," laughed Maude
Seaton. "Do you know where they come from?" she
said, speaking in at the open office-window to the boy.

"I guess they come to sell berries from a place the
folks round here call 'The Lost Nation,'" he replied,
grinning.

"'The Lost Nation!' Do you hear that?" said Sam
Grayson. "Let's have a nearer view of the natives." They

all went to the end of the veranda nearest the cart.   Sam
Grayson and Jack went out to investigate.

Two boys in faded blue overalls and almost brimless
straw hats jumped down before the wagon stopped, and
began lifting out six-quart pails of shining blackberries
from beneath an old buffalo robe.   Jack, with his hands
in his pockets, sauntered up to the tail of the cart.

" Buy them all, do — do ! " cried Miss Seaton, clapping
her hands.   " We need them to-morrow for our picnic ;
and pay a good price," she added, "for the sake of the
looks.   I would n't have missed it for anything ? "

" How do you sell them ? " said Jack to the tall boy
who stood with his back to him, busied with the berries.

The boy turned at the sound of the pleasant voice, and
lifted his brimless hat by the crown with an air a Harvard
freshman might have envied.   Jack, seeing it, was sorry he
was bareheaded, for he hated to be outdone in such courtesy.

" Ten cents a quart, sir."

" What a handsome fellow ! " whispered Mrs. Fenlick.
" You rarely see such a face ; and where did he get such
manners ? "

" How many quarts have — halloo, Little Sunbonnet !
Look out ! " said Jack, laughing, as he caught the owner
of the yellow sunbonnet, who, perched on the side of the
wagon, suddenly lost her balance because of Bess's uneasy
movements in fly-time.

" Well, you *are* an armful," he laughed as he set her
down and tried in vain to peer up under the drooping
bonnet and discover a face.

"Whoa — ah, Bess!" shouted the driver, as Bess reared and snorted and shuddered and finally rid herself of the tormenting horse-fly. "All right, Cherry Bounce?" he said, turning at last when the horse was quieted.

But Cherry was dumb with embarrassment, and Jack answered for her.

"Little Sunbonnet's all safe, but what —" He got no further with that sentence. To the amazement of the group on the veranda and Jack's overwhelming astonishment, a wild, gleeful "Oh-ee!" issued from the depths of another sunbonnet in the cart, and the owner thereof precipitated herself recklessly over the side, and cast herself upon Jack's neck, hugging and "oh-eeing" with all her might.

"Why, Hazel! Hazel!" Except for that, Jack was dumb like Cherry, but not with embarrassment. Was this Hazel? Her sunbonnet had fallen off, and the dark blue gingham dress set off the wonderful richness of coloring that helped to make Hazel what she had become, "a perfect beauty."

"Oh, Jack, you old darling, why did n't you let us know you were coming? Chi, Chi!" Hazel was fairly wild with joy at seeing a dearly loved home-face. "This is my Cousin Jack we 've talked about. Jack, this is my friend, Chi."

Chi put out his horny brown hand, and Jack grasped it.

"Guess she 's givin' you away pretty smart, ain't she?" said Chi, with a twist of his mouth and a motion of his thumb backwards to the veranda.

"Well, rather," said Jack, laughing, for he felt that Chi's keen eyes had taken in the whole situation at a glance. "I meant to surprise her, but she has succeeded in surprising me." He stood with his arm about Hazel. "And these are your friends, Hazel?" he inquired; he felt he must make the best of it now.

"Oh, Jack, I'm ashamed of myself; I'm so glad to see you I've forgotten my manners. Rose," she spoke up to the other sunbonnet that had kept its position straight towards the horse and never moved during this surprise party. Then Rose turned. "Rose, this is Cousin Jack."

The sunbonnet bowed stiffly, and Jack heard a low laugh behind him. It was Maude Seaton's. Rose heard it, too; so did Chi and March. It affected each in the same way. As Chi said afterwards, he "b'iled" when he heard it. Then Rose spoke: —

"I'm very glad to see you, Mr. Sherrill, we've heard so much of you." Her voice rang sweet and clear; every word was heard on the veranda. "And these berries aren't to be preserved; but evidently you are going to buy them just the same, — as well as your friends," she added, looking towards the veranda.

Jack bit his lip. "I should like to introduce all my friends to you," he said, without much enthusiasm, however. "I know this is March;" he turned pleasantly to him, but dared not offer his hand, for the look on the boy's face warned him that March had resented the laugh. "Will you come?" He held up his hand to Rose to help her down.

"Thank you." Rose sprang down, ignoring the proffered help.

She knew just how she looked, and her face burned at the thought. Her old green and white calico dress was shrunken and warped with many washings; her shoes were heavy and patched; fortunately her sunbonnet with its green calico cape was of a depth to hide her burning face. But that laugh had been like a challenge to her pride.

"Drive up to the front veranda, Chi," she commanded rather brusquely; and Chi, muttering to himself, "She's game, though; I would n't thought it of Rose-pose; but I glory in her spunk!" drew up to the front door in a truly rattling style.

Then Rose and Hazel were introduced to them all; but in vain did Maude Seaton try to get a look into her face. It was only a ceremony, and Rose felt it as such; nevertheless she said very pleasantly, "Hazel, would n't you like to invite your friends up to tea on the porch to-morrow? that is, if you are to be here?" she added, addressing Mrs. Fenlick.

"Oh, Rose, that would be lovely. Then they can see the chickens!" said Hazel. There was a general laugh.

"I fear it will be too much trouble, Miss Blossom," said Mrs. Fenlick, courteously, for she felt like apologizing for that laugh of Maude Seaton's; "there are so many of us."

"Oh, no, my mother will be glad to meet you," Rose replied with serene voice; "won't she, Chi?"

"Sure," said Chi, addressing the general assembly; "the

more the merrier; 'n' if you come along about four, you 'll get a view you don't get round here, 'n' a wholesale piazzy to eat it on. How many do you count up?" Jack winced at the burst of merriment that followed the question.

"We 'll line up, and you can count," said Sam Grayson, the fun getting the better of him. "Here, Miss Seaton, stand at the head."

"Miss Blossom, there are ten of us; are you going to retract your invitation?" said Mrs. Fenlick, shaking her head at Sam.

"Not if you wish to come," said Rose, pleasantly. "We will have tea at five. Come, Hazel, we must be going; there are the berries to sell — or shall we leave you here with your cousin till we come back?"

"No, I won't leave you even for Jack," said Hazel, earnestly; "besides, I 've never had the fun of selling berries."

"I 'm thinkin' you 've lost your fun, anyway," said Chi, "for Budd says the tavern-keeper has taken all; guess *he 's* goin' into the jam business, too."

"I 'll pick some more, then, to-morrow, and you 'll have to buy some of them, Jack," said Hazel, "for I 'm bound to sell some berries this summer."

"We 'll take all you can pick, Hazel," said Maude Seaton, sweetly. Then, as the cart rattled away with the three sunbonnets held rigid and erect, she turned to Mrs. Fenlick and the other girls: "What an idea that was of Doctor Heath's to put Hazel away up here in such a family — a girl in her position!"

"She seems to have thriven wonderfully on it," remarked Mrs. Fenlick; "she will be the prettiest of her set when they come out. I am delighted to have a chance to see Doctor Heath's mountain sanatorium."

"Oh, I 'm sure it will be amusing," replied Maude, dryly. Then she shook out her light draperies, pulled down her belt, and went down the road a bit to meet Jack and Sam Grayson, who had accompanied the cart for a few rods along the village street.

When they had turned back to the inn, the storm in the apple-green cart burst forth.

"Did you hear that girl laugh?" demanded March, with suppressed wrath in his voice.

"Just as plain as I hear that crow caw," said Chi.

"I can't bear her," said Hazel; "telling me she would buy my berries when I only meant Jack."

"Kinder sweet on him, ain't she?" asked Chi, carelessly.

"I should think so!" was Hazel's indignant answer. "I heard Aunt Carrie tell papa she was always sending him invitations to everything. But is n't Cousin Jack splendid, Rose?"

Rose's sunbonnet was still very rigid, and Chi knew that sign; so he spoke up promptly, knowing that she did not care to answer just then: —

"He 's about as handsome as they make 'em, Lady-bird; if he wears well, I sha'n't have nothin' against him."

Hazel felt rather depressed without knowing exactly why. March returned to the charge.

"Did you hear that laugh, Rose?"

"Yes, I did," said Rose, shortly. March looked at her in surprise, but Chi managed to give him a nudge, which March understood, and the subject was dropped on the homeward way.

That the berry-sellers were under a cloud was evident to Mrs. Blossom as soon as they drove up to the woodshed.

"Did you have good luck, children?" she called to them cheerily.

"We 've sold all our berries," said Budd.

"But March and Rose are cross, Martie," added Cherry.

"Tired 'n' hungry, too, Mis' Blossom," Chi hastened to say, trying to shield Hazel and the other two. "I wish you 'd just step out to the barn with a spoonful of your good lard. Bess has rubbed her shin a little mite, 'n' I want to grease it good to save the hair." Mrs. Blossom, reading his face, took the hint.

He made his confession in the barn.

"I don't know what we 've done, Mis' Blossom; but Rose has invited 'em all up here to-morrow to supper, — they 're regular high-flyers, girls 'n' fellers, 'n' the Colonel and his wife. There 's ten of 'em; 'n' it 's a-goin' to make you an awful sight of work, but, by George Washin'ton! that pesky girl — Miss Seaver, or somethin' like it — riled me so, that I ain't got over it yet, 'n' I 'd backed up Rose if she 'd offered to take the whole of 'em to board for a week. I just b'iled when I heard her laugh, 'n' she can't hold a candle to our Rose; 'n' she 's that sassy — although you can't put your finger on anything special — that you can't sass back; the worst kind every time; 'n' she's set her cap for the straightest sort of chap — that's Hazel's cousin — there is goin', 'n', by George Washin'ton! I'm afraid he's fool enough to catch at that bait.

"There!" said Chi, stopping to draw breath, "I've had my blow-out 'n' I feel better. Now, what are we goin' to do about it?"

"We'll manage it, Chi," said Mrs. Blossom, smiling in spite of herself at Chi's wrath. "After all, the children have been carefully guarded in our home up here, and, sometimes, I think too much, — it won't hurt them to take a prick now and then. Besides, Chi," she added, laughing outright as she turned to go into the house, "the children did look perfectly ridiculous in those old berry-picking rigs. I laughed myself when I saw you drive off with them."

But she left Chi grumbling.

That night, after the children were in bed, and Mrs. Blossom was sure they were all asleep except Rose, she went upstairs a second time and spoke softly at the door:

"Rose."

"Yes, Martie; oh, you're coming! I'm so glad." And as Mrs. Blossom knelt by the bed, whispering, "Now tell me all about it," Rose threw one arm over her mother's shoulder and whispered her confession.

"They were n't rude to you, dear, were they?"

"No, Martie," whispered Rose, "it was n't that, but I just *hated* them for a minute, — Hazel's cousin and all."

"That is n't like you, Rose dear, to hate anyone without reason."

" Oh, Martie, I 'm ashamed to tell you — " the arm came close about her mother's neck, "I 'm too old to have such feelings, but I could n't bear them because I looked as I did. I was ashamed of my looks and the children's; and I was ashamed even of Chi — dear, old Chi! — " there was a smothered sob and an effort to go on. "And they were all dressed so beautifully, and Hazel's cousin had on a lovely white flannel suit, and I was just a little rude to him; but it was nothing but my dreadful pride! I did n't know I had it till to-day, — oh, dear!" The head went under the counterpane to smother the sound of the sobs.

"But, my dear little girl — " (When Rose cried, which was seldom, Mrs. Blossom called her daughter who was as tall as herself, "little girl," and nothing comforted Rose more than that.) So now, hearing the loving words, the head emerged from the bedclothes, and a tear-wet face was meekly held over the side of the bed for a kiss.

"But, my dear little girl," Mrs. Blossom went on after the interruption, " surely you were courteous and thought-ful of Hazel's happiness, at least, to ask them all up here to tea. You have n't that to regret."

There was a fresh burst, smothered quickly under the sheet. "Oh, Martie, that 's the worst part of it! I did n't ask them for Hazel's sake, but just for myself, because I knew — I knew — " Rose smothered the rising sob; " that if they came, I could have on my one pretty dress, and they 'd see that I — that I — " Rose was unable to finish.

" Could look as well as they did? " said Mrs. Blossom, completing the sentence.

" Yes," sighed Rose, "and I feel like a perfect hypocrite towards every one of them; — and, oh, Martie! the truth is, I was ashamed of being poor and selling berries — " again the head went under the coverlet, and Mrs. Blossom caught only broken phrases : —

" I am so proud of — of you and Popsey — poor Chi made it worse — they laughed — March was mad, too, — and Miss Seaton's so pretty — clothes — Hazel's cousin tried to be polite — Hazel — just her dear own self — but she's rich — and Cherry f-fell into his arms — and I know — and I know — I know he wanted to be out of the whole thing — oh dear ! "

Mrs. Blossom patted the bunch under the clothes whence came the smothered, broken sentences, and smiled while a tear rolled down her cheek.   After all, this was real grief, and she wished she might have shielded her Rose from just this kind of contact with the world.   But she was wise enough not to say so.

" Well, Rose dear, let's look on the other side now the invitation has been given.   I, for my part, shall be glad to see what they are like.   I know you looked queer in those old clothes, but, after all, would n't it have been just as queer to have been all dressed up selling berries ? "

" Yes, I think it would, Martie," said Rose, emerging from her retreat.   " I'm not such a goose as not to realize we must have looked perfectly comical."

" Well, now comfort yourself with the thought, that to-morrow you need only look just as nice as you can in honor of our guests.   I'm sure I shall," said Mrs. Blos-

som, laughing softly. " I 'm not going to be outdone by
all those ' high-flyers,' as dear, old Chi calls them. We 'll
put on our prettiest — and there is n't much choice, you
know, for we have just one apiece — and we 'll set the
table with grandmother's old china out on the porch, and
we 'll give them of our best, and queens, Rose-pose, can
do no more. That 's *our* duty ; we 'll let the others look
out for theirs. Now, what will be nice for tea ? "

" Not preserves, Martie, for Chi said — " Her mother
interrupted her, —

" Never mind what Chi said now, dear, but plan for the
tea. We shall have to work as hard as we can jump
to-morrow forenoon to get ready. I 'm sorry father can't
be at home."

" Could n't we have blackberries and those late garden
raspberries Chi has been saving ? " said Rose.

" Yes, those will look pretty and taste good; and then
hot rolls, and fresh sponge and plum cake, and tea, and
cold chicken moulded in its jelly, the way we tried it last
month — "

" Oh, that will be lovely, Martie," whispered Rose,
eagerly.

" And if Chi and March have the time," went on Mrs.
Blossom, entering heart and soul into the hospitable plan,
" I 'll ask them to go trout-fishing and bring us home two
strings of the speckled beauties, and if those served hot
don't make them respect old clothes — then nothing on
earth will," concluded Mrs. Blossom, with mock solemnity.

" Oh, Martie Blossom, you 're an angel ! " cried Rose,

softly, rising in bed and throwing both arms about her mother's neck — "there !" — a squeeze, "and there — " another squeeze and a kiss, "and now you won't have to complain of me to-morrow."

"That's mother's own daughter Rose," said Mrs. Blossom, smoothing the sheet under the round chin. "Now, good-night — sleep well, for I depend upon you to make those rolls to-morrow forenoon."

XI

JACK

JACK SHERRILL had always had a particularly warm interest in his Cousin Hazel. He, too, was motherless. The fifteen-year-old lad had gone into one of the great preparatory schools with the terrible mother-want in his heart and life. Like Hazel, he, too, was an only child, and consequently without the guidance and help of an elder brother or sister. His father was all that a man, absorbed in large business interests, could be to the son whom he saw in vacation time only.

"You are born a gentleman, Jack," he had said to him when he was about to enter Harvard; "remember to conduct yourself as such. You 'll not find it an easy matter at times — I did n't — but you will find it pays; and — and remember your mother." Then Mr. Sherrill had wrung his boy's hand, and hurried away.

It was the only time in the three years since she had been lost to him, that his father had borne to mention the lad's mother to him. To Jack it was like a last will and testament, and he wrote it not only in his memory, but on his heart.

He had tried, yes, honestly, amid the manifold temptations of his life and his " set," to live up to a certain ideal of his own, but it had been slow work; and the last three months of his sophomore year had been far from satisfactory to himself.

He was thinking this over as he rode slowly up the steep road to Mount Hunger. He had come up that morning to call on Mrs. Blossom, for he knew that the social law of hospitality demanded that he should pay his respects to Rose Blossom's mother and Hazel's guardian before his friends should break bread in the house.

That tall girl in the sunbonnet was a disappointment — but then, he had been a fool to expect anything else just because she happened to sing one of Barry Cornwall's love-songs. He rode out of the leafy woods'-road, and came unexpectedly upon the farmhouse. Chi saw him from the barn, and came out to meet him.

"Is Mrs. Blossom at home?" asked Jack, lifting his cap.

Chi patted Little Shaver's neck, shining like polished mahogany. "Yes, she's home, 'n' she'll be glad to see you. You'll find her right in the kitchen, 'n' I'll tend to this little chap — what's his name?"

"Little Shaver, he's my polo pony."

"George Washin'ton! He knows a thing or two. He most winked at me," laughed Chi.

"Oh, he knows a stable when he sees it," said Jack, smiling; "but where's the kitchen?"

"Right off the porch. — There's Rose singing now; guess that'll be as good a guide-post as you could have. Come along, Little Shaver, — a good name for you."

Jack went up on the porch, but stopped short at the open door. Rose was at the kitchen table, patting out the dough for the rolls. Her sleeves were turned up above the elbows, and the round, yet delicate, white arms and the pretty hands were working energetically with the rolling-pin. She was singing from pure lightheartedness, and she emphasized the rhythm by substantial thumps with the culinary utensil.

> " ' I told thee when love was hopeless ; (thump)
> But now he is wild and sings — (thump)
> That the stars above (thump ! thump ! !)
> Shine ever on Love — (thump —)' "

Jack knocked rather loudly, and Rose turned with a little "Oh !" and an attitude that made Jack long for a button-hole kodak.

" Come in, Mr. Sherrill," she said, cordially, but thinking to herself, " Caught again ! well, I don't care."

" I hope I haven't come too early this morning to be received," said Jack, extending his hand.

" I can't shake, Mr. Sherrill," laughed Rose, " and if I stop to wash them, you won't have any rolls for tea."

" Do go on then," said Jack, eagerly, " only don't let me be a bother. I was afraid it might be too early and incon-venience you, but — "

" Not a bit," said Rose as she turned to the kneading-board again. " If you don't mind, I'm sure I don't ; only these rolls must be attended to."

" You're very good to let me stay and watch the pro-cess," said Jack, humbly, deferentially taking his stand by

the table. "I hope I shall not interfere so much with Mrs. Blossom; I forgot that — that — " Jack grew red and confused.

"That we did our own work?" Rose supplied the rest of his thought with such winning frankness, that Jack succumbed then and there to the delight of a novel experience.

"I'll be out in a few minutes, Mr. Sherrill," called a cheery voice from the pantry behind him. Jack started, — then laughed.

"Am I interrupting you, too Mrs. Blossom?" he said, addressing a crack in the pantry door.

"I don't mean to let you, or you will have no sponge cakes for tea; I'm beating eggs and can't leave them or they'll go down."

"Can't I help, Mrs. Blossom? I've no end of unused muscle," said Jack, entering into the fun of the situation.

"No, thank you, I shall be but a few minutes. Rose dear, just feel the oven, will you?"

Jack began to think himself a nonentity in all this domesticity. "'Feel the oven,'" he said to himself. "Do girls do that often, I wonder." He watched Rose's every movement.

"Now, confess, Mr. Sherrill, have you ever seen anyone make biscuit before?" said Rose, cutting off a piece of dough, flouring it, patting it, cuddling it in both hands, folding it over with a little slap to hold a bit of butter, and tucking it into the large, shallow pan.

"No — " Jack drew a long breath, "I never have. You

see I have always thought it a kind of drudgery, but this —" Jack sought for a word that should express his feelings in regard to the process as performed by Rose — " this is, why — it's poetry!" he exclaimed with a flashing smile that became his expressive face wonderfully, and caused Rose to fail absolutely in making a shapely poem of the next roll.

She laughed merrily. "There now, they'll soon be done — in good shape too, if you don't compliment them too much."

"I'll eat a dozen of them, I warn you now." Jack was waxing dangerous, for he was already possessed with an insane desire to become a piece of dough for the sake of having those pretty hands pat him into shape.

"Do you hear that, Martie?" cried Rose, flushing with pleasure.

"Yes. That's the best compliment you can pay them, Mr. Sherrill. I hope my cakes will fare as well," she said, coming from the pantry with extended hand.

It was strange! But when Jack Sherrill returned the cordial pressure of that same hand, small, shapely, but worn and hardened with toil, his eyes suddenly filled with tears. This, truly, was a home, with what makes the home — a mother in it.

Mrs. Blossom saw the tears, the struggle for composure, and, knowing from Hazel he was motherless, read his thought; — then all her sweet motherhood came to the surface.

"My dear boy," she said with quivering lip, "it is very

thoughtful of you to come up and pioneer the way over the Mountain for all your city friends."

Jack found his voice. " Mrs. Fenlick wanted to come, too, Mrs. Blossom, but I managed to put it so she thought it would be better to wait until afternoon. They are all looking forward to it."

" I 'm sorry Hazel is n't here; she is out picking berries with the children. If Rose had n't so much to do, I 'd send her to hunt them up."

Jack protested. He had come to call on Mrs. Blossom and had detained them altogether too long.

" I don't want to go," he said laughingly, " but I know I ought. It seems almost an imposition for so many of us to come up here and put you to all this trouble. Why did you ask us, Miss Blossom?" At which question, Rose did not belie her name, for a sudden wave of color surged into her face, and she looked helplessly and appealingly at her mother.

" I 've put my foot into it now," was Jack's thought, as Mrs. Blossom responded quickly, " For more reasons than one, Mr. Sherrill."

They were out on the porch; Chi was bringing up Little Shaver.

" It will be a regular stampede this afternoon," said Jack, gayly, as he vaulted into the saddle. " Have you room enough for so many horses?" He turned to Chi.

" Plenty 'n' to spare, 'n' I 'm goin' to give 'em a piazzy tea of their own. Little Shaver knows all about it: I 've told him. I never saw but one horse before that could most talk, 'n' that 's Fleet."

Little Shaver whinnied, and with a downward thrust and twist of his head tried to get it under Chi's arm.

" Did n't I tell you ? " said Chi, delightedly.

" Can I get on to the main road by going over the Mountain ? " Jack asked him.

" Yes, you can get over, if you ain't particular how you get," said Chi.

" No road ? "

" Kind of a trail ; — over the pasture 'n' through the woods, an acre or two of brush, 'n' then some pretty steep slidin' down the other side, 'n' a dozen rods of swimmin', 'n' a tough old clamber up the bank — 'n' there you are on the river road as neat as a pin."

Jack laughed. " Just what Little Shaver glories in ; I 'll try it, and much obliged to you, Mr. — " he hesitated.

" Call me, Chi."

" Chi," said Jack, in such a tone of good comradeship that it brought the horny hand up to his in a second's time.

Jack grasped it ; " Good-bye till this afternoon." He spoke to Little Shaver, who ducked his head and fairly scuttled across the mowing, scrambled up the pasture, took the three-rail fence at the top in a sort of double bow-knot of a jump, and then disappeared in the woods, leaving the three gazing after him in admiration.

" That feller 's got the right ring," said Chi, emphatically ; " but if he had n't come up here this mornin', first thing, after that invite of Rose-pose's, I 'd have set him down alongside of that Miss Seaver — 'n' a pretty low seat that would be!"

" I'll put up some lunch, Chi, for you and March, and, if you can find him, you would do well to start now for the trout."

Mrs. Blossom turned to Rose. "Come, dear, we've a hundred and one things to do to be ready in time. You may set the table on the porch, and we'll all picnic for dinner to-day; I've no time to get a regular one, and father isn't at home."

It was a perfect afternoon on that second of September. At a quarter of five Mrs. Blossom and Rose and Hazel were on the porch, looking down upon the lower road for the first glimpse of the party.

The table was set on the huge rough veranda that Mr. Blossom and Chi had built just off the kitchen long-room. Clematis and maiden-hair ferns, which abounded on the Mountain, were the decorations, and set off to good advantage Mrs. Blossom's mother's old-fashioned tea-set of delicate green and white china.

On one end was a large china bowl heaped with blackberries, on the other stood a common glass one filled with luscious, red raspberries. The sponge cakes gleamed, appetizingly golden, from plates covered with grape-vine leaves for doilies.

The chicken quivered in its own jelly on a platter wreathed with clematis. The delicious odor of fried trout floated out from the long-room, and the rolls were steaming hot in snow-white napkins.

"Oh, dear!" moaned Rose. "Everything will get cold, it's so late."

Just then there was a shout from the advance-guard of the twins, and the cavalcade came into view; Jack on Little Shaver, who, after his thirty-mile morning ride, was as fresh as a pastured colt — riding beside Maude Seaton on Old Jo.

There was a general dismounting, assisted by Chi; a gathering and looping up of riding habits; a bit of general brushing down among the men; then, with one accord they turned to the broad step of the porch.

Mrs. Fenlick, telling of it afterwards, said that, for a moment, she did nothing but look with all her eyes; for there on the porch step stood a woman still in the prime of life and beautiful. She was dressed in an India mull of the fashion of a quarter of a century ago, with a lace kerchief folded in a V about the open neck, and fastened with an old-fashioned brooch.

"At her side," said Mrs. Fenlick, "stood one of the loveliest girls off of canvas I have ever seen. She had on a gown of old-fashioned lawn — pale blue with a rose-bud border. She was tall and straight, and the skirt was a little skimpy, and so plain that had she designed it to set off the grace of her figure she could n't have succeeded better. And the face and head!" Mrs. Fenlick used to wax eloquent at this point — "were simply ideal. Hazel, of course, looked as handsome as a picture in her full, dark blue frock of wash silk trimmed with Irish lace, and with that rich color in her cheeks — but that girl's face was simply divine! Just imagine a complexion of pure white, and dark blue eyes — real violet color — black almost in her pretty excitement of welcoming us, and the loveliest golden brown hair just plaited and puffed a little at the temples, and a braid, that big—" Mrs. Fenlick generally put her two delicate wrists together at this point, — "that fell below her waist fully half a yard! I never saw such hair!"

Mrs. Fenlick used to pause for breath at this point, and then add, " Well, the whole thing was too lovely to be described. Of course, we ate — lots; for that ride and the air were enough to make a saint hungry in Lent, but I was only dimly conscious of ever so many good things I was eating, for that face fascinated me. And manners! Just as if those two women had had nothing to do all their lives but entertain royalty!

" I had sense enough, however, to notice that Jack Sherrill said very little and ate a great deal. I *counted* twelve rolls — of course they were small — for one thing; and I don't blame him, — I wanted more. Well, the whole thing was perfect — the valley and the great mountains were just in front of the porch, and everything harmonized. Even that lovely girl had a bunch of purple-blue pansies at her belt and a few in the bit of cotton lace at her throat; and the sunset and the mountains matched them — as if she had had the whole thing made to order."

Mrs. Fenlick always ended with, " I 've got one bone to pick with that dear Doctor Heath — a mountain san- atorium! I 'd be willing, almost, to get nervous prostra- tion to be sent up there.

"But oh! you should have seen Maude Seaton!" And thereupon, Mrs. Fenlick would go off into a fit of laughter at the remembrance. "She was looking about for the 'rigid sunbonnet,' as she called it, of the day before, and did n't hear when Rose Blossom spoke to her; and when she did realize that the two were one and the same, her look was the kind 'Life' likes to get hold of, you know.

"As for Jack Sherrill," Mrs. Fenlick concluded in her most serious manner, "I have my own thoughts about some things." More than that she would not say, for fear it might get back to Maude Seaton's ears.

Jack, too, had his own thoughts about some things — and kept them to himself.

XII

It was the middle of October. A wild, cold wind was sweeping over the Mountain, and driving black clouds in quick succession across the tops of the woodlands. It howled around the farmhouse and, as now and again a more furious blast hurled itself against doors and windows, the children drew nearer together on the rug before the huge fireplace with a delightful sense of safety and cosiness.

A kettle of molasses was simmering on the stove, and Chi was wielding the corn-popper with truly professional skill before the open fire.

It was such fun to see the hurry, and scurry, and hustle, and rattle, and pop, and sudden white transformation of the heated kernels! A huge, wooden bowl received the contents of the popper, and March salted them. Oh, how good it smelt! And Rose was going to make molasses corn-balls to put aside for the next evening.

"It's just like having a party every night, there are so many of us," said Hazel, clapping her hands in delight.

"I should think you'd miss some of your real parties, Hazel," said Rose, thoughtfully.

"Miss them! Not a bit; why, they are n't half so nice as this, and at home it's so lonesome when papa is n't there. Is n't it lovely to think he's coming up Christmas? Even up here, you know, it would n't be quite Christmas for me without him. That makes me think, I must write him very soon about some things." Hazel looked mysterious.

"We hung up our stockings last year, but we did n't get what we wanted," said Cherry rather mournfully.

"Why not?" asked Hazel.

"Coz Popsey was so sick he could n't go out to the Wishing-Tree, and so he did n't know."

"What is the Wishing-Tree?" said Hazel, consumed with curiosity.

Cherry's mouth was full of corn, so Budd carried on the conversation between mouthfuls.

"I 'll show you to-morrow. It's a big butternut up in the corner of the pasture, an' there's a little hollow in the trunk where the squirrels used to hide beech-nuts, but March has made a door to it with a hinge and put a little padlock on it — that's the key hanging up on the clock."

Hazel saw a tiny key suspended by a string from one of the pointed knobs that ornamented the tall clock.

"'N' nobody touches it till All-hallow-e'en," said Cherry, when the sound of her munching had somewhat diminished, although her articulation was by no means clear. "'N' then Chi goes up with us in the dark, 'n' we put in our wishes, 'n' — "

"Let me tell Hazel," said Budd. "You've begun at the wrong end. You see, we write what we want for Christmas down on paper, an' seal it with beeswax, an' then don't tell anybody what we've written; an' then Chi goes up there with us after dark, an' we're all dressed up like Injuns — "

"Indians, Budd," corrected March.

"Well, Old Pertic'lar, Indians, then," said Budd, a little crossly, " an' then — "

"Oh, you've forgot the dish-pan and the little tub," Cherry's voice came muffled through the corn. "We take the dish-pan, Hazel, 'n' the little wash-tub, me 'n' Budd between us, 'n' beat on them with the iron spoon 'n' the dish-mop handle, 'n' play 'tom-toms' — "

"Yes, an' March gives an awful war-whoop — " Budd, in his earnestness, had risen and gone over to Chi's side, and now sat down by the big bowl, but, unfortunately, on the popper which Chi had just emptied. There was a smell of scorched wool, and, simultaneously, a wild, " Oh, gee-whiz !! " from Budd, who leaped as if shot, and stood ruefully rubbing the seat of his well-patched knicker-bockers, while the rest rolled over on the rug in their merriment.

"Oh, do go on, Budd!" cried Hazel, wiping the tears of mirth from her eyes. Cherry had laughed so hard that she was hiccoughing with outrageous rapidity; and March — forgetting May — chose that opportune moment to give forth a specimen of his best war-whoop, for the purpose, as he explained afterwards, of frightening her out of them.

By the time order had been restored, Cherry was able
to take up the thread of the story;

" 'N' we join hands — Chi 'n' all of us — 'n' sing as loud
as we can sing:

> " ' Intery, mintery, cutery corn,
> Apple seed, apple thorn;
> Wire, briar, limber lock,
> Five geese in a flock —
> Sit and sing by the spring;
> You are OUT.'

Then we all give a great shout and grunt like In-di-ans —,"
said Cherry, emphatically, looking at March; and March
nodded approval.

"How's that?" asked Hazel, who was listening with
all her ears.

" A hánnah — a hánnah — a hánnah," grunted the children as well as they could, hampered by mouths full of
corn. "An' then," went on Budd, "we drop the wishes
into the hollow in the tree-trunk, an' Chi locks the door
an' keeps it, an' — "

" 'N' each of us ties two feathers from a rooster's tail to
different colored strings, 'n' fastens them on to a branch
of the tree, 'n' that brings us good luck; March calls
it 'winging the wishes.' That's the way we get our
presents."

"Oh, what fun!" cried Hazel. "May I do it this
year?"

"Course," replied Budd, "but how will your father
know anything about it?"

" I never thought of that," said Hazel, all her Christmas castles toppling over suddenly.

" We 'll fix it somehow, Lady-bird," said Chi, who, having finished his labors, had seated himself in a chair behind the children and provided himself with a private bowl of his own.

" But now, speakin' of roosters, I 'd like to know how you 're comin' out about chicken money. I sold the last lot but one down in Barton's to-day. There 's been a lot of express to pay, 'n' I thought I 'd better pay dividends to-night, 'n' get it off my mind, seein' it 's most Wishin'-Tree time."

Rose took her little account book from her pocket. " We cleared one hundred and ten dollars on our preserves and jams after we 'd paid Hazel what we had borrowed for the jars and sugar, and paid for the express and boxes. I 'm awfully sorry we could n't fill all the orders, but we 'll try to next year. I 'll go and get the money. I like to look at it, knowing it means so much to us all."

She ran upstairs and came back with a little wooden box that Chi had made for her years ago. The children crowded about her. " There," said Rose, proudly, as she took out the money and smoothed it, one crisp bill after another, on her knees ; " they 're all in ones, so it will seem as if we had more when we divide. Now we 've agreed to divide this equally, so that 'll make just twenty-two apiece."

" Let 's play ' Hold-fast-all-I-give-you ' in earnest," said Cherry, sitting down again on the rug and holding out her hands. " That'll be twenty-two times round and make it seem a lot more."

" Good for you, Cherry," said March, approvingly, and they all followed her example. With a gravity befitting the occasion, the " truly-bruly " game, as Budd called it, went on to the supreme satisfaction of those interested as well as the enjoyment of father and mother and Chi; for to the two former the money-making had long been, of necessity, an open secret.

Chi, after watching them a little while, left the room. When he reappeared a few minutes later, he was greeted with a prolonged " Ah ! " of satisfaction ; for in one hand he held his old account-book, and in the other a long, dark blue woollen stocking which bulged fearfully from the toe halfway up the leg, where it was tied with a stout piece of leather whip-lash.

The whole business of disposing of the chickens had been intrusted to Chi, and the members of the N. B. B. O. O. Society had pledged themselves not to ask him any questions in regard to the sale of them until he should tell them of his own accord. This pledge they had kept, and now they were to have their rewards.

" If this is going to be a meeting of the N. B. B. O. O. Society, I move we ask those who aren't members to adjourn to the bedroom," said March, looking significantly at his mother and father. Mr. and Mrs. Blossom took the hint, and, without waiting for anyone to " second the motion," betook themselves, laughing, into the other room.

" Guess we 'll sit up to the table 'n' count it out," said
Chi, " coz we don't want any of it to fly up chimney. We
should never find it again in this gale."

He emptied the stocking of its contents — bills, pennies,
and silver pieces of all denominations — upon the table, and
the children drew up their chairs.

" Now we 'll sort," said Chi. " You take the bills, Rose,
'n' the rest take the other pieces, 'n' make little piles before
you of a dollar each. Then we can reckon up easy. I 'll
take the pennies and the nickels."

" I choose the ten-cent pieces," said Cherry, " an' you
take the quarters, Budd." March and Hazel took the
rest.

" This is a kind of stockholders' meetin'," said Chi, as
the piles were completed. " We 'll divide the proceeds
accordin' the number of hens each set; coz I could n't
keep run of so many chicks after they 'd struck out for
themselves."

He opened his book.

" Here 's some items you better hear, before you find any
fault with the management:

" Mem.   July.   15 chicks killed by hen-hawks.

" Mem.   August.   21 chicks died of the pip.

" Mem.   September.   Skunks stole ten.

" Mem.   October.   2 can't find.

" There 's a dead loss to all the stockholders, share 'n'
share alike. Now for expenses:

" Mem.   Corn for feed till October — 7 bushels.

" Mem.   October.   Express, $5.50.   Crates for expressin' — $1.10. Now for the profits!" said Chi, with a ring of triumph in his voice. "Count up your piles."

How the cheeks flushed and the eyes grew dark with excitement as the counting proceeded: "One hundred — one hundred and thirty-two — one hundred and seventy-seven — two hundred!"

"Oh-ee!" cried Hazel, as March fairly thundered "Two hundred!" "There's more, there's more!"

"Go on, go on!" she cried again, almost beside herself with excitement.

"Two hundred and seven — TWO HUNDRED AND SEVENTEEN!!"

"Chi!" exclaimed Rose, almost breathless, "How *did* you make all that?" and thereupon, without waiting for his answer, she sprang up from her chair, and, to Chi's amazement, took his weather-worn face between her two hands, and popped a kiss upon his forehead.

Chi cleared his throat and attempted to make his explanation, but was interrupted by March, who got hold of his right hand and wrung it without speaking. Chi saw the boy turn a little white about the mouth and his gray eyes flash through tears; words were not needed.

Budd and Cherry did not realize all this meant to the elder brother and sister, but they did not wish to be outdone by the others in expressing their appreciation of Chi. So Budd thumped him unmercifully on the back, saying, "You're a trump, Chi; tell us how you did it," in a most patronizing tone, and Cherry danced around the table, singing; "I love my Love with a big, big C!"

Hazel looked on, rejoicing in their joy, but wondering why such a little sum, less than her yearly allowance, should create all that happiness.

" But tell us how you did it, Chi," said Rose again.

" Well, I sold most of them for broilers, they bring a pretty good price; 'n' then I sold the feathers; 'n' you forget all those forty hens have been layin' the last two months, 'n' I sold the eggs.   Then, too, — " a slow smile wrinkled Chi's eyes — " I was n't interfered with, 'n' that made a great difference in the business.   How much have you got altogether ? "

" Three hundred and twenty-seven dollars," said March.

" What you goin' to do with it ? that 's the next question. You can't let your money lay round in wooden boxes 'n' old stockin's.   It ought to be bringing you in interest."

" I 'm going to give my share to Rose, to prepare for college with," said Hazel.

" Indeed, I sha'n't take your money, Hazel; you 've earned it fairly for yourself.   I should be ashamed to accept it, but it 's lovely of you to think of it —   Why, Hazel ! " she cried, throwing her arm around her, for the tears were rolling down Hazel's cheeks, and her chest heaving with a bona fide sob.

But Hazel flung off the encircling arm and threw herself full length upon the settle in an abandonment of woe.

"I don't care anything about your old money," she sobbed.   " I did n't want it for myself, and I 've worked so hard picking berries and all — and you said you 'd keep the by-law — and I 've been so happy working to help others, and I never would have believed it of you, Rose Blossom, that you 'd go back on your word — you promised — you promised to help others — a regular solemn pl-pledge, Chi says, and now — and the only way you could help me — was to let — to let me help y-ou-oo-oo ! "

March and Rose looked at each other aghast at this unwonted outburst from Hazel, and Mrs. Blossom, hearing the wail, made her appearance from the bedroom.

" Why, Hazel dear, what is the matter ? " she said.

" They 've spoiled all my good times," sobbed Hazel, refusing to be comforted even when Mrs. Blossom, sitting down by her, stroked her head and begged her to sit up and tell her all about it.

" Oh, mother ! " cried Rose, holding back the tears as well as she could, " it 's all my fault. It 's my old pride that keeps coming up at every little thing, somehow, and I know it 'll be the death of me ! March has it, too ; and between us we have made it just horrid for Hazel."

" Why, Rose, what do you mean ? " asked her mother, gravely.

" Things that we 've kept from you, Martie. Hazel wanted to give us the jars and the sugar, and we would n't let her ; and she wanted to give me a blue wash silk like hers, because I said I wished I could afford one like it, — and I — and I was a little angry, and showed it ; and March spoke up and said we would n't be patronized if we were poor — "

" Why, March Blossom ! " was all his mother said.

"Yes," broke in Budd, ready to place himself on the side of righteousness, "an' Cherry told her that March called her 'a perfect guy,' an' that meant she was homely; an' that Chi said she was awful poor, an' we were a great deal richer than she was, an' that you would n't have had her here if you had n't pitied her —"

"Children!" Not one of them ever remembered to have heard their mother speak with such stern anger in her voice. "I'm ashamed of you; you have disgraced your parents' name." Then she turned to Hazel, drew her up into her arms, and said, tenderly:

"Hazel, my dear little girl, why did n't you come to me with this trouble?"

"Because — because you were n't *my mother*, you were theirs; but, oh! I wish you were mine! I love you so —" Hazel flung both arms around Mrs. Blossom's neck and sobbed out, — "I've wanted to call you Mother Blossom and hug and kiss you like the rest — but Cherry was so jealous — the first time I did it — that she — she stuck burrs in my bed and led me through the nettle-patch when we were raspberrying, because she knew I did n't know nettles; and Chi told me we'd got to be brave if we joined the N. B. B. O. O., and I knew I ought to bear it — for I *do* love to be here — and I love them all, for most of the time they're lovely to me; — and I don't think you've been horrid, Rose, only you did hurt my feelings when you would n't let me give you the blue silk — and — and it is n't my fault if I *am* rich, and it is n't fair not to like me for it!"

"No more it ain't, Lady-bird," said Chi, who, after drawing the back of his hand across his eyes, was apparently the only dry-eyed one in the room. March had flung himself on the other end of the settle and buried his face deep among the patch-work cushions. Rose was sobbing outright with her head on her arms as she sat at the dining-room table.

Cherry, in her shame and misery — for she had come to love Hazel dearly without wholly conquering her jealousy — softly opened the pantry door and slipped inside where she sniffed to her heart's content. As for Budd, he stood over the wood-box, repiling its contents while the tears ran off his nose so fast that he saw all the sticks double through them.

"You may go to bed, children," said Mrs. Blossom, still holding Hazel in her arms. At this fiat, there was a general increase in the humidity of the atmosphere; and, knowing perfectly well when their mother spoke in that tone, that words, tears, or prayers would not avail, they, one and all, — for Cherry had been listening at the pantry door, — made a rush for the stairs and stumbled up, blinded by their tears.

Mrs. Blossom led Hazel still sobbing into her own little bedroom, and shut the door.

Chi, president of the vanished N. B. B. O. O. Society, was left alone. He gazed meditatively awhile at the little piles of money and the vacant chairs opposite each. Then he gathered them up carefully and placed them in orderly rows in the wooden box. His next move was to the shed door. As he opened it, a gust of wind extinguished the lamp on the table.

" Guess I 'll go to bed, too," said Chi to himself, coming back for the box, which the firelight showed plainly enough. " The barometer 's dropped, 'n' it always makes me feel low in my mind."

He heaved a prodigious sigh and went out into the shed and up the back stairs. The wooden box he put under the head of the mattress ; he barricaded the door and placed his rifle beside it against the wall. Then he turned in and drew the coverlet up over his head with another sigh, so long, so profound, that it mingled with the wind as it swept through the cracks of the shed beneath, and made a part of the dismality of the night.

Mrs. Blossom returned to the long-room, and, sitting down in her low rocker before the fire, waited. She knew her children.

Soon, it might have been within half an hour, she heard Rose call softly at the top of the stairs : —

" Martie."

" Yes, Rose."

" May I come ? "

" Yes, dear."

" O Martie ! may I, too ? " wailed Cherry.

" Yes."

" I 'm coming, mother," said March, speaking in a low, determined voice through the knot-hole.

" Very well, March."

" Come along, Budd," said March, and Budd was only

too glad to grip his brother's pajamas and follow after.

Down they came, tiptoeing in their bare feet, Rose heading the penitential procession. She knelt by her mother's side, and March and Budd and Cherry knelt, too.

Then, to their mother's, " Are you *truly* ready, children ? " they answered heartily, " Yes, Martie."

Together they said in subdued but earnest tones, " Our Father; " together they prayed, " ' Forgive us our trespasses as we forgive those who trespass against us ' " — and after the heart-felt, " Amen," each received a kiss by way of absolution; and together, until the clock struck ten, they talked the whole matter over and resolved to fight their Apollyons daily and hourly, and, with God's grace, conquer them.

These were the rare hours, the memory of which held March Blossom in the way of right and honor when he went out to battle for himself in the world. These were the hours, the memory of which kept him in his college days unspotted from the world. It was such an hour that ripened Rose Blossom into a thinking, feeling woman, and made Budd into a knight of the Twentieth Century.

It was for such an hour that Jack Sherrill would have given his entire fortune.

XIII

A SOCIAL ADDITION

IT was a chastened household that gathered about the breakfast table the next morning; and for a week afterwards, every one was so thoughtful and considerate of everybody else that Mrs. Blossom said, laughing, to her husband; "They're so angelic, Ben, I'm afraid they are all going to be ill. I declare, I miss their little naughtinesses."

Several things had been settled during the week and, apparently, to everyone's satisfaction. At a very serious-minded meeting of the N. B. B. O. O., it had been decided to keep the larger part of the money in order to start March on his career. Not without protest, however, on March's part. But he was overruled. Rose argued that if he were going to college, he must begin to prepare that very winter, and if their earnings were divided among the five, no one would reap any special benefit from them, least of all, March.

"I can wait well enough another year, perhaps two," she said; "and, meanwhile, we'll be earning more. But you, March, ought to be in the academy at Barton's this very minute."

"I know it," said March, dejectedly; " but I do hate to take girls' money ; somehow, it does not seem quite — quite manly."

" Better remember what your mother talked to you 'bout last Sunday, 'bout its bein' more of a blessin' to give than to get," said Chi, sententiously.

" I do remember, and there 's nobody in the world I 'd be more willing to take it from than from you, all of you, but — "

" Me, too ? " interrupted Hazel, leaning nearer with great, eager, questioning eyes.

" Yes, you, too, Hazel," March replied gently, with such unwonted humility of spirit shining through his rare, sweet smile, that Hazel bounced up from her seat at the table, and, going behind March's chair, clasped both arms tightly around his neck, laid the dark, curly head down upon the top of his golden one, exclaiming delightedly :

" Oh, March, you are the dearest fellow in the world. I never thought you 'd give in so — and I love you for it ! There now," — with a big squeeze of the golden head — " you 've made me superfluously happy." Hazel took her seat, flushed rosy red in pleasurable anticipation of being allowed, at last, to give to those she loved, and wholly unmindful of her slip of the tongue.

" Now that 's settled, I move that each of you keep three dollars of that money 'gainst the Wishin'-Tree business. Chris'mus 'll be here 'fore you can say ' Jack Robinson.' "

" Second the motion," said Budd and Cherry in the same breath.

It was a unanimous vote.

"There is just one thing I want to say," said March, who, in a bewilderment of happy emotions, had been unable to reply one word to Hazel, "and that is, that I want you to consider that you have lent it to me and let me have the pleasure of paying back, sometime, when I am a man."

"That's fair enough," said Chi. "I glory in your independence, Markis. That's the right kind to have. Put it to vote."

Again there was a unanimous vote of approval, for they all knew that to one of March's proud spirit it meant much to accept the money, from the girls especially; and they felt it would make him happier if he were to accept it as a loan.

"I can save a lot by not boarding down at Barton's, and by working for my board at the tavern, or in some family," said March, thoughtfully.

"No you don't," said Chi, emphatically. "'T ain't no way for a boy to be doin' chores before he goes to school in the mornin' 'n' tendin' horses after he gets out in the afternoon. If you 're goin' to try for college in two years, you 've got to buckle right down to it — 'n' not waste time workin' for other folks that ain't your own. Here comes Mis' Blossom, we 'll ask her what she has to say about it."

"Why, Martie, where have you been all this afternoon? I saw you and father driving off in such a sly sort of way, I knew you did n't want us to know where you were going. Now, 'fess!" laughed Rose.

"'Fess, 'fess, Martie!" cried Budd and Cherry, hilariously breaking up the meeting. "We've got you now!" And without more ado they anchored her to the settle, each linked to an arm, while Hazel took off her hood, March drew off her rubbers, and Rose unpinned her shawl.

Mrs. Blossom laughed. "No, you guess," she replied.

"Down to the Mill Settlement?"

"Wrong."

"Over to Aunt Tryphosa's?"

"No."

"Down to see the Spillkinses?"

"Wrong again."

"Over eastwards to the Morris farm," said Chi.

"Right," said Mrs. Blossom, smiling. "How did you know, Chi?"

"I didn't, just guessed it; coz I knew the new folks was goin' to move in this week."

"What new folks?" chorussed the children in surprise.

"An addition to the Lost Nation," replied their mother, "and a very charming one. Now there are five families on our Mountain."

"Who are they, Martie?" — "Are you going to ask them to Thanksgiving, too?" — "What's their name?" — "How many are there of them?" — "Any boys?" They were all talking together.

"One at a time, please," laughed Mrs. Blossom, putting her hands over her ears. "I never heard such mill-clappers!"

"Do hurry up, mother," said March, appealingly.

"A young man from New Haven has taken the lease of

the farm for three years. He has his mother and sister with him. He was in the law school at Yale until last spring; then his father died, and his sister, a little older than you, Rose, was injured in some accident — I don't know what it was — and now she is very delicate. The doctor says if she can live in this mountain country for a few years, she may recover her health. The brother and mother are perfectly devoted to her. She calls herself a 'Shut-in' — "

"Then she can't come over for Thanksgiving dinner," said Rose, interrupting.

"Not this year, but I hope she may next."

"Did he give up college for his sister's sake?" asked March.

"He gave up the last year of his law course; they could not afford to travel so many years for the benefit of her health, so they came up here. I do pity them; it must be such a change. But, oh, March! how you will enjoy that house! They have been there only a week, yet it looks as if they had lived there always. They have such beautiful framed photographs of places they visited when they were in Europe with their father, and cases of books, and a grand piano — I don't see how they ever got it up the Mountain. The young man and his mother both play, and he plays the violin, too."

The children and Chi were listening open-eyed as Mrs. Blossom went on enthusiastically : —

"It's just like a fairy story, only it's all true. Just two weeks ago, when your father and I drove by there,

10

that long, rambling house looked so bleak and bare and desolate — your father and I always call it the 'House of the Seven Gables,' for there are just seven — and the spruce woods behind it looked fairly black, and the wind drew through the pines by the south door with such an eerie sound, that I shivered. And to-day, what a change! All the shutters were open, and muslin curtains at the windows, and the sun was streaming into the four windows of the great south room that they have made their living-room. There was a roaring big fire in the hall fireplace, and plants — oh, Rose, you should see them! palms and rubber trees and sword ferns, — and lovely rugs, and — I can't begin to tell you about it; you must go and see for yourselves." Mrs. Blossom paused for breath, with a glad light in her eyes.

"It sounds too good to be true," said Rose, "and you look as if you had been to a real party, Martie."

"Well, I have, my dear. Just to see such people and such a house is a party for me."

"And you can keep having it, too, can't you, Martie? because they're going to be neighbors," cried Cherry, every individual curl dancing and bobbing with excitement.

"Is the young man good-looking?" asked Hazel, earnestly.

"Very," replied Mrs. Blossom, smiling.

"As handsome as Jack?" said Hazel.

"Very different looking, Hazel; quiet and grave, but genial. Not so tall as Mr. Sherrill, I should say; talks but little, but what he says is well worth listening to —

and when he smiled! I did n't hear him laugh, but I know
he can enjoy fun. He has a fine saddle horse, Chi, and
he wants you to come and give him some advice about
selecting stock."

" 'Fraid he 's too high-toned for me," said Chi, modestly;
"but if I can help him anyway, I 'd like to. Seems a
likely young man from all you say."

" He 's more than 'likely,' Chi," returned Mrs. Blossom,
with a twinkle in her eye that only Chi caught.

"Speakin' of horses, Mis' Blossom, we 've decided to
send March to the Academy at Barton's, 'n' if I let him
have Fleet, he could come 'n' go, a matter of sixteen miles
a day, without bein' from home nights. I don't approve
of that for boys."

" No, indeed, neither his father nor I would think of
such a thing for a moment. But how kind of you, Chi, to
let March have Fleet."

" I want to help on the college education all I can; 'n'
if our boy wants to go, he 's goin' to have the best to get
him there so far as I 'm concerned."

"I don't know how to thank you, Chi," said March,
" but I 'll treat Fleet like a lady and I 'll study like a —
like a house on fire. I don't envy that other fellow his
saddle horse if I can have Fleet. What 's his name,
mother? you have n't told us yet."

" Why, so I have n't — Ford, Alan Ford, and his sister's
name is Ruth."

"When can we go over and see them, Martie?" said
Rose.

" I thought two or three days after Thanksgiving, and then you can take a little neighborly thank-offering with you."

" What can we take ? " queried Cherry.

" Oh, a mince pie or two, some raspberry preserves, a comb of last summer's honey, a pat of butter, a nice bunch of our white-plume celery, and, perhaps, Chi could find a brace of partridges."

" M-m — does n't that sound good-tasting ! " said Cherry, patting her chest ecstatically.

" Who 's coming for Thanksgiving, Martie ? " asked Budd.

" All the Lost Nation — the Spillkinses and Aunt Tryphosa and Maria-Ann, Lemuel and his wife and — who else ? Guess."

" Why, that 's all."

" Not this year, you forget your new teacher, Budd. She boards around, and it 's the Mountain's year, so she is at Lemuel's now."

" Oh, good ! " cried Budd enthusiastically. " She 's a daisy. I know you 'll like her, Hazel. All the fellows are awfully soft on her, though — bring her butternut candy, an' sharpen her pencils, an' black the stove, an' wash off the black-board ; an' I saw Billy Nye sneak out the other day and wipe the mud off her rubbers with his paper lunch-bag ! Catch me doing it, though," he added, his chest swelling rather pompously as he straightened himself and thrust his hands deep into the pockets of his knickerbockers.

"Why not?" his mother asked with an amused smile.

"Oh, coz," was Budd's rather sheepish reply, and thereupon he followed Chi out to the barn, whistling "Dixie" with might and main.

XIV

THE four families on Mount Hunger were known to the towns about as The Lost Nation. Two of them, the Blossoms and the Spillkinses, were, in reality, lumber-dealers rather than farmers. The third, Lemuel Wood, had a sheep farm, and Aunt Tryphosa Little with her granddaughter, Maria-Ann, was the fourth. The two women owned a spruce wood-lot and let it out to men who cut the bark. They cultivated a small garden-patch of corn, beans, and squash, kept a cow and a few hens, and eked out their scanty income with a day's work here and there in fine weather.

Every two weeks they did the washing and ironing for the Blossom family, as Mrs. Blossom's cares were too heavy for her, and she felt that not only could she afford it this year, but that in putting it out she was giving a little help to her poorer neighbors.

Chi or March took the huge basket of linen over on the wagon or sledge, and always left with it a neighborly gift — a peck of fine russets or greenings, a bunch of celery, a pound or two of salt pork, a bunch of delicious parsnips, or a dozen eggs when the old dame's hens were moulting.

Aunt Tryphosa and Maria-Ann were not to be outdone
in neighborly kindnesses, and, regularly, the willow basket,
full to overflowing with snow-white clothes, was returned
with something tucked away under the square covering
of oil-cloth — a tiny bunch of sage or summer savory, an
ironing-holder made of bits of bright calico or woollen
rags, a little paper-bag of spruce gum, a pair of woollen
wristers for Mr. Blossom or Chi, a new recipe for spring
bitters with a sample of the herbs — sassafras, dockroot,
thoroughwort, wintergreen, and dandelion — gathered by
Aunt Tryphosa herself.

They had one cow which they regarded as the third
member of their family. She had been named Dorcas,
after Aunt Tryphosa's mother, and proved a model animal
of her kind. She gave a more than ordinary amount of
creamy milk; presented her mistress with a sturdy calf
each year; never hooked or kicked; never, during the
bitter winter weather, grew restless in her small shed
which adjoined the woodshed, and never broke from pasture in the sweet-smelling summer-time.

Aunt Tryphosa and Maria-Ann vied with each other in
petting her. They brushed her coat as regularly as they
did up their own back hair. They gave her a weekly
scrubbing as conscientiously as they took their Saturday
bath. For cold nights Aunt Tryphosa had made for her
a nightdress of red flannel (although she had never heard
of "Cranford"), which she and Maria-Ann had planned to
fit the cow-anatomy, and it had proved a great success.

For the midsummer fly-time they had contrived a wonderfully fashioned garment of coarse fish-netting, into which they had knotted a cotton fringe. They claimed, and rightly, that freedom from chill and irritation, incident upon zero weather and August dog-days, affected the milk most favorably, both in quantity and quality; and, as it all went to make delicious small cheeses, which sold at Barton's River for twenty-five cents apiece and were renowned throughout the county, people had ceased to laugh at the cow's appearance.

It had become one of Hazel's great treats to be permitted to go with March or Chi to the little house — not much more than a cabin — on the east side of the Mountain; and when she knew that the two were to be guests for Thanksgiving, but not for Christmas, she began to lay plans accordingly.

The Spillkinses were an aged set, not one was under seventy.

There were the Captain and his wife, who had celebrated their Golden Wedding, and his wife's two maiden sisters, Melissa and Elvira, of whom he always spoke as the "girls." They were funny old maidens of seventy one and two, who did up their hair in curl-papers, precisely as they did a half a century ago; wore black cotton mitts when they went to church, and white silk ones when they went out to tea; called each other "Lissy" and "Elly," and were still sensitive in regard to their ages.

In addition to these, the old, gray-shingled, vine-covered farmhouse on the lower mountain-road, sheltered the Captain's elder brother, Israel, who was just turned ninety.

three, hale and hearty, and Israel's eldest son, Reuben, a youth of seventy, who in our North Country parlance " was not all there," but harmless, kindly, and generally helpful.

All these, together with Lemuel Wood and his wife, and the new teacher, were to be Thanksgiving guests, and wonderful preparations went on for days beforehand.

Such a sorting and paring and chopping of apples! Such a seeding of raisins, and whipping of eggs, and compounding of cakes! Such a tucking away of chickens beneath the flaky crust of the huge pie! Such a moulding of cranberry jelly, so deeply, darkly, richly red! Such a cracking of butternuts, and a melting of maple sugar! Such a stuffing of an eighteen-pound turkey, and such a trussing of thin-linked sausages! Such a making of goodly pies, pumpkin, mince, and apple! Such a quartering of small cheeses contributed by Aunt Tryphosa! Such an unbottling of sweet pickles, and unbarrelling of sweet cider; — and, on the final day, such a general boiling, and baking, and roasting, and basting, and mashing, and grinding, and seasoning, and whipping, and cutting, and kneading, and rolling, as can occur only once a year in an old-fashioned, New England farmhouse.

Hazel was in her glory. Arrayed in a checked gingham apron, which she had made herself, she beat eggs, whipped cream, helped Rose set the table, wiped the dishes and baking-pans, basted the noble Thanksgiving bird once, as a great privilege, although in so doing, she burned her fingers with the sputtering fat, scorched her apron, and parboiled her already flushed face with the escaping steam. But she was happy!

"Oh, papa!" she wrote the day after the party, "I never had such a good time in my life! If only you could see the things we made! — apple and lemon tarts, and mince and cranberry 'turnovers,' and doughnuts all twisted into a sort of French bow-knot such as Gabrielle used to make of her back hair, and a queer kind of cake they call 'marble,' all streaky with chocolate and white, and butternut candy made with maple sugar, and an *Indian* pudding, and little bits of nut-cakes with a small piece of currant jelly inside and all powdered sugar out; and — oh, I can't begin to tell you, for this is only a part of the dessert.

"I'll try to paragraph this letter in the right places so you'll understand about the party.

"All the Lost Nation was invited; Captain and Mrs. Spillkins, Miss Melissa and Miss Elvira, Uncle Israel and Poor Reub, Mr. Lemuel Wood and his wife, and Aunt Tryphosa and Maria-Ann, and — Oh, I forgot Miss Alton. She's awfully sweet; she is Budd and Cherry's teacher in the district school at the Mill Settlement. She's more like a city person than the others. I wish you'd been here! for I can't tell it half as nice as it was; but I'll do my best because you wrote you wanted me to tell you everything.

"We were already for the party at eleven o'clock — in the morning, I mean — (I can't remember the sign for forenoon). We don't have any lunch up here, as you know, but the dinner comes between 12 and 1, so everything was ready then. I got up at five o'clock! and worked hard till it was time to change my gown.

"It was awfully cold. Chi said the thermometer was shivering when he looked at it just after breakfast; he means by that, it's below zero — a good deal; and I could n't help thinking how cosy and warm and deliciously smelly it would be for the Lost Nation when they came in out of the cold into the long-room and saw the table (it looked beautiful, with baskets of red apples, and nuts and raisins, and a big centre-piece of red geranium) just loaded with goodies.

"March had driven over for Aunt Tryphosa and Maria-Ann, and they arrived first — Mrs. Blossom says they always do. (I want you to go over and call on them when you are up here Christmas; it's just like a story in Hans Andersen; they keep a cow, Dorcas, who wears a kimono on very cold nights.)

"March helped Aunt Tryphosa out just as if she had been Queen Victoria. (I forgot to tell you she and Maria-Ann do our laundry work.)   March is perfectly splendid about such things — and Maria-Ann sort of bounced out, although Chi held out his hand to help her. It's so funny to see them together! Aunt Tryphosa is so small and wrinkled and thin that, some-times, Chi says he has known a good wind to knock her right over; and Maria-Ann is almost as tall as Chi, and stout and rosy-cheeked, with nice brown eyes that talk to you.

"And, oh, papa! — I 'll tell you, but it 's a confidence — I saw Aunt Tryphosa shiver hard when she came into the house, and I'm afraid she did not have enough warm things on.   I know her shawl was n't *very* thick, for I went into the bedroom afterwards and felt of it; and she had no furs at all!   Think of that with the thermometer way down below zero, papa! I 'll tell you all about it when you come.

" Well, after Mrs. Blossom had given the old lady a cup of hot tea, she felt better and began to talk; and, honestly, papa, she never stopped talking all day long!   March said he timed her.   She lives away over on the east side of the Mountain away from everybody, and yet she knows everything that is going on, on the Mountain, and at the Mill Settlement, and at Barton's River, and that, as you know, is quite a large place.

" She told us all about the new neighbors in the seven-gabled-house ; how they had their dinner at bed-time, and what ' help ' they have, and whom they are going to have for hired man, and how they have music every night after dinner, and how the lights were n't put out in the north-east chamber till one o'clock. She even knew the pattern of lace on the underclothes that were hung out to dry ! and Maria-Ann was trying to crochet some in imitation ; I saw it myself.

" And she said that one of the chambers was all lined with books, and another just covered, floor and walls, with pictures — what can she mean, papa? and that down stairs off the living-room in what used to be old Mrs. Morris's milk-room, there were ropes, and weights, and pulleys, and a stretcher, and iron balls, and that every one said it did n't have the right look.   But she said she meant to stand up for them, because the young man had come over to call just two or three days ago and said, as she was his nearest neighbor, they ought to become acquainted before winter set in ; and he ordered a half a dozen cheeses and brought word from his mother that she would like them to come over and see her daughter, for she thought Maria-Ann might be able to do something for her. Now, what do you suppose it all means?

" Of course, it makes us all wild to go over there, and I hope we shall go soon.

" But, oh ! if you could see the Spillkinses ! I had to go off up stairs and bury my face in Rose's feather bed so I could laugh without being heard.   They 're the funniest lot of people I ever saw.   They all came over in a big wagon filled with straw, and before they came in sight, Chi said, ' They 're coming, I know by the cackle ; ' and, papa, that is just what it was.

" They are all awfully aged, but they act just like young people, and Mrs. Blossom says it 's their young hearts that keep them so young.

"Uncle Israel, he's ninety-three, but he wears a dark brown wig and looks younger than his son, Poor Reub, who is seventy and has snow-white hair. Mrs. Spillkins wears what they call up here a 'false front;' it's just the color of Uncle Israel's, so she looks more like his sister. But her two sisters, Miss Melissa and Miss Elvira, are perfectly comical. They're just as small as Aunt Tryphosa, but they don't talk; only nod and smile and bow as if they were talking. They have little cork-screw curls, three on each temple, and they bob and shake when they nod and smile and sort of chirrup; it's the Captain and his wife and Uncle Israel who cackle so when they laugh. Poor Reuben does n't say much either, only he looks perfectly happy, and always sits by his father when he can get a chance. Chi was just lovely to him all the afternoon.

"Well, after Mr. Wood and his wife and the new teacher came, we all sat down to dinner, and Mr. Blossom said 'grace,' and all the Spillkinses said 'Amen,' which surprised us all very much.

"We don't have courses up here, because there is nobody to serve us; so everything is put on your plate at once, except, of course, dessert, and papa! — I would n't say it to any one but you, but I never saw any one eat so much as Aunt Tryphosa for all she is so small and thin. Mr. Blossom piled her plate up twice with turkey, and squash, and onion, and potato, and turnip, and then she helped herself to cranberry jelly and sweet pickles three times; and yet she managed to talk all the time; and the queer part of it was that she did n't cut herself once, they all eat with their knives — except, of course, our family and Miss Alton.

"Rose and Cherry and I removed the dinner plates, and that was all the waiting there was.

"We sat till half-past three at the table; then Uncle Israel said another 'grace' — 'after-grace,' he called it, — and Mr. Blossom and Chi took the — the gentlemen part out to see the horses and cows, and all the rest went to work to clear off the table and do up the dishes. There were so many of us it did n't take long, and then we lighted the lamps, and all the — the ladies took out their knitting and began to work as fast as they could.

"Then in a little while all the — the gentlemen came in, and the ladies put up their work, and they all sat round the room and sang Auld Lang Syne. Rose led, and Miss Alton sang a lovely alto. It was lovely, and I longed to have you with me. Then Captain Spillkins said it was time to hitch up, and Chi said it was time to be going as it was very dark and cold. He drove Aunt Tryphosa and Maria-Ann home, and Mrs. Blossom filled a large basket with all sorts of goodies, and Mr. Blossom set it in behind in the apple-green cart without their knowing it; so now they can have a surprise party of their own and Thanksgiving for a whole week.

"There! This is the longest letter I ever wrote in all my life. I 've written it at different times during the day. I ate so much yesterday, that I don't feel very bright to-day, so you must excuse any mistakes, although I 've used the dictionery as you wanted me to.

"Always your loving, and now your dreadfully sleepy

"DAUGHTER HAZEL.

"P. S. I think I shall feel better, if I tell you that we all had a very unhappy time two weeks ago. I had a really dreadful heartache, papa, and, for the first time, was homesick for you.

"You see, March and Rose are very proud of spirit, and I don't think they liked it in me because we are rich — but you and I understand each other, don't we? and know that being rich does n't mean anything to us, does it? and then, too, Chi says we 're poor because we have n't so much family to love as the Blossoms have, and that 's true, too, is n't it? — and I think that kind of poorness ought to balance our riches, don't you?

And — well, I can't explain how it all came about, but now they are willing to let me give them things when I want to, and that makes me very happy, and we are all a great deal happier than we were before, and I'm going to call Mrs. Blossom, ' Mother Blossom,' after this, she says she wants me to, and she takes me in her arms just as she does Rose and Cherry, and we talk things over together; so everything is all right now.

"Please send up my violin by express when you receive this. There is a very good-looking young man, the new neighbor at the seven-gabled-house, and he plays the violin, too, and his mother the piano. Love to Wilkins and Minna-Lu. I'll send him a present from here — Oh, I forgot! don't forget to write Chi within a week sure, to inform you about the Wishing-Tree, and don't buy any presents for anybody till you hear from him. H. C."

When Mr. Clyde read this long letter at the breakfast table, his face was the despair of Wilkins, who hovered about, seeking, ineffectually, for an excuse to ask about Miss Hazel.

" Doan know what kin' er news Marse John get from little Missy," he told Minna-Lu, the cook; " but he laffed pow'ful part de time, an' den he grow pow'ful sober, an' de fust ting I know, de tears come splashin' onto de paper, an' he speak up rale sharp, ' Wha' fo' yo' hyar, Wilkins?' an' sayin' nuffin', I jes' makes tracks, case I see he wan's nobuddy see dem tears. — Fo' Gawd, I'se be glad when little Missy come home."

Mr. Clyde took this manuscript, as he called it, over to the Doctor.

" There, Dick, read that," was all he said.

After the Doctor had read it, he whisked out his handkerchief in a remarkably suspicious manner, and Mr. Clyde busied himself with a medical journal without reading one word, till the Doctor spoke :

"I say, Johnny, let's get up a theatre party of us two for the Old Homestead to-night; it's the nearest thing we can get to this of Hazel's."

" You always hit the right thing, Dick, I'll call for you at eight."

XV

WISHING—TREE SECRETS

ALL-HALLOW-E'EN had come and gone.

The exercises about the tree had been carried out with great success — tom-toms, war-whoop, song and dance. After supper, the apples had been roasted, and the whole family "bobbed" for them in the wash-tub; father, mother, Chi, and even little May joining heartily in the fun. Then they had melted lead, sailed nutshells freighted with wishes, and finally "loved their Loves" with all the letters of the alphabet.

When all were off to bed and sound asleep, Chi took his lantern, and went up again to the old butternut tree in the corner of the pasture.

It was preparing to snow. A chill wind drew through the bare branches, and caused a wild commotion among the roosters' tail feathers that dangled from one of the lower ones.

Chi unlocked the little door, and from the hollow took out a handful of notes. He thrust them into the side pocket of his coat, relocked the door, and went back to his room over the shed. There, by the light of the lantern, he read them and rejoiced over them; re-read them and cried a little over them, nor was he ashamed of his

11

tears; for in the precious missives, Rose and Hazel, March and Budd and Cherry, had shown, as in a mirror, the workings of their loving hearts.

All-hallow-e'en.

MY DEAR MOTHER, — I have a great favor to ask of you and father. Will you hang up *your* stockings this year and let us children fill them instead of your filling ours? I don't want you to take one cent of the money you are earning by having Hazel here to buy me anything. I want every penny of it to go to pay off that mortgage you told us of — for I feel just as you do about it, and only wish I had known it last Hallow-e'en when I asked for the paints and brushes. It makes me sick just to think of all we asked for, and you not having any money to buy them with — and never telling us! Oh, mother!

Your devoted son,
MARCH BLOSSOM.

All-hallow-e'en.

MY DEAR POPSEY, — Me and Cherry want to help you and Martie pay off that morgige she told us about. March says it is a dreadfull thing that we must get rid of just as soon as we can. So Cherry and me are going to give you 2 dollars apeace out of our $3 we saved for ourselves out of the jam and the chickens as we voted in the N. B. B. O. O. That will make four dollars and March says it will be just $\frac{1}{300}$ of what you owe and will help a great deal. I think the other $1 we have left will be enough to buy presents for the rest of the famly, don't you?

Your Son,
BUDD BLOSSOM.

P. S. I meant to say I don't expect anything this year 'cause last year I asked for a double-runner and a bat and a new cap with fir on the edges like the boys at Barton's and 20 cents to buy marbles with and I did n't get them 'cause you were sick

and I 'm sorry I asked for so much to bother you when you
were sick.   B. B.

DEAR FRIEND CHI, — Do you think you can find out in some
way what March and Budd would like for Christmas? And if
you know anything *special* that Rose wants very *specially*,
please let me know at your earliest convenience so I can send
to New York for it.   I should like to consult you about some
gifts for Aunt Tryphosa and Maria-Ann, and if you could get
a chance to take me down to the Barton's River shops all alone
by myself, I should esteem it a great favor.

Your true friend,

HAZEL CLYDE.

All-hallow-e'en.

P. S.   I 'm rather anxious about the note I put in the Wishing-Tree for papa.

All-hallow-e'en.

DARLING PATER NOSTER, — When I think of last year, my
heart aches for you and my precious Martie.   Oh, why did n't
she tell us before!   I never should have asked for that dress
and the French grammar and dictionary and the cheap set of
Dickens', if I had only known.

Do, Pater dear, let us know in the future if you are in
trouble, and let us help share it.   Would n't that make it easier
for you?

Now a favor; I want you and Martie to play boy and girl
again this year and hang up *your* stockings for a change; and
please, *please*, father dear, don't give us anything this year —
we don't want anything but you and Martie, and besides, we
have money of our *own!*   Chi calls us " bloated bond-holders,"
and says we have formed a " combine."

Your loving daughter,

ROSE BLOSSOM.

DEAREST COUSIN JACK, — I have n't answered your letter because I 've been having too good a time. This is only a Wishing-Tree note; I want you to do me a favor, please; find out what I can buy nice for papa with a dollar. I 've earned it myself (and a great deal more, Jack, you would be surprised if you knew how much the preserves and chickens came to) and want him to have a present out of it. Then, I would like to buy something for Doctor Heath, about 'fifty cents' worth, and another fifty cents' worth for Mrs. Heath. I want to give Aunt Carrie a little something, too, *out of my own earnings;* (I 've all my two quarterly allowances besides,) I can afford fifty cents for her; and then I would like to remember Wilkins with a little gift out of *my earnings* for mamma's sake as well as my own, and then I shall have twenty-five cents left of the money I worked for. The rest we all voted to put aside for March to help him through college. He wants to be an arcitect, you know, and he draws beautifully. I shall be glad of your advice.

In haste, yours devotedly,

HAZEL.

All-hallow-e'en, MOUNT HUNGER.

DEAR CHI, — May wants a doll the kind she saw last summer down at Barton's River. I ve got only a doller to spend for all the famly, so will you plese ask the pris for me as I am afrade it will be to high. There is a big french one in the right hand window at Smith's store with a libel on it 7$, and I play it 's mine when I am down there and you are buying horse-feed. I have named her Emilie Angelique. Rose spelt it for me.

Your loving CHERRY BOUNCE.

DEAR OLD CHI, — If you can find out what Hazel would like specially for Christmas, just let me know.

MARCH.

Dear Chi, — Can you manage to get us all down to Barton's some Saturday to do some Christmas shopping?

Your Rose-pose.

All-hallow-e'en.

Dearest Papa, — Will you please ask Aunt Carrie to please help you buy these Christmas things? I enclose fifty dollars ; (your check.)

A white serge dress pattern, like mine.

A book of lovely foreign photographs of buildings and pictures for March.

2 pairs of white kid gloves, number 6.

2 pairs of tan kid gloves, number 6¼.

1 pair fur-lined gloves for March.

1 pair ditto for Mr. Blossom.

A year's subscription for the Woman's Hearthstone Journal for Maria-Ann.

A small shirt waist ironing-board for Aunt Tryphosa.

1 pair brown woolen gloves and one pair of those fleece-lined beaver gauntlet driving gloves like those of yours, for Chi.

1 blue Kardigan jacket for Chi.

The other things I think I can get at Barton's River.

Your devoted daughter,

Hazel Clyde.

" Well," said Chi, thoughtfully, as he finished reading them a second time, " I 've got more than one string to my bow this year. Beats all, how Chris'mus limbers up a man's feelin's ! Guess 't was meant for all of us children of a lovin' Father." So saying, Chi knelt beside his bed, and, dropping his face in his hands, remained there motionless for a few minutes, while his loving, gentle, manly " soul was on its knees."

XVI

A CHRISTMAS PRELUDE

"It's goin' to be an awful cold night, grandmarm," said Maria-Ann as she stepped to the door just after sunset on Christmas eve. The old dame followed her and looked out over her shoulder.

"I know 't is; my fingers stuck to the latch when I went out to see after Dorcas. While your gettin' supper, I 'm goin' to bundle up the rooster and the hens, or they 'll freeze their combs, sure 's your name 's Maria-Ann; looks kinder Chris'musy, don't it?"

"I was just thinkin' of that, grandmarm; just look at that star in the east!" She pointed to a shoulder of the Mountain, where a serene planet was ascending the dark blue heavens. "An' there 's been just enough snow to make all the spruces look like the Sunday School tree, all roped over with pop-corn. Do you remember that last one, grandmarm?"

"I ain't never forgot it, Maria-Ann; that 's ten year ago, an' I sha'n't never see another?" She shivered, and drew back out of the keen air.

"Nor I," said Maria-Ann, shutting the door.

"I don't know why not," snapped Aunt Tryphosa, who always contradicted Maria-Ann when she could. "I guess we can have a Chris'mus tree same 's other folks; we 've got trees enough."

"That 's so," replied Maria-Ann, laughing. "Let 's have one to-morrow, grandmarm. I don't see why we can't have a tree just as well as we can have wreaths — see what beauties I 've made! I 've saved the four handsomest for Mis' Blossom an' Mis' Ford."

"You do beat all, Maria-Ann, making wreaths with them greens and bitter-sweet; I wish you 'd hang 'em up to-night; 't would make the room seem kinder Chris'musy."

"To be sure I will." And Maria-Ann bustled about, hanging the beautiful rounds of green and red in each of the kitchen windows, on the panes of which the frost was already sparkling; then, throwing her shawl over her head, she stepped out into the night and hung one on the outside of the narrow, weather-blackened door. Again within, she set the small, square kitchen table with two plates, two cups and saucers of brown and white crockery, the pewter spoons and horn-handled knives and forks that her grandmother had had when she was first married. Finally, she put on one of the pots of red geranium in the centre and stood back to admire the effect.

"Guess we 'll have a treat to-night, seein' it 's night before Chris'mus — fried apples an' pork, an' some toast; an' I 'll cut a cheese to-night, I declare I will, even if grandmarm does scold; she 'll eat it fast enough if I don't say nothin' about it beforehand."

Maria-Ann had formed the habit of thinking aloud, for she had been much alone, and, as she said, "she was a good deal of company for herself."

" Oh, hum ! " she sighed, as she cut the pork and sliced the apples, " a cup of tea would be about the right thing this cold night, but there ain't a mite in the house." Then she laughed: " What you talkin' 'bout luxuries for, Maria-Ann Simmons? You be thankful you 've got a livin'. I can make some good cambric-tea, and put a little spearmint in it; that 'll be warmin' as anything." She began to sing in a shrill soprano as she busied herself with the preparations for the supper, while the kettle sang, too, and the pork sizzled in the spider:

> " 'Must I be carried to the skies
>   On flowery beds of ease,
> While others fought to win the prize
>   And sailed through bloody seas?' "

Meanwhile, Aunt Tryphosa, with her lantern in one hand and a bundle of red something in the other, had repaired to the hen-house which was partitioned off from the woodshed.

Had either one of them happened to look out down the Mountain-road just at this time, they would have seen a strange sight.

Along the white roadway, sparkling in the light of the rising moon, came six silent forms in Indian file. Two were harnessed to small loaded sledges. Sometimes, all six gesticulated wildly; at others, the two who brought up the rear of the file silently danced and capered back and forth across the narrow way. They drew near the house on the woodshed side ; the first two freed themselves from the sledges, and left them under one of the unlighted windows. Then all six, attracted by the glimmer of the lantern shining from the one small aperture of the hen-house, stole up noiselessly and looked in.

What they saw proved too much for their risibles, and suppressed giggles and snickers and choking laughter nearly betrayed their presence to the old dame within.

On the low roost sat Aunt Tryphosa's noble Plymouth Rock rooster, and beside him, in an orderly row, her ten hens. Every hen had on her head a tiny flannel hood — some were red, some were white — the strings knotted firmly under their bills by Aunt Tryphosa's old fingers trembling with the cold.

She was just blanketing the rooster, who submitted with a meekness which proved undeniably that he was under petticoat government, for all the airs he gave himself with his wives. The funny, little, hooded heads twisting and turning, the " aks " and " oks " which accompanied Aunt Tryphosa in her labor of love, the wild stretching and flapping of wings, all furnished a scene never to be forgotten by the six pairs of laughing eyes that beheld it.

The moment the old dame took up her lantern, the spectators sped around the corner. Under the dark windows they noiselessly unloaded the wood-sleds, and silently carried bundles, baskets, and burlap-bags around to the front door.

At last they had fairly barricaded it, and the tallest of the party, after fastening a piece of paper in the Christmas wreath that Maria-Ann had hung up only a half-hour before, motioned to the others to step up to the kitchen window.

Just one glimpse they had through the thickening frost and the wreathing green: a glimpse of the kitchen table, the steaming apples, the pot of red geranium, the two cups of smoking spearmint tea, and of two heads — the one white, the other brown — bent low over folded, toil-worn hands in the reverent attitude for the evening "grace."

"For what we are now about to receive, may the Lord make us truly thankful," said Aunt Tryphosa, in a quavering voice.

"Amen," said Maria-Ann, heartily — "Land sakes, grandmarm! how you scairt me, looking up so sudden!" she exclaimed, almost in the same breath.

"Thought I heerd somethin'," said the old dame, holding her head in a listening attitude — "Hark!"

"I don't hear nothin', grandmarm. Now, just eat your apples while they're hot. What did you think you heard?" she continued, dishing the apples.

"I thought I heerd it when I was out in the shed, too."

"I shouldn't wonder if 't was a deer. I saw one come into the clearing this afternoon, an' seein' 't was Christmas evening, I put a good bundle of hay out to the south door of the cow-shed."

"Guess 't was that, then," said Aunt Tryphosa. "You clear up, Maria-Ann, an' I'll keep up a good fire, for I want to finish off them stockings for Ben Blossom an' Chi. I s'pose you've got your things ready in case we see a team go by to-morrow?"

"Yes, they're all ready," said her granddaughter, rather absently, and set about washing the few dishes.

When all was done, neatly and quickly as Maria-Ann so well knew how, she flung on her shawl, saying:

" I 'm goin' out a minute to see if the bundle of hay is gone, and besides, I want to look at the moon on the snow; it 's the first time I 've seen it so this year." She opened the door —

" Oh, Luddy ! " she screamed, as bundle, and basket, and bag toppled over into the room.

" Land sakes alive ! " quavered Aunt Tryphosa, hurrying to the rescue. " Did n't I tell you I heerd somethin' ? What be they ? "

"Presents ! " cried Maria-Ann, pulling, and hauling, and gathering up, and finally getting the door shut.

" Seems to me I see somethin' white catched onto the door 'fore you shut it," said Aunt Tryphosa. " Better look an' see." Again her granddaughter opened the door, and found the strip of paper on which was written ;

" Merry Christmas ! with best wishes of
  Benjamin and Mary Blossom and May,
  Malachi Graham and Rose Eleanor Blossom,
  March Blossom and Hazel Clyde,
  Benjamin Budd Blossom and Cherry Elizabeth Blossom of
  the N. B. B. O. O., and of
  John Curtis Clyde of New York; U. S. A.; N. A.; W. H."

" Oh, grandmarm ! It 's just like a romantic novel ! " cried Maria-Ann, who was as full of sentiment as an egg is full of yolk. " It makes me feel kinder queer, comin' just now right after we was talkin' 'bout our tree. You open first, an' then we 'll take turns." Aunt Tryphosa, who was winking very hard behind her spectacles, was not loath to begin.

"Let's haul 'em up to the stove; it's so awful cold," she said, shivering.

"Why, you've let the fire go down; that's the reason. Don't you remember you was goin' to put on the wood just as the things fell in?"

"So I was," said her grandmother, making good her forgetfulness; in a few minutes there was a roaring fire, and the room was filled with a genial warmth. Then they sat down to their delightful task, Maria-Ann kneeling on the square of rag carpet before the stove.

"My land!" cried Aunt Tryphosa, clapping her hands together as she opened the largest burlap bag; "if that boy ain't stuffed this two-bushel bag chock full of birch bark! Look a-here, Maria-Ann, you read this slip of paper for me; my specs get so dim come night-time."

The truth was, the tears were running down Aunt Tryphosa's wrinkled cheeks and filming her eyes to such an extent that she saw the birch bark through all the colors of the rainbow.

"'For Aunt Tryphosa from Budd Blossom to make her fires quick with cold mornings.' Did you ever?" said Maria-Ann, untying another large burlap bundle — "What's this? 'Made by Rose Blossom and Hazel Clyde to keep Aunt Tryphosa snug and warm o' nights when the mercury is below zero.' O grandmarm, look at this!"

Maria-Ann unrolled a coverlet made of silk patch-work (bright bits and pieces that Hazel had begged of Aunt

Carrie and Mrs. Heath and others of her New York friends) lined with thin flannel and filled with feathers.

But Aunt Tryphosa was speechless for the first time in her life; and, seeing this, Maria-Ann took advantage of it to do a little talking on her own account.

" She don't seem like a city girl in her ways; she ain't a bit stuck up — Oh, what's *this* ! " She poked, and fingered, and pinched, but failed to guess. Aunt Tryphosa grew impatient.

" Let me *see*, you've done nothin' but feel," she said, reaching for the package, and Maria-Ann handed it over to her.

Again Mrs. Tryphosa Little was nearly dumb, as the miscellaneous contents of the queer, knobby parcel were brought to light.

" These are for you, Maria-Ann," she said in an awed voice, laying them on the kitchen table one after the other: — A copy of the Woman's Hearthstone Journal, with the receipt for a year's subscription pinned to it; — A small shirt waist ironing-board; — A pair of fleece-lined Arctics that buttoned half-way up Maria-Ann's sturdy legs when, an hour later, she tried them on; — Six paper-covered novels of the Chimney Corner Library including Lorna Doone (Hazel had discovered in her frequent visits, that Aunt Tryphosa's granddaughter at twenty-nine was as romantic as a girl of seventeen); — A box of preserved ginger; — Two pounds of Old Hyson Tea; — (upon which Maria-Ann bounced up from the floor, and without more ado made two cups, much to her grandmother's amazement); — Six pounds of lump sugar ; — A dozen lemons ; — A dozen oranges ; — A white Liberty-silk scarf tucked into an envelope ; — Six ounces of scarlet knitting-wool ; — All for " Miss Maria-Ann Simmons, with Hazel Clyde's best wishes."

Then it was Maria-Ann Simmons's turn to break down and weep, at which Aunt Tryphosa fidgeted, for she had not seen her granddaughter cry since she was a little girl.

" Don't act like a fool, Maria-Ann," she said, crustily, to hide her own feelings; " take your things an' enjoy 'em. I 've seen tears enough for night before Chris'mus," she added, ignoring the fact that she had established a precedent.

" Well, I won't, grandmarm," said her granddaughter, laughing and crying at the same time; " but I 'm goin' to have that cup of tea first to kind of strengthen me 'fore I open the rest," she added decidedly. " Besides, I don't want to see everything at once ; I want it to last."

" I don't mind if I have mine, too. Guess you may put in two lumps, seein' as we did n't have to pay for it," and the old dame sipped her Hyson with supreme satisfaction, as did likewise her granddaughter.

As the latter pushed back her chair from the table, her grandmother cautioned her: — " Look out! you 're settin' it on another bag ! " But it was too late. To Aunt Tryphosa's amazement and Maria-Ann's horror, the bag suddenly flopped up and down on the floor, the motion being accompanied with such an unearthly, " A — ee — eetsch — ok — ak — ache — eetsch ! " that the two women's faces grew pale, and they jumped as if they had been shot.

Then Maria-Ann, with her hand on her thumping heart, burst into a shrill laugh, and Aunt Tryphosa quavered a thin accompaniment. How they laughed! till again the tears rolled down their cheeks.

"Scairt of hens!" chuckled the old dame as she undid the strings of the bag — "at my time of life! Oh, my stars and garters, Maria-Ann! ain't they beauties?"

She drew out by the legs two snow-white Wyandotte pullets, and held them up admiringly. "They're from March, I know; but just to think of this, Maria-Ann!" Again words and, curiously enough, eyes, too, failed her, and her granddaughter read the slip of paper tied around the leg of one of the hens: —"'One for Aunt Tryphosa, and one for Maria-Ann; have laid three times; last time day before yesterday; I hope they'll lay two Christmas-morning eggs for your breakfast. March Blossom.'"

"I'm goin' to put 'em on some hay in the clothes-basket, Maria-Ann, an' keep 'em right under my bed where it's good an' warm," said Aunt Tryphosa, decidedly. "They're kinder quality folks and can't be turned in among common fowl. Besides, I ain't got another hood, an' if they *should* freeze their combs, I'd never forgive myself."

"Well, I would, grandmarm," said Maria-Ann, still laughing, as she untied the last two bundles. "Laws!" she exclaimed, "Here's New York style for you." She read the visiting card:

" To Mrs. Tryphosa Little, with the Season's compliments from John Curtis Clyde.   4 East——th Street."

" Well, I 'm dumbfoundered," sighed Mrs. Tryphosa Little, and more she could not say as she took out of the large pasteboard box, a white silk neckerchief, a cap of black net and lace with a " chou " of purple satin lutestring, a black fur collar and a muff to match, in all of which she proceeded to array herself with the utmost despatch, forgetful of the two hens, which, after wandering aimlessly about the kitchen, had roosted finally on the back of her wooden rocking-chair, where they balanced themselves with some difficulty.

But suddenly, as she was thrusting her hands into the new muff, she paused, laid it down on the table, and said, rather querulously, " Help me off with these things, Maria-Ann; I 'm all tuckered out.   I can stan' a day's washin' as well as anybody, if I am eighty-one come next June, but I can't stan' no such night 'fore Chris'mus as this, an' I 'm goin' to bed, an' take the hens."

" I would, grandmarm," said her granddaughter, gently, taking off the unwonted finery and kissing the wrinkled face. " You go to bed; I put the soap-stone in two hours ago, so it 's nice an' warm.   I 'll clear up, an' don't you mind me — here, let me take one of those hens."

" No, I can take care of hens anytime," snapped Aunt Tryphosa, for she was tired out with happiness, " but I can't stan' so many present, an' I 'm too old to begin." She disappeared in the bed-room, the two Wyandotte hens hanging limply, heads downward, from each hand.

Maria-Ann picked up the paper and the wraps, and made all tidy again in the kitchen. She put her hand on the last bag that was so heavy she had not moved it from the door. "It's a bag of cracked corn — hen-feed," she said to herself, "an' it's from Chi, I know as well as if I'd been told."

Then she sat down in the rocker before the stove and put her feet in the oven to warm. She blew out the light and sat awhile in silence, thinking happy thoughts.

The fire crackled in the stove, and dancing lights, reflected from the open grate, played on the wall. The moon shone full upon the frosted window panes, and the Christmas wreaths were set in masses of encrusted brilliants. The kettle began to sing, and so did Maria-Ann — but softly, for fear of waking Aunt Tryphosa:

> " 'My soul, be on thy guard;
>   Ten thousand foes arise;
>   The hosts of sin are pressing hard
>   To draw thee from the skies.' "

XVII

HUNGER-FORD

SUCH a line of communication as was soon established between Mount Hunger and New York, Mount Hunger and Cambridge, the Lost Nation and Barton's River, Hunger-ford — the Fords' new name for the old Morris farm — and the Blossom homestead on the Mountain!

Uncle Sam's post, the Western Union Telegraph Company, the American Express, a line of freight, saddle horses, sleds, and the old apple-green cart on runners were all pressed into service; in all the United States of America there were no busier young people than those belonging to the Lost Nation.

They wrote notes to one another with an air of great mystery; they drove singly, in couples, or all together to Barton's River with Chi; they smuggled in bundles and express packages of all sorts and sizes; looked guilty if caught whispering together in the pantry; took many a sled-ride over to Hunger-ford, and audaciously remained there three hours at a time without giving Mrs. Blossom any good reason either for their going or remaining.

The acquaintance formed between the Blossoms and the Fords just after Thanksgiving, was fast ripening into friendship. March, usually shy with strangers, fairly adored the tall, quiet son with the wonderful smile, and expanded at once in his genial presence. With Ruth Ford he had much in common; and regularly once a week since Thanksgiving he had drawn and painted with her in her studio, the room that Aunt Tryphosa had so graphically described. His gift was far more in that direction than hers; and Ruth, recognizing it, encouraged him, spurred his ambition, and placed all her materials at his disposal.

Rose's sweet voice had proved a delight to them all, and Hazel's violin was being taught to play a gentle accompaniment to Alan Ford's, that sang, or wept, or rejoiced according to the player's mood.

"I am so thankful, Ben, that our Rose can have the advantage of such companions just at this time of her life," said Mrs. Blossom, on the afternoon before Christmas when the two eldest, with Hazel, had gone over to Hungerford with joyful secrets written all over their happy faces.

"So am I, Mary. When I see young men like Ford, I realize what I lost in being obliged to give up college on father's account," said Mr. Blossom, with a sigh.

"I do, too, Ben; and what I've lost in opportunity when I see that gifted woman, Mrs. Ford. She has travelled extensively, she reads and speaks both German and French, she is a really wonderful musician, and keeps up with every interest of the day, besides being a splendid housekeeper and devoted to her children."

"Do you regret it, Mary?" said her husband, looking straight before him into the fire.

"Not with you, Ben," was Mary Blossom's answer.

Taking her husband's face in both her hands and turning it towards her, she looked into his eyes, and received the smile and kiss that were always ready for her.

" If we did n't have all this when we were young people, Mary, we 'll hope that we may have it in our children," he said, earnestly.

Just then Chi came in, and gave a loud preliminary, " Hem !" for to him, Ben and Mary Blossom would always be lovers. " Guess 't is 'bout time to hitch up, if you 're goin' clear down to Barton's to meet the train, Ben ; I 've got to go over eastwards with the children."

" All right, Chi, I 'd rather drive down to the station to-night ; it 's good sleighing and our Mountain is a fine sight by moonlight."

" Can't be beat," said Chi, emphatically. " S'pose you 'll be back by seven, sharp? I kind of want to time myself, on account of the s'prise."

" We 'll say seven, and I 'll make it earlier if I can. You 're off for Aunt Tryphosa's now ? "

" Just finished loadin' up — There they are !" and in rushed the whole troop, hooded and mittened and jacketed and leggined, ready for their after-sunset raid.

" Good-bye, Martie !" screamed Cherry, wild with excitement, and made a dash for the door ; then she turned back with another dash that nearly upset May, and, throwing her arms around her mother's neck, nearly squeezed the breath from her body. " O Mumpsey, Dumpsey, dear ! I 'm having such an awfully good time ; it 's so much happier than last Christmas ! "

" And, O Popsey, Dopsey, dear ! " laughed Rose, mimicking her, but with a voice full of love, and both mittens caressing his face, " it's so good to have you well enough to celebrate this year ! "

Hazel slipped her hand into Chi's, and whispered, " Oh, Chi, I wish I had a lot of brothers and sisters like Rose. Anyway, papa's coming to-night, so I'll have one of my own," she added proudly.

" Guess we'd better be gettin' along," said Chi, still holding Hazel's hand. " It's goin' to be a stinger, 'n' it's a mile 'n' a half over there."

"Come on all ! " cried March; " we'll be back before you are, father."

" We'll see about that," laughed his father, as he caught the merry twinkle in his wife's eye.

But March was right by the margin of only a minute or two; for just as the merry crowd entered the house on their return from their errand of " goodwill," they heard Mr. Blossom drive the sleigh into the barn. In another moment Hazel had flung wide the door and was caught up into her father's arms.

In the midst of their cordial greetings there was a loud knock at the door. They all started at the sound, and Budd, who was nearest, opened it.

" Please, Budd, may I come in, too ? " said a voice everyone recognized as the Doctor's.

Then the whole Blossom household lost their heads where they had lost their hearts the year before. Rose and Hazel and Cherry fairly smothered him with kisses; Budd wrung one hand, March gripped another; May clung to one leg, and the monster of a puppy contrived to get under foot, although he stood two feet ten.

Jack Sherrill, looking in at the window upon all this loving hominess, felt, somehow, physically and spiritually left out in the cold. " What a fool I was to come! " he said to himself. Nevertheless he carried out his part of the program by stepping up to the door and knocking. This time Mrs. Blossom opened it.

" Have you room for one more, Mrs. Blossom? " he said with an attempt at a smile, but looking sadly wistful, so wistful and lonely that Mary Blossom put out both hands without a word, and, somehow, — Jack, in thinking it over afterwards, never could tell how it happened so naturally — he was giving her a son's greeting, and receiving a mother's kiss in return.

In a moment Hazel's arms were around his neck; — " Oh, Jack, Jack! I 've got three of my own now; I 'm almost as rich as Rose! "

Rose, hearing her name, came forward with frank, cordial greeting, and May transferred her demonstrations of affection from the Doctor's trousers to Jack's; Cherry's curls bobbed and quivered with excitement when Jack claimed a kiss from " Little Sunbonnet," and received two hearty smacks in return; March took his travelling bag; Budd kept close beside him, and the puppy, who had been christened Tell, nosed his hand, and, sitting down on his haunches, pawed the air frantically until Jack shook hands with him, too.

By this time the wistful look had disappeared from Jack's eyes, and his handsome face was filled with such a glad light that the Doctor noticed it at once. He shook his head dubiously, with his eyebrows drawn together in a straight line over the bridge of his nose, and, from underneath, his keen eyes glanced from Jack to Rose and from Rose back again to Jack. Then his face cleared, and explanations were in order.

"Why, you see," the Doctor said to Mrs. Blossom, "my wife had to go South with her sister, and could not be at home for Christmas — the first we've missed celebrating together since we were married — and when I found John was coming up to spend it with you, I couldn't resist giving myself this one good time. But Jack here has failed to give any satisfactory account of how or why he came to intrude his long person just at this festive time. I thought you were off at a Lenox house-party with the Seatons?" he said, quizzically.

Jack laughed good-naturedly. "I don't blame you for wondering at my being here; but I've been here before," he said, willing to pay back the Doctor in his own coin.

"The deuce you have!" exclaimed the Doctor. "I say, Johnny, are we growing old that these young people get ahead of us so easily?"

"I don't know how you feel, Dick, but I'm as young as Jack to-night."

"That's right, Papa Clyde," said Hazel, approvingly, softly patting her father on the head; "and, Jack, you're a dear to come up here to see us, for you've just as much right as the Doctor."

The Doctor pretended to grumble : — " Come to see you, indeed, you superior young woman — *you* indeed ! As if there weren't any other girls in the world or on Mount Hunger but you and Rose — much you know about it."

"Well, I'd like to know who you came to see, if not us ? " laughed Hazel, sure of her ultimate triumph.

"Why, my dear Ruth Ford, to be sure."

" Ruth Ford ! " they exclaimed in amazement.

" Why not Ruth Ford? You didn't suppose I would come away up here into the wilds of Vermont in the dead of winter, did you ? just to see — " But Hazel laid her hand on his mouth.

" Stop teasing, do," she pleaded, " and tell us how you knew our Ruth."

" *Our* Ruth ! Ye men of York, hear her ! " said the Doctor, appealing to Mr. Clyde and Jack. " The next thing will be ' our Alan Ford,' I suppose. How will you like that, Jack ? "

" I feel like saying ' confound him,' only it wouldn't be polite. You see, Doctor, I thought I had preëmpted the whole Mountain, and was prepared to make a conquest of Miss Maria-Ann Simmons even; but if Mr. Ford has stepped in " — Jack assumed a tragic air — " there is nothing left for me in honor, but to throw down the gauntlet and challenge him to single combat — hockey-sticks and hot lemonade — for her fair hand.":

At the mention of Maria-Ann, Rose and Hazel, Budd

and Cherry and March went off into fits of laughter. They laughed so immoderately that it proved infectious for their elders, and when Chi entered the room Budd cried out, " Oh, Chi, you tell about the — we can't — the rooster and the hoods, and — Oh my eye ! — " Budd was apparently on the verge of convulsions.

" I stuffed snow into my mouth and made my teeth ache so as not to laugh out loud," said Cherry ; at which there was another shout, and still another outburst at the table when Chi described the scene in the hen-house.

" Now, children," said Mrs. Blossom, after the somewhat hilarious evening meal was over, the table cleared, the dishes were wiped and put away, " we 're going to do just for this once as you want us to — hang up our stockings ; but I want all of you to hang up yours, too. If you don't, I shall miss the sixes and sevens and eights so, that it will spoil my Christmas."

" We will, Martie," they assented, joyfully ; for, as March said, it would not seem like night before Christmas if they did not hang up their stockings.

" Yes, and papa, and you," said Hazel, turning to the Doctor, " must hang up yours, and you, too, Jack."

" Why, of course," said Mrs. Blossom, " everybody is to hang up a stocking to-night, even Tell."

" Oh, Martie, how funny ! " cried Cherry, " but he has n't a truly stocking."

" No, but one of Budd's will do for his huge paw — won't it, old fellow ? " she said, patting his great head.

Then Budd must needs bring out a pair of his pedal

coverings and try one brown woollen one on Tell, much
to his majesty's surprise ; for Tell was a most dignified
youth of a dog, as became his nine months and his famous
breed.

Early in the evening the stockings were hung up over
the fireplace, all sizes and all colors : — May's little red
one and Chi's coarse blue one ; Mr. Clyde's of thick silk,
and Budd's and Tell's of woollen ; Hazel's of black cashmere beside Jack's striped Balbriggan.   What an array !

Then Mrs. Blossom and May went off into the bedroom,
and Mr. Blossom and his guests were forced to smoke
their after-tea cigars in the guest bedroom upstairs, while
the young people brought out their treasures and stuffed
the grown-up stockings till they were painfully distorted.

" Don't they look lovely ! " whispered Hazel, ecstatically
to March, who begged Rose to get another of their mother's
stockings, for the one proved insufficient for the fascinating
little packages that were labelled for her.

" Let 's go right to bed now," suggested Budd, " then
mother 'll fill ours — Oh, I forgot," he added, ruefully,
" we are n't going to have presents this year — "

" Why, yes, we are, too, Budd," said Rose, " we 're going
to give one another out of our own money."

" Cracky !   I forgot all about that — "   Budd tore upstairs in the dark, and tore down again and into the bedroom, crying : — " Now all shut your eyes while I 'm going
through ! " which they did most conscientiously.

Soon they, too, were invited laughingly to retire, and by
half-past ten the house was quiet.

" 'T WAS THE NIGHT BEFORE CHRISTMAS, AND ALL THROUGH THE
    HOUSE,
NOT A CREATURE WAS STIRRING, NOT EVEN A MOUSE;"
Stretched out on the hearth-rug lay Tell snoring loudly,
And above from the mantel the stockings hung proudly;
When down from the stairway there came such a patter
Of stockingless feet — 't was no laughing matter!
As the good Doctor thought, for he sprang out of bed
To see if 't were real, or a dream in its stead.

But no! with his eye at a crack of the door
He discovered the truth — 't was the Blossoms, all four,
With Hazel to aid them, tiptoeing about
Like a party of ghosts grown a little too stout.
They pinched and they fingered; they poked and they squeezed
Each plump Christmas stocking — then somebody sneezed!
Consternation and terror!! The tall clock struck one
As the ghosts disappeared on the double-quick run!

" 'T WAS THE NIGHT BEFORE CHRISTMAS, AND ALL THROUGH THE
    HOUSE,
NOT A CREATURE WAS STIRRING, NOT EVEN A MOUSE;"
Without in the moonlight, the snow sparkled bright;
The Mountain stood wrapped in a mantle of white,
With a crown of dark firs on his noble old crest
And ermine and diamonds adorning his breast;
And the stars that above him swung true into line
Once shone o'er a manger in far Palestine.

What a Christmas morning that was!

Chi was up at five o'clock, building roaring fires, for it
was ten degrees below zero.

With the first glint of the sun on the frosted panes the
household was astir. At precisely seven the order was
given to take down the thirteen stockings. But bless

you! You're not to think the stockings could hold all the gifts. In front of each wide jamb were piled the bundles and packages, three feet high!

Rose hesitated a moment when the children sat down on the rug with their stockings, as was their custom every Christmas morn; then she plumped down among them, saying, laughingly:

"I don't care if I *am* growing up, Martie — it's Christmas."

Upon which Jack, hugging his striped Balbriggan, sat down beside her.

Such "Ohs" and "Ahs"! Such thankings and squeezings! Such somersaults as were turned by March and Budd at the kitchen end of the long-room! Such rapturous gurgles from May! Such hand-shakes and kisses! Such silent bliss on the part of Chi, who, though suffering as if in a Turkish bath, had donned his new, blue woollen sweater, drawn on his gauntleted beaver gloves, and proceeded to investigate his stocking with the air of a man who has nothing more to wish for. And through all the chaotic happiness a sentence could be distinguished now and then.

"Chi, these corn-cob pipes are just what I shall want after Christmas when I give my Junior Smoker."

"Oh, Martie, it can't be for me!" as the lovely white serge dress, ready made and trimmed with lace, was held up to Rose's admiring eyes.

Budd was caressing with approving fingers a regular "base-ball-nine" bat and admiring the white leather balls.

"I say, it's a stunner, Mr. Sherrill; but how did you know I wanted it?"

Mr. Clyde, who was touched to his very heart's core by Hazel's gift of a dollar pair of suspenders which she had earned by her own labor, felt a small hand slipped into his, and found Cherry Bounce looking up at him with wide, adoring, brown eyes, which, for the first time, she had taken from her beautiful Émilie Angélique, whom she held pressed to her heart: —

"I want to whisper to you," she said, shyly. Mr. Clyde bent down to her; — "After I said my prayers to Martie, I asked God to give me Émilie Angélique — every night," she nodded — "but I only told Budd, so how *did* you know?"

March was lost to the world in his volume of foreign photographs, in his boxes of paints and brushes, and a whole set of drawing materials. He had not as yet thanked Hazel for them.

Everybody was happy and satisfied. Everybody said he or she had received just exactly *the* thing. Tell alone could not express his gratification in words. He had been given his woollen stocking, and nosed about till he had brought forth three fat dog-biscuit, a deliciously juicy-greasy beef bone, wrapped in white waxed paper and tied at one end with a blue ribbon, a fine nickelplated dog collar with a bell attached, and last, from the brown woollen toe, three lumps of sugar.

One by one he took the gifts and laid them down at Mrs. Blossom's feet; putting one huge paw firmly on the waxed-paper package, he waved the other wildly until she took it and spoke a loving word to him. Then, taking up his beloved bone, he retired with it to the farthest end of the long-room, under the kitchen sink, and licked it in peace and joy.

Jack and Chi in the joyful confusion had slipped from the room.

Soon there was a commotion in the woodshed, and the two made their appearance dragging after them a brand-new double-runner and a real Canadian toboggan, which Jack had ordered from Montreal for March.

Breakfast proved to be a short meal, for the whole family was wild to try the new toboggan with Jack to engineer it. Then it was up and down — down and up the steep mountain road ; Jack and Doctor Heath, Mr. Clyde, Mr. Blossom and Chi, all on together — clinging for dear life, laughing, whooping, panting, hurrahing like boys let out from school, while March and Budd and Rose and Hazel and Cherry flew after them on the double-runner, the keen air biting rose-red cheeks, and bringing the stinging water to the eyes.

But what sport it was !

" Now, this is something like," panted Jack, drawing up the hill with Chi, his handsome face aglow with life and joy.

" By George Washin'ton ! it 's the nearest thing to shootin' Niagary that I ever come," puffed Chi.

" Did n't we take that water-bar neatly ? " laughed Jack.

" 'N inch higher, 'n' we 'd all been goners ; — I had n't

a minute to think of it, goin' to the rate of a mile a minute; but if I had — I'd have dusted! Guess I'll make
it level before I try it with the children, — 'n' I want you
to know there's no coward about me, but I'm just speakin' six for myself this time."

So the morning sped. Even Mrs. Blossom and May
were taken down once, and the Doctor stopped only because he wanted to make a morning call on his patient,
Ruth Ford; for it was by his advice the family had come
to live for three years in this mountain region.

The horn for the mid-day meal sounded down the Mountain before they had thought of finishing the exciting
sport, and one and all brought such keen appetites to the
Christmas dinner, that Mrs. Blossom declared laughingly
that she would give them no supper, for they had eaten
the pantry shelves bare.

Such roast goose and barberry jam! Such a noble
plum-pudding set in the midst of Maria-Ann's best wreath,
for she and Aunt Tryphosa had sent over their simple
gifts by an early teamster. Such red Northern Spies and
winter russet pears! And such mirth and shouts and
jests and quips to accompany each course!

It was genuine New England Christmas cheer, and the
healths were drunk in the wine of the apple amid great
applause, especially Doctor Heath's:

" Health, peace, and long life to the Lost Nation — May
its tribe increase!"

And how they laughed at Chi, when he proposed the
health of the Prize Chicken (which, by the way, he had

kept for the next season's mascot,) and recounted the episode in the barn.

What shouts greeted Budd, who, rising with great gravity, his mouth puckered into real, not mock, serious-ness — and that was the comical part of it all — said earnestly :

"To my first wife!" and sat down rather red, but grati-fied not only by the prolonged applause, but by the enthu-siasm with which they drank to this unexpected toast from his unsentimental self.

Directly after dinner Mr. Clyde declared that a seven-mile walk was an actual necessity for him in his present condition, and invited all who would to accompany him to call in state on Mrs. Tryphosa Little and Miss Maria-Ann Simmons. Only Doctor Heath and Jack went with him, for Mr. Blossom and Chi had matters to attend to at home, and Rose and Cherry and Hazel were needed to help Mrs. Blossom. Even March and Budd turned to and wiped dishes.

"I'll set the table now, Martie," said Rose, "then there will be no confusion to-night — there are so many of us."

"No need for that to-night, children," replied Mrs. Blossom, with a merry smile. "'The last is the best of all the rest,' for we were all invited a week ago to take tea and spend Christmas evening at Hunger-ford."

"Oh, Martie!" A joyful shout went up from the six, that was followed by jigs and double-shuffles, pas-seuls and fancy steps, in which dish-towels were waved wildly, and tin pans were pounded instead of wiped.

When the din had somewhat subsided there were numberless questions asked; by the time they were all answered, and Rose and Hazel had donned their white serge dresses, the gentlemen had returned from their walk, and it was time to go.

"That's why Mrs. Ford had us learn all those songs," said Rose to Hazel. "Don't forget to take your violin."

A merrier Christmas party never set forth on a straw-ride. Mr. and Mrs. Blossom and May went over in the sleigh, but the rest piled into the apple-green pung, and when they came in sight of the seven-gabled-house, a rousing three times three, mingling with the sound of the sleigh-bells, greeted the pretty sight.

Every window was illumined, and adorned with a Christmas wreath. In the light of the rising moon, then at the full, the snow that covered the roof sparkled like frosted silver. The house, with its background of sharply sloping hill wooded with spruce and pine, its twinkling lights and the surrounding white expanse, looked like an illuminated Christmas card.

Within, the hall was festooned with ground hemlock and holly; a roaring fire of hickory logs furnished light and to spare. In the living-room and dining-room, Mr. Clyde and Jack Sherrill found, to their amazement, all the elegance and refinement of a city home combined with country simplicity. The tea-table shone with the service of silver and sparkled with the many-faceted crystal of glass and carafe. For decoration, the rich red of the holly berries gleamed among the dark green gloss of their leaves.

At first, the younger members of the Blossom family felt constrained and a little awed in such surroundings; for although they had been several times in the house, they had never taken tea there. But the Fords and the other city people soon put them at their ease, and, as Cherry declared afterwards, "It was like eating in a fairy story." There was a real pigeon pie at one end and a Virginia ham at the other, as well as cold, roast duck with gooseberry jam. There were sparkling jellies, and the whole family of tea-cakes — orange, cocoanut, sponge, and chocolate ; and, oh, bliss ! — strawberry ice-cream in a nest of spun cinnamon candy, followed by Malaga grapes and hot chocolate topped with a whip of cream.

After tea there was the surprise of a beautiful Christmas Tree in the library. Ruth Ford had occupied many a weary hour in making the decorations — roses and lilies fashioned from tissue paper to closely copy nature ; gilded walnuts; painted paper butterflies; pink sugar hearts, and cornucopias of gilt and silver paper, in each of which was a bunch of real flowers — roses, violets, carnations, and daisies, ordered by Jack Sherrill from New York. On the topmost branch, there was a waxen Christ-child. The tree was lighted by dozens of tiny colored candles. When the door was opened from the living-room, and the children caught sight of the wonderful tree, they held their breath and whispered to one another.

But more lovely than the tree in the eyes of the older people were the radiant faces of the young people and the children. Rose, with clasped hands, stood gazing up at

the Christ-child that crowned the glowing, glittering mass
of dark green. She was wholly unconscious of the many
pairs of eyes that rested upon her in love and admiration.
There was nothing so beautiful in the whole room as the
young girl standing there with earnest blue eyes, raised
reverently to the little waxen figure. Her lips were parted
in a half smile; a flush of excitement was on her cheeks;
the white dress set off the exquisite fairness of her skin;
the shining crown of golden-brown hair, that hung in a
heavy braid to within a foot of the hem of her gown,
caught the soft lights above her and formed almost a halo
about the face.

Suddenly there was a burst of admiration from the children, and, under cover of it, Doctor Heath turned to Mr.
Clyde, who was standing beside him : —

"By heavens, John! That girl is too beautiful; she
will make some hearts ache before she is many years older,
as well as your own Hazel — look at *her* now!"

The father's eyes rested lovingly, but thoughtfully, on
the graceful little figure that was busy distributing the
cornucopias with their fragrant contents. Yes, she, too,
was beautiful, giving promise of still greater beauty. He
turned to the Doctor and held out his hand : —

"Richard, I have to thank you for this transformation."

"No — not me," said the Doctor, earnestly, "but," pointing to Mrs. Blossom, "that woman there, John. Hazel
needed the mother-love, just as much as Jack does at this
moment."

Jack had turned away when the Doctor began to speak

of Rose, and, joining her, said, " Won't you wear one of my roses just to-night, Miss Blossom ? "

" Your roses ! Why, did you give us all those lovely flowers ? "

" Yes, I wanted to contribute my share, and flowers seemed the most appropriate offering just for to-night."

" They 're lovely," said Rose, caressing the exquisite petals of a La France beauty. " Of course I 'll wear one —" she tucked one into her belt; " but why — why ! —has n't anyone else roses ? "   She looked about inquiringly.

" No, — the roses were for their namesake," said Jack, quietly.

Rose laughed merrily, — a pleased, girlish laugh. " Then won't the giver of the roses call their namesake, ' Rose '? — for the sake of the roses ? " she added mischievously.

Now Jack Sherrill had seen many girls — silly girls, flirty girls, sensible girls, charming girls, smart girls, nice girls, and horrid girls, and flattered himself he knew every species of the genus, but just this once he was puzzled. If Rose Blossom had been an arrant flirt, she could not have answered him more effectively ; yet Jack had decided that she had too earnest a nature to descend to flirting.   Somehow, that word could never be applied to Rose Blossom — " My Rose," he said to himself, and knew with a kind of a shock when he said it, that he was very far gone.   But in the next breath, he had to confess to himself that he had " been very far gone " many a time in his twenty-one years, so perhaps it did not signify.

Indeed, in the next minute, he was sure it did not signify, for, before he could gather his wits sufficiently to
reply to her, Rose had slipped away to the other side of
the room, where she was busying herself in fastening one
of Jack's roses into the buttonhole of Alan Ford's Tuxedo.
In consequence of which, Jack turned his batteries upon
Ruth Ford with such effect, that she declared afterwards
to her mother he was one of the most fascinating *young* men
— for Ruth was twenty-one! — she had ever met.

Mrs. Ford and Hazel and Mr. Ford had done their best
to persuade Chi to remain with them for the tree. Even
Rose urged — but in vain. True, the girls had insisted
upon his taking one look, then he had begged off, saying,
as he patted Hazel's hand that lay on his arm:

"Not to-night, Lady-bird. I don't feel to home in there.
I'll sit out here and hear the music, then I can beat time
with my foot if I want to." He remained in the hall, just
outside the living-room door, enjoying all he heard.

First there was a lovely piano duet, an Hungarian waltz
by Brahms, Mrs. Ford and the grave, quiet son playing
with such a perfect understanding of each other, as well as
of the music, that it proved a delight to all present. Then
there was a carol by all the children, Rose leading, and
Mrs. Ford playing the accompaniment:

" 'Cheery old Winter! merry old Winter!
 Laugh, while with yule-wreath thy temples are bound;
 Drain the spiced bowl now, cheer thy old soul now,
 "Christmas *waes hael !*" pledge the holy toast round.
 Broach butt and barrel, with dance and with carol
 Crown we old Winter of revels the king;

And when he is weary of living so merry,
He 'll lie down and die on the green lap of Spring.
Cheery old Winter! merry old Winter!
He 'll lie down and die on the green lap of Spring! ' "

This won great applause, and a loud thumping could be heard in the hall. Jack went out to try his powers of persuasion with Chi, and found him sitting close to the door with one knee over the other and a La France rose (!) in his buttonhole.

" Come in, Chi, do."

" Ruther 'd sit here."

" Oh, come on. "

" Nope."

Jack laughed at the decided tone. " Where did you get this ? " he asked, touching the boutonnière.

" Rose-pose," answered Chi, laconically, but with a happy smile.

" Out of her bunch ? "

" Nope — took it out of her belt," said Chi, with a curious twist of his mouth.

Jack went back crestfallen, and Chi smiled.

" I 'm afraid I cut him out, just for once; kind of rough on him, but 't won't hurt him any to have a change. He 's had his own way a little too much," said Chi to himself.

Again there was music, a Schubert serenade, with the two violins, and after that, the children begged Hazel to dance the Highland Fling as she did once in the barn. Hazel, nothing loath, borrowed a blue Liberty-silk scarf from Ruth Ford; the rugs being removed and Alan Ford tuning his violin, she made her curtsy, and, entering heart and body into the spirit of the thing, danced like thistle-down shod with joyousness.

It was a pretty sight! and Chi edged into the room, while the company made believe ignore him in order to induce him to remain there; but when the singing began, he slipped out again. Such singing! Everybody joined in it. They sang everything; — "Oh, where, tell me where, is your Highland laddie gone?"; — "Star-spangled Banner"; — "Marching Along"; — "John Anderson, my Jo"; — "Ye banks and braes o' Bonnie Doon"; — "Twinkle, twinkle, little star"; — "Annie Laurie"; — "A grasshopper sat on a sweet-potato vine"; — "Ben Bolt"; — "Fair Harvard" and, finally, "Old Hundred."

It had been arranged that Mr. Blossom should take his wife and the younger children home in the pung; the rest were to walk. Chi, meanwhile, had driven home in the single sleigh.

On the walk home Jack tried what he had been apt to term — of course, to himself — his "confidential scheme" with Rose. He had tried it before with many another, and it had never failed to work. The thought of one of his roses in Alan Ford's buttonhole still rankled, and the best side of Jack's manhood was not on the surface when he entered upon the homeward walk.

"Miss Blossom," — somehow Jack had not quite the courage to say "Rose," although he had been so frankly invited to — "I want to tell you why I came up here; it must have seemed almost an intrusion."

" Oh, no, indeed," said Rose, earnestly, " and I know why you came; Hazel told me."

" Oh, she did," said Jack, rather inanely, and a little uncertain as to his footing, figuratively speaking; for he had given her the chance to ask " Why ? " — and she had n't taken it; in which she proved herself different from all those other girls of his acquaintance. To himself he thought, " Well, for all the cordial indifference, commend me to this girl."

" Yes, I 'm sure it would have seemed like anything but Christmas to you in New York with your father in Europe; you must miss him so."

Jack felt himself blush in the moonlight at the remembrance that he had seen his father but little in the last three years, and did not know what it was in reality to miss him. He never remembered to have missed anything or anybody but his mother, and that indefinite something in his life which he had not yet put himself earnestly to seek.

" I suppose you 'll be shocked, Miss Blossom, but I don't really miss my father. I 'm only awfully glad to see him when I get the chance — which is n't often. He 's such a busy man with railroads and syndicates and real estate interests. I wonder often how he can find time to write me even twice a month, which he has done regularly ever since — " he stopped abruptly.

" Since what ? " asked Rose, innocently.

" Since my mother died," said Jack, in a hard, dry voice that served to cover his feeling.

" Yes," Rose nodded sympathetically, " Hazel told me."
Then — for Rose's love for her own mother was something
bordering on adoration — she said softly, under her breath,
but with her whole heart in her voice; " Oh, I don't see
how you could bear it — how you can live without her ! "

" I don't," Jack replied with a break in his voice, " not
really live, you know. I've always felt it, but never
realized it until last night, when I stood out on the veranda and looked in at the window at you — all.   Then I
knew I'd been hungry for that sort of thing for the last
seven years — "

Now Rose's heart was swelling with pity for the loneli-
ness of the tall, young fellow swinging along beside her,
and at once her inner eyes were opened to see a, to her,
startling fact.   She turned suddenly towards him.

" Is that why you kissed Martie last night, and came up
here to us ? " she demanded rather breathlessly.

" Yes ; " Jack had forgotten his scheme, and was in dead
earnest now.

" Then," cried Rose, impulsively — but at the same time
thinking, " I don't care if he is engaged to that Miss
Seaton " — " I hope you'll come to us whenever you feel
like it ; for," she added earnestly, " I'm beginning to
understand what Chi means when he talks about Hazel's
being poor and our being rich, and — and I'd love to share
mine with you."

" You're awfully good," said Jack, rather awkwardly
for him ; for, suddenly, in the presence of this young girl,
as yet unspoiled by the world, he realized that Life was

dependent upon something other than polo and club theatricals, railroad syndicates and Newport casinos, stocks and bonds and marketable real estate.

Jack was young, and the moonlight was transfiguring the face that, framed in a white, knitted hood, was turned towards him full of a frank, loving sympathy for him in his "poverty." — And, seeing it, Jack suddenly braced himself as if to meet some shock, thinking, as he strode along in silence, "Oh, I'm gone! — for good and all this time."

Rose, a little surprised at the prolonged silence, welcomed the sound of sleigh-bells behind them.

"Why, that's Chi!" she exclaimed. "I thought he was at home long before this. I'm sure he left long before we did. Where have you been, Chi?" she called so soon as the sleigh was within hailing distance.

"I've been Chris'musin'," said Chi. "It ain't often you get just such a night on the Mountain as this, and I've made the most of it. Can I give you a lift?"

"No, thank you, Chi, we're almost home," said Rose.

"Well, then I'd better be gettin' along — it's pretty near midnight — chk, Bob — " And Chi drove away down the Mountain, chuckling to himself:

"Ain't a-goin' to give myself away before no city chap that has cut me out as he has. George Washin'ton! When I peeked into the window 'n' saw Marier-Ann sittin' there in front of that kitchen table with all those presents on it, 'n' the little spruce set up so perky in the middle of 'em, 'n' she a-wearin' a great handful of those red, spice pinks in her bosom, 'n' her cheeks to match 'em, 'n' her eyes a-shinin' — I knew *he* 'd come it over me ; he 'd made the first call, 'n' given her the first posies. Guess I won't crow over him after this." Chi undid his greatcoat, and bent his face until his nose rested upon Jack's rose : —

"It ain't touched yet, but it 's a stinger ; must be twenty below, now." Suddenly Chi gave a loud exclamation : "I must be a fool ! — I 've broken one of the N. B. B. O. O. rules not to be afraid of anything, and did n't dare to give my posy to Marier-Ann ! — Anyhow, she don't know I was goin' to give it to her, so I need n't feel so cheap about it — Go-long, Bob ! "

XVIII

BUDD'S PROPOSAL

BEFORE Mr. Clyde and Jack left the next day, Budd sought an opportunity to interview the latter on a subject, that, for a few weeks past, had been occupying many of his thoughts. The applause, with which his Christmas-day toast had been greeted, had encouraged him to seek an occasion for acquiring more definite knowledge on a subject which lay near his heart. It came when Jack was packing his dress-suit case in the guest chamber.

There was a knock on the half-opened door.

"Come in," said Jack, and Budd made his appearance.

"Halloo, Budd! What can I do for you? Any commissions in New York, or Boston?"

"Don't know what you mean by commissions," replied Budd, cautiously, thrusting both hands deep into the pockets of his knickerbockers, and spreading his sturdy legs to a wide V.

"Anything I can buy with that hen-and-jam money you helped to earn? — you did well, Budd, on that. I congratulate you."

"I have n't any of that money left. You see, we voted to give it to March to go to college with. But I 've got two quarters an' a dollar — Christmas presents, you know; an' that 'll do, won't it?" he asked rather anxiously.

"Well, that depends on what you buy," said Jack, with due seriousness.

"You 'll keep mum, Mr. Sherrill, if I tell you?" said Budd, inquiringly.

"Mum 's the word, if you say so, Budd; out with it."

"Well, I want two things; one thing to make me feel grown up, an' I 've wanted it for a year."

"What 's that, Budd?" asked Jack, immensely amused at Budd's swelling manhood — "A pair of long trousers?"

"No —" Budd hesitated for a moment, then went on in rather an aggrieved tone; "I hate to wear waists with buttons; it 's just like a baby, an' a fellow can't feel grown up when he has to button everything on. I want to hitch things up the way March an' Chi do, an' I want you to buy me a shirt like that one you 're rolling up — only not flannel, — with a flap, you know, to tuck in."

"Oh, that 's it, is it?" said Jack, endeavoring to keep his face and voice from betraying his inward amusement. "Well, I think you can get one for seventy-five cents — plain or striped?"

"I like those narrow blue striped ones like yours best," he replied, pointing to one of Jack's.

"Like mine it shall be, Budd; but you 'll want a pair of suspenders, or there 'll be too much hitching to be agreeable to you."

"March has an old pair, an' I 'm going to borrow them."

"That's an idea; now, what's the second thing?"

"A ring."

"A ring?" Jack looked amazed.

Budd nodded.

"For yourself?" Jack questioned further.

"No — for somebody else."

"Do you mean a finger ring?"

Budd nodded again emphatically.

"Engagement?" laughed Jack, at last, the fun getting the better of him.

Budd's mouth puckered into solemnity; "No — wedding."

Jack gave up the packing, and sat down, shaken with laughter, on the first convenient chair.

"Pardon me for laughing, Budd, but I can't help it. What do you want of a wedding ring? Is it for that 'first wife' of yours you toasted yesterday at dinner?"

Budd nodded again. "I don't see anything to laugh at," he said, with a reproachful glance. "You wouldn't if you was me."

"No, I don't think I should; you're right there, Budd," he replied, sobering suddenly after his outburst of laughter. "When is the wedding to be?"

Budd looked thoughtful. "I haven't proposed yet," was his matter-of-fact answer.

"Well, why don't you?" Jack, sinner that he was, scented some fun at Budd's expense.

"I'm going to when I know how," said Budd, humbly.

"Why don't you take lessons?" suggested Jack.

"I have."

" Of whom ? "

" Chi."

Jack shouted. " What did Chi say ? " he demanded when he had regained his breath.

" He said if he wanted to marry a girl, he 'd say what he wanted to — tell 'em he was fond of 'em."

" ' Fond of them ' — hm," repeated Jack, thoughtfully.

" What do *you* say ? " questioned Budd, turning the tables rather suddenly on Jack.

" I don't say — never said," replied Jack, shortly.

" That 's what Chi said. He said if I begun early I 'd find out how."

" You seem to be on the right road for it."

" Would you say ' fond of her ' ? " persisted Budd.

" Yes, I think I should," Jack replied with a peculiar smile; "but, of course, it would depend on the girl."

" Why, that 's just what Chi said ! "

" He did, did he ! " Jack laughed ; " Chi knows a thing or two."

" But I thought you 'd know more." Budd's face began to wear a puzzled look

Just then Jack heard Rose's voice in the long-room asking where Mr. Sherrill was, and the sound brought home to him a realizing sense of the fact that there was but an hour before they left for the station, and every moment too precious to be wasted on Budd. Rising, and proceeding with his packing, he said with perfect seriousness : —

" Well, Budd, all I can say is, that if I were going to

ask a girl to marry me, I should ask her if she thought enough of me to take me with all my imperfections and —"

"Where are you, Jack?" called Hazel, at the foot of the stairs; "Chi has to go an hour earlier than he said, and the sleigh is at the door."

In the hurry of Jack's good-byes and departure, the sentence was never finished, and the ring forgotten by him. But Budd remembered.

He was a sturdy little chap, broad of shoulder, strong of limb. His sandy red hair bristled straight up from his full forehead. His pale blue eyes, with thick reddish-brown lashes, were round and serious. His nose was a freckled pug, and his small mouth puckered, when he was very much in earnest, to the size of a buttonhole. From the time he had championed Hazel's coming to them, nearly a year ago, he had never wavered in his allegiance to her, and in his small-boy way showed her his entire devotion. Hazel had been so grateful to him for his whole-souled welcome of her, that she took pains to make his boy's heart happy in every way she could.

For Hazel, Budd was never in the way; never asked too many questions for her patience; never teased her beyond endurance. He found in her a ready listener, a good sympathizer, a capital playmate, and a loving girl-friend, who reproved him sometimes and, at others, praised him. What wonder that his ten-year-old heart had warmed towards her with its first boy-love? and that in his manly, practical way, he made of her an ideal?

"I love Hazel, and when I am big enough, I shall marry

her," was what he said to himself whenever he stopped his play long enough to think about it at all. Naturally it seemed the wisest thing to tell her this when he should find the opportunity, and at the same time recall the fact.

Fortified by the testimony of Chi and Jack, he bided his time.

One Saturday afternoon in January, Rose said suddenly to Hazel: "I wish I could do some of the things that you do, Hazel." Hazel looked up from her book in surprise.

"What can I do that you can't do, Rose?"

"You dance so beautifully, and I've always wanted to know how. I feel so awkward when I see you dance the Highland Fling."

"Is that all?" Hazel laughed a happy laugh. "I can teach you to dance as easy as anything, if you'll let me."

"Let you!" Rose exclaimed, flushing with pleasure; "just you try me and see. But where can we practise?"

"Oh, out in the barn," cried Hazel. "It'll be lots of fun; of course, it's awfully cold, but the skipping about will keep us warm. I'll tell you what — I'll play on the violin, and you and March and Budd and Cherry can learn square dances first."

"What fun!" said Rose.

"What's the joke?" asked March, coming in at that moment with Budd and Cherry.

"We're going to have a dance in the barn; Hazel's going to teach us. She says she can do it easy enough."

"Oh, bully!" Budd threw up his tam-o'-shanter, and

14

Cherry, attempting to charge up and down the long-room as she had seen Hazel at the Fords', tripped on the rug and fell her length. When March had picked her up she rubbed her nose, which was growing decidedly pink, and sniffed a little, then asked suddenly: —

"Who's going to be my partner? They always have partners in the story books."

"Sure enough," Rose laughed. "Whatever will we do, Hazel?"

"I never thought of that," said Hazel, ruefully. "Of course, it takes eight."

"Why can't we have chairs for partners?" said Cherry. "We can bow to them just as if they were alive, and make them move round, can't we?"

They all laughed at Cherry's inspiration.

"You 're a brick, Cherry Bounce?" said March, approvingly. "All choose your partners!" And, thereupon, he seized one of the kitchen chairs, and the rest followed his example. Hazel took her violin, and hooded and mittened and coated and muffled, they trooped out to the barn, each lugging a wooden chair.

"Now I 'll give you the first four changes," said Hazel, illustrating, as well as she could in trying to be two couples at once, the first movements. "Form your square and get ready."

They obeyed with alacrity, and Hazel drew her bow across the strings.

"All curtsy to your partners!" she shouted, and the chair-partners received a bow, and, in turn, were made to thump the floor by being laid over on their backs, and righted suddenly.

"First couple forward and back!" shouted Hazel, and away went Rose dragging her chair after her to meet March and his chair — thumpity-thump — thumpity-thump.

They were in dead earnest, and the chairs were made to behave in a most human way.

All went well until they came to the Grand Right and Left; then there arose such a medley of shrieks of laughter, wild wails from the violin, thumps from sixteen chair-legs, and stampings from eight human ones as was never heard before. In a few minutes all was inextricable confusion, and the noise might have been best compared to a Medicine Dance among the Sioux Indians.

Upon this scene Mr. Blossom and Chi, on their return from the wood, looked with amazement.

"They seem to be havin' a regular pow-wow," Chi remarked dryly, as the exhausted dancers and musician sat down, panting for breath, on their wooden partners. "Rose-pose is about as young as any of 'em — but it beats all, how she's shootin' up into womanhood."

"She's no longer my little Rosebud Blossom," said her father, rather sadly. "I dread the time when the birds begin to fly from the nest, and I see it coming with March and Rose."

Just then Rose caught sight of her father, and ran to him linking her arm in his. "We've had such fun, father! We're learning to dance; you must be my partner sometime, for Hazel's going to teach us the schottische next."

Rose never forgot the look of love her father gave her, nor the feel of his hand as he laid it on her hooded head: " Be my little Rose-pose, as long as you can, dear; you 're growing up too fast."

She recalled afterwards that this first dance in the barn marked the last time that she abandoned herself to the children's fun with a girl's careless heart.

The winter twilight was fast closing about the Mountain and the children just returning to the house, when Chi went out to milk. Leaving his lantern, stool, and pails in the first stall, he entered the third one to tie one of the cows to a shorter stanchion. Before he had finished he heard Budd's voice, and, looking over the partition, saw him standing with Hazel in the circle of light about the lantern. In another minute he began to feel like an eavesdropper.

"What did you want me to come here for, Budd?" said Hazel, dancing on the barn floor to warm her feet.

" I want to tell you something," said Budd, blowing on his cold fingers.

"Well, hurry up and tell; it 's simply freezing here. Is it a secret?"

"Kinder," replied Budd, blowing harder; then, suddenly ceasing the bellows movement, he drew a step nearer to Hazel, and, putting the tips of his pudgy fingers together to make a triangle, he puckered his mouth solemnly and said, looking up at her with earnest eyes : —

"I 'm very fond of you."

Hazel laughed merrily. " Why, of course you are, you

funny boy; you 've always been fond of me, have n't you?
I 'm sure I 've always been fond of you. Is *that* what you
kept me out here in the cold to say?"

"Not all;" Budd nodded seriously. "I 'm very fond
of you, an'—an' if you 'll take me with all my perfections
—I think that 's the way it goes—if I have n't got the
ring yet, it will be just the same, you know." He paused,
and in the circle of light Chi could see the entire earnestness of his attitude.

"Goodness me, Budd! What do you mean about rings
and things?"

"I want to marry you when I 'm big—an' I thought
I 'd speak 'fore anyone else did to get ahead of 'em."
Budd hastened to explain, as Hazel showed signs of im-
patience.

"Oh, is that all!" Hazel breathed a sigh of relief. "I
thought something was the matter with you. Why, of
course you 're fond of me, Budd; but I could n't marry
you, for I 'm older than you, you know."

"I never thought of that," said Budd, beginning to
blink rather suspiciously, "I thought—"

"Now, look here, Budd," said Hazel, in a business-like
way; "I think everything of you, too, and I 'll tell you
what you can be—"

"What?" interrupted Budd, eagerly, balancing himself
on the tips of his toes.

"My knight!" said Hazel, triumphantly, "and wear my
colors. I 'll give you a bow of crimson ribbon—I 'm
Harvard, you know—and you must wear it till you die.

And I have a white kid party glove I'll give you, too, and that will mean I'm your lady-love, and it will be just like the days of chivalry, you know we were reading about them the other day."

"And you won't mind about the ring?" queried Budd, rather wistfully.

"Not a bit — a glove is much nicer than a ring, and —"

"Moo — oo — oo — " came from the next stall.

"Oh, goodness gracious! How that made me jump. I'm not going to stay out here another minute; so come along if you're coming" — and the knight meekly followed his lady-love into the house.

XIX

"It seems queer to settle down the way we have, ever since Christmas. We had such fun up to that time." Hazel heaved a long sigh as she wrestled with her Latin and the Third Conjugation.

Rose looked up from her Cicero and smiled at the bored expression on Hazel's face. "I know, Latin is awfully dull at first, but when you can read it, you 'll like it. If only you could hear Cicero give this horrid Catiline — the old traitor — 'Hail Columbia' as March says, you could n't help liking Latin. Then, too, if we had n't settled down, where would my French have been?"

But Hazel still pouted a little. "I wish papa had n't wanted me to study at all this winter — I don't see why, when Doctor Heath is always talking about its 'effect on my health —'"

She was interrupted by a merry laugh. Rose threw down her Cicero, caught away the grammar from Hazel, and, seizing her by the hand, drew her into the little bedroom. Then, taking her by the shoulders, she whirled her about until she faced the small looking-glass.

"There!" she exclaimed, still laughing, "look at that face before you talk about any 'effect on your health.'"

Hazel looked at the reflection in the mirror, and smiled in spite of herself. What a contrast to what she was a year ago! For to-morrow would be St. Valentine's day. There were real American Beauty roses on her cheeks; the dark eyes were full of sparkling life; the chestnut-brown hair fell in heavy curls upon her shoulders. She had grown tall, too, but rounded in the process, and the healthful, bodily exercise had given her grace of carriage — she was straight as an arrow, and as lithe as a willow wand.

"Perhaps I shall feel more interest when Miss Alton is here, for she is a regular teacher. When is she coming, Rose?"

"The very last of the month, when the spring term opens. It's our turn to have the district-school teacher board with us, and I've never liked it before. But now I can't wait for Miss Alton to come. I think she's lovely."

"She isn't half as lovely as you are, Rose," said Hazel, turning suddenly from the glass, in which she had been scrutinizing her reflection, and giving Rose an unexpected squeeze and a hearty kiss. "I think you are the most beautiful girl I have ever seen, I heard Doctor Heath say so; and — I told Jack so on Christmas night."

"I'll warrant he didn't agree with you," said Rose, with a pleased smile. "You forget Miss Seaton."

"I know." Hazel shook her head dubiously. "He didn't say a word to me about you — I don't care if he didn't, Rose-pose, you're worth all the Maude Seatons in the world, and I'd give anything to have you for my real cousin instead of her, if only Jack — "

" I don't know what you are talking about, Hazel," said Rose, interrupting her shortly and sharply.

" And I don't know why you are speaking to me in that tone, Rose Blossom," retorted Hazel, both angry and hurt. "I've said nothing I'm ashamed of, and I shall say it whenever I choose and to whomever I please, so now." She flung out of the room, but not before Rose had laid a firm hand upon her shoulder.

"Hazel Clyde, if ever you speak of that again to any-one, I 'll break friendship with you, see if I don't."

" Break then," Hazel twitched her shoulder from under the detaining hand. "I 'll speak whenever I choose. I only said I thought you were the most beautiful girl I had ever seen, and I wished that you were going to be my real cousin, instead of Miss Seaton, and you need n't get mad just because Jack does n't happen to think as I do — "

" Hazel Clyde ! " Rose stamped her foot, " don't you speak another word to me; I 'll not hear it." Rose stuffed both fingers into her ears, and beat an ignominious retreat to her own room, where she shut herself in, and was invisible until tea-time.

The family were late in sitting down to the table, for Mrs. Blossom wanted to wait for Chi, who had driven down to Barton's River to take Mr. Blossom to the train, and had arranged to bring March home with him.

It was seven already. " We won't wait any longer, children," said Mrs. Blossom. " Something must have

detained Chi. Budd, you may say 'grace' to-night?"
she added as she took her seat.

Budd looked up in amazement. "Why, Martie, Rose
is here and you always — "

"That will do, Budd," said his mother, quietly, ignoring
the flame that shot up to the roots of Rose's hair, and the
cool look of indifference on Hazel's face. Budd folded
his pudgy hands and repeated reverently the words he had
heard father, or mother, or sister say ever since he could
remember. Scarcely had he finished when Tell's deep
note of welcome sounded somewhere from the road, and
the sleigh-bells rang out on the still air.

"There they are!" cried Cherry. "May I go to meet
them?"

"Yes — but put your cape over you, it's so chilly
to-night."

In a minute Cherry was back again, every single curl
bobbing with excitement.

"Oh, Martie! Chi's bringing in something all done
up in the buffalo robe, and March won't tell me what
it is."

She was followed by March, who walked up to his
mother, put both arms about her and gave her a quiet kiss.

"There, little Mother Blossom, is my valentine for you,"
he said half-shyly, half-proudly, and placed in her hands
his first term's report and a set of books.

"Oh, March, my dear boy!" said his mother, rising from
the table and placing both hands on the broad, square
shoulders of her six foot specimen of youth, "I'm afraid

I'm getting too proud of you. *Did* you get the first Latin prize?"

"You bet I did, Martie." March's rare smile illumined his face. "There is n't another fellow at Barton's, who can boast of such a mother as I have, and I was n't going to let any second-class mothers read those books before you did. By Cicky!" (which was March's favorite name for the famous orator) — "But I 've worked like a Turk, and I 'm hungry as a Russian bear. Why, Rose, what 's the matter with you? You look awfully glum, and Hazel, too. Here comes Chi; he 's bringing something that will cheer you up. The truth is, mother, these girls miss *me*."

"Indeed, I do, March?" said Hazel, looking straight up into his eyes and showing the amazed lad tears trembling in her own.

"Guess there 'll be some breakin' of hearts, this year, Mis' Blossom." Chi's cheery voice was welcome to them all for some unknown reason. He came in loaded with huge pasteboard boxes.

"Your arms will break first, Chi," said Mrs. Blossom, hastening with March to relieve him.

"It ain't the heft of 'em, it 's the bulk. Valentines are generally pretty light weight. Romancin' 'n' sentiment don't count for much, nowadays, though they take up considerable room." He deposited the last box on the settle. "'N' there 's a whole parcel of things come by mail. I ain't looked at the superscribin's — you read 'em out, Rose-pose."

Rose read the addresses; there was more than one missive for each member of the family.

"Let's have supper, first, mother," said March, "then, after the table is cleared, we can sit round and guess who they're from."

This proposition was welcomed by Budd and Cherry. Rose and Hazel gave a cordial assent, but there was a frigidity in the atmosphere which the outside temperature did not warrant. Chi and March were aware of this so soon as they entered the room, and Mrs. Blossom had known it the moment she saw the girls' faces at the table. She thought it not wise to interfere, but let matters straighten themselves in good time. She felt she could trust them both to see things in their right light, without the aid of her mental glasses.

"Now let's begin," said Chi, rubbing his hands in glee as, directly after supper, he piled the boxes on the table while March laid the envelopes in their proper places before each member of the family. "This top one says 'Miss Hazel Clyde.' Show us your valentine, Lady-bird."

"They're violets — from Jack, I know. He always sends them. What's yours, Rose?" She spoke rather indifferently.

"Oh, roses!" Rose was having the first look all to herself. "The loveliest things I have ever seen. Look, Martie!" Rose held up the mass of exquisite bloom, and the children oh'ed and ah'ed at the sight.

"They're from Mr. Sherrill," said Rose, trying to speak

in a most common-place tone, but, in her excitement, failing signally.

"They are lovely," Hazel remarked, shooting an indignant glance at Rose. "They're just like the ones he sent Miss Seaton last year, only they were formed into a great heart. Papa gave me one just like it; he got his idea from Jack."

Rose suddenly put down the flowers, in which she had buried her face to inhale their fragrance, as if something had stung her.

"Mr. Sherrill is very impartial with his favors," she said in a tone that increased the pervading chill of the domestic atmosphere.

"Why, Rose!" exclaimed Mrs. Blossom. "It is not like you to receive a favor so ungraciously; you've never had flowers sent you before, and I'm sure you would never have them again if the donor could witness your reception of them."

"I don't care for them again, thank you," Rose retorted with flaming cheeks; "I'd give more for this of yours, Chi —" she opened a huge yellow envelope, and took from it a scarlet cardboard heart, with a small, white, artificial rose glued to the centre and a gilt paper arrow transfixing both rose and heart.

Chi hemmed rather awkwardly, thinking: "Beats the Dutch what's got into Rose-pose to-night. I ain't ever known her to treat a livin' soul so shabby as that in all her life. Beats all what gets into women 'n' girls, sometimes; when a feller thinks he's doin' 'em just the best

turn he knows how, they up 'n' get mad with him, 'n' turn
the cold shoulder, 'n' upset things generally." But aloud
he said:

"I 'm glad it pleases you, Rose. Can't most always tell
when it 's goin' to please a girl or not. I suppose Jack,
now, thought you 'd be tickled to get those posies just in
the dead of winter. They don't grow round here on *our*
bushes. What 's in the other box?"

"Why!" Hazel exclaimed, laughing rather half-heart-
edly, "it 's addressed to ' Miss Maria-Ann Simmons ' — and
just look, Mother Blossom! See what that dear old Jack
has sent her! He 's just too dear for anything." She
added emphatically; — "I 'd like to give him a kiss for
thinking of that poor girl all alone over there on the
Mountain. I don't believe she ever had a valentine before.
Look! Oh, look!"

She took out of the many layers of wadding a mass of
yellow tulips, their closed golden cups shining in the lamp-
light as if gilded by sunbeams.

"Sho!" was all Chi said, leaning nearer to examine the
beautiful blossoms.

"You 'll take them over in the morning, early, won't
you, Chi?" said Hazel, replacing them.

"First thing, Lady-bird; guess you 're right, Rose,
about that young feller 's bein' 'n all-round man with his
favors. Don't seem to be much choice between you and
Marier-Ann, 'n' that Miss Seaver. Kind of a toss-up, hey,
Rose-pose?"

But Rose was too busy with another package to answer

Chi. She grew wildly enthusiastic over the calla lilies that Alan Ford had sent her, and caressed their white envelopes, and praised their pure loveliness, until Hazel, growing jealous for poor Jack and his discarded gift, rose to put the neglected beauties in water, saying as she did so:

"I'm sure, Rose, if Jack had known you cared so much for lilies, he would have sent you some Easter ones, they're out now. I'll tell him to next time."

"Hazel!" Rose burst forth indignantly, "do you mean to tell me you told Mr. Sherrill to send me these flowers for a valentine?"

Then Hazel, stung by the tone and the words, yielded to temptation — for it had been the last straw. "What if I did?" she said with irritating calm, "he's my cousin. I suppose I can say what I choose to him."

Rose answered never a word; but, rising, took the La France roses from the pitcher in which Hazel had just placed them, and, going over to the fireplace, deliberately cast the mass of delicate pink bloom into the fire.

Mrs. Blossom looked both puzzled and shocked; this was wholly unlike Rose. What could it mean? The children were too awed by the proceeding to speak or exclaim. March looked gravely at Hazel, who burst into tears — it was such an insult to Jack! — and rushed into her bedroom and shut the door.

"I'm going to bed; good-night, Martie," said Rose, quietly, after she had watched the last leaf shrivel in the flame, and, kissing her mother, she lighted her candle and went upstairs. Mrs. Blossom, following her with her eyes, felt that she had lost her "little Rose" in that hour.

March looked grave, complained of feeling tired, and said he would go to bed, too, as to-morrow was the last day of school and there were two more examinations to take. Budd and Cherry kissed their mother twice, bade her good-night in suppressed tones and crept upstairs. "It's just as if somebody was sick in the house," said Cherry, in an awed voice. Budd's was sepulchral: —

" It's just as if somebody was dead and all the flowers had come for the funeral."

Across the dining-room table, loaded with boxes and brilliant with valentines, Chi looked at Mrs. Blossom, and Mrs. Blossom looked at Chi. The whole affair was so incomprehensible, and the result so painfully disagreeable, that, for a while, they found no words with which to give expression to their feelings. Chi broke the silence: —

"Well! I wish I was one of those clairivoyants they tell about, 'n' could kind of see into the meanin' of this flare-up of Rose-pose's. Don't seem natural for Rose to go flyin' off at a tangent that way. What's she got against him, anyway? He's about as likely as you'll find. Beats me ! " Chi leaned both elbows on the table, unmindful that he was crushing some of the flowers, sank his chin in the palms of his hands and thought hard for full a minute.

"I know Hazel and Rose have had some little trouble this afternoon — the first quarrel they have had — but

Rose is too old to allow herself to lose her control in that way. I can't imagine what made her — " Mrs. Blossom broke off suddenly, for Chi had raised his head and sent such a look of intelligence across the table, handing her, as he did so, Jack Sherrill's card, which Rose in her confusion had neglected to read, that, in a flash, something of the truth was revealed to Mrs. Blossom.

She took the card. On the back was written, enclosed in quotation marks : —

> "For I am thine
> Whilst the stars shall shine,
> To the last — to the last."

"O Chi!" was all Mary Blossom said; but the tears filled her eyes, and, reaching across the table, her hand was clasped in Chi's strong one.

"I wish Ben was to home," sighed Chi, so lugubriously that Mrs. Blossom laughed through her tears.

"Oh, it is n't so bad as that, Chi. Girls will be girls, and grow up, and hearts will ache even when we 're young. We won't make too much of it. I don't understand the ins and outs of it, but I do know Hazel has said her family thought he was engaged to Miss Seaton. I 'm sure I 've thought so all along, and it never occurred to me there could be any danger for Rose under the circumstances. The mere fact of his name being connected so closely with Miss Seaton's would be a safeguard. Then, too, I fear he is spoiled by women on account of his riches."

"I don't know about that Miss Seaver, — but if it's as you say, I kind of wish Rose could cut her out."

"Sh-sh, Chi!" said Mrs. Blossom, reprovingly.

"Well, I do," Chi retorted with some warmth. "She ain't fit to tie Rose's old berryin' shoes, 'n' I saw her lookin' at her feet that day we was sellin' berries down to Barton's to the tavern, 'n' snickerin' so mean like, 'n' Rose just showed her grit — 'n' I wish she 'd show it again 'n' cut her out. I *do*, by George Washin'ton!" Chi rose up in his wrath, lighted his lantern, and started for the shed. At the door he turned: —

"I wish Ben was to home," he said again. "There 's goin' to be the biggest kind of a snow-down before long, 'n' he 'll get blocked on the road, sure as blazes."

"He 'll be back in two days, at the most, Chi; I would n't worry."

"I ain't worryin'; I 'm just sayin' I wish he was to home," repeated Chi, doggedly, and shut the door.

Mrs. Blossom smiled. She knew Chi's crotchets. When there was any disturbance of the family peace, Chi was apt to be depressed, and sometimes despondent. She put away the flowers in the cold pantry, smiling as she tied up Maria-Ann's box:

"He *is* universal," she said to herself. "I know it irritated Rose to be classed with her and Miss Seaton; but things will work around right with time. I can trust to Rose's common-sense. — Not a prayer to-night!" she added thoughtfully. "Well, we 'll make it up to-morrow." She took up the prize books. "That dear March! What a manly fellow he is getting to be — and *so* handsome. I wonder — " here Mary Blossom checked herself, laughing softly. " Goodness ! if Ben were here what a goose he would think me — a regular old Mother Goose — " And again she laughed as she put out the light.

XX

THEY were all on the porch the next morning to see March off. It was not so very cold, but there was a marked chill in the air and the sky was leaden.

"It's my last day, mother, then vacation for two weeks. Hooray!" He leaped into the saddle, and Fleet reared gently to show her approval.

"Don't you get out a little earlier to-day, March?" said his mother, looking up at the leaden sky. "I'm afraid it's going to snow heavily. Promise me not to start from Barton's if the storm is a hard one; you can stay at the inn or at the principal's. I would rather you remained away from home two days, or over Sunday, than to have you attempt the Mountain in too severe a storm."

"I'll be careful, mother."

"Better give your promise to your mother, March; she'll feel better 'bout you 're not startin' out," said Chi.

"I promise, little Mother Blossom." He threw himself off the horse, and gave her another kiss; "I wouldn't go to-day except for the exams. — I can't miss them."

"Good luck, dear," said his mother, and her eyes followed the horse and rider down the Mountain.

"I'll go over the first thing 'n' give them posies to Marier-Ann, 'n' then I'll make tracks for home, 'n' get my snow-shed up before it begins to come down."

"Do you think we shall need it?"

"Sure's fate," replied Chi, laconically, and went into the barn to harness Bess.

It was noon before Chi had set up his snow-shed, a long, low, wooden tunnel, which he had manufactured to connect the woodshed door with a side door of the barn. By means of this he was enabled, in unusually heavy storms, to communicate with the barn and attend to the stock without "shovelling out."

It was about three in the afternoon when the first flakes began to fall, or rather to "spit," as Chi expressed it, and the snow fell intermittently and lightly until four, when there was a sudden change of wind. It veered to the north-east, and blast after blast, charged with icy particles, hurled itself against the Mountain. Within half an hour it was almost as dark as at midnight, and the snow swept in drifting clouds over woodlands and pasture. When the wind ceased for a moment, white, soft avalanches descended upon farmhouse, barn, and mountain-road, until, by six o'clock, the road was impassable and the drifts at the back of the house a foot above the bedroom windows. Chi had made all snug for the night.

"This beats anything I ever saw, Mis' Blossom. I'm mighty glad Ben ain't comin' home to-day, 'n' that March gave you the promise to stay at Barton's if it stormed hard."

"You don't think he would venture to start, do you, Chi?" asked Mrs. Blossom, trying not to appear anxious for the sake of the others.

"Bless you, no;" was Chi's hearty response. "March has got too level a head to risk himself 'n' Fleet in such a storm — it's a regular howler of a blizzard. If he *did* start," he added, "he'd go in somewheres on the road — he couldn't get far."

After tea there was no settling down to the cosey evening pastimes or employments. If such a thing could be, the storm seemed to increase in severity. The wind struck the house at times with terrific force; the intermittent drift of snow and ice against the window panes startled the inmates of the long-room like the rattle of small shot. Chi had put out the fire in the fireplace before supper, for the wind drove flame and ashes out into the room.

Again and again Mrs. Blossom went to the windows — first one then another, and pressed her face close to the pane; but they were plastered so thick with snow that her efforts to see into the night were fruitless. Chi sat by the kitchen stove, which he had filled with wood. His boots rested on the fender, and, apparently, he was indifferent to the storm. But, in reality, not the creak of a beam, not the springing of a board, not an unwonted sound within or without the house escaped his notice.

In marked contrast to Chi's apparent apathy was Tell's restlessness. Since six o'clock he had shown signs of uneasiness. With strides, heavy and long, the huge beast

paced up and down the long-room. Sometimes he followed
Mrs. Blossom to the window, and, sitting down on his
haunches beside her, rested his nose on the window sill
and gazed at the whitened panes. At others he took his
stand beside Chi and looked into his face, their eyes meeting on a level as the man sat and the dog stood. The
dog looked as if he were questioning him dumbly.

As the evening wore on the dog's pace grew more rapid,
more uneven ; his tail waved in a jerky, excited manner.
At last he lay down by the shed door, and, placing his
nose on the threshold, gave vent to a long, low, half-stifled
moan. At the sound Chi brought down his heels and the
tipped chair-legs with a thump, and started to his feet.
Mrs. Blossom turned to him with a white face, and Rose
cried out : —

"Oh, Chi! What is the matter with Tell? He never
acted this way before."

"Don't know," said Chi, shortly; "dumb beasts are
curious creatures. Guess he don't like the storm. I 'll
go out, Mis' Blossom, 'n' see if the stock 's all right. Kind
of looks as if Tell was givin' us a warnin'."

"Oh, Chi, don't go through the tunnel now," cried Mrs.
Blossom, all the pent-up anxiety finding expression in her
voice.

Chi manufactured a laugh: "That's all safe, Mis'
Blossom. I chained it and roped it down, both — it can't
get away, 'n' the snow can't crush it. Don't you worry
about me. I 'll be back inside of fifteen minutes." He
took his lantern from the shelf over the sink : — "Get up,

Tell." The dog rose, but, as Chi opened the door, he tried to push past him. Chi crowded him with his leg: — "No you don't, old feller! there ain't room only for just one of us to-night. Lay down!"

And Tell lay down, with his nose on his paws, and both nose and paws pressed close to the crack on the threshold. Another long crescendo moan, that, at the last, sounded like a sharp wail, filled the long-room, and Budd and Cherry clung to their mother in terror.

"You must go to bed, children," said Mrs. Blossom, her face white as the snow on the window panes, but with a voice of forced calm. "When you 're asleep, you won't hear all this trouble the storm is raising to-night."

"But I don't want to sleep upstairs alone without March, Martie," protested Budd, trying to be brave, but showing his fear.

"You can sleep in Hazel's room to-night, Budd, and Cherry can get into my bed and sleep with me."

The twins looked relieved. "Oh, that 's different, Martie," said Budd, with a grateful look. Cherry begged for a little cotton wool to stuff in her ears: — "Then I can't hear Tell and this awful noise." A novel idea, which Budd at once adopted and put into practice. Th .r mother looked relieved when they were safely bestowed in their new quarters.

About ten minutes afterwards they heard Chi's steps in the shed. Then the door opened slowly, as he shoved Tell aside. When he entered the room Mrs. Blossom gave one look at his face.

"Oh, Chi, what has happened!" She cried out as if hurt.

Chi's face showed grayish white and drawn in the lamp-light. His hand shook a little as he reached for a second lantern, turning his back on the three terrified faces.

"Horse stalled, that's all. Had a tough tussle to get him round, but he's all right now." His voice sounded hoarse.

"Was it Bob or Bess?" asked Rose.

Chi, without answering, turned quickly to Tell, who was pressing him nearly off his feet, and at the same time, lashing his tail as if in fury.

"What ails you, anyway?" said Chi, roughly. "D' you want to get out?"

For answer the dog rushed to the front door that opened on the porch, rose on his hind legs, stemmed his powerful forepaws against the panels and, throwing back his massive head, sent forth from his deep throat a roar that seemed to shake the rafters.

"Mis' Blossom," Chi's voice shook and his hand trembled till the glass globe of the lantern tinkled in the wire frame, "I'm goin' to let him out, 'n' I'm goin' to follow on — there's trouble somewhere on the Mountain, 'n' I'm goin' to find out where 't is."

All three cried out, protesting, entreating, praying him to desist. But Chi shook his head.

"I tell you I've *got* to go, Mary Blossom " — Chi had never called her that but once before, and Mrs. Blossom, recalling the time, felt her heart as lead within her —

"you 're brave, — brave as a woman can be; don't say nothin', but let me go. Have plenty of hot water 'n' flannels, 'n' some spirits ready 'gainst I come back —

" Lady-bird, give me the dog collar with the bell you gave Tell last Chris'mus; 'n' Molly Stark, fill your mother's hot water-bag — 'n' hurry up; 'n' Mis' Blossom, give me Ben's brandy flask, he did n't take it with him."

Chi, while issuing these orders, was strapping down his trousers over his long boots; then he poured out a brimming cup of hot water, and mixed with it some of the brandy from the flask. He put the collar on Tell, the bell ringing loud and clear with every movement. He opened the door; the dog bounded out into the night. Chi followed him, a coil of rope around his neck, a shovel over one shoulder with a lantern suspended from the handle, and in his hand a second lantern. The hot-water bag he had put beneath his sweater, and a leathern belt girded him.

So equipped he went out into the drifting snows and the night of storm. The terrified women were left alone.

" Mother, oh, mother! " cried Rose, wringing her hands, " I know it 's something dreadful; Chi would never look that way."

Mary Blossom could not answer. Her silence was prayer. It was all of which she was capable at that time.

" I don't know what the matter was in the barn, mother," again cried Rose, in an agony of fear. " Chi did n't tell us all, I 'm sure. Let me go through the tunnel and find out, do, mother! "

"Oh, Rose, I can't — I can't!" Mrs. Blossom spoke under her breath.

"Please, mother. It's all safe, and the wind has gone down a little since Chi went; let me go — I can't rest till I do. You can hold the light at the shed door end and I won't be gone but a minute or two. I'll take the dark lantern with me — Oh, mother! do, do — !"

"Well, Rose, perhaps it's for the best. I'll watch you through."

"May I watch, too?" asked Hazel, eagerly.

"No, dear, I want you to stay here in case the children should wake. Come, Rose."

They were gone but a few minutes; then Mrs. Blossom came in followed by her daughter. The girl's teeth were chattering; she looked blue and pinched.

"What did you find, Rose?" Her mother's voice was scarce above a whisper.

"*I found Fleet !*"

The two women sat down on the settle, holding each other close; and the wind rose again in its fury.

Wrapping a heavy shawl about her Hazel crept away upstairs to the back garret and the window overlooking the woods'-road, which formed the approach to the house. There was a little snow-drift beneath it where the flakes had sifted through; but the wind was felt less severely on that side of the house. She opened the window a few inches, propping it on a corn cob she had stepped upon; then, kneeling, she put her ear to the opening and strained her hearing in every lull of the storm.

At last — she knew not how long she had listened — she heard Tell's deep roar. It came muffled, but distinct. She scarce trusted her ears; but again she heard it, and, this time, in a dead silence, she caught the sound of the bell. Surely Tell was nearing the house. She ran downstairs.

"They're coming!" she cried, hardly realizing what she said in her excitement. Mrs. Blossom and Rose leaped to their feet. They threw open the door.

"Chi! Chi!" they called out into the night. There was a joyous bark for answer — then a groan, and Chi staggered across the snow-laden porch and fell with his heavy burden on the threshold.

At midnight the wind went down, but the snow continued to fall. All the next day it fell steadily, but at sunset it ceased, and a young moon looked over the shoulder of Mount Hunger upon an unbroken white coverlet that, in some places, was drifted to the depth of twenty feet.

There was twilight in Aunt Tryphosa's little cabin "over eastwards," for the snow was piled to the eaves, and the tulips furnished their only sunshine for two days.

There was consternation at Hunger-ford, for the family were cut off from their neighbors and the outside world of letters and papers.

There were councils at Lemuel's and the Spillkinses' — for how could they gather their forces to break out the Mountain?

There were heavy hearts and reddened eyelids in the farmhouse, for March, rescued by Chi and revived by vigorous treatment, had succumbed to the exposure and chill, and lay unconscious in fever — and no help at hand.

Chi, spent to exhaustion, had rallied at midnight, but knew that it was beyond human powers to attempt to reach Barton's or even Lemuel Wood's, their next neighbor, through the drifts.

So they waited, helpless — one day, two days. On the second day the white expanse showed no tracks. Then March began to wander, and clutch his breast, where his mother had found the telegram, which his father had sent to him from Ogdensburg : —

"Heavy blizzard. Roads blocked. Tell mother at once. Don't worry."

Chi walked the house night and day in his misery of helplessness. At last, on the third day, looking eastwards he descried a black blotch on the white, — it was a four-ox team breaking out from the Fords'. Later in the day, when the men were within two hundred yards of the house, he saw another black spot on the lower road. It was the Mill Settlement road-team, with a full equipment of men and tools, to cut a way through the drifts.

Soon there was help and to spare. Alan Ford was riding down the narrow way between high walls of glittering white to Barton's for aid, and bringing back telegrams of anxious inquiry from Mr. Blossom and Mr. Clyde. On

the fourth day, the blockade was raised, and the south-
bound express to Barton's River brought Mr. Blossom
from the north, and another train brought Mr. Clyde from
the south.   Two days after all the Lost Nation knew that
March would live.

XXI

IT was days before March himself was aware of that fact.

Budd and Cherry were at the Fords'. May was with Aunt Tryphosa and Miss Alton at Lemuel Wood's. Maria-Ann had come over to help Mrs. Blossom with the work, and Chi had taken care of the stock. Rose and her mother watched and waited in the sick room, relieved on alternate nights by Mr. Blossom and Chi.

The great storm was a thing of the past. The sun shone in a deep blue heaven, and the white world of the Mountain showed daily life and movement. The teamsters were at work loading the sledges with logs, and the ponderous drags squeaked and grated as they slid down the crisping highway.

A crow cawed loudly on the first of March, and the hens came out to find a warm nook in the south-east corner of the barn-yard, where a heap of sodden straw was thawing.

All in the farmhouse were rejoicing, for March had spoken in his weakness — a few words, but clear, coherent, for the frost and fever, both, had left his brain. When he spoke the second time it was to ask for Chi; and Chi had tiptoed into the room in his stocking-feet and laid his hand on March's thin, white one, gulped down the tears and the rising sob that was choking him, and — spoke of the weather !

The next day March turned to his mother, who was sitting by the bed, brooding him with her great love, and asked suddenly, but in a clear and much stronger voice :

" Where 's Hazel ? "

Mrs. Blossom hesitated for a moment, then spoke quietly : — " Hazel is at home with her father for a few weeks."

March turned his face to the wall and was silent for several hours.

When he was stronger Mrs. Blossom gave him the little note Hazel had left for him, and, with mother-tact, knowing March's reserve of nature, went out of the room while he read it. She saw no signs of it when she returned and asked no questions, but March's gray eyes spoke a language for which there was but one interpretation. With his rare smile, he held out his hand for his mother's, and clasped it closely.

Soon he was able to be up and about, and the children were again at home. Life in the farmhouse resumed its old course — but with a difference. Just what it was no one attempted to define. But each felt it in his own way. March was more gentle with Budd and Cherry, more often with his mother and Chi, more companionable for his father. Rose was quieter, but, if possible, more loving towards all. Budd was at times wholly disconsolate, and wasted sheets of his best Christmas note-paper in writing letters to Hazel which were never sent.

Chi went oftener to the small house "over eastwards," where he was sure of willing ears and sympathetic hearts when he unburdened himself in regard to his "Lady-bird."

"Fact is," he said to Maria-Ann, as she stood with her apron over her head watching him plough their garden plot (that was his annual neighborly offering), "she's left a great hole in that house, 'n' there isn't one of us that don't know it 'n' feel it; — kind of empty like in your heart, you know, just as your stomach feels when you've ploughed an acre of sidlin' ground, before breakfast — Get up, Bess, whoa — back! — you don't hear that laugh of hers in the barn, nor out in the field, nor up in the pasture; 'n' you don't see those great eyes lookin' up at you when you're harnessin', nor peekin' round the corner of the stall to see if you're most through milkin'. 'N' you don't hear a fiddle makin' it lively after supper, 'n' the children ain't danced once in the barn this spring." Chi sighed heavily.

"Don't Mr. Ford go over there pretty often?" queried Maria-Ann. "I see him gallopin' by two or three times a week."

"Well, what if you do?" Chi answered grumpily, much to Maria-Ann's surprise. "He can't fiddle the way Lady-bird does, 'n' they all sit 'n' jabber some kind of lingo — French, they call it, but I call it, good, straight Canuck —

16

'n' act as if they were at a party, — Rose, 'n' Miss Alton, 'n' the whole of 'em. 'T ain't much company for me. I get off to bed about dark. 'N' the worst of it is, when he is n't to our house, they 're all to his — Come around!" Chi jerked the reins, to Bess's resentful surprise.

" They say he 's payin' attention to Rose," ventured Maria-Ann, her eyes following the furrow, which was running not quite true.

" They 're a parcel of fools," growled Chi, eyeing the furrow with a dissatisfied air, " Rose need n't look Alan Ford's way for attention. She can have all she wants most anywheres. — Get up, Bess! what you backin' that way for! — 'n' folks tongues can be measured by the furlong 'twixt here and Barton's."

" Well, there ain't any harm in Rose's havin' attention, Chi," said Maria-Ann with some spirit, and ready to stand up for her sex.

" Did n't say there was," retorted Chi, in mollified tones. " There ain't no more harm in Rose's havin' attention than in your havin' it."

" Me!" exclaimed Maria-Ann, pleasantly surprised out of her momentary resentment. " I ain't had any chance to have any."

" Ain't you ?" said Chi, busying himself with the plough preparatory to leaving. " Well, that ain't any sign you won't have — Get along, Bess! — I 'll leave this plough here till to-morrow; I ain't drawn those last two furrers straight, 'n' I 've got too much pride to have any man see that — Malachi Graham, his mark. — No, sir-ee," said

Chi, emphatically, "straight or starve is my motto every time, just you remember that, Marier-Ann Simmons."

" I will, Chi," laughed Maria-Ann, and went back to her washing, singing joyfully to her rubbing accompaniment : —

> " Come, sinners all, repent in time,
> The Judgment Day is dawning;
> Sun, moon, and stars to earth incline,
> The trumpet sounds a warning."

Meanwhile letters were coming to every member of the family from Hazel. As March regained his strength there came as special gifts to him, books and magazines, and from time to time a beautiful photograph of an old-world cathedral — Canterbury, or York; a stately castle like Warwick, or Heidelberg; a peasant's châlet, or an English cottage to gladden his artist soul and eye, and transform the walls of his room into dwelling-places for his ideals.

" Mother," he said rather wistfully to Mrs. Blossom, on the first May day as they sat together under the old Wishing-Tree, talking over the plans for his future, " how can I go to work to make it all come true ? "

He held in his hand a large photograph of the interior of Cologne Cathedral, which Hazel had given him.

" There are many ways, dear, which are most unexpectedly opened at times. No boy with health and perseverance has much to fear."

" But, mother, father had both, and he was n't able to go through college. He told me all about it the other day, and how he had missed it all through his life."

"I know, March, father failed in attaining to that which was his great desire, but he succeeded so immeasurably in another direction, that I think, sometimes, it must have been all for the best."

"Why, mother, father is poor now — how do you mean he has succeeded?"

"My dear boy, you are only in your seventeenth year, and I don't know that I can make it plain to you because you *are* young; but when your father conquered every selfish tendency in him, put aside what he had striven so hard for and what was just within his reach, and turned about and did the duty that the time demanded of him; — when he took his dead father's place as provider for the family, and, by his own exertions, placed his mother and sisters beyond want, before he even allowed himself to tell me he loved me, he proved himself a successful man; for he developed, in such hard circumstances, such nobility of character, that he is rich in love and esteem, — and that, March, and only *that*, is true wealth."

"I see what you mean, mother, but it does n't help me to see how I 'm to get through college, and get the training I need in my profession." March uttered the last word with pride. "There is so much a man has to have for that. Look at that now," he continued, holding up the photograph; "I need all that, and that means Europe, and Europe means money and time, and where is it all to come from?"

His mother smiled at the despairing tone. "As for time, March, you are only in your seventeenth year. That means ten years before you can begin to work in your profession; and as for the means — " she hesitated — " I think it is time to tell you something I 've been keeping and rejoicing over these last two weeks." She drew a letter from her dress-waist and handed it to him. " Read this, dear, and tell me what you think of it." Wondering, March took it and read : —

HAWKING VALLEY, NORTH CAROLINA,
April 15, 1897.

MY DEAR MRS. BLOSSOM, — Just a year ago to-day I sent my one child to you, trusting the judgment of my dear friend, Doctor Heath, in a matter which he felt concerned the future welfare of my daughter. My home has been very lonely without her. You, as a parent, can know something of what this separation has entailed.

It seemed wise to me, and I know you concurred in my opinion, to take her away from the conditions, in which she has thriven so wonderfully, while you were burdened, both in heart and hands, by such a critical illness as your son's. The result confirms the wisdom of my action, for March's convalescence has been slow and long; I am thankful to be assured it is sure. The burden of an extra member in your family at this time would, in the long run, prove too heavy for you.

I cannot tell you how I appreciate what you have done for Hazel. I have no words to express it. She returns to me full of life and joy, with no apparent unwillingness to take up her life again with me, which must seem dull to her in contrast to that which she had with you. Yet I know in her loyal little heart she belongs to you, is a part of your family henceforth — and I am glad to know it is so, for she needs, and will need, as a young girl, your motherly influence at all times.

I 'm not taking her away from you for good. Oh, no ! That

would be her loss as well as mine; but I am testing her a little. I have said I had no words with which adequately to express my gratitude. I am your debtor for my child's physical well-being — for much else which I do not find it easy to define. Will you allow me to make some compensation for your year of devotion? I do not care what form it take, providing you will permit me to try to discharge something of the debt — the whole can never be repaid. Will you not let me send that splendid son of yours through college? and give him two years of Europe afterwards? That future profession of his has always been of great interest to me. If the boy is too proud, as I suspect is the case, to accept the necessary amount other than as a loan, make it plain to him that I will even yield a point there — a pretty bad state of affairs for me as a debtor to find myself in. If he won't do this for me — won't Rose help me out by permitting me to aid her in cultivating that voice of hers? I know your magnanimity, and depend upon you to help me in this.

Hazel does not know I am writing to you, or she would send loving messages.

My kindest regards to Mr. Blossom, with hearty congratulations for March, and all sorts of neighborly remembrances for all others of the Lost Nation.

Sincerely your friend,

John Curtis Clyde.

To Mrs. Benjamin Blossom.

" Oh, mother ! "

A wave of crimson surged into March's pale face, and the sensitive nostrils quivered; then two big drops plashed down upon the letter which he handed to his mother.

" Oh, mother! if only I could — but I can't ! "

He rolled over on the soft pasture turf, face downwards, his head resting on his arms.

"Why, March dear," said his mother, tenderly, "why can't you? I think it 's beautiful, so does father."

A sob shook the long, thin frame. His mother laid her hand on the back of the yellow head. "What is it, my dear boy? Can't you tell me?"

The head shook energetically beneath her hand, and muffled words issued from the grass.

"But, March, we thought it would please you to have such an opportunity. You have read what Mr. Clyde says — you can look upon it as a loan. I hope you won't have any false pride in this matter — "

" 'T is n't false, mother," came forth from the grass, "and I would like to accept his offer, if only it were n't just his."

"Why not his, March? Surely, Hazel has been like one of us — a real little sister — " Another vigorous wagging of the yellow head arrested his mother in the midst of her sentence.

"Hazel is n't my sister."

"Why, of course, you can't feel as near to her as to Rose, but then, you must see how dear she has become to us all — and Mr. Clyde has put it in such a way, that the most sensitive person could accept it without injury to any feeling of true pride. Take time and think it over, March. It has come upon you rather suddenly, and I have been thinking about it for two weeks."

"It 's no use to think it over." Deep tragedy now made itself audible, as March rolled over and sat up, displaying eyes bright with excitement, flushed cheeks, and a generally determined air of having it out with himself.

" Well, I can't understand you, March."

" I wish you could."

His mother smiled in spite of the gravity of the situation. " Can't you tell me? or give me some clue to this mysterious determination of yours? "

March cast a despairing glance at his mother. " Mother, will you promise never to tell? "

" Not even your father, March? "

" No, father, nor any one — ever, mother."

" Very well; I promise, March, for I trust you."

" Oh, mother, have n't you seen? — don't you know, that I — that I love Hazel! And how can I take the money from her father, when I 'm going to try to make her love me and marry me sometime, when I get through studying, and — and — Oh, don't you see? "

And Mrs. Blossom did see — at last.

She spoke very gently, after a minute's silence, in which March's ears burned red to their tips, and his fingers were busy digging up a tiny strawberry-plant by the roots. " My son, I see, and I honor you for feeling as you do; but, March, have you thought of the difference between you and Hazel? "

" What difference, mother? "

Now Mary Blossom was not a worldly woman, neither was she a woman of the world — and she found it difficult to answer.

" You know how Hazel is placed in life, although you

do not know with what luxury she is surrounded in her home. She has beauty, a large circle of friends, immense wealth. There will be many who will seek her hand in four years' time, for she has a wonderful charm of her own, for all who come close to her. — Is it worth while to attempt, even, to win this little daughter of the rich? You, a poor boy, with his way to make?"

"But, mother," — there was strong protest in the voice — "she didn't have any beauty till she came up here to us — and if she *was* a rich girl, she wasn't a healthy one till she lived up here, and I don't see the good of money and a lot of things, if you 're sick, and homely, too." March waxed eloquent in his desire to convince his mother of the justice of his cause. "And if she hadn't come up here she wouldn't have got well, and then she wouldn't have grown so beautiful — and she *is* beautiful, mother." (Mrs. Blossom nodded assent.) "And I don't see why I haven't just as much right to try to make her love me as any other fellow. You 've told us children, dozens of times, it 's just character that counts, and not money, and if I try as hard as I can to keep straight and be a good man like father, I don't see why things wouldn't be all right in the end."

Mrs. Blossom was silenced, — "hoist with her own petard." "How can I destroy this lovely, young ideal? I dare not," was her thought. But aloud, she said: — "You 're right, March. Nothing but character counts. Make yourself worthy of this little love of yours. We 'll keep this in our own hearts, and when you are tempted to wrong-doing — and there are fearful temptations for every young man to meet, March, — temptations of which you can form no conception here in the shelter of your home — just remember this little talk of ours, and keep yourself un- spotted by the world just by the thought of this dear girl whom you hope some day to win. There is nothing, March, that will keep a young man in the right way like his love for just 'the one girl in the world ' — if only she be worthy of his love. And I think Hazel will be — even of you."

March flung his arms about her neck and kissed her heartily :

" Dear, little Mother Blossom, I 'll try, and even if I fail, just the thought of such a glorious-filorious mother that does n't laugh at a fellow — I was afraid you would, though, — will keep me straight enough. Why, Mother Blossom! I 'd be ashamed to look you in the eyes, if I did a down- right mean thing."

His mother laughed through her tears. " I wonder if many mothers get such a compliment? Come, dear, the dew is beginning to fall — it 's been such a heavenly day, I had forgotten it is early spring. Do you feel chilly ? "

" Not I," laughed March, and proceeded to relieve his feelings after his favorite method — by turning a double- back somersault down the pasture slope.

As Mrs. Blossom leaned over to kiss tired, sleepy Budd that night, she thought complacently to herself : —

" Well, thank fortune, here 's one who is heart-free," and

*l*aughed softly to herself.   Chi had not told her of Budd's proposal.

" Wilkins, tell Miss Hazel to come down into the library when she is dressed for dinner."

" Yes, Marse Clyde."   Wilkins sprang upstairs two steps at a time, and, knocking at Hazel's door, delivered his message.

" Tell papa I'm going to dress early, for I've some things to attend to about the table, Wilkins."

" Fo' sho', Miss Hazel," said Wilkins, with a broad smile of delighted surprise.

" And tell Mrs. Scott I'll choose the service, if she will take out the linen, and I have ordered the flowers.   Papa said I might."

Wilkins skipped downstairs, delivered his message to the amazed housekeeper, and then flew into the kitchen to impart his news to the cook, his confidante and co-worker for years in the Clyde household.

Minna-Lu was preparing a confection, and giving her whole soul to the making, when Wilkins made his appearance.   She looked up grimly, the ebony of her countenance shining beneath the immaculate white of her turban : —

" Wa' fo' yo' hyar ? "

Wilkins slapped both knees with the palms of his hands, and bent nearly double with noiseless laughter; then, straightening himself, approached Minna-Lu with boldness, despite the repelling wave of the cream-whip that she held suspended over the bowl, and confided to her the change of régime, to her edification and delight.

She put down the bowl and whip, stemmed her fists on her broad hips, and gurgled long and low. " 'F little missus done take rale hol' er de reins, dere ain't no kin' er show fo' sech po' trash." She indicated with an upward movement of her thumb the upper regions where the housekeeper was supposed to be.

" When I wan's a missus, I wan's quality folks, an' little missus do take de cake. Nebber see sech er chile. Dem great, shinin' eyes, lookin' at yo' out o' all de do's, an' dat laff soun'in' jes' like de ol' mocker dat nebber knowed nuffin' 'bout bedtime — yo' recollecks ? " Wilkins nodded emphatically, but was unprepared for Minna-Lu's next move : —

" Git out o' hyar, yo' good-fo'-nuffin' niggah. Huccome yo' stan'in' roun' wif yo' legs stiffer 'n de whites er dese yer eggs, an' yo' jaw goin' like de egg-beatah, an' de comp'ny comin' at rale sharp eight." Minna-Lu took up her bowl, and Wilkins beat a hasty retreat.

It was a warm first of May, and just about the hour when March and his mother were leaving the Wishing-Tree, that Hazel appeared in the dining-room. Wilkins gazed at her in a species of adoration. Her orders appeared to him revolutionary, but he obeyed them implicitly and unhesitatingly.

"Take off the candelabra, Wilkins, it is too warm to-night to have them on ; besides, people don't have a nice time talking when they have to peek around them to

get a glimpse of the people they 're talking to." Wilkins whisked off the candelabra as if they had been made of thistledown.

" Dat 's so, fo' sho', Miss Hazel. I see de folks doan' talk when dey ain' comf'ble; but I nebber tink ob de can'les."

" When it 's dark you can light all the sconces. I want you to use the pale green, Bohemian dinner set to-night; and I want just as little silver as possible."

Wilkins looked blank, and Hazel laughed. " Oh, we 'll make it up with some cut glass, I 'll manage it. I want the table to look cool and simple, just to-night."

Cool and simple. Wilkins failed to comprehend it, but such was his faith in " little Missy," that he carried out her orders to the letter, and the result was, according to Mrs. Fenlick, "a dream of beauty."

When she had made her preparations to her entire satisfaction, as well as Wilkins's, and the latter had called Minna-Lu from her culinary tug-of-war to witness "little Missy's " triumph, Hazel ran into the library.

Her father looked at her in amazement. Could this radiant, young girl be the same Hazel of a year ago? They had gone directly to North Carolina when Hazel had left Mount Hunger, and had been at home but two days. This little dinner was given to Mr. Clyde's intimate friends as an informal celebration and recognition of his daughter's return to the New York house.

Now, as she ran into the room and linked her arm in his, her father looked down upon her with such evident pride and love, that Hazel laughed joyfully, laid her cheek against his coat-sleeve and patted his hand.

"Do I look nice, Papa Clyde?"

"Nice! that's no word for it, Birdie." And thereupon he took her in his arms and gave her such a hug and a kiss, that the pretty dress must have suffered if it had not been made of the softest of white China-silk.

"Oh, my flowers! you'll crush them!" she cried, shielding with both hands a bunch of flowers at her belt.

"Where did you get all this — this style, daughter mine? It's — why, you're nothing but a little girl, but it's 'chic.'"

Hazel enjoyed her father's admiration to the full. She drew herself up, straight and tall, graceful and slender — her head was already above his shoulder — exclaiming: —

"Little girl! Well, your little girl designed this gown herself. I wouldn't have any fuss or frills about it; it's just plain and full and soft and clingy, and this sash of soft silk — isn't it a pretty, pale green? — feel — " She caught up a handful of the delicate fabric and crushed it in her hand, then smoothed it again, and it showed no wrinkles. "I've put it on to match the dinner. I've had it all my own way — Wilkins did just as I said — and it's all cool and green and springy. You'll see."

"Where did you get these flowers?" Mr. Clyde touched the bunch of arbutus, that showed so delicately pink and white against the white of her dress and the green of her sash.

A wave of beautiful color shot up to the roots of the

little crinkles of chestnut hair on her temples ; she touched
the blossoms caressingly.   "I wrote March about this
dinner-party, and how it was the first at which I had been
hostess, and he wrote back and wanted to know what I
was going to wear, and I told him — and this morning
these lovely things came by mail all done up in cotton
wool in a tin cracker-box, the kind Chi uses to put his
worm-bait in, when he goes fishing.   Are n't they lovely ?
And was n't March lovely to think of them, papa ? "

   " They are n't half as lovely as you are," said Mr. Clyde,
earnestly, replying to half of her question only.   " You
are my unspoiled Hazel-blossom — "   Then a sudden, in-
trusive thought caught and arrested his words.   " Hazel
Blossom," he repeated to himself, looking at her unconscious face as he uttered the last word, " Good heavens !
Could such a thing be ? "

   " De Cun'le an' Mrs. Fenlick," announced Wilkins.

   And when they were all seated at the table — the
Colonel and Mrs. Fenlick, Doctor and Mrs. Heath, Aunt
Carrie and Uncle Jo, the Masons and the Pearsells — with
no candelabra to interfere with the merry speech and
glances, with the light from the candles in the sconces
shining softly on the exquisite napery, on the low bed of
white tulips in the centre and the grace of the pale, green
porcelain, with the tall Bohemian Römer-glasses before
the plates — what wonder that Mrs. Fenlick pronounced
it a "dream of beauty"?

   When their guests had gone, Mr. Clyde turned to
Hazel: — "I shall be glad to open the Newport cottage

again, Birdie, with such a little hostess to help me entertain."

"The Newport house, papa!" Hazel exclaimed, a distinct note of disappointment sounding in her voice.

"Why not, dear? I thought of getting down there by
the tenth; in fact, gave my orders to Mrs. Scott to begin
packing to-morrow."

Hazel was evidently struggling with herself. She fingered the arbutus nervously; took them out of her belt;
inhaled their fragrance. Then she looked up with a smile,
although the corners of her mouth drooped and trembled
a little : —

"Why, of course, why not, papa? It's so much pleas-
anter there in May, than when everybody is down for the
summer."

Her father sat down in an easy-chair, put an arm around
his daughter, and drew her down to a seat on the arm of
the chair.

"Now, Hazel, I want you to tell me all about it. Don't
you want to go?"

"Yes, if you're there, papa, but —" she turned suddenly and her arm stole around his neck — "don't leave
me there alone, papa, please don't."

"Leave you — I? Why what do you mean, dear?"

"Oh, it is so lonesome when you are away, papa, when
you go off yachting with the Colonel — and the house is
so big, and there's nobody to talk to and say good-night to
— and — and, oh, dear!" The tears began to come, but
she struggled bravely for a few minutes.

"Why, little girl, you have never told me you were lonesome without me: indeed, you have never shown any sign of it, or of wanting me around much. I never thought — why, Hazel." Down went the curly head on his shoulder, and the sobs grew loud and frequent.

"There, there, Birdie," he said soothingly, stroking her head, "you're all tired out; this party has been too much for you — "

An energetic, protesting head-shake was followed by broken sentences — "It wasn't that — I'm not tired — you don't know, papa — I didn't know — know I was lonesome, and that I was — I think I was homesick — dreadfully — but Barbara Frietchie, you know — I had to be brave— and, I have tried not to show it to make you feel unhappy — and I love you so! but, oh, dear! I miss them so dreadfully, and I hoped — I was a member of the N. B. — B. O. — O., Oh — dear me, — Society, and the by-law says — I mean March read it — Oh, papa!"

"Well, well, there, there, dear," said the somewhat mystified father, bending all his efforts to soothe this evidently perturbed spirit, "why didn't you tell me before?"

"Because I was Barbara Frietchie."

"Now, Hazel, sit up and look me in the face and tell me what you mean. I supposed I was holding Hazel Clyde in my arms and not old Barbara Frietchie. Please explain."

"I thought I wrote you, papa," Hazel could not help smiling through her tears, for it did strike her as rather funny about papa's holding the patriotic, old lady in his arms.

" Well, you did n't tell me that." So Hazel explained.

Mr. Clyde nodded approval. " Very good, I approve of the N. B. B. O. O. Society, and of the present Barbara Frietchie's heroism — but no more of it is called for. You see, I fully intended you should pay your friends — my friends — a visit this summer, but I thought it would be much better later in the season when Mrs. Blossom would be rested from the fatigue of March's illness — "

" Oh, papa! " A squeeze effectually impeded further utterance. " I don't care how soon we go to Newport, or anywhere — of course, if *you* are with me — as long as I can go to Mount Hunger sometime this summer. And, besides," she added eagerly, " we planned next winter's visit from Rose, did n't we ? "

" I should rather think we did. We shall be very proud of our beautiful friend, Rose, and delighted to have our friends meet her, shan't we ? " Another squeeze precluded, for the moment, articulate speech.

" Yes," Hazel cried, enthusiastically, " we 'll take her to concerts and operas — just think, papa, with that lovely voice she has never heard a concert! — and we 'll take her to the theatre and — "

" And," her father went on, growing enthusiastic himself at the prospect, for he was the soul of hospitality, " and we 'll give her a dainty dinner or two, and possibly a little dance — few and early, you know — "

" Oh — ee! " cried Hazel, forgetting her woe, " and Mrs. Heath will give a lunch-party for her, and, perhaps, Aunt Carrie a tea, and Mrs. Fenlick a reception — "

"Heavens!" interrupted her father, "you'll kill her with kindness — that fresh, wild rose can't stand all that —"

"Oh, yes, she can, papa; she can stand that just as well as I stood going up there where everything was so different."

"True," said Mr. Clyde, thoughtfully, "it was different."

"Oh, it was, papa! I never had to go to bed alone. Mrs. Blossom always came to say good-night and to kiss me, and to — to —"

"To what?" asked her father.

"You won't mind if I tell you?" Hazel asked, half-shyly.

"Mind! I should say not; I should mind if you did n't tell me."

"— to say 'Our Father' with me, papa; you know no one ever said it with me before, and it's — it's such a comfy time to feel sorry and talk over what you've done wrong; and it's *that* I miss so."

"I don't blame you, Birdie," said her father, quietly. "But now see how late it is!" — he pointed to the clock — "Eleven! This will never do for a *débutante*. Good-night, darling. Sweet dreams of Rose and the N. B. B. O. O. Society."

"Good-night, Papa Clyde; Doctor Heath says you are the most splendid fellow in the world — but I know you are the dearest father in the world; good-night, I've had a lovely party."

She ran upstairs, but, in a moment, her father heard her tripping down again. Her head parted the portières. "I just came back to tell you, that this kind of a talk we've had is just as good as the Mount Hunger bedtime-talks. I shan't be homesick any more." And away she ran.

Now John Curtis Clyde was a pew-owner — as had been his father and grandfather before him — in one of the Fifth Avenue churches, and duly made his appearance in that pew every Sunday morning. He entered, too, into the service with hearty voice, and made his responses without, the while, giving undue thought to the world. But when he had said "Our Father" with his little daughter by his side, he had supposed his duty performed to the extent of his needs — of another's, his child's, he gave no thought.

To-night, however, as he sat in the easy-chair where Hazel had left him, it began to dawn upon him slowly that his little daughter, during her fourteen years, might have had other needs, for which he had not provided, nor, perhaps, with all his riches was capable of providing.

The clock chimed twelve, — one, — two —; John Clyde, with a sigh, rose and went up to bed — a wiser and a better man.

XXII

ROSE

WHAT a summer that was! Mr. Clyde sent Hazel up to the Blossoms for July and again for September, when he, the Colonel and Mrs. Fenlick, the Pearsells and the Masons, Aunt Carrie and Uncle Jo took possession of the entire inn at Barton's River, and for a month coached and rode throughout the "North Country," all in the cool September weather. Jack Sherrill joined them for the last three weeks, and, this time, Maude Seaton was not of the party.

"I just headed her off every time she made a dead set at any one of us for an invitation," said Mrs. Fenlick one day in confidence to her intimate, Mrs. Pearsell, as they sat on the vine-covered veranda of the inn, "but she proved a regular octopus. She got the Colonel in her toils one morning at the Casino, and I pretended to be faint — yes, I did — just to get his attention for a sufficient time to make a fuss, and get him alone in the carriage; then, of course, I settled it. Oh, dear! men are so guile-less in spots!" — Mrs. Fenlick gave a weary sigh — "What I have n't been through with that girl! Anyway, she's been out two winters, now, and she has n't caught

Jack Sherrill yet. I don't think there is much chance after the first season for a girl to make a really fine match, do you?" Then they fell to discussing the pros. and cons. of the question with evergreen interest.

Jack Sherrill, for one, had no thought of Miss Seaton. He had sent the valentine-flowers, and the sentiment from Barry Cornwall's love-song, with a strange kind of "kill or cure" feeling.

He had communed with himself, at twilight of one February day, as he lay at full length on the cushioned window-seat of his room from which he looked down upon the darkening, snow-covered campus and the anatomy of the elms showing black against it. His pipe had gone out, but he derived some satisfaction in pulling away at it mechanically, while he thought out the situation for himself.

"What's the use of a man's hanging fire when he *knows?*" he thought. "Now, I love her — love her." (Jack's hand stole into the breast of his jacket and crushed a bit of paper there; he smiled.) "Of course she does n't know, and won't know for a while, but it shan't be through any neglect of mine that she does n't; and when she knows — there 's the rub! — will she care for me, Jack Sherrill? I've never done anything in my life to make a girl like that care for me.

"But there's one thing I'd stake my life on — she would n't marry a man for his money. A man 's got to be loved for himself — not for what he can give a woman, or do for her, but just for himself, if it 's going to be the

real thing, and *last*. And what am I that a girl like that
should love me —" Jack was growing very humble. He
pulled himself together: "Anyhow, I'll send the flowers
and the sentiment, *I mean it;* I don't care what she
thinks!" Jack's courage rose as he began to feel something like defiance of Fate.

Just then his chum came in.

"There's no use, Sherrill," he said, flinging himself
down upon the cushioned seat Jack had just vacated; "we
can't have the theatricals unless you take the girl's part.
It won't put you out any — smooth face and no scrub.
You've been it once, and it will be a dead failure if you
are n't in it now."

"I don't see how I can," replied Jack, shortly, for this
intrusion on his mood irritated him. "I told you, all of
you, at the Club last year, that I would n't play after I was
a Junior."

"Well, what if you did?" rejoined his chum, a little
crossly. "You're not so uncompromisingly steadfast in
other things that you can't afford to change your mind in
such a trifle as this."

"Come, don't be touchy," said Jack, good-humoredly.
"Hit right out from the shoulder, old man, and tell me
what you mean."

Dawns smiled, clasped his hands under his head, and
raised his merry blue eyes to Jack, who was lighting up.

"They say over at the Club that you have thrown
Maude Seaton over, but Grayson took up the Seaton
cudgels and made the statement that *she* had thrown you

over, and you won't take the girl's part in the play because
she is coming on for it."

Jack hesitated. He hated to play at any comedy of love
when his heart was throbbing with the genuine article.
But, after all, it might be the best way to silence the
Club's tongues as well as some others in Boston and New
York.

"I'll help you out this once, Dawns, but I tell you
plainly I won't have anything more to do with the Club
theatricals while I'm in college," he replied, ignoring both
of Dawns' statements, which omissions his chum noticed,
and made his own thoughts: "Just like Sherrill. You
can't get any hold of him to know what he really feels
and thinks."

Jack played his part accordingly, repeating the success
of the year before, and scoring new triumphs. He was
glad when it was over, and he could go back to his room
"dead tired," as he said to himself, but with the conviction
that he had settled matters to his own satisfaction if not to
that of one other.

The room was in such disorder! Evidently, Dawns had
been having a little spree before Jack's late return, and the
smoke had left the air heavy.

Jack dropped his paraphernalia in the middle of the
floor — peeling himself as he stood yawning and thanking
his lucky star that he was not born a woman to be handi-
capped by such things! — *décolleté* white satin waist, long-
trained satin gown, necklace — Jack gave the string a
twitch, for it had knotted, and the Roman pearls rolled

into unreachable places all over the floor. Off flew one
white satin slipper — number ten, broad at the toes! —
with a fine "drop kick" hitting the ceiling and landing on
the book-shelves; the other followed suit. White fan with
chain, white elbow gloves, corsage bouquet — all dropped
in a promiscuous heap. A general stampede loosened silk
under-skirt and dainty muslin petticoat, lace-trimmed. A
wrench, — corset-cover and corsets were torn from their
moorings. Jack groaned — or something worse — at the
flummery, and, leaving everything as it had dropped,
rushed off into his bedroom, only to find that he had
forgotten to take off the blonde wig and wash off the
rouge.

At last, however, he was asleep, and slept the sleep of
the justified.

He slept both soundly and late, but when he awoke the
next morning his first thought was of the flowers for Mount
Hunger and the appropriate sentiment. Accordingly, having reckoned the arrival of train, departure of stage, etc.,
to a minute, he selected the flowers, wrote the sentiment,
not without forebodings of the usual kind, and despatched
both to Mount Hunger with high hopes, notwithstanding
prescient feelings. Then, metaphorically, he sat down to
await an answer. He waited just two months, and during
that time had turned emotionally black and blue more
than once at the thought of his temerity in sending such
a message.

Hazel had written him at once from North Carolina to
tell him of March's illness, and on the same day she sent

a penitent note to Rose, confessing her shame at her attempt at deception, and explaining that it was because she loved her cousin so dearly she could not bear to see his gift slighted.

When March was out of danger, Rose had written to Hazel a frank, loving letter, blaming herself for her want of self-control, and begging Hazel's forgiveness for her harsh words:

"It's all my old pride, Hazel dear," she wrote, "that I have to fight very often. It was most kind of Mr. Sherrill to remember me when he has so many, many other friends whom he has known longer, and I shall write and tell him so. Now that my heart is lighter on account of dear March, I can write more easily.

"We miss you so! when are you coming back to us? Chi looks perfectly disconsolate, and we all feel a great deal more than we care to say.

"I wish you were here to have the fun of the French evenings, three times a week. You speak it so beautifully, Mr. Ford says, and I thank you so much for all the help you gave me in teaching me. Mr. Ford speaks it very well, too, so Miss Alton says. We all meet at our house once a week on March's account, and then one evening in the week, Miss Alton and I (she's lovely) go over to the Fords' for music. He has sent for some lovely songs for me — old English ones, and we're going to have a little celebration for March's birthday in May. How I wish you were to be here!

"March is lying on the settle, dreaming over that exquisite photograph of Cologne Cathedral you sent him; I've just asked him if he had any messages for you, and he smiled — oh, it's so good to see his dear smile again! You can't think

how tall he's grown since his illness, and he's so thin — and
said, ' I sent one to her this morning myself; she can't have two
a day.'   But you know March's ways.

" Now I must stop ; Mr. Ford is coming over on horse-
back and I am riding Bob now.   I wear an old riding-
habit of Martie's — it fits fine!   I have more to tell you, but
will finish after I get back from the ride — there comes Mr.
Ford — "

This letter Hazel duly forwarded to her cousin.   " He 'll
know by what she says in it that she really was pleased,
for all she acted so queer," she said to herself as she enclosed it in one to Jack, in which she took special pains
to inform him that he had never told her whether he had
given those verses Rose sang to Miss Seaton.

" I told Rose I was sure they were for Miss Seaton, and
Rose said she did n't mind copying them herself for you if you
wished them.   Do tell me if you gave them to her.   I told
Rose your valentine to her last year was a rose-heart.   I hope
you don't mind my telling, for, you know, Jack, all our family
think you are engaged to her — "

Jack dropped Hazel's letter at this point and gave a
decided groan.

" What luck ! " he muttered.   " It 's all up with the
whole thing now.   No girl of any spirit would stand all
that — and Hazel meddling so ! thinking she is doing her
level best to explain matters ; — What an ass I was to
send that flower-valentine to Maude — and she thinks I
gave her those verses ! and there 's this Ford skulking
round and having it all his own way ; he 's just the kind

a girl would care for — those musical cranks are no end sentimental. Hang it all!"

Jack thrust his hands deep into his pockets, took several decided turns up and down the room, squared his shoulders, pursed his lips, cut his two classroom lectures, ordered up Little Shaver and rode out to the polo grounds, where, finding himself alone, he put the little fellow through his best paces, ignoring the fact that snow and ice wore on the pony's nerves — and had a game out to himself.

When just two months had passed, he received a note from Rose, his first, and it was accorded the reception due to first notes in particular. After this, Jack developed certain wiles of diplomacy, he had thus far, in his various experiences, held in abeyance. He wrote sympathetic notes to Mrs. Blossom; commissioned Chi to find him another polo pony — Morgan, if possible — among the Green Hills; sent March a set of illustrated books on architecture, and complained to Doctor Heath of a pain that racked his chest; at which the Doctor's eyes twinkled. He said he would examine him later, but he was convinced it was heart trouble, the symptoms were apt to mislead and confuse. He added gravely: "Too much hard polo riding, Jack; get away into the country — mountains if you can, and you'll recuperate fast enough. I'll make an examination in the fall."

Jack obeyed to the letter, and what a month of September that was!

There were glorious rides with Rose along the beautiful river valley and over the mountain roads. There were delightful evenings at the Fords', and silent, beatific walks with Rose homewards beneath the harvest moon. There were morning rambles with Rose up over the pastures and deep into the woodlands for late ferns and hooded gentians. There were adorable hours of doing nothing but adore, while Rose was busy about her work, setting the table for tea (Jack paid his board at the inn, but he lived at the Blossoms'), or laying the cloth for dinner, or on Saturday morning even making rolls for the tea to which the whole party at the inn were invited.

Chi was in his glory. Little Shaver came trotting regularly every day up through the woods'-road, and whinnied " Good-morning " first to Fleet, then to Chi. There were general coaching-parties to Woodstock and Brandon, in which Mrs. Blossom was guest, and a grand tea at the Fords' for all the guests, with a musicale for a finish, and an informal dance in the Blossoms' barn to which all the Lost Nation were invited.

They accepted, one and all. Captain Spillkins was in his element, so he said. He and Mrs. Fenlick danced a two-step in a manner to win the commendation of the entire assembly. Miss Elvira and Miss Melissa went through the square dance escorted by Jack and Uncle Jo. There were round dances and contra dances. Uncle Israel contributed an " 1812 " jig, and Mr. Clyde passed round the hat for his sole benefit. There were waltzes for those who could waltz, and polkas for those who could polka, and schottische and minuet. " There never was such a dance since before the Deluge!" declared Mrs.

Fenlick, when Captain Spillkins escorted her to a seat on a sap-bucket; and then they all went at it again in a grand finale, the Virginia Reel — Chi and Hazel, Mr. Clyde and Aunt Tryphosa for head and foot couple; Maria-Ann with Jack; Alan Ford with Mrs. Fenlick; the Colonel with Mrs. Blossom whom he admired greatly; March and Miss Alton — such a double row of them!

Poor Reub sat in one of the empty stalls and watched the fun with slow, half-understanding smile, and Ruth Ford reclined in a rocking-chair in the corner, and with merry laughter and sparkling wit soothed the dull ache in her heart that the knowledge that she was henceforth to be a "Shut-out" from all that life had at first given her.

The next day after the dance there was a grand dinner given at the inn by the Newport party to all the Lost Nation; and, later on, private entertainments for Mr. and Mrs. Blossom and the Fords. At last, when the first maple leaves crimsoned and the frost silvered the mullein leaves in the pasture, Hazel, her father, Jack, and their friends bade good-bye to the Mountain and all its joys of acquaintance, and in some cases, friendship, and turned their faces, not without reluctance on the part of some of them, city-wards.

"Oh, mother! hasn't it been too beautiful for anything?" exclaimed Rose, turning to her mother, as the last of the riding-party waved his cap in farewell to those on the porch. It was Jack.

"We have had a happy summer, Rose; — I think they have, too," her mother added, shading her eyes from the setting sun. "You'll be very lonely here at home, dear, after all this gayety."

"Lonely! Why, Martie Blossom, how can you think of such a thing!" said Rose, still scanning the lower road for a last glimpse of the riders. "See, see, they are all waving their handkerchiefs!"

The whole Blossom family laid hold of what they could — napkins, towels, a table-cloth, and Chi seized his shirt, which he had hung on the line to dry, and waved frantically until the party was no longer to be seen.

"Lonesome! the idea," said Rose, turning to her mother. "Think of all the studying March and I have to do, and the French evenings, and the Fords, and Thanksgiving coming, and then Christmas, and then —"

"Then," said Mrs. Blossom, interrupting her, "my Rose takes a little plunge into that whirlpool of gay life and fashion in New York."

"Yes," said Rose, with a happy smile that spoke volumes to her mother, "I do look forward to it, Martie dear; but the whirlpool shan't suck me under; I shall come home just your old-fashioned Rose-pose."

"I hope so, dear," said her mother, a little wistfully, and called the children in to supper.

Indeed, they found little opportunity to miss their friends in the ensuing months; for there came kindly letters, and friendly letters, and something very nearly resembling love-letters. The mail brought papers, books, and magazines. The express brought to Barton's River many a box of lovely flowers. At Christmas came more than

one remembrance for them all, including Aunt Tryphosa
and Maria-Ann, and four special invitations for Rose to
visit in New York directly after the holidays. One was
from Mr. Clyde — with an urgent request from Hazel to
say "yes" by telegram and "relieve her misery," so she
put it —; one from Mrs. Heath; one from Aunt Carrie,
and a gushingly cordial one from Mrs. Fenlick! Each
claimed her for a month. But Mrs. Blossom shook her
head.

"No, no, dear, you would wear your welcome out. I
shall need you at home by the last of February. I think
you can accept only Mr. Clyde's and Mrs. Heath's. You
can accept social courtesies from the other four of course."

"But, mother," Rose's face was the image of despair,
"what shall I wear? Just hear what Hazel has planned
—'lunches, dinners, theatre, concerts'— why! I can never
go to all those things."

"I've thought of that, too, Rose; but the little colt
shan't go bare this time — it will take some courage, dear,
to wear the same things over and over again, not to mention the puzzle of planning for it all."

"I'm not 'Molly Stark' for nothing," laughed Rose,
and the two women began to plan for what Chi called
"Rose's campaign." The pretty white serge was lengthened and made over to appear more grown up, as Cherry
put it; the dark blue wash silk — Hazel's gift that had
never been made up — was fashioned into a "swell affair"
— so March pronounced it; the old-fashioned blue lawn
was cut over into a dainty full waist, and then Mrs.

Blossom added her surprise — a delicate blue taffeta skirt to match the waist. Rose went into raptures over it, and sought the best bedroom regularly three times a day to feast her girl's eyes on the silken loveliness as it lay in state on the best bed. A new dark blue serge was to do duty for a street suit, with a plain felt hat. For best, there was a turban made of dark blue velvet to match the wash silk.

"And four pairs of gloves! Martie Blossom, you are an angel, to give me these that Hazel gave you a year ago last Christmas. Have you been keeping them for me all this time?"

Mrs. Blossom smiled assent, and was rewarded by a squeeze that interfered decidedly with her breathing apparatus.

The night before she left, Rose "costumed" for the benefit of the entire family, who were assembled in the long-room, together with Aunt Tryphosa and Maria-Ann, to see Rose in her finery.

"I'll make it a climax," said Rose, laughing half-shamefacedly, as she slipped upstairs to change her street suit, which had brought forth admiring "Ohs" and "Ahs" from the children, and favorable criticism from their elders.

Down she came in her white serge; there were nods and smiles of approval.

Her reappearance in the wash silk and velvet turban was the signal, on March's part, for a burst of applause, and cries of admiration from Budd and Cherry.

"Grand transformation scene!" cried March, as Rose

tri_ped down in the blue taffeta, looking like a very rose herself.

"Beats all!" murmured Chi, who had become nearly speechless with admiration, "what clothes'll do for a good-lookin' woman; but for a ravin', tearin' beauty like our Rose — George Washin'ton! She'll open those high-flyers' eyes."

"Cinderella — fifth act!" shouted March as, after a prolonged wait, he heard Rose on the stairs.

But was it Rose?

The beautiful India mull of her mother's had been transformed into a ball-dress. She had drawn on her long white gloves and tucked into the simple, ribbon belt three of Jack's Christmas roses.

Maria-Ann gasped, and that broke the, to Rose, somewhat embarrassing silence.

Marshalled by March, the whole family formed a procession, and Rose was reviewed: — back breadths, front breadths, flounces, waist, gloves; all were thoroughly inspected.

Chi touched the lower flounce of the half-train gingerly with one work-roughened forefinger, then, straightening himself suddenly, sighed heavily.

"What's the matter, Chi?" Rose laughed at the dubious expression on his face.

"You ain't Rose Blossom nor Molly Stark any longer. You're just a regular Empress of Rooshy, 'n' you don't look like that girl I took along to sell berries down to Barton's last summer, 'n' I wish you —" he hesitated.

" What, Chi ? " said Rose.

" I wish you was back again, old sunbonnet, old calico
gown, patched shoes 'n' all — "

" Oh, Chi, no, you don't," said Rose, laughing merrily;
" you forget, I shall probably see Miss Seaton down there
in New York, and you would n't want me to appear a
second time before her in that old rig."

" You 're right, Rose-pose," replied Chi, his expression
brightening visibly. He drew close to her and whispered
audibly :

" Just sail right in, Molly Stark, 'n' cut that sassy girl
out right 'n' left. She never could hold a candle to
you."

" Sh-sh, Chi ! " said Mrs. Blossom, meaningly, but with
a twinkle in her eye.

" I mean just what I say, Mis' Blossom. Folks can't
come up here on this Mountain to sass us to our faces, 'n'
she *did ;* — I 've stayed riled ever since, 'n' I hope she 'll
get sassed back in a way that 'll make her hair stand just
a little more on end than it did, when she gave that mean,
snickerin' giggle — "

" Chi, Chi," Mrs. Blossom interrupted him in an appeas-
ing tone.

" You need n't Chi me, Mis' Blossom. These children
are just as near to me as if they was my own, 'n' when
they 're sassed, I 'm sassed too; 'n' my great-grandfather
fought over at Ticonderogy, 'n' I ain't bound to take any
more sass than he took — "

By this time the whole family were in fits of laughter

over Chi's persistent use of so much "sass," and, at last,
Chi himself joined in the laugh at his excessive heat : —

"Over nothin' but a wind-bag, after all," he concluded.

On the following morning, Mr. Blossom, Chi, March
and Budd drove down to Barton's to see Rose off. The
old apple-green pung had been fitted with two broad
boards for seats, and covered with buffalo robes and horse
blankets.   There was just room in the tail for Rose's old-
fashioned trunk and a small strapped box, which held two
dozen of new-laid eggs, six small, round cheeses, and a
wreath of ground hemlock and bitter-sweet — a neighborly
gift from Aunt Tryphosa and Maria-Ann to Hazel and
Mr. Clyde.

As the train moved away from the station, Chi watched
it with brimming eyes.

"She 'll never come back the same Rose-pose, livin'
among all those high-flyers — never," he muttered to himself; but aloud he remarked, with forced cheerfulness,
turning to Mr. Blossom while he dashed the blinding
drops from his eyes with the back of his hand:

"Looks mighty like a thaw, Ben; kind of wets down,
don't it ? "

" Yes, Chi," said Mr. Blossom, busy with conquering his
own heartache, " we 'd better be getting on home ; " and the
masculine contingent of the Blossom household climbed
into the pung and took their way homeward in silence.

But what a reception that was for the transplanted
Rose !

Mr. Clyde met her at the Grand Central Station, and

Rose felt how welcome she was just by the hand-clasp, and his first words:

"We have you at last, Rose; I would n't let Hazel come because I thought the train might be late, and there 's a cold rain falling. Martin, take this box — "

"Oh, no ; I must carry that myself," laughed Rose, looking up at the liveried footman with something like awe. "I promised Aunt Tryphosa and Maria-Ann I would n't let any one take them till they were safe in the house; thank you," she bowed courteously to Martin, who confided to the coachman so soon as they were on the box: "Hi 'ave n't seen nothink so 'ansome since Hi 've bean in the States."

As the brougham whirled into the Avenue, and the electric lights shone full into the carriage, Rose could see the luxuriously upholstered interior, and a sudden thought of the old apple-green pung and the buffalo robes dimmed her eyes. But it was only for a moment; Mr. Clyde was telling her of Hazel's impatience, and how the coachman had had special orders from her to hurry up so soon as he should be on the Avenue, and he had hardly finished before the coachman drew rein, slackening his rapid pace as he turned a corner, Martin was opening the door, and Hazel's voice was calling from a wide house entrance flooded with soft light:

"Oh, Rose, my Rose ! Is it really you, at last ? "

"And this, I am sure, is Wilkins," said Rose, when finally Hazel set her arms free. "We 've heard so much of you, that I feel as if I had known you a long time."

Rose held out her hand with such sincere cordiality that Wilkins' speech was suddenly reduced to pantomime, and he could only extend his other hand rather helplessly towards the box that Rose still carried. But Rose refused to yield it up.

"Here, Hazel, I promised Maria-Ann and Aunt Tryphosa I would n't give it into any hands but yours. Oh! be careful — they 're eggs!"

"Eggs!" repeated Hazel, laughing. "Here, Wilkins, unstrap it for me, quick — Oh, papa, look!" She held out the box to Mr. Clyde, and, somehow, John Curtis Clyde for a moment thought with Chi, that there was going to be a "thaw." Each egg was rolled in white cotton batting and wrapped in pink tissue paper. The six little cheeses were enclosed in tin-foil, and cheeses and eggs were embedded in the Christmas wreath. On a piece of pasteboard was written in unsteady characters:

To Mr. John Curtis Clyde of New York City, with the season's compliments.
MOUNT HUNGER, VERMONT, January 6th, 1898.

"And you 've had such lovely flowers come for you, five boxes of them, Rose, and piles of invitations. I 'm sure you 're engaged up to Ash Wednesday."

"Come, Chatterbox," said her father, smiling at her volubility, "Rose has just time to dress for dinner; you know Aunt Carrie and Uncle Jo are coming to-night."

"Oh, I forgot all about them; you 'll have to hurry, Rose. Wilkins, bring up the flowers. Come on."

Hazel ran up the broad flight of stairs, carpeted with velvety crimson, to the first landing, from which, through a lofty arch in the hall, Rose caught a glimpse of softly lighted rooms, the walls enriched with engravings and etchings, with here and there a landscape or marine in watercolors. Rose drew a long breath. This, then, was what Chi meant when he said "Hazel was rich as Crœsus."

" But, Hazel, my trunk has n't come," said Rose, as she followed her hostess into the spacious bedroom, which was separated from Hazel's only by a dressing-room.

" It 'll be here in a few minutes; papa has a special man, who always delivers them almost as soon as we get here."

Sure enough, the trunk came in time; and Rose, as she unpacked, finding evidences of the loving mother-care in every fold, cried within her heart, looking about at the exquisite appointments of her room and dressing-room :

" Martie, Martie, what would all this be without you ! — Oh, I know now, what dear old Chi meant when he said Hazel was poor where we are rich — only a housekeeper to see to all Hazel's things — "

" Rose, what flowers are you going to wear ? " called Hazel from her room.

" I have n't had time to look," Rose called back, surveying her white serge with great satisfaction in the pier-glass.

" Do look, then, and see who they 're from."

" Oh, Hazel, do come and see.   How kind everybody

has been! Here are cards from Mrs. Heath and Doctor Heath, and your Aunt Carrie, and Mr. Sherrill, and Mrs. Fenlick, and even that Mr. Grayson who was up at our house to tea a year ago!"

"They are lovely. Whose are you going to wear?"

"I'll make up a bunch of one or two from each, that will show my appreciation of all their favors."

Hazel looked slightly crestfallen. "I hoped you'd wear Jack's — they're the loveliest with white —." she lifted the white lilacs — "and they're so rare just now. I heard Aunt Carrie say that one of the girls had put off her wedding for six weeks, just because she couldn't have white lilacs for it."

"They'll last with care three days surely, and I can wear them to-morrow evening," replied Rose, bending to inhale their delicate fragrance.

"So you can, for papa is going to give a dinner for you to-morrow night, and afterwards, he has promised to take you to a dance at Mrs. Pearsell's. I can't go, you know, for I'm not grown up; but you can tell me all about it. We're going to have lots of fun this week, for school does not begin for several days. Come."

Together they went down to the drawing-room, and Wilkins announced that dinner was served.

After it was over he sought Minna-Lu in her own domains, and gave vent to his long pent emotions.

"Minna-Lu," he whispered, mysteriously, ".dere's an out an' out angel ben hubberin' 'bout de table —"

"Fo' de Lawd!" Minna-Lu turned upon him fiercely,

for she was superstitious to the very marrow. " Wa' fo' yo' come hyar, skeerin' de bref out a mah bones wif yo' sp'r'ts ! Yo' go long home wha' yo' b'long."

But Wilkins was not to be repulsed in this manner. " Nebber see sech ha'r, an' jes' lillum-white — "

"Oh, go 'long ! Lillum-white ha'r," interrupted Minna-Lu, with scathing sarcasm. "Huccome yo' know de angels hab lillum-white ha'r ?"

" Huccome I know? — 'Case I see de shine, jes' lake yo' see in de dror'n-room."

" De shine ob lillum-white ha'r in de dror'n-room ! 'Pears lake yo' head struck ile — "

"Yo' hol' yo' tongue, Minna-Lu," retorted Wilkins, irritated at the continued evidence of disbelief on the part of his coadjutor. " Jes' yo' hide back ob de dumb-waitah to-morrah ebenin' when de dessert comes on, an' see fo' yo'se'f ! " He departed in high dudgeon, and Minna-Lu gurgled long and low to herself, but, in her turn, was interrupted by the sound of tripping steps on the basement flight.

Minna-Lu hastily put her fat hands up to her turban to see if it were on straight, and smoothed her apron, muttering :

" Clar to goodness, ef it ain't jes' mah luck to hab little Missus come into dis yere hen-roost ? " she rapidly surveyed her immaculate kitchen with anxious eye.

" Minna-Lu, this is my friend, Miss Rose ; the one who did up those lovely preserves, and here are some new-laid eggs and some cheeses that Miss Maria-Ann Simmons—

you know I told you all about her and the hens — has sent papa."

Minna-Lu gazed at Rose in open admiration. The faithful colored retainer had her thorny side and her blossom one.

Rose put out her hand, and Minna-Lu took it in both hers. " I 'se mighty glad yo' come, Miss Rose, dere ain't no strawberry-blossom nor no rose-blossom can hol' a can'le to yo' own honey se'f. Dese yere cheeses is prime." She examined one with the nose of a connoisseur. " Jes' fill de bill wif de salad-chips to-morrah." She stemmed her fists on her hips, and her mellow, contented gurgle caused Rose and Hazel to laugh, too.

"What is it, Minna-Lu ? " said Hazel, reading the signs of the times.

"Dat Wilkins done tol' me to git back ob de dumb-waitah, to-morrah ebenin' to see Missy Rose, but I 'se gwine to ask rale straight to jes' see her 'fo' de comp'ny come."

" Of course you may. Come up to my room about seven, and we 'll be ready."

" Fo' sho'," said Minna-Lu, with beaming face.

" Good-night," said Rose, beaming, too, for she found the black faces and ways irresistibly amusing.

" De Lawd bress yo' lily face, Missy Rose."

When the two girls were alone, at last, in Hazel's room, there was no thought of bed for an hour. There were numberless questions on Hazel's part concerning all the dear Mount Hunger people, and speechless astonishment on Rose's at the number of invitations that were waiting for her. They chatted all the time they were undressing, calling back and forth to each other as one thing or another suggested itself. Finally, Hazel made her appearance in Rose's room. She went up to her, put her arms about her neck, and, looking up with eyes full of loving trust, said:

"Rose-pose, won't you come into my room and say 'Our Father' with me as Mother Blossom used to do on Mount Hunger? You can't think how I miss it."

"Why, Hazel darling, of course I will — then I shan't feel homesick missing that precious Martie."

She followed Hazel into her room, and after she was in bed, Rose knelt by her side, and together they said, "Our Father." Then Rose bent over to receive Hazel's loving kiss and whispered, "Oh, Rose, I'm so happy to have you here," and whispered back, "And I'm so happy to be with you, Hazel — good-night."

"Good-night."

Rose went back to her room. At last she was alone. She drew one of the easy-chairs up before the wood-fire that was dying down, put her bare feet on the warm fender, and, for a while, dreamed waking dreams. It was all so strange. The cathedral clock on the mantel chimed twelve. They were all asleep in the farmhouse on the Mountain — it was time for her to be. She rose, tiptoed softly into the dressing-room, took from the bowl the spray of white lilacs she had worn with the other flowers that evening, shook off the water, and drew the stem through a buttonhole in the yoke of her simple night-dress. She tiptoed back again into her room, looked up at the dainty, canopied bed, then laid herself down within it, and, almost immediately, fell asleep — with her hand resting on the white fragrance that lay upon her heart.

XXIII

BEHOLD HOW GREAT A MATTER A LITTLE FIRE KINDLETH

It was so delightful! The weeks were passing all too quickly, and the letters to Mount Hunger waxed eloquent in praise of everybody's kindness.

Jack had come on to lead a cotillion with Rose at Aunt Carrie's. It was a weighty affair — the selecting of the flowers for her. White violets they must be, and white violets were about as rare as white raspberries. Jack gave the florist his own address.

"I 'll see them, myself, before I send them up; for I won't trust anyone's eyes but my own," he said to himself as he hurried home to dress for dinner with a friend. "I wish I had n't promised Grayson to meet him at the Club before seven. I 'm afraid they won't come in time." He looked at his watch. "I 'm going to make them a test — and see what she 'll do. She 's so friendly and frank and all that, I can't find out even whether she 's beginning to care."

Jack's absorption in the theme was such that he put his latch-key in wrong-side up, and, in consequence, wrestled with the lock till he had worked himself into a fever of impatience; finally he touched the button before he discovered the trouble.

"Any packages come for me, Jason?" he inquired of the butler, whose dignified manner of locomotion had been rudely shaken by Jack's unceasing pressure on the electric-bell.

"Yes, Mr. John. Just taken a box up to the rooms."

Jack looked relieved, and sprang upstairs two steps at a time. He opened the box. There they were in all their exquisite freshness. "Like her," he thought, touching his lips to them; then, suddenly straightening himself, he felt the blood surge into his face.

"I like Dord's way of putting up his flowers, no tags, nor fol-de-rols. Jason," he said, as he ran down stairs again, "I shall be back in an hour; tell Thomas to have everything laid out — I'm in a hurry. And have a messenger-boy here when I come back, and don't forget to order the carriage for quarter of eight, sharp."

"Yes, Mr. John."

"Messenger-boy come?" he inquired as Jason opened the door on his return.

"Yes, sir, waiting in the hall."

Jack raced up stairs. There was the precious box on his dressing-table. He hastily took a visiting card, and, writing on it the sentiment that was uppermost in his heart, slipped it into the envelope, gave it, together with the box, to the waiting boy, and bade him hand it to the man, Wilkins, with the request that it be sent up at once to the lady to whom it was addressed. Then he made ready for dinner.

An hour later, Rose was dressing for the dance, and Hazel was watching her, chatting volubly all the while.

"That's the loveliest dress, Rose, I heard Aunt Carrie say, you couldn't buy such, nowadays."

"It was Martie's wedding-dress. An uncle of her mother's, who was a sea-captain, brought it from India. But if I wear it many more times, it will be known throughout the length of New York. This is my sixth time."

"I shouldn't care if it were the hundredth; it's just lovely. Besides, Jack hasn't seen it, you know."

Rose laughed. "Oh, yes, he has — on Martie; that night of the tea on the porch."

"Oh, well, that's different. What flowers are you going to wear?"

"I thought I wouldn't wear any, just for a change." Rose's face was veiled by the shining hair, which she was brushing, preparatory to coiling it high on her head; otherwise, Hazel would have seen the clear flush that warmed even the roots of the soft waves at the nape of her neck. Just then there was a knock. The maid opened the door, and Wilkins' voice was distinctly audible : —

"Jes' come fo' Miss Rose; dey wuz to come up right smart, so de boy say."

"Oh, more flowers. Who from?" cried Hazel, eagerly, while Wilkins strained his ears to catch the reply.

"From Mr. Sherrill," said Rose, opening the little envelope.

What she read on the card caused the blood to mount

higher and higher, till temples and forehead flushed pink, then as suddenly to recede.

"May I open them, Rose, and won't you wear some if they're from Jack?"

"Yes," said Rose, simply. The two girls leaned over the box as Hazel took off the wrapper — then the cover — then the inner tissue papers — then —

Suddenly a shriek of laughter, followed by another, penetrated to Wilkins, who was lingering on the stairs; he came softly back again. Peal after peal of wild merriment issued from Rose's room. Within, Rose in her petticoat and bodice had flung herself on the bed in an ecstasy of mirth, and Hazel was rolling over on the rug as was the wont of Budd and Cherry in the old days on Mount Hunger. The maid looked from one to the other, and, no longer able to keep from joining in the merriment, although she did not know the cause, left the room, only to find Wilkins with perturbed face just outside the door.

"'Pears lake dere wor sumfin' queah 'bout dat yere box —" he began; but the maid only shook with laughter and laid her finger on her lips, motioning him into the back hall.

"Did you ever?" cried Hazel, when she recovered her breath.

"No, I never," said Rose, wiping away the tears, for she had laughed till she cried. "Let's take another look."

They bent over the box, and took out its contents; then went off again into fits of seemingly inextinguishable laughter; for, neatly folded beneath the tissue paper, lay

four sets of Jack's new light-weight, white silk pajamas, which he had purchased that afternoon, in order to take back to Cambridge with him. On the card, which Rose still held in her hand, was written, " Wear these for my sake."

"What will you say to him, Rose?" said Hazel, sitting up on the rug with her hands clasped about her knees.

"I don't know," said Rose, proceeding to dress. "I can't *wear* them, that's certain." And again the absurdity of the situation presented itself to her. "And I can't apologize for not wearing them. Neither can I take it for granted that he was going to send me flowers, and explain that he sent me these instead."

"How awfully careless," said Hazel, interrupting her; "he must have had something on his mind not to take the pains to look, even."

Rose flushed. "It will be best to let the matter drop, and say nothing about it," she replied in a cool, toploftical tone that amazed, as well as mystified, her little hostess.

"Why, Rose, I think Jack ought to know about it. I'll tell him, if you don't want to."

"Thank you, Hazel, but I don't need your good offices in this matter."

Hazel rose from the rug, and going over to Rose, laid both hands on her shoulders and looked straight up into her eyes.

"Now, Rose Blossom, please don't speak to me in that way. You're so queer! First you're nice about Jack, and then you're horrid; and when you're that way, you aren't nice to *me* a bit — and I don't like it, and I don't

19

blame Jack for not liking it either," she added emphatically. "I remember papa said a year ago that Jack was 'all heart' for a good many girls, old and young — but I can tell you what, he won't have any for you, if you whiff round so."

Hazel in her earnestness gave Rose a little shake. Rose smiled, and, bending her head, kissed her, saying, "F. and F. and you know, Hazel."

"Oh, I know all about 'forgiving and forgetting,' but I don't like it just the same. He's my cousin and the dearest fellow in the world, and I don't like to have him treated so."

"How about his treating me?" said Rose, pointing to the innocent box of underwear, "forgetting even to look, or not caring enough, to see if I had the right package?"

"Oh, that's different — perhaps the florist made a mistake."

"The florist!" Rose laughed merrily. "I never knew that gentlemen's underwear and roses grew on the same bush. — There's Wilkins, and I'm not ready."

"De coachman say it's a pow'ful col' night, an' Miss Rose bettah take some mo' wraps."

"Thank you, Wilkins," Hazel flew into the dressing-room for a long fur cloak of her mother's which she had used to wear to the dancing-classes. She wrapped it about Rose, who stooped suddenly and kissed her again, whispering, "Hazel, you've all spoiled me, that's what's the matter, — but I'll be good to Jack, for your sake as well as for my own."

" Now you 're what Doctor Heath calls papa, the most splendid fellow in the world. There now — I won't crush your gown — " A kiss — " Good-night. You look like an angel ! "

Mr. Clyde thought so, too, as he watched her coming downstairs. She slipped off the cloak as she stood beneath the soft, but brilliant hall lights. " Do I look all right ? " she asked earnestly, for she had fallen into the habit, before going anywhere with him or Hazel, of asking for their criticism.

" I should say so — but where are the flowers ? I miss them."

"I thought I would n't wear any to-night, just for a change."

" A woman's whim, Rose. But I can't say that you need them — Now, what 's to pay ? " he said to himself, as he helped her into the carriage. " I saw Jack at Dord's this afternoon, and, evidently, something was in the wind. I hope it has n't been taken out of his sails."

" Sumfin' mighty queah 'bout dat yere box," murmured Wilkins to himself, as he closed the door, " but Miss Rose doan' need no flow's. Nebber see sech h — Fo' de good Lawd ! Wha' fo' yo' hyar ? Yo' Minna-Lu, — skeerin' mah day-lights out o' mah, shoolin' 'roun' b'hin' dat por' chair, — jes' lake bug'lahs."

Minna-Lu gurgled. " Yo' jes' straight, Wilkins ; nebber see sech ha'r. Huccome I 'se hyar ? Jes' to see dat lillum-white angel — "

" Yo' go 'long, wha' yo' b'long," growled Wilkins, not

yet having recovered from his fright. And Minna-Lu went, with the radiant vision still before her round, black eyes.

Jack felt a queer tightening about his lower jaw, and one heart-throb, apparently in his throat, as he entered Aunt Carrie's reception-room. Then, as with one glance he swept Rose from the crown of her head to the hem of her dress, a hot, rushing wave of indignant feeling mastered him — he knew he had staked his all (so a man at twenty-two is apt to think) and lost. He braced himself, mentally and physically. He was n't going to show the white-feather — not he.

But Rose — Rose was mystifying, captivating, cordial, merry, and altogether charming. She knocked out all Jack's calculations as to life, love, women, girls in general, and one girl in particular, at one fell swoop. He was brought, necessarily, into unstable equilibrium, so far as his feelings were concerned — his head he was obliged to keep level on account of the various figures. Several other heads were variously askew, and would have been turned, likewise, for good and all, had the wearer of her mother's India-mull wedding-dress been possessed of a fortune.

Rose developed social powers that evening that furnished food for conversation for Aunt Carrie and Mr. Clyde, who watched her with pride and pleasure. She was evidently enjoying herself thoroughly, and her enjoyment proved contagious.

" After all," said Jack as, between figures, he found

opportunity for a whispered word or two; "this is n't half so fine a dance as the one in the barn, last September."

"Why, that's just what I was thinking, myself, that very minute!"

"You were?"

"Yes."

The brown eyes and the blue ones met with such evidence of a perfect understanding, that Jack failed to see Maude Seaton, who had approached him for the purpose of taking him out in the four-in-hand.

"Oh, I beg your pardon," said Jack, starting to his feet, "it's the 'four-in-hand.'"

"Yes, and I think you 'll have to be put into the traces again," she said, with a meaning smile.

"Not I," retorted Jack, merrily, "I kicked over them nearly a year ago."

"So I heard," replied Miss Seaton, sweetly; and Jack wondered what she meant.

When Jack found himself again beside Rose, he decided that, flowers or no flowers, he would ask for an explanation. But his first attempt was met with such a bewilderingly merry smile, and such confident assurance that explanations were not in order, that it proved a successful failure.

When, at last, in the early morning hours he was seated before the open fire in his bedroom, pulling away reflectively at his pipe, he had time to think it over. He came to the conclusion that it was trivial in him to have staked his all on her wearing those flowers, for she certainly —

certainly had led him to think that she was anything but indifferent to him.

"That look now," mused Jack. "I don't believe that a girl like Rose Blossom would look that way if she did n't mean it — if she did n't care. No other girl *could* look that way." He reached for his watch on the dressing-case. "I shall get good two hours' sleep before that early train. — What's that?" He noticed for the first time, that on the bed lay a familiar-looking box in a brown paper wrapper. In a trice he had broken the string, whisked off the cover, scattered the tissue paper right and left. — There lay the violets, white, and sweet, and almost as fresh as when he gave them his virgin kiss nearly twelve hours before.

Jack sat down stupefied on the bed. *What had he given her, anyway?* He thought intensely for a full minute.

"Great Scott! the pajamas!" And then Jack Sherrill rolled over on the bed, ignoring the damage to dress suit and violets, and, burying his face in the pillow, gave vent to a smothered yell.

There was a merry exchange of notes between Cambridge and New York during the next two weeks, and Rose had promised to wear any flowers — and only his — he might send her for the ball at Mrs. Fenlick's the middle of February, and for which Jack was coming on. It would occur during the last week of Rose's visit, and Jack thought that possibly — possibly, — well, he could n't define just what " possibly;" but it proved to be an infinitely absorbing one, and Jack felt it was "now or never" with him.

Mrs. Heath had claimed Rose as her guest for the last three weeks, and the days were filled with pleasures. On the Saturday before the ball, and a week before Rose was to return to Mount Hunger, two seats in a box at the opera had been sent in to Mrs. Heath from a friend.

"Look at these, Rose!" Mrs. Heath exclaimed, showing her the note. "Just exactly what you were wishing to hear, and we thought we could not arrange it for next week. That opera has been changed for to-day's matinée, and now you can hear both Lohengrin and Siegfried."

Rose clapped her hands. "I've just longed to hear Lohengrin; Mrs. Ford and her son have played so much of it to me. I think it's perfectly beautiful."

"I'm so sorry I can't go, dear; but I made a positive engagement for this afternoon and it must not be broken. But I'll send round for Cousin Anna May. She does n't care much for the opera, but she will chaperone you. She's not much of a talker either, so you can enjoy the music in peace. People chatter so abominably there."

From the moment the orchestra sounded the first notes of that pathetic and thrillingly appealing fore-word of the overture, Rose was lost to the world about her. She was glad of the darkness, glad no one could see or notice her intense absorption in the opening scene. Even when the lights were turned on between the acts, and the subdued murmur in the house rose to a confusing babble, she was living in the story of Elsa and her lover Knight. Elderly

Cousin Anna May, seeing this, let her alone, thinking to herself : — "One has to be young to be so enthusiastic over this wornout theme."

The curtain fell ; the house was brilliant with lights ; confusion of talk, confusion of merry chat and laughter were all about Rose ; but she sat unheeding, wondering if the element of evil would be turned into a factor of good. Her heart was aching with the intensity of feeling for the two lovers. Suddenly, a few words behind her arrested her attention. She sat with her back to the speakers — two girls in the next box, who had annoyed her more than once by their ceaseless, whispering gabble.

"I told Maude I did n't believe it."

"What did she say?"

"She said it was gospel truth."

"Do tell me what it was, I won't tell."

"Sure?"

"Not a soul."

"Promise?"

"Why, of course. They say he 's got oceans of money."

"Piles —. He 's got his mother's fortune and will have his father's. Besides, his Uncle Gray is a bachelor, and so Jack will have that, too. Maude says he 's the best catch in New York."

"I heard Sam say he was in an awfully fast set in college ; but Sam likes him awfully well. Have you seen him ?"

"Oh, yes, lots. Maude let me see him one night before dinner at Newport. I used to see him playing polo at the grounds. I think he 's fascinating — just like Lohengrin."

" But what was it? Hurry up, do."

" You 'll never tell ? "

" Never."

The voice was slightly lowered — confused with the munching of Huyler's; and Rose, with hypersensitive hearing, could distinguish only a word or two, or a detached sentence.

" I don't think that's so awful. Sam does that, too, and he 's just as nice a brother as I want."

" Oh, I don't know anything about that; but I know it 's true, for Maude said so." In the increasing confusion of talk in the house, the voices were suddenly raised, and Rose caught every word.

" I 'll ask Sam — " began the other, dropping her opera glass and stooping to pick it up.

" If you do, Minna Grayson, I 'll never speak to you again."

" Oh, I forgot — " laughed the other. " Tell us some more, it 's awfully exciting."

" I won't either," said the other, in a huffy tone. Evidently, they were school-girls in for the matinée.

" Oh, *do;* what *did* Maude say ? "

" She said, ' No,' " chuckled the other triumphantly.

" But think of his money ! "

" She said she did n't mind; she 's got money enough of her own, anyway, if she does skimp me on allowance ever since grandmamma died."

"I heard Sam say last Christmas when I was home for vacation, that he was perfectly devoted to that new girl the Clydes have taken up."

"Yes. Maude says it's one of his fads. She gives him six months more to get over it."

"Everybody says she is a perfect beauty. Sam says that Mrs. Fenlick says she is the most beautiful creature off of a canvas she has ever seen."

"Oh, Maude says Mrs. Fenlick raves over everything new. She, the girl, I mean, made a dead set at him a year ago when he happened to meet her up in the mountains. You know they had a riding-party last August. But now they say she seems to be setting her cap for Hazel's father — he has a million or two more than Jack, and she's as poor as a church-mouse."

"I didn't know that, — poor?"

"Yes, awfully. Why, Maude says she's seen her selling berries for a living somewhere up in the mountains — oh, way back in them. People call them the Lost Nation, they're so far back; and Maude says she wore patched shoes and an old calico dress — Sh! — Now we're going to have that bridal march, isn't it dandy? It ought to be a part of the marriage ceremony, Maude says. I'm so glad it's coming; — Tum, tum, ty tum — tum, tum, ty tum — here's just one more candied violet — tum, tum, ty tum, tum, ty tum, ty ty tum, ty tum — Oh, look! Isn't Elsa just lovely — "

A burst of applause greeted the beautiful prima donna. Upon Rose's ears it fell like the thunder of a cataract, like the crash and roll of an avalanche. She stared at the exquisite scene before her with strained eyes. The music went on with all the troublous-sweet under-tones of love, and longing, and forever-parting. Not once did Rose stir until the curtain fell, then she turned to her companion : —

"Can we get out soon, Mrs. May? The air is a little close here."

"Certainly, my dear;" but to herself she said, "How intense she is. I'm thankful I never was so strung up over music."

XXIV

"OLD PUT"

"WHERE 's Rose?" said the Doctor as he came in that Saturday evening, and heard no welcoming voice from the library or the stairs.

"She came home from the opera with a frightful headache and has gone to bed. She said she did n't want any dinner, but I have insisted upon her having some toast and tea," replied his wife.

"Humph!" growled the Doctor; "Our wild rose can't stand such hot-house atmosphere. When does the Fenlicks' ball come off?"

"Next Wednesday; it will be a superb affair. Rose showed me her card the other day, and if you will believe me, it 's full, although Jack Sherrill gets the lion's share."

"How do you think things are coming on there, wifie?"

"Why, he 's devoted to her whenever he can be; you know what Mrs. Pearsell told us about last summer, but — "

"But what?" said the Doctor, a little impatiently. "Generally, wifie, you can see prospective wedding-cake *if* two young people so much as look twice at each other."

Mrs. Heath laughed and nodded. " Yes, I know; but in just this case, I don't know. You can't tell anything by her — and I fear, hubbie, that Jack Sherrill is n't *quite* good enough for her."

" Not quite good enough for her ! " The Doctor almost shouted in his earnestness. " Jack Sherrill not quite good enough for — "

" Sh — sh, dear ! " His wife held up her hand in warning. " Someone might hear."

" Let 'em hear, then," growled the Doctor. " I say Rose is n't a bit too good for him. — Look here, wifie, — " he drew her towards him and down upon the arm of his easy-chair, " Jack 's all right every time — do you understand ? *All right !* "

" Ye-es," admitted his wife rather reluctantly. " I know he 's a great favorite of yours. But Mrs. Grayson says he 's in a very fast set at Harvard — "

" Now look here, wifie, don't you let those women with their eternal hunger for gossip say anything to you about Jack. I tell you there is n't another fellow I know, who, placed as he is, can set up so many white stones to mark his short life's pathway as John Sherrill's only son. For heaven's sake, give him the credit for them. I know what I saw on Mount Hunger a year ago, and I know and believe what I see."

" Well, I only hope he won't flirt with her — " began Mrs. Heath. Her husband interrupted her:

"Flirt with *her!*" The Doctor chuckled. "I'll warrant Jack won't do any flirting with her — it'll be the
other way round sooner than that! Just say good-night
to Rose for me when you go up stairs, and tell her if she
isn't down bright and early Sunday morning, I'll prescribe
for her."

But there was no need for the Doctor's prescription; for
Rose was down for breakfast, and although white cheeks
and heavy eyes caused the Doctor to draw his eyebrows
together in a straight line over the bridge of his nose,
nothing was said of there being any need for a prescription.
But after breakfast he drew her into the library and
placed her in an easy-chair before the blazing fire.

"There now," he said in his own kindliest tones, "sit
there and dream while wifie makes ready for church, and
after that you shall go with me for an official drive. The
air will do you good. I can't send such white roses" —
he patted her cheek — "back to Mount Hunger; what
would mother say?"

To his amazement Rose buried her face in both hands;
a half-suppressed sob startled him.

"Why, Rose-pose! What's the matter, little girl?
Headachey — nerves unstrung — too much opera? Here,
come into the office where we shan't be disturbed, and
tell me all about it."

But Rose shook her head, lifted it from her hands, and
smiled through the welling tears.

"I'm a perfect goose, but — but — I believe I'm getting
just a little bit homesick for Mount Hunger, and I'm not

going to stay for Mrs. Fenlick's ball. I know mother needs me at home — I can just feel it in her letters, and I know I want — I want her."

"Don't blame you a bit, Rose, — but is n't this rather sudden? Any previous attacks?"

"No — and I know it seems dreadfully ungrateful to you and dear Mrs. Heath to say so, and it is n't that — I 'd love to be with just you two; but it 's this dreadful feeling comes over me, and I know I ought to go."

"And go you shall, Rose," said the Doctor, emphatically, but oh! so kindly and understandingly. "Go back to all the dear ones there — and when you come again, don't give us the tail-end of your visit, will you?"

"Indeed, I won't," answered Rose, earnestly, "and if it were only you and Mrs. Heath, I 'd love to stay, but — but — "

"No need to say anything more, Rose, wifie and I understand it perfectly — " ("I wish the dickens I did!" was his thought) — "Tell wifie when she comes down, and meanwhile I 'll send round for the brougham and we 'll take a little drive in the Park before office hours."

Rose patted his hand, and her silence spoke for her.

"Here 's a pretty kettle of fish!" said the Doctor to himself as he went to the telephone. "I wish I could get to the bottom of it."

And thus it came about that a cool, dignified note, not expressive of any particular regret, was mailed to Cambridge on Sunday afternoon, and a long letter to Mount

Hunger telling them to be sure to meet her on Tuesday at Barton's, and filled with wildly enthusiastic expressions of delight in anticipation of the home-coming. And on Tuesday afternoon, as the train sped onwards, following the curves of the frozen Connecticut, and the snow-covered mountains on the Vermont side began to crowd its banks, Rose felt a lightening of the heart and an uplifting of spirits.

The bitterness and shame and shock she had experienced, in consequence of that one little bite of the fruit of the Tree of the Knowledge of Good and Evil, seemed to diminish with every mile that increased the distance between her and the frothing whirlpool of the great city's gayeties. All the way up, until the mountains loomed in sight, there had been hot, indignant protest in her thoughts. At first, indeed, it had been hatred.

"I hate it all — hate it, *hate* it!" she found herself saying over and over again after the good-byes had been said at the station, and Hazel and Mr. Clyde and Doctor Heath had supplied her with flowers and magazines for the long day's journey. It was all she could think or feel at the time; but soon the little pronoun changed, and the thought grew more bitter:

"I hate him! How could he — how dared he do as he did! Because I am poor, I suppose. Oh! I wish I could make him pay for it. I wish I could make him love me really and truly, and then just *scorn* him! But what a fool I am — as if he *could* love after what I heard — oh, why did I hear it! I wish I may never see his face again, and I wish I'd stayed at home where I belong — I hate him!" — And so on "da capo" hour after hour, and the incessant chugetty-chug-chug of the express furnished the rhythmic, basal tone for the bitter motive.

It was long after lunch time, and the train of thought had not changed, when Rose's eye fell upon the dainty basket Martin had placed in the rack.

"This is a pretty state of mind to go home to Martie in!" she said to herself, rising and taking down the basket. "I have n't eaten a good meal since last Saturday at lunch, and I 'm — why, I believe I 'm hungry!"

She opened the basket, and loving evidence of Minna-Lu's admiration tempted her to pick a little here and there — a stuffed olive or two, a roast quail, a delicate celery sandwich, a quince tart, a bunch of Hamburg grapes. Soon Rose was feasting on all the good things, and her harsh thoughts began to soften. How kind they all were! And *they* truly loved her — and what had they not done for her comfort and pleasure! Rose, setting her pretty teeth deep into a third quince tart, looked out of the window and almost exclaimed aloud at the sight. The vanguard of the Green Mountains closed in the upper end of the river-valley along which they were speeding. It was home that was behind all that! The thought still further softened her.

What? Carry her bitterness and disappointed pride back into that dear, peaceful home? Not she! "They shall never know — never!" she said to herself — "I 'm not Molly Stark for nothing, and there are others in the

20

world beside Jack Sherrill." And so she continued to speak cold comfort to herself for the next four hours until the brakeman called "Barton's River!"

There beyond the platform was the old apple-green pung!—and yes! father and March and Budd and dear old Chi anxiously scanning the coaches.

Home at last! and such a home-coming! How busy the tongues were for a week afterwards! How wildly gay was Rose, who kept them laughing over the many queer doings of the metropolis, over Wilkins and Minna-Lu and Martin and Mrs. Scott! And how lovingly she spoke of Hazel's charming hospitality and of Mr. Clyde's thoughtfulness for her pleasure, although, as she mentioned his name, a wave of color mounted to the roots of her hair at the ugly thought that would intrude. Chi listened with all his ears, enjoying it with the rest; but once upstairs in his room over the shed, he would sit down on the side of his bed to ponder a little the gay doings of his Rose-pose among the " high-flyers," and then turn in with a sigh and a muttered:

"'T ain't Rose-pose. I knew how 't would be. — There's a screw loose somewhere ; but she 's handsome ! — handsome as a picture, 'n' I 'd give a dollar to know if she 's cut that other one out."

" Valentines seem kind of scarce this year," he remarked rather grimly, a few days after her arrival, as late in the afternoon, he returned from Barton's with little mail and no boxes of flowers. " It 's the sixteenth day of February, but it might be Fast Day for all that handful of mail would

show for it!" He placed the package on Mrs. Blossom's
work-table at which Rose was sitting busy with some
sewing. They were alone in the room.

Rose laughed merrily. "Goodness, Chi! you want us
to have more than our share. We had a perfect deluge
last year when Hazel was here; you know it makes a
difference without her. You said yourself that there was
a good deal of bulk, but it was pretty light weight — don't
you remember?"

Chi elevated one bushy eyebrow. "I ain't forgot; but I
don't know about it's bein' any *Deluge* — it appeared to
me it was a Shadrach, Meshach, 'n' Abednego kind of a
business — " He gave the back log a kick that sent the
sparks up the chimney in a grand pyrotechnic show.
"Seems as if I could see those posies, now, a-shrivellin'
in the fireplace. Never thought you treated those innocent
things quite on the square, Rose-pose!"

Rose's head was bent low over her work. Chi went on,
bracing himself to the self-imposed task of enlightening
her : —

"I don't want to meddle, Rose, in anybody's business,
but it ain't set well with me ever since — the way you
treated those roses; 'n', after all, we're both members of
the Nobody's Business But Our Own Society, 'n' if anybody's goin' to meddle, perhaps I'm the one. I've thought
a good many times you would n't have been quite so harsh
with 'em, if you had n't overlooked this in your flare-
up — " He drew out of his breast pocket a card — Jack's
— with the verse on the back. "Read that, 'n' see if you

ain't dropped a stitch somewhere that you can pick up in time." He handed her the card.

Rose looked up surprised, but with burning cheeks. She took the card, read the verse, turned it over on the name side, and rose from her chair. Every particle of color had left her face. She went over to the fireplace, and, bending, dropped the little piece of pasteboard upon the glowing back-log.

" The sentiment belongs with the roses, Chi; don't let's have any more Shadrach, Meshach, and Abednego business — I'm tired of it." She spoke indifferently; then, resuming her seat, called out in a cheery voice :

" Martie, won't you come here a minute, and see if I have put on this gore right?"

" I'll come, dear."

Chi, nonplussed, irritated, repulsed, set his teeth hard and abruptly left the room.

Outside in the shed he clenched his fist and shook it vigorously at the closed door of the long-room: " — By George Washin'ton!" he muttered, " I'll make you pay up for that, Rose Blossom. You can't come any of your high-flyers' games on me — Just you put that in your pipe and smoke it! Thunderation! what gets into women and girls, sometimes?" He seized the milk-pails from the shelf and hurried to the barn nearly running down Cherry in his wrathful excitement.

" Look out there, Cherry! You're always getting round under foot!" he said, harshly, and stumbled on, regaining his balance, only to be met by Budd in the barn.

"Just clear out now, Budd! I ain't goin' to stand your foolin'. Let alone of that stanchion," he roared. "Always worryin' the cow if she looks once at you sideways. Get *up*, there — " His right boot helped the amazed cow forwards into the stall, and the milk drummed into the pail as if the poor creature were being milked by a dummy-engine with more pressure of steam on than it could well stand.

Budd flew into the woodshed and found Cherry still standing, in a half-dazed condition, where Chi had left her. They compared notes immediately to the detriment and defamation of Chi's character. Then they carried their budget of woe to their mother.

"Chi is worried, children; you must n't mind if he is a little cross now and then. He feels dreadfully about the prospect of this war, as we all do, and that's his way of showing it."

"Well, if he's going to be so cross at us, I wish he'd clear out an' go to war!" retorted Budd, smarting under the unjust treatment.

"I'm only afraid he will if we have one," said Mrs. Blossom, sadly. "But, oh, I hope and pray we may be spared that!"

But Budd continued to grumble, and Cherry to be suspiciously sniffy, until their father's return; and then at the supper table they listened greedily to all the talk of their elders, that had for its absorbing theme the prospective war.

As the spring days lengthened, and the sun drew northward, the tiny cloud on the country's peaceful horizon grew larger and darker, until it cast its shadow throughout the length and breadth of the land, and men's faces grew stern and troubled and women prayed for peace.

With the lengthening days Chi showed signs of increasing restlessness. "It ain't any use, Ben," he said, one soft evening in early May, as the family, with the exception of the younger children, sat on the porch discussing the latest news, "I 've got to go."

"Oh, Chi!" broke from Mrs. Blossom and Rose. They cried out as if hurt. Mr. Blossom grasped Chi's right hand, and March wrung the other.

"I can't stand it," he went on; "we 've been sassed enough as a nation, 'n' some of us have got to teach those foreigners we ain't goin' to turn the other cheek just coz we 're slapped on one. When I wasn't higher than Budd, my great-grandfather — you remember him, Ben, lived the other side of the Mountain — put his father's old Revolution'ry musket (the one, you know, Rose-pose, as I 've used in the N. B. B. O. O.) into my hands, 'n' says: 'Don't you stand no sass, Malachi Graham, from no foreigners. — Just shoot away, 'n' holler, "Hands off" every time, 'n' they 'll learn their lesson easy and early, 'n' respect you in the end.' And I ain't forgot it."

"Chi," Mrs. Blossom's voice was tremulous, "you won't go till you 're asked, or needed, will you?"

"I ain't goin' to wait to be asked, Mis' Blossom; I 'd ruther be on hand to be refused. That 's my way. So I thought I 'd be gettin' down along this week — "

" This week ! " Rose interrupted him with a cry and a half-sob. " Oh, Chi! dear old Chi! *must* you go? What if — what if — " Rose's voice broke, and Chi gulped down a big lump, but answered, cheerily :

" Well, Rose-pose, *what if?* Ain't I Old Put? 'n' ain't you Molly Stark? 'n' ain't Lady-bird Barbara Frietchie? — There, just read that — " he handed a letter to March, who gave it back to him, saying, in a husky voice, that it was too dark to read.

" Well, then we 'll adjourn into the house, 'n' light up. — There now," he said, as he lighted the lamp and set it on the table beside March, " here 's your letter, Markis, read ahead."

March read with broken voice :

4 EAST —TH STREET, NEW YORK,
May 5, 1898.

DEAR FRIEND CHI, — I never thought when I joined the N. B. B. O. O. Society, that I 'd have to be really brave about real war ; — and now dear old Jack is going off to Cuba with Little Shaver and all those cow-boys, — and it 's dreadful! Uncle John is about sick over it, for, you know, Jack is all he has. Papa is going to keep the house open all summer; he says there is no telling what may happen.

We have made no plans for the summer, for our hearts are so heavy on Jack's account — his last year in Harvard, too! He told me to tell you he would find out if there is a chance for you in the new cavalry regiment he has joined. He looked so pleased when I told him; he read your letter, and I told him how you wanted to go with him, and he said: " Dear old Chi, I 'd like to have him for my bunkie " — and told me what it meant. He told me to tell you to be prepared for a telegram at any moment.

I must stop now; papa wants me to go out with him. Give my love to *all*, and tell Mother Blossom and Rose I will write them more particulars in a few days.

If you come to New York, you know a room will be ready for you in the home of your

Loving friend,

HAZEL CLYDE.

There was silence for a while in the room; then Mr. Blossom spoke:

"How are you going, Chi?"

"I'm goin' to jog along down with Fleet, 'n' take it kind of easy — thought I'd cross the Mountain, 'n' strike in on the old post-road; 'n' follow on down by old Ticonderogy, — I've always wanted to see that, — then across to Saratogy 'n' Albany, 'n' foller the river. You can't go amiss of New York if you stick to that."

Again there was a prolonged silence. Chi hemmed, and moved uneasily on his chair, while he fumbled about in his trousers' pocket. He pulled out a piece of crumpled, yellow paper.

"S'pose I might just as well make a clean breast of it." He tried to laugh, but it was a failure. "Jack's telegram came along last night, 'n' I thought, maybe I'd better be gettin' my duds together to-night, Mis' Blossom, as 't will be a mighty early start — before any of you are up," he added, hastily.

The two women broke down then, and Mr. Blossom and March followed Chi out to the barn.

The household, save for the younger children, was early astir — before sunrise. Mrs. Blossom had prepared a hearty breakfast, and Rose was rolling up a few pairs of her father's stockings to put in the netted saddle-bag which Chi was wont to use in hunting.

"Tell March to call Chi, Rose," said her mother. "His breakfast is ready, I hear him in the barn."

Rose ran out in the dawning light to find her father and March just coming towards the house.

"Why, where's Chi?" she cried.

For answer, her father pointed to the woodlands. She looked just in time to see in the soft gray of the early morn the horse and rider rise to the three-railed fence that separated the pasture from the woodlands. He was following the trail he had indicated to Jack — "through the woods 'n' acre or two of brush, 'n' then some pretty steep sliding down the other side, 'n' a dozen rods or so of swimmin', 'n' a tough old clamber up the bank —"

Some ten days afterward, late on a warm afternoon in May, there rode into New York City by the way of the Bronx and Harlem, a middle-aged man on a bright bay horse. The animal's gait was a noticeable one, a long, loping gallop, that covered the ground in a manner that roused the admiration of the drivers on the speedway. The tall, loose-jointed body of the rider apparently loped along with the horse — their movements were identical. The saddle was an old-fashioned cavalry one of the early sixties. A netted saddle-bag and a rolled rubber coat were fastened to the crupper. A light-weight hunting rifle was slung on a strap over the man's shoulder. At the northern entrance to the Park he drew rein beside a mounted policeman.

"Can you tell me if I'm on the right track to this house?"

He took a card from the pocket of his dusty blue flannel shirt and handed it to the policeman.

The city guardian nodded assent. "But you can't take that gun along with you; you're inside city limits and liable to arrest."

"'Gainst the law, hey? Well, I've come from a pretty law-abiding state, 'n' ain't goin' to get into rows with you fellers —" He laid a brown, knotty, work-roughened finger on the policeman's immaculate blue coat — "I'd trust that color as far as I could see. Where shall I leave the rifle?"

The city guard unbent as the kindly voice yielded such undefiant obedience to his demand. "You can leave it with me now, — I'm off my beat by seven, and live over east of this —" he handed back the card — "and I'll leave it at the house if you're going to be there."

"All right, that'll suit me. Yes, I'm goin' to put up there for a day or two, maybe."

"Off on a hunting trip?"

"You bet — goin' on a big, old, U. S. A. hunt for a lot of darned foreigners in Cuby."

The policeman held out his hand and grasped the stranger's. "You're one of them?"

"Yes, I come down to join a cavalry regiment. Jack

Sherrill, he belongs, too. Great rider — can't be beat.
Ever seen him round here on Little Shaver?"

The policeman smiled. "No, but I'd like to see *you*
again — "

"Maybe you will; but I'd better be getting along before sundown, — 'gainst the law to ride this horse a piece
through those woods?" He pointed into the Park.

"Oh, no, that's all right. Keep along till you come to
Seventieth Street, and inquire; and then turn into Fifth
Avenue — east — and you're there."

"Much obliged. Like to show you a trail or two up
in Vermont when you come that way. Get, Fleet." The
animal set forward into a long, loping gallop.

The brilliant, light green of the May foliage was en-
hanced by the level rays of the setting sun, as the man
turned his horse into Fifth Avenue and drew rein to a
rapid walk. Many a one paused to look at him as he
paced over the asphalt. He was looking up at the man-
sions of the Upper East Side. Soon he halted at the
corner of a side street and gazed up at the first house, the
end of which, with the conservatory, was on the Avenue,
but the entrance on the side street. "That's the place,"
he spoke to himself, — "don't see a hitchin'-post handy, so
I'll just have to tie up to this electric light stand. Iron,
by thunder! — Well, there ain't any risk so long as 't isn't
lit, 'n' there ain't a tempest."

Leaving his horse firmly tied to the standard he
stepped up on the low, broad stoop of "Number 4," and
looked for the bell. Not finding any he knocked forcibly

on the carved iron grill that protected the plate-glass doors.

The great doors flew open, and a face — "blacker 'n thunder" — as the man said to himself, scowled on the interloper.

"Wha' fo' yo' come hyar, yo' — " He got no further. A horny hand was extended, and a cheery voice, that broke into a laugh, spoke the assuaging words:

"Guess you 're Wilkins, ain't you? I 've heard Lady-bird tell 'bout you till I feel as if we 'd been pretty well acquainted goin' on nigh two year now."

By this time Wilkins' face was one broad beam. He slapped his free hand on his knee:

"Yo 's Mister Chi, for sho' — dere ain't no need yo' tellin'. Yo' jes' come straight in, Mister Chi; Marse John an' little Missy jes' gone fo' ah drive in de Park. Dey 'll be in any minute. Yo' room 's all ready, an' little Missy put de flow'rs in fresh dis yere mornin' — ' 'Case,' she say, ' Wilkins, dere ain't no tellin' when Chi 's comin'.' "

"Sho'," Chi interrupted him, brushing the back of his hand hastily across his eyes. "I can't come in now, Wil-kins, coz I 've got to stay here 'n' watch my horse — I 'll sit here on the steps a spell 'n' cool off till Mr. Clyde gets home, 'n' he 'll help me see to puttin' up Fleet for the night. His legs are a little mite swollen near the hocks, 'n' I 'm goin' to rub him down myself."

"De coachman jes' tend to yo' hoss like 's ef 't wor yo'se'f, Mister Chi. I 'll jes' call up de stable bo', 'n' he 'll rub him down wif sp'r'ts, an' shine him up till he look jes' lake new mahog'ny. Jes' yo' come — dere dey come now ! "

Chi was at the curbstone to welcome them.

"Chi! O Chi!" Hazel rose up in the trap at sight of the well-known figure, and Chi, laying his hand firmly on Martin's shoulder, put him aside as he sprang to open the door and let down the steps, reached up both arms, and took Hazel out as tenderly as on the night of her first arrival at the farmhouse on the Mountain. And then and there Hazel gave him a kiss, and Mr. Clyde grasped his hands in both his, and the wide hall doors that Wilkins had thrown open to their fullest extent closed upon the re-united friends.

"'E 's a 'ansome 'oss," Martin remarked to the coach-man, as he mounted Fleet to take him to the stable; " Hi 'ave n't seen a 'ansomer since Hi 've bean in the States."

A few days after the hall doors were again flung wide, but not to their fullest extent, and Wilkins' face grew strangely tremulous when he heard Hazel and Mr. Clyde, Jack and Chi coming down the broad hall stairs. Martin was proudly leading Fleet and Little Shaver up and down in front of the house.

"Jack! O Jack! I can't bear to have you go — but I *will* be brave." Hazel smiled through the raining tears. She clung to him and kissed him. He put her aside, ran out to Little Shaver, and flung himself on before Chi had said good-bye.

"Take care of Jack, Chi," she whispered, patting his hand.

" I will, Barbara Frietchie." He pointed to the flag that, in the east wind blowing in from the Sound, was waving over the entrance, gripped Mr. Clyde's hand, then Wilkins', and, apparently, stepped into the saddle.

" Quick, quick, Wilkins! lower the flag, and let me have it." Wilkins sprang to obey. Hazel seized it, and rushed up stairs to the drawing-room, the windows of which over-looked the Avenue. One of them was open; she leaned out; and as Fleet and Little Shaver turned the corner, their riders, looking up, saw the young girl's figure in the opening. She was waving the symbol of their Country's life and their manhood's loyalty.

They halted, baring their heads for a moment — then without once looking back, galloped down the Avenue.

XXV

SAN JUAN

NOTWITHSTANDING it was a hot day in the first week of July, Mrs. Spillkins had decided to have a " quilting-bee." Having made up her mind, after consulting with Miss Melissa and Miss Elvira, she lost no time in summoning Uncle Israel from the barn, and making known her plans. Uncle Israel mildly objected.

" Kinder hot fer er quiltin'-bee, ain't it, Hannah ? "

" 'T is pretty hot," Mrs. Spillkins admitted, wiping the perspiration from her face with her apron, " but we 'll have it to-morrow 'long 'bout four. You get the frames and rollers out, Israel, from the back garret, an' then I want you to go up to Mis' Blossom's an' ask 'em to come, an' get word to the other folks on the Mountain."

" I 'll go, Hannah, but I dunno 'bout Mis' Blossom 'n' Rose comin' ter er quiltin'-bee jest 'bout this time. They 're feelin' pretty low 'bout Chi off thar in Cuby ; news hez come thet ther 's ben fightin' — "

" I know that, Israel ; I 've thought of that, too ; but, mebbe, it 'll do 'em good, just to change the scene a little. Anyway, you ask 'em."

" Jest ez ye say, Hannah."

The sun was setting when Uncle Israel made his appearance on the porch where the whole family was assembled with Alan Ford. They had but one topic for conversation.

Uncle Israel gave his invitation, and added: "Hannah thought ye 'd better come 'n' change the scene a leetle — she knowed ye 'd be kinder low-spereted 'bout now."

Mrs. Blossom held out her hand. "Thank you, Uncle Israel. Tell Mrs. Spillkins we will both come."

"Hannah wants your folks ter come, tew, Alan."

"Much obliged, Uncle Israel. I 'll tell mother and Ruth; I 'm sure they will enjoy it. Ruth said the other day she wished she might have a chance to see a quilting-bee while we are here. Shall I take your message over to Aunt Tryphosa?"

"Much obleeged, Alan. Thank ye, Rose," — as Rose brought out the large arm-chair and placed it for him; "I 'll set a spell 'n' rest me."

It was a typical northern midsummer night. Across the valley the mountains loomed, softly luminous, against the pale green translucent stretch of open sky in the west. There were no clouds; but high above and around there swept a long trail of motionless mist, flame-colored over the mountain tops, but darkening, with the coming of the night, into gray towards the east. The stars were not yet out. The veeries were choiring antiphonally in the woodlands.

An hour afterwards Alan Ford rose to go, and Uncle Israel soon followed his example.

"I 'll go down the woods'-road a piece with you, Uncle Israel," said Rose.

As she came back up the Mountain a cool breath drew

through the pines, and the spruces gave forth their resin-
ous fragrance upon the dewless night.   The stars were
brilliant in the dark blue deeps.

A midsummer night among the mountains of New
England! And far away in the sickening heat and wet,
the fever-laden exhalations of the tropics rose into the
nostrils of a man, who sat motionless in the rude field-
hospital, hastily improvised on the slope of San Juan,
watching, with his knees drawn up to his chin and his
hands clasping them, for some faint tremor in the still
face on the army blanket spread upon the ground.

The lantern cast its light full upon that still face. Suddenly the watcher bent forward; his keen eyes had de-
tected a twitch of an eyelid — a flutter in the muscles of
the throat. " Don't move him," the surgeon had said;
" the least movement will cause the final hemorrhage."

There was a catch of the breath — the eyes opened,
partly filmed.

" Jack ! " The watcher spoke, bending lower; his ear
over the other's lips.

" Chi — " it was a mere breath, but the man heard —
" I 'm — done for."

The watcher's hand, muscular, toil-hardened, sought the
nerveless one that was lying on the other's breast, and
closed upon it with a brooding pressure.   There was
silence for a few minutes. Then the horny hand felt a
feeble stirring of the fingers beneath the hardened palm —
they were fumbling weakly at a button.

The strong hand undid the button, gently — very gently,

without apparent movement. There was a motion of the nerveless fingers towards the place. Another breath : —

"Give — love — "

A long silence fell.

Mrs. Spillkins heaved a sigh of satisfaction: " We 've done an awful sight of work," she said, surveying the five quilts "run" and "tacked" and "knotted" in even rows and mathematically true squares; "but it seems as if they did n't eat a mite of supper, an' that strawberry short-cake was enough to melt in your mouth."

" What 'd I tell ye, Hannah? They 're worretin' 'bout Chi," said Uncle Israel. "They 've fit agin; Ben told me while he wuz waitin' with the team fer the womin-folks. He hed the mail, 'n' er telegram thet thet young feller, we see ridin' 'roun' here las' summer, wuz mortal wounded. He did n't want the womin-folks ter know it till he got 'em hum. They sot er sight by him."

Mrs. Spillkins threw up her hands: " Dear suz'y me ! " she exclaimed in a distressed voice. " What 'll they do ! I hope an' pray Malachi Graham ain't hurt none. I feel as if I ought to go right up there, an' see if there 's any-thing I can do."

"Better wait till the Cap'n comes hum, Hannah; he 'll hev the papers."

" I guess 't would be better," and Mrs. Spillkins pro-ceeded to fold up her quilts and " clear up" the best room.

The hot July days warmed the breast of the Mountain.

Over in the corn-patch the stalks had spindled and the swelling ears were ready to tassel. By word or look Rose had given no sign — and her mother wondered. The days wore on; the routine of daily work and life went on; but the younger children's voices were subdued when they spoke lovingly and longingly of Chi, and Rose sang no longer when she kneaded bread. They were days of suspense and heart misery for them all.

Two weeks had passed since that evening when Mr. Blossom had read to them the fatal despatch. No word had come from anyone save Hazel, who wrote that her father and Uncle John had started at once for Cuba, and that she hoped to be with the Blossoms the third week in July, for by that time they would know the whole truth.

They had been making ready Hazel's little bedroom, for she was expected in a few days. Rose was tacking up a white muslin curtain at the small window, when she heard her father call:

" Rose, come here a minute."

" Yes, father."

She went out on the porch with the hammer in her hand. " What is it, Popsey dear ? — Why, father, what — oh what —!"

With shaking hand her father held out a letter to her. Rose looked once — it was from Chi!

" I wish mother were here, daughter — but she'll be back soon. Let me know how it is with them all —." Mr. Blossom could say no more, for Malachi Graham was as near to him as a brother, and he was agonizing for his child. He went off to the barn, leaving Rose standing on the porch, staring as if fascinated at the superscription of the letter:

> To Miss Rose Blossom,
> Mill Settlement,
> Barton's River,
> Vermont.
> N. B. B. O. O. — To be opened by nobody but her.

Rose laid down the hammer mechanically, opened the envelope, and unfolded the piece of brown paper from out of which fluttered to the floor another and thicker slip, stained almost beyond recognition. With staring eyes and face as white as driven snow she read the few words scrawled in pencil on the brown slip: —

> DEAR ROSE-POSE, — I ain't no wish to meddle with anybody's business — but I 'm just obeying orders. The last words I heard Jack Sherrill speak, was "Give — love," and he fumbled at his breast to get out this enclosed. I ain't read it — but it 's his heart's blood that 's on it. Give my love to all.
> Yours forever,
> CHI.

"His heart's blood!" For a moment the words conveyed no meaning. She picked up the iron-rusty brown slip from the floor; unfolded it; read — Barry Cornwall's love-song in her own handwriting!

"His heart's blood!" She pressed one hand hard upon her own heart, crushing with the other the dark-stained slip. Then, with one wild look around her as if searching for help, she ran down the steps, across the mowing, over into the pasture and up into the woodlands. Deep, deep into the heart of them she made her way, as her mother, Mary Blossom, had done before her; but now there was no kneeling, no prayer, no petition to take from her the intolerable pain.

She was young, and she loved as the young love. It was not God whom she wanted; it was "Jack! Jack! Jack!" She cast herself face down upon the ground, and moaned in her agony: "His heart's blood — his heart's blood." She pressed the stained paper to her lips, over and over again. Then she opened her blouse and baring her bosom, laid the love-song against it — "His heart's blood — his heart's blood!"

So her mother found her.

XXVI

MARIA-ANN'S CRUSADE

OF late Aunt Tryphosa had been growing suspicious of Maria-Ann, and the latter felt she was being watched; to use her own words, "it nettled her."

One afternoon, late in August, her grandmother, coming upon her rather suddenly in the pasture as she sat under the shade of a patriarchal butternut, ostensibly watching Dorcas, asked her sharply :

" What you doin', Maria-Ann ? "

" 'Tendin' to my own business," retorted Maria-Ann, with an unwonted snap in her voice, and hurriedly folded something out of sight beneath the Hearthstone Journal which lay upon her lap.

This was the signal of open revolt on the part of her granddaughter, and the like had occurred but once before in all the time of her up-bringing with Aunt Tryphosa. The old dame's lips drew to a thinner line than usual, as she fired the second shot into the hostile camp:

" You been cryin', Maria-Ann."

" What if I be ? " demanded her granddaughter, with a flash of indignation from beneath her reddened eyelids. " S'pose I have a right to have feelin's same as other folks."

Suddenly Aunt Tryphosa swooped like a hen-hawk upon a small piece of bright scarlet flannel, that the breeze had caught away from the protecting folds of the Hearthstone Journal, and landed in the covert of sweet fern just at her feet.

"What's that?" She held up the glowing bit of color, dangling it before Maria-Ann's eyes.

Upon poor Maria-Ann's inflamed sense of injustice, it had much the same effect as a red rag waved before the eyes of an infuriated bull.

She sprang to her feet, snatched the bit of cloth from between her grandmother's thumb and fore-finger, and thrust it into her dress waist, crying out shrilly in her unwonted excitement:

"You let that be, Grandmarm Little! It's my cross and I'm going on a crusade — so now!"

Aunt Tryphosa sat down rather suddenly in the middle of the sweet-fern patch. Was Maria-Ann going crazy? Her breath came short and sharp; she drew her thin lips still more tightly, and, although really alarmed, braced herself for the combat.

"What'd you say you was goin' on, Maria-Ann?"

"I never knew you was growin' deef before, grandmarm; I said a crusade." She had raised her voice to a still higher pitch, as she stooped to gather up the Hearthstone Journal, the bits of red cloth, her scissors, and thimble which had fallen from her lap as she sprang to her feet.

"Is that the thing you read me about last winter in the

Journal, with the soldiers with crosses on their backs on hosses startin' out for Jerusalem?" demanded the old dame, but in a strangely agitated voice.

"Yes," responded Maria-Ann, promptly, but with less acerbity of manner.

"And is that red rag you hid away a *cross*, Maria-Ann Simmons?" No words can do justice to the old dame's tone and its implied impiety of her granddaughter's conduct.

Maria-Ann was silent.

"Be you a Christian girl, or an idolater, Maria-Ann?"

Her grandmother's voice shook pitiably. Maria-Ann's conscience gave a twinge, when she heard it; but she felt the time was ripe, and she must put in the sickle.

"I hope I 'm a Christian, grandmarm, but I 'm an idolater, too, —" Aunt Tryphosa drew in her breath, as if hurt. "But, anyway, I guess I was an American 'fore I was a Christian, an' I jest *idolize* my Country —" Maria-Ann's eyes filled with tears —"an' I can't do anything for her, nor make sacrifices same as other women do who can send their husbands —," a sob, "an' lovers —," another sob, "an' nuss 'em, an' help on their Country's cause livin' 'way up here in an old back paster with an old cow — an' an old wo — Oh, grandmarm!" Maria-Ann broke down utterly, laid her head upon her knees, and sobbed unrestrainedly.

It was an unusual sight, and Aunt Tryphosa was troubled. She felt it necessary to beat a retreat in the face of such genuine grief, but she was determined that it should be a dignified one.

"I ain't never seen you give way so, Maria-Ann, and you're thirty-one year old come next January. I've done my best to bring you up right, an' now you're old enough to know your own mind, *I hope;* so, if you want to leave me, you can go jest as soon as you can get ready. I come up for Dorcas, an' now I'm goin' home." In spite of her effort her old voice trembled, but her pride sustained her nobly, and Maria-Ann was all unaware that the tears were rolling down the wrinkled furrows in the old cheeks as her grandmother drove Dorcas before her down the fern-scented pasture slope.

Her granddaughter followed her half an hour later, and after a silent supper, except for Aunt Tryphosa's murmured "grace," and a faint "amen" from the other side of the table, Maria-Ann lighted a lamp and shut herself into her small bedroom.

She placed a chair against the door, lest she might be suddenly raided, and drew the other splint-bottomed one up to the head of the bed. Lifting the feather-bed she thrust her hand far under and drew out a square, white pasteboard box. It was tied with a narrow, white ribbon. She undid it carefully, and took out a layer of tissue paper. The lamp-light shone upon a large, gilt heart, some ten by eight inches, with a thickness of two inches.

Maria-Ann turned the box this way and that, watching the play of light on it, for the heart was skewered with a large, silver-gilt arrow, and the shaft, where it penetrated, held a small, white card with simulated blood-drops in carmine splashed on in one corner, and the sentiment, written in the same, straggling diagonally across the other corner:

> "In thy sight
> Is my delight."

Maria-Ann shut her eyes and leaned back in her chair. "Don't seems as if he'd sent me that if he hadn't meant somethin'," she murmured, and dreamed for a little while. Then she opened her eyes, prepared for new delights. Raising the gilt top with tender care, she took out a faded rose:

"Don't seem as if he'd come back that nex' mornin' after Chris'mus an' give me that, 'thout he'd had *some* notion." She laid the rose carefully upon the tissue paper, and began to lift the leaves of the heart-shaped book, until she had lifted every one of the three hundred and sixty-five! She smiled to herself.

"'T ain't likely he'd 'a' sent me jest such a cook-book, 'thout he'd been tryin' to give me a hint." She began to read the recipes — it was absorbing: puddings, cakes, preserves. She was lost to time as she read; "An' he took that pair of socks I knit him last Chris'mus 'long with him, Rose said — " There was a fumbling at her door. Maria-Ann blew out the light.

"That you, grandmarm?" she called pleasantly.

There was no answer, and Maria-Ann laughed softly to herself as she undressed in the dark, and lay down to sweet dreams.

"I'm goin' over to Mis' Blossom's, grandmarm," she announced the next afternoon, " to see if they've had any news. I ain't heard for two days."

Her grandmother made no reply, but when her grand-daughter was well on her way to the Blossoms', Mrs. Try-phosa Little's conscience deemed it prudent to issue a private search-warrant and investigate Maria-Ann's prem-ises — even to the under side of the feather-bed. The re-sults perfectly justified the search, and upon Maria-Ann's return just before tea, she was amazed to have her grand-mother offer her a wrinkled cheek to kiss.

"Why, grandmarm!" exclaimed Maria-Ann, in joyful surprise, "I 'm so glad you ain't laid it up against me — "

"I can see through a barn-door when 't is wide open, even at my time of life, Maria-Ann Simmons," said the old dame, interrupting her.

"What did you hear over to Ben's?"

"Hazel 's just had a letter from her father, and he says they 've got Mr. Sherrill home to New York, an' if nothin' new sets in, he 'll get over it, but his lungs 'll be weak, mebbe, for two years. He was shot clean through the lungs."

"What do they hear from Chi?"

Maria-Ann's face grew suddenly radiant. "Oh, he 's been awful sick with the fever, an' ain't left Cuby yet, but he 'll come North jest as soon as he can be transported. I 've been talking over my plans with Mis' Blossom an' Rose an' Hazel, an' they 're goin' to do everything they can for me."

"So you 're a-goin' to Cuby, Maria-Ann?"

"Yes, grandmarm, I 've got a call to go an' nuss our sick an' wounded; I 've been readin' a lot 'bout the Red

Cross nusses in the Hearthstone Journal, an' I 'm goin' to wear a cross, an' Hazel 's goin' to pay my fare, an' I 'm goin' to stop to Mr. Clyde's when I get to New York, an' he 'll start me all right for Cuby —"

"Them beets are burnin' on, Maria-Ann; guess you 'd better stop for jest one more meal on the Mountin, had n't you?" said her grandmother, dryly.

Maria-Ann laughed merrily. "I know, grandmarm, it seems kinder queer and foolish to you, but I feel as if I could go now with nothin' on my mind, for you know Mandy's girl is comin' to stay all September an' October, an' she 's grand help. You won't begin to miss me 'fore I 'll be back — an' I 'll own up, grandmarm, ever since Rose Blossom went to New York last winter, I 've hankered after seein' more of the world 'sides Mount Hunger."

"When you goin' to start?"

"I calc'late 'bout the last of next week, that 'll be into September — here, let me pare them beets, grandmarm;" and forthwith she seized the pan, and began peeling the steaming, deep-red balls, singing heartily the while:

"'Must I be carried to the skies
On flowery beds of ease,
While others fought to win the prize,
And sailed through bloody seas?'"

"Now be careful, and change at White River Junction," were Mr. Blossom's parting words at the station. "After that you go right through to New York."

"I 'll take good care, don't you any of you worry 'bout me!" She waved her handkerchief from the back platform

of the car to the little group she was leaving, — Mr. and
Mrs. Blossom, Rose, March and Hazel, Captain Spillkins
and Susan Wood, with Elvira and Melissa. She was
inflated with heroic resolve, and felt ennobled to be going
forth to do battle, as she termed it to herself, for her Country's cause. Moreover she was seeing the world, and even
at the start she found it most interesting, for she had been
but ten miles at most by train, and here she was speeding
towards White River Junction, distant forty miles from
Barton's River.

She longed to communicate her enthusiasm to the occu-
pants of the car, but found only one opportunity. She
offered to hold a baby, one of a family of five, while the
mother fed and watered the other four. She continued to
dandle it recklessly till the woman protested:

"Guess you ain't had a fam'ly," she remarked sternly,
rescuing her child; "a woman of your age ought to know
better 'n to shake a baby up so when he 's teethin' — 't ain't
good for their brains—like enough bring on chol'ry morbis."
She pulled down the small clothes, turned the atom over on
its stomach, and patted its back with a broad hand and a
dove-like settling motion that bespoke the mater-familias.

Maria-Ann looked out of the window. True, she had n't
any family — only Grandmarm Little and Aunt Mandy's
one daughter who had just come to visit them. What was
Aunt Tryphosa doing now? She was dreaming again, and
before she could realize it, the brakeman called, "White
River Junction! Change cars for all points south via
Windsor, Springfield, New York."

Hearing that, Maria-Ann felt as if she had already travelled a thousand miles, so far away seemed Mount Hunger and its uneventful life.

She found herself on the platform. She had been so confident of taking care of herself — and now ! She looked helplessly about. Trains to the right of her, trains to the left of her, trains in front of her and behind her switched, and shifted, and thundered. Engine-bells, dinner-bells, train-bells ; stentorian voices of baggage-men, brakemen, call-men ; frantic women, screaming babies, hurrying porters, indifferent travellers, fashionable women and city men ; farmers, children, baskets, shawl-straps, dress-suit cases, golf bags, boys ; dogs, yelping and crying, in arms or in leash ; canaries in their wooden cages shrilling over all ; and hither and thither and yon a bustling, and rustling, and rattling, and roaring, and clanking, and hissing, and shrieking, and hurrying, and scurrying, and pushing, and hauling, and prodding, and rushing ! For a minute Maria-Ann was dazed and almost stunned. Then her courage rose to the occasion. *This* was the famous Junction of which she had heard so much. *This* was the great world. *This* was Life !

" I 'll stand stock-still an' wait till it clears up a little. I 've got an hour here, an' mebbe I 'll see somebody from Barton's," she said to herself, and had just put down her valise when a hoarse voice cried in her ear, — " Hi, there ! get out of the way ! "

She dodged a baggage truck piled high with toppling trunks, only to be caught in the surging, living stream, and carried with it up a step into the restaurant of the station.

To Maria-Ann it was a marvellous sight. She set down her valise by a window and, standing guard in front of it, gazed about her with intense satisfaction. In truth this was seeing the great world, of which she had read so much in the Journal and for which she had longed, at first hand. Around the counter — a long oval — were perched on the high, wooden, spring stools "all sorts and conditions of men," with a sprinkling of women and children. There was perpetual motion of knives, forks, teaspoons, arms, hands, mouths, — and a noisy conglomerate beyond description, accented by the shriek and toot of the switch-engines.

Suddenly the clangor of a gong-like bell and a stentorian voice rose above the chaos of sound ; — there was a momentary lull in the confusion of masticating utensils, followed by a general slipping, sliding, and jumping off the round wooden perches, — and to Maria-Ann's amazement, the room was nearly vacant.

"*Now's* my time," said Maria-Ann, with considerable complacency, and forthwith proceeded to hoist herself, by means of the foot-rail, upon one of the seats, at the same time placing her valise on another at her right. She looked at the varied assortment of delectables — an embarrassment of riches : jelly-roll cakes, pickles, squash pie, baked beans, frosted tea-cakes, sage cheese, ham sandwiches, lemon pie, cold, spice-speckled custards, doughnuts, great as to their circumference, startling as to their cubical contents.

"I've heard tell of them," said Maria-Ann to herself, as her eye, ranging the oval marble slab, encountered a pyramidal pile of New England's doughty cruller. "I'll have two of them, I guess," she said to the indifferent attendant, "an' a cup of coffee; that'll last me for a spell, and I can keep my lunch for supper." She expected some response to her explanation, but there was none forthcoming, save that a cup of coffee, half-pint size, was shoved over the counter towards her, and the huge glass dome that protected the doughnuts was removed with a jerk, and the towering pile set down in front of her.

Maria-Ann helped herself. It seemed rather tame, after so much excitement, to be eating a doughnut the size of a small feather-bed, without company. She looked around. There were but three or four at the entire counter. Farther down to the left, his tall, gaunt figure silhouetted against the blank of the large window, a man was seated, bestriding the perch as if it were a horse. He wore the undress uniform of the volunteer cavalry. When Maria-Ann discovered this, she felt for a moment, to use her own expression, "flustered." The mere presence of the uniform brought to her a realizing sense of the importance of her mission; it seemed to bring her at once into touch with far-away Cuba, and the feminine knights of the Red Cross; with — her heart gave a joyful thump — with Chi! She felt in a way ennobled to be eating her doughnut within speaking distance of a hero (they were all that in Maria-Ann's idealizing imagination).

She had bitten only halfway into the periphery of the

doughnut, when the man stepped from his seat. She watched him as he moved slowly towards the door; his back was turned to her. How feebly he moved! Almost seeming to drag one foot after the other.

A great flood of patriotic pity engulfed Maria-Ann's whole being. She forgot the doughnuts; she left the coffee; she forgot even her valise; her one thought was as she slid from the stool: "I ain't no call to wait till I get to Cuby; I'm just as much a Red Cross nuss right here in White River Junction, Vermont, as if I was a thousand miles away." The girl at the counter looked after her in amazement — she had n't even paid! But there was her valise.

She saw Maria-Ann whisk something out of her dress-waist and stop halfway down the room to pin it on her sleeve, and lo and behold! — it was a cross of bright red flannel. She saw her hurry after the man, who had dragged himself to the doorway, and stood there leaning heavily against the jamb.

"If you're goin' to take a train, just you let me help you aboard," she said, speaking just at his elbow. The man's head half turned with a jerk. "You ain't fit to stan' more 'n an eight months baby, an' I'm a Red Cross nuss on my way to Cuby — "

A gaunt, yellow face with haggard eyes was turned slowly full upon her, and a hand, shaking, as that of a man in drink, was laid on her arm:

"Don't you know me, Marier-Ann?"

Maria-Ann sat down suddenly on the doorstep at the

22

man's feet. There was no strength left in her. Then she
put her head into her hands, and began to cry softly;
there were few to see her, and had the whole world been
there, she would not have cared.

"Just help me into the waitin'-room, Marier-Ann, where
we can talk."

She bounced to her feet, with streaming, tear-blinded
eyes, and Chi, linking his arm in hers, led *her* into the
"Ladies' Room."

A porter followed them in; he addressed Chi. "She
ain't paid for what she ordered, and she ain't eat it neither,
and she 's left her valise."

Chi pulled out a ten-cent piece and put it into his hand.
"Bring 'em all in," he said, "grub 'n' all, 'n' I 'll pay for
'em. We 'll sit here a spell till train time." Maria-Ann
sobbed afresh.

The porter brought in the plate with the doughnuts, the
cup of coffee, and the valise, and set them down on the
wooden settee. He pointed to the ten-cent piece that
lay within the inner ring of a doughnut:

"I don't take nothin' of that kind from you fellers."
He touched the bit of braid on the cuff of Chi's coat; Chi
smiled, and pocketed the money.

"Guess you was n't expectin' to meet an old friend so
soon, was you?" said Chi, gently, setting the plate in her
lap.

Maria-Ann shook her head vigorously, but she could
not control the sobs. Chi crossed one leg over the other,
and waited.

The flies buzzed on the smoke-thickened panes, and an empty truck rattled down the platform. There were no other sounds.

"When does your train go, Marier-Ann?"

There was another sob, but no answer.

"Did n't I hear you say you was on your way to Cuby?"

Maria-Ann nodded.

"Bad place for women — 'n' men, too. What you goin' for?"

Maria-Ann's answer was only half audible : "To nuss."

"To nuss? Ain't there enough nussin' you can do nearer home?"

Maria-Ann looked up with tear-reddened eyes. "I did n't think so — " a sob — "till I saw you, Chi. I did n't know you — I thought I 'd begin right now, before I got there — " her hands covered her eyes again.

Chi's trembling ones, weak from the fever, drew her cold ones down from her face.

"You did just right, Marier-Ann, to want to begin right now. — The Barton's River train is due to start from here in fifteen minutes ; — s'posin' you give up Cuby, 'n' come along home, 'n' try nussin' me. I need it bad enough."

"Oh, Chi, do you mean it?" Maria-Ann caught her breath.

"You bet I do," said Chi, emphatically, "only" — he paused and took up the plate from her lap, spilling the coffee, for the trembling of his hand had increased — "if you 're goin' to undertake it with me, it 's got to be a life job, Marier-Ann."

The flies continued to buzz on the smoke-thickened panes. The train for Barton's River steamed in from the siding. The couple in the waiting-room boarded it. The porter watched them with a queer smile. Then he took up the plate of uneaten doughnuts and the cup of cooled coffee, and handed them to the girl behind the counter.

"She ain't eat 'em, after all," she said. "She acted kinder queer for a Red Cross nurse."

"He's the chap I give the telegram to when he got here on the up-train last night."

"What was it?"

"Twenty-five cent one from Barton's River — 'M. A. starts for Cuba Thursday stop her at Junction.'"

The girl laughed, and the restaurant filled again.

XXVII

"— The stars above
Shine ever on Love — "

"I 'm goin' up into the clearin', Mis' Blossom, to see if there ain't some late blackberries," said Chi, a few days after his triumphal return with Maria-Ann. "Seems as if the smell of the sun on that spruce-bush up yonder would put new life into me — I feel so kind of shif'less."

"I would, Chi," said Mrs. Blossom; "you have n't begun to get your strength back yet, and the more you 're out in this air, without overworking, the better it will be for you."

"I 'll go with you, Chi," said Rose, looking up from her work, as she sat sewing on the lower step of the porch.

"That 's right, Rose-pose; it 'll seem like old times." Chi followed her with wistful eyes as she turned to go up stairs.

"I 'll be down in a few minutes, Chi; we 'd better take the two-quart pails, had n't we?"

"Maybe we 'll find enough for one or two messes."

He turned to Mrs. Blossom when Rose had left the room. "Can't there nothin' be done 'bout it, Mis' Blossom?" He spoke almost wistfully.

Mrs. Blossom's eyes filled with tears. She hesitated a moment before she spoke: "I know Rose so well, Chi, that I *dare* not interfere. I doubt if she would accept anything, even from me, her mother."

"It beats me," Chi sighed heavily. "He's just a-pinin' for a word or sign, 'n' there ain't no use talkin' — *she's* got to give it; I'd back him up every time, he's done enough — "

"Sh — !" Mrs. Blossom held up her finger; she heard Rose on the stairs. Chi looked up — his old Rose-pose stood before him: old, faded, green and white calico dress, old sunbonnet, patched shoes! Chi turned away abruptly to get his pails; and her mother wondered, but said nothing.

They found more than one "patch," where the berries hung in luscious clusters of shining jet. Chi pummelled his chest, and drew deep, deep breaths of the balsamic mountain air. "This sets a man up, Rose-pose; there ain't nothin' like the air on this Mountain for an all-round tonic. Let's sit here a spell, right by this sweet fern."

She pushed back the sunbonnet as she sat down beside him. "Tired, Chi?"

"No — rests me clear through just to sit 'n' look off onto those slopes, just about as green as in June."

They sat awhile in silence; then Chi turned and picked up the sunbonnet that had fallen from her head. He touched it gently.

"Remember the first time you sold berries in that rig, Rose-pose?"

The blood surged into Rose's face, and receded, leaving it strangely white. Chi felt his heart contract at the change, but he went on:

"First time Jack ever saw you was in that rig. — You ain't changed so much but he 'd know you again if he saw you in Chiny."

Still there was silence. Chi moistened his lips.

"Can't say as much for him; never saw such a change; he 's all fallen away to nothin' but skin and bones. Doctor Heath told me just before I left — 'n' he put me aboard the train — that nothin' could set him up again but this Mountain air, 'n' good food, 'n' — " Chi paused; his mouth was uncomfortably dry. Rose's face was turned from him, but he saw a contraction of her delicate throat, as if a dry sob were suddenly suppressed. Then she spoke in a monotone:

"Why does n't he come, then?"

"*Why!* — " Chi fairly startled himself with his thundering "why," and Rose half started from the ground. The blood leaped to her very temples; seeing which, Chi took heart — "Coz he 's every inch a man, Rose Blossom; 'n' he 's got too much grit of the right sort to ask a girl twice, he 's about given his heart's blood for.

"He ain't a-goin' to come crawlin' up here to ask no favors of you after he knows that you *know* — 'n' I glory in his spunk. But I can tell you, if you don't look out, you 'll come nearer to bein' a real Molly Stark than you ever thought you could be when you joined the N. B. B. O. O., 'n' by George Washin'ton! it goes against me to see you breakin' the by-laws you pledged yourself to stand by, every minute of your life that you keep so dumb towards Jack Sherrill; — for you 're provin' yourself a coward in your love, 'n' you 'll have a widowed heart to pay for it

mighty soon, if you keep on, that'll be worse than Molly
Stark's any day — "   A whisper stopped him:

" Chi, Chi, tell him to come — I want him so; oh, Chi ! "

Chi's hand was laid on the bowed head with its crown of
shining, golden-brown braids: " Rose Blossom, may God
Almighty bless you for proving yourself a true woman,
'n' worthy of the mother that bore you. I can't say any
more."

An hour later March Blossom, with a telegram in his
hand, was speeding on Fleet to Barton's River; and two
days afterwards Mr. Blossom and Alan Ford in the double
wagon, and Chi alone in the buggy, drove down to Barton's
to meet the up-train. Mrs. Blossom and Rose stood on
the porch straining their eyes in the quickly-falling September twilight to see any movement on the lower road.
The children had been sent over to Hunger-ford till after
tea, for Jack was not strong enough to bear a too joyful
home-coming.

" They're coming, Rose," said Mrs. Blossom, in a low
tone; then she turned abruptly, and went into the house,
leaving Rose alone on the step.

" Here we are, safe 'n' sound," said Chi, in an affectedly
cheery voice, as he drove out of the woods'-road. " Just
wait a minute, Jack, 'n' I'll give you an arm gettin' out."
He laid the reins on the dasher. Then he assisted the tall,
gaunt figure of the man beside him to alight. Jack half
stumbled, for his eyes were seeking Rose — and Rose ?

All her womanhood, all the sacred privileges of wifehood,
came to her aid at that moment. She sprang to the carriage, and, with one hand, put Chi aside; with the other,

she lifted Jack's half-nerveless arm and laid it over her shoulders; then, encircling him with her own slender one, she said gently, guiding him to the porch step:

"*Lean on me, dearest.*"

On the first of November, one of the short-lived Indian Summer days, the farmhouse on Mount Hunger literally blossomed like a rose.

A week beforehand there had been an animated discussion as to what should be the wedding decorations of the "long-room." Hazel, who had been with them a week already, settled it.

"As if there could be any choice!" she exclaimed. "It's been great fun to hear you all suggesting this, that, and the other, from ground hemlock and bitter-sweet, to everlasting! But Jack and I settled it three weeks ago — how could there be anything for Rose, but roses? Anyway, that's what Jack wrote, and our florist looked fairly dazed when I gave him the order — just bushels of them, Rose-pose, lovely La France ones, like those you threw into the — No, I won't tease you, Cousin mine," she said, with a merry laugh, as Rose looked at her appealingly.

And now, on the wedding morning of the first of November, the great box that Chi had brought up from Barton's the night before was opened, and in Hazel's skilful fingers the exquisite pink blooms lent to the "long-room" a wonderful grace and beauty.

She was flitting about in her pale pink cashmere dress — "Made specially to match the roses," she said to March, as she dropped him a curtsy preparatory to pinning a rose

into his buttonhole. " We must all wear Rose-pose's badge
to-day.   Where are you, Budd ? "

" Here," said her knight, promptly appearing with Cherry
from the pantry, where they had been counting the frost-
ing-roses on the wedding-cake.   He looked down at the
slender fingers as they pulled the stem of the pink bud
through the buttonhole of his jacket, and thought — of the
ring !   Then he looked up at the tall, beautiful girl bending
over him, and, somehow, the day of his proposal seemed
very far away in the Past.   Hazel was so grown up! — as
tall as Rose.   Still, he was n't going to be afraid, if she
was grown up.   Now was his time ; — and " Ethan Allan "
always made the most of his opportunities.   Budd was in
United States History, this term, and he knew this for a
fact.

He drew forth from his breeches' pocket a something
that might once have been white, but, at present, looked
more like a shoe-rag, it was so dingy and soiled.

" I 've kept it, you see, Hazel," he said, his small mouth
puckering, his round, light-blue eyes growing rounder, as
he looked up at Hazel, with twelve-year-old earnestness.

" Kept what ? " said Hazel, mystified, and holding up
the offering gingerly between thumb and forefinger to
examine it.

" Why, don't you know ? — the glove you gave me when
you said you 'd be my Lady-love ? don't you remember, —
in the barn ? " answered Budd, slightly crestfallen.

Hazel laughed merrily.   " Oh, you funny boy ! " she
said, " to keep an old glove of mine for nearly a year and
a half ! Why, it 's nearly black and blue.   Have you kept

't in your best Sunday-go-to-meeting trousers' pocket all this time ? "

Budd nodded, but soberly. Seeing which, Hazel gave him a pat on the top of his head, and assured him she would give him one of her cleaned party gloves once a year till he was twenty-one, if only he would promise not to keep it in his pocket with spruce-gum, chalk, chestnuts, lead-pencil sharpenings, top-twine, jack-knives, and ginger cookie crumbs.

"How'd you know I had all those things in my pocket?" demanded Budd, in his amazement forgetting his sentiment.

"Oh, a little bird told me," replied Hazel. "Run and ask Chi to come in, will you? I have his rose ready for him, and it's most time for them all to come."

It was a quiet wedding. Only those nearest and dearest were about them; Mr. Sherrill, Aunt Carrie and Uncle Jo, Mr. Clyde and Hazel, Doctor and Mrs. Heath, the Blossoms and Chi.

Afterwards all the Lost Nation came in to give their heart-felt blessings and good wishes. They were all there —from Maria-Ann, radiant in the realization of her own romance, to Miss Alton and the Fords, who were to leave on the night train to remain six weeks in New York, and had placed Hunger-ford at the disposal of Rose and Jack during the first weeks of their marriage. They remained but a little while, for the excitement was almost more than Jack was able to bear.

The moon rose between six and seven, largely luminous

and slightly reddened through the soft, warm haze of the Indian Summer night.   Rose had insisted, that, if the night were mild, Jack should ride over to Hunger-ford at a snail's pace on Little Shaver, and that she should lead him.   At first Jack protested, but in the end Rose had her way.   Chi, on Fleet, was to ride on a little ahead to be within call, if anything should be needed.   " Kind of scoutin' to remind us of Cuby, Jack," he said, laughing, as he helped him into the saddle.

They were all on the porch to see the little cavalcade set forth, the pony whinnying his delight to find his master on his back.   Rose took the bridle.   Suddenly she dropped it, turned, and came back to the steps where Hazel stood between Mrs. Blossom and March.   She put up her arms, and clasping the young girl about the waist, drew her down to kiss her, and whisper:

"Oh, Hazel!   What if you had n't come to us! — All this happiness is through you."

And Hazel, but dimly perceiving Rose's meaning, whispered back as she kissed her:

"And if I had n't come, Rose-pose, *I* should never have been rich as I am now; Chi can't call me 'poor' any longer — for you 're all mine, now that you are Jack's; are n't you?"

March, hearing those whispered words, found his mother's hand, somehow, — and Mrs. Blossom understood.

"Good-night, Martie dear," cried Rose, love and tears and laughter struggling in her voice.

"Good-night, Rose dear."

"Good-night, Rose — Good-night, Jack!" cried the twins.

A white slipper filled with rice flew after Little Shaver, and hit him on the left hock. But he was a well-bred polo pony, and a white satin slipper with a little rice was as nothing to a swift, long-distance polo ball; so he gave no sign.

Chi stopped at the little house "over eastwards." Maria-Ann was on the lookout.

"They're comin' along just by the turn of the road," he spoke low, "can you see 'em?"

The road lay white in the moonlight. "Yes, yes," cried Maria-Ann excitedly, "Oh, Chi, ain't it beautiful!"

"Sh — sh!" said Chi, "they'll hear you. Hark! By George Washin'ton! she's singin' — Get, Fleet." The horse loped along over the moonlit road, and Maria-Ann went in and shut the door — all but a crack. To that she put her ear, to hear what the clear, sweet voice was singing:

> " 'I told thee when love was hopeless;
> But now he is wild and sings —
> That the stars above
> Shine ever on Love,
> Though they frown on the fate of kings.' "

Mount Hunger stood bathed in white radiance. The stars came out, but faintly; — still, they were shining.

www.ingramcontent.com/pod-product-compliance
Lightning Source LLC
Chambersburg PA
CBHW032227010726
47494CB00002B/390